I AM
THE
STORM

ALSO BY W.J. CHERF

THE MANUSCRIPTS OF THE RICHARDS' TRUST

BOW TIE

RECOVERY

CHILDREN OF PTAH

IMHOTEP

MAAT-KA-RE. MEMOIRES OF A TIME TRAVELER

THE ADVENTURES OF J.J. STONE

THE FIRST SOUL

THE LICTOR OF MAGIC

I AM THE STORM

BOOK III

THE ADVENTURES OF J.J. STONE

BY

W.J. CHERF

FOXBAT PUBLISHING

Foxbat Publishing
ISBN: 978-0-9989318-2-1

DEDICATION

Dear Sweet Sue.
This is the last of my madness.
But, as always, this one is for you.

A GPS Adventure Book

How many times did you wish you could go where the story took place? That mummy's tomb? That Caribbean pirate ship? Normandy Beach or the Alamo?

For Harry Potter, there is Platform 9¾ at King's Cross Station, the Reptile House at the London Zoo, Leadenhall Market, and the Tower Bridge. Universal has an entire Wizarding World devoted to the famous J.K. Rowling series.

But did you ever read a book that told you where to go? To actually see what inspired the writer? Or where the action took place?

Well, now you can. Sleuth out any of the following GPS coordinates of J.J. Stone's first adventure. Be sure to have a USB adaptor handy that is appropriate for your device.

Good hunting!

1: GPS: Lat: 47°29' 14.27" N. Long: 19°03' 10.03" E.

2: GPS: Lat: 52° 30' 37.16" N. Long: 13° 25' 10.03" E.

3: GPS: Lat: 41° 23' 50.87" N. Long: 2° 11' 56.58" E.

4: GPS: Lat: 48° 51' 04.60" N. Long: 2° 17' 34.14" E.

5: GPS: Lat: 39° 37' 01.34" N. Long: 104° 47' 54.97" W.

6: GPS: Lat: 41° 48' 36.70" N. Long: 88° 09' 15.44" W.

7: GPS: Lat: 40° 45' 36.88 N. Long: 73° 58' 33.87" W.

8: GPS: Lat: 40° 43' 09.22" N. Long: 73° 59' 56.08" W.

PROLOGUE

What may seem to us as irreconcilable, the old ones took as complementary, and thus as confirmation of the manifold powers of the gods. Although ancient logic is not ours, it has its own consistency and integrity. Consequently, one must leave behind the world of rational and scientific causality in order to gain entrance to the world of magic.

The Knot of Eternity. A Commentary. T. Good. (Old Oaks Academy Press, 1963), 1.

Let me be clear, I am fully human.

Many of my opponents … not so much.

I'm the latest in a long line that has held the righteous title of Lictor of Magic. That makes me an actual demon slaying exorcist. The International Integrated Interface Society trained me for this gig and I have become … proficient. I still have a long way to go, in my mind, a long, long way.

From demon-possessed politicians to hellish fiends conjured by despicable practitioners, I have dispatched them all. Fortunately, these *things* are easily identified by their horrific auras, which are dark, black, and in the most hard-core cases, wriggle and squirm about like slimy obsidian eels.

I have a lot of work ahead of me. How much? At last count about eight hundred years' worth of demons to hack through, ever since they began to illicitly seep into the mortal realm.

That leak was mended a year or so back. In truth,

the soul I carry, the First Soul of Creation, actually performed all the fancy stitching, I just got us to the right place, at the right time. Now it's up to us to put things back into balance once again. As I said, about eight hundred years' worth of demons need slaying.

That's lots of practice.

*   *   *

About two weeks earlier, the ever-venerable Mr. Henry and I sat under a weathered pine overhang at a scenic upland gas stop. Shaded from a cloudless New Mexican sun, we were frankly parched and hungry after our hike. Several guzzled beers later, we wolfed down some potato chips and a couple of god-awful microwaved hot dogs.

Then, in a burping, beery moment, the aged white haired man looked me in the eye and declared, "You've evolved. You're now J.J. 2.0."

Mr. Henry's words launched me back several hours, to an obscure cave opening blocked with spider webbing. A swipe from a handy stick and we entered its split-rock opening, stepping over a tiny stream that dribbled out, mercury-like, into the sunshine.

Dark, quiet, and smelling vaguely moldy, we shined our flashlights within this narrow passage, skimming our beams over its towering walls. It then opened up into a chamber that swallowed our beams. Our shoes crunched on a dry, sandy floor.

"Well, J.J.," Mr. Henry said, "we're here. Can you feel it?" His voice echoed.

"Feel what?"

"A faint thrum ... almost a harmonic that hits your inner ear."

I concentrated. "Yeah. It sounds like a river flowing near us, in the rock, just beyond our reach."

I reached out and touched the gently vibrating side wall. And that's all she wrote, until I came to, on the floor, with Mr. Henry kneeling over me with a worried look on his face.

"J.J! J.J! Are you all right?"

"What happened?" I asked, dazed and confused. I won't sugar-coat it, something had leveled me. I tasted copper in my mouth. I must have bitten my tongue.

Mr. Henry, clearly relieved at my return, said, "You've been out for a full minute. Boy, you gave me a fright. I even had to catch you before you cold-cocked yourself good on the floor."

"I reached out to feel that wall. Never have felt anything like it before. It knocked me for a loop."

"Oh," the Fourth-Class Adept said laconically, as he hovered the palm of his hand over where I had pointed.

"That's a powerful hot spot, got to be a side branch of the Silver Nile."

I attempted to get up.

"J.J., stop. Take a good inventory. Are you okay?"

"I think so. But give me a hand. I don't want to touch any more walls."

Once up, I felt light-headed, but everything else seemed to work just fine.

"Jesus, Mr. Henry, you're glowing. Your aura is really amped up."

Looking down at his hands, then at me, Mr. Henry corrected. "No, it's not me, it's you. Your usual aura has become sparkly somehow. I think you've been charged up. Now, as a test, try to read my mind."

I did, as easily as if I were looking into a beer cooler, and said so.

"*Well, now*, that's mighty interesting. I indeed had a frosty beer in mind, but I had my blocks on full. How hard did you try?"

"I didn't. I just did it. This is really freaking me out. What else did the Silver Nile do to me?"

"There's no telling, son. But just for safety, let's get out of this god-forsaken cave. But take it slow."

"By the way, Mr. Henry, where's your flashlight?"

"I must have dropped it somewhere."

"I can see you clear as day. Now let me find the flashlight. It's got to be around here somewhere near. I can feel it."

*   *   *

That's why Mr. Henry called me, J.J 2.0. I had accidentally tapped into *the* ley line of the American Southwest—the Silver Nile—and received a dose of its psychic energy. That alone explained why I conked out, and my amplified physical and paranormal senses.

What do I mean? Consider this. I was born with an Innate Paranormal Ability Rating of ten. The scale doesn't go any higher. Sixth Class Adepts, the highest known by my society, typically are rated at five to six on the IPAR scale.

On top of that, my Soul Numeral was one, meaning, I carried the First Soul of Creation. So right out of the block, I grew up as a hyper-sensitive paranormal who routinely perceived and interpreted the auras of living creatures.

To be completely honest, I'm not sure *what* the Silver Nile did to me. Just that afterward, I found my senses and abilities highly enhanced.

Since that experience, I have noticed that auras appeared brighter, more detailed, even rippled with signs of strength or exhaustion. My sixth sense sharpened to a preternatural level where my intuition became so sure that reality sometimes got fuzzy; as in "did that happen yet?" My motor reflexes, much augmented, were altered to a cheetah-like twitch. My ability to exorcize a demon from an unfortunate mortal, by touch alone, came naturally. It was like I had become their Kryptonite.

Once again, I found myself in uncertain territory at the worst possible time. Unsure of myself and my newly augmented abilities, I rode my brand new bike like it had training wheels. Meanwhile, I was on the run—staying two steps ahead of an evil international paranormal organization bent on putting me in the ground.

Truth be told, I had earned the rapt attention of the *Consilium magorum et sagarum.* Yes, I single-handedly eliminated one of their hit squads in the Santa Fe National Forest. Yes, I ruined their North American headquarters in Manhattan. And yes, I assassinated their regional director and stole his much-coveted *Book of Spells.*

By all counts, I admit these deeds made me a high-priority target. Fortunately, they didn't know I had assassinated their international chairman as well—a man whose own blood-sworn oracle wanted removed. As they say, "he was not greatly loved."

On the other hand, and in my defense, never forget that since my birth, CMES had targeted me for destruction several times. Why you might ask? Chiefly because I carried the First Soul. Add to that, each and every one of my actions against CMES I undertook in response to one of their horrible atrocities—like infant human sacrifice, crucifixion, and assassination.

Seldom had the biblical adage, "an eye for an eye," been more rigorously applied. Usually, the paranormal community smoothed over such injuries with the more peaceful concept of *Wehrgeld*, "man-money." Yes, this tit-for-tat feud between my society and CMES had spiraled into a low-grade paranormal war between good and evil.

When I first signed up to be the muscle for the paranormal "good guys," TIIIS, little did I know how rapidly I would get such a long rap sheet. So who were these good guys I work for? Think of them as Nature's own counter balance that represented good versus evil, light versus darkness, freedom versus oppression. Without question, TIIIS was an odd anagram for an obscure paranormal society made up of sensitives, telepaths, telekinetic athletes, and outright gifted white witches and wizards. Were they perfect? Hardly.

Before I showed up, TIIIS' external policy had been that of a box turtle—passive, and defensive, with precious little desire for anything offensive or retaliatory in nature. CMES would dish it out, and TIIIS was content to absorb it and survive.

However, when I became their Lictor of Magic— their enforcer of external policy—that all changed. Since I was a decorated U.S. Marine veteran and non-com officer, I knew what a battlefield smelled like. Crucially, I had killed—many times. TIIIS' then president recognized the opportunity and turned me loose.

In spite of TIIIS' many odd turns of tradition and policy, I remained a man of moral conscience, who stood apart and jealously held to my own true nature. I could say no, and often did. But throughout all the mayhem I was never truly alone, for I had an ally, the First Soul itself. This spiritual companion I conversed with quite often.

Given my role in shaping TIIIS' external policy, President Silver Moon directed me to lay low and off the grid. I wasn't really all that surprised. I had been busy giving CMES fits. At the same time, I was on call on a twenty-four/seven basis. Which sorta puts a crimp in your social life, though management didn't see it that way.

Then things got really interesting.

CHAPTER 1
The Raid of Late 2010

A choking gray smoke tried to fill my lungs, but the respirators in my urban combat suit's facemask held it at bay. Instead, I tasted my own recycled bad breath of pizza, garlic, and onions. I licked lips covered with nervous sweat. My mask's goggles, in one sense, protected my eyes from all the soot in the air, but not from what they beheld—the grotesque human carnage.

A portion of the TIIIS campus at Old Oaks Academy, nestled in a southwestern Pennsylvania forest, had been transformed into a modern battlefield. The blackened limestone remains of the campus' once graceful gothic chapel amounted to one intact flying buttress and an adjacent wall fragment. The burned near-dead, looking like darkened and broken twigs, wailed for release, while the truly dead had been reduced to ash during the initial, surprise attack.

It was Christmas Eve and a fairytale-like snowfall had made it perfect and serene. The remaining holiday population, students and staff alike, had filed into the chapel's spacious confines for Midnight Mass, about one hundred in all. In hindsight, it made for an-all-too-easy target, so very ripe for harvesting. It was payback for our ruination of their Manhattan headquarters.

* * *

The displays of Marauder One's cockpit bathed its pilots' helmets and goggled faces in red, making them look more like blood-thirsty praying mantises than men.

"Marauder One to flight. Engage IR and acquire target," the lead pilot transmitted to his three comrades, who, one by one, promptly acknowledged.

Meanwhile, his copilot and weapons officer pressed his face into the soft foam padding of his IR camera's targeting sight.

"Target acquired," he confirmed into his stalk mike as his thumb caressed the fire button's stub in anticipation. The sight was amazing. From this range and altitude he could make out row upon row of thermal blobs through the tall, spear-shaped stained glass windows. Three individuals stood at one end of the structure before the flickering pinpoints of six altar candles.

"Fire on my mark ... FIRE!" the lead pilot ordered.

As one, four weapons officers pressed their fire buttons. The result was a something right out of the Fourth of July, but instead of going up, luminous trails arched down from the horizontal. All met at the gracefully built stone structure. And it was no more.

The weapon's officer of Marauder One, upon firing his rockets, whispered, "Trick or Treat, motherfuckers."

The first volley of eight Hellfire missiles simultaneously struck, ignited, and crumpled the four sides of the chapel, illuminating the surrounding grounds in a ghastly scarlet glare.

"FIRE."

The second volley intersected and pulverized the collapsing roof before it had a chance to hit the ground.

"FIRE."

The rockets of the last salvo flew right through the leveled structure, now engulfed in flame and smoke, impacting in a crisscross pattern the surrounding terrain. Many exploded leaving dirty scars in the white terrain, some did not. Instead, they simply burrowed into the earth or skipped across the snow-covered surface. Finally coming to rest, they transformed into dangerous liabilities for the bomb disposal units.

"Cease fire. Prepare to deploy."

*   *   *

I saw them as they swooped in silently like owls in the night. Their heavily muffled engines and broad rotor blades made such stealth possible. After their rocket attack upon the chapel, they dared to land, full with bold intent, to mop up and plunder.

That's when I got into the act, for I had been late to that doomed midnight service. I had been on the phone with mom and dad several time zones away. That was when I first heard the unmistakable sounds of full scale combat, something that I hadn't experienced since my Marine days in Iraq. I got geared up and ran out of my dorm.

Moving about in my one piece UCS, its light-bending fabric making me an indistinguishable wraith, I hid behind the heavy snowfall and smoke. Methodically, I went about my grim task of hunting down and slaughtering their assault teams. My ceramic Bone Sword quickly claimed forty-three. These losses were quickly noted by their squad leaders as unit recall whistles began blowing all around me, echoing oddly against the curtains of snow.

Their departure, too, I would disrupt. They would not escape this horror they'd brought on.

I gutted all in the first helicopter as I ran up its lowered cargo ramp, silently claiming anyone in my path, transforming its hold into a splattered butchery. Its pilots, tucked away within their cramped and heavily armored confines, I dispatched with my 9mm—two rounds for each.

The second transport I caught just as it spooled up for takeoff. For whatever reason, its copilot had his side curtain ajar. Through that convenient opening I slam-dunked a thermite grenade, which I had liberated from a dead soldier. The lumbering machine, its cockpit transformed into an inferno, immediately augured into the ground, flipping the massive twin-rotor Chinook onto its back. Its rotor blades surreally wind-milling into a once manicured lawn, slewing out ragged clumps of shrapnel-like sod.

I sprinted away, sending danger. Moments later, an aviation-fuel-fireball engulfed the stricken airframe and plumed skyward, lighting up the scene with stark, hellish shadows. In the process, I saw yet another transport on the ground.

I made for it without a thought as to how to cripple it. All I knew was it was dead meat.

*   *   *

The pilot of Marauder Two overheard the terrified chatter of the ground troops and their squad leaders as something unseen attacked them left and right. No one had expected a hot landing zone. Wisely, Marauder One signaled for their immediate recall, but suddenly went off the air in mid-sentence.

Marauder Two's copilot frantically asked, "How long will we wait?"

His seasoned pilot answered tersely, "Two mikes. Those grunts deserve that, at the very least."

"Two minutes! That's an eternity on a hot LZ!"

Almost as an exclamation point to the copilot's concerns, a helicopter blew up in a fiery plume.

"Holy shit! Get us out of here!" the copilot begged.

"Steady, Freeman. I see a group of stragglers boarding in my mirror. Do something useful. Man the chain gun. Give them some cover fire."

KRUMMP! The massive report of a second transport blowing up rolled over them. The shockwave shook Marauder Two's airframe as if it were a toy.

The pilot checked his mirrors and seeing a partially filled cargo hold, made a hard decision, "Things are heating up fast. Time to fly." With a heavy sigh of resignation he pulled back on his stick and lifted off.

"Jesus, Peters," Freeman said while craning his head around, "there must be twenty guys we left back there. They're waving at us to come back and pick them up!"

"They're all dead men," Peters said. "Just watch."

As they gained altitude, the copilot saw the stragglers were now falling like puppets without strings.

There's something out there mowing them down.

BRRRRRRRRR! Freeman stitched the earth with the chain gun in frustration while hoping to hit something he couldn't see.

"How did you know?" the copilot gasped wide-eyed.

"Someone, or something, shut down three of our transports. I wasn't eager to join them."

*   *   *

Eighty-three dead. Twenty-seven injured.

That was the latest casualty report on the TIIIS

personnel. Still full of blood-lust, I walked about in a daze, frisking my kills for any intel I could find, anything that would answer the questions of "who," or "where from."

I counted them, all the time wishing for more, like those poor bastards left behind by the last helicopter.

Among them I found no goons—half-human, half-demon surrogates. No. All were fully human. That fact alone shook me to the bone.

Examining closely a corpse while down on one knee, I thought, *Who in their right mind would willingly go to into battle on Christmas Eve? Much less fire volley after volley of Hellfire missiles into a packed chapel?*

You already know the answer to that question, Soul Carrier, the First Soul commented, my spiritual partner-in-crime since birth.

Yeah. You're right. It's just hard to figure.

Not at all, Soul Carrier. We are dealing with evil, pure and simple, and it comes in all guises. They all knew what they were doing and getting into.

That clinical observation caused me to pause. But this fragile moment of introspection was broken by the voice of President Betsy Silver Moon, which instantly brought me back to the here and now.

"Lictor of Magic. Stand down." She crisply ordered.

In response, I stood up, erect and at attention, with my Bone Sword in hand, and stared back at the feisty and diminutive Native American. I marveled at her command presence. In my eyes she stood ten feet tall in that dark trench coat.

"Yes, ma'am." I replied hoarsely as I sheathed my

sword across my back.

"Lictor of Magic, remove your facemask so I can better see you. That's better, but you still look like hell. Do you have anything to report?"

"Yes, ma'am. All were humans. None had any ID or personal papers; that makes them pros. Their nationality appears mixed. My best guess, and you will not like this, is predominately Eastern European, maybe Chechen. Their weapons and ammo are all Eastern European knock-offs. Totally untraceable. I think their thermite grenades are of Chinese manufacture."

The president paused a moment while she digested my intel. Her face took on a look of resignation, or, was it confirmation?

"Mr. Stone, do you even know what time it is?"

"No, ma'am."

"It's ten-thirty in the morning. How long have you been on duty?"

"Not sure, ma'am. Probably, maybe, nine, ten hours."

"Then hit the showers, eat, and get some rack time, soldier. You got that?"

"Yes, ma'am. Is Old Main even open?"

"Yes, it is. Go there. Now." She pointed. "They're expecting you."

*　　*　　*

Silver Moon could not believe her eyes. Before her stood this sword-wielding, blood splattered giant. His gore-covered UCS tried to blend into its blindingly bright white surroundings, but failed miserably, constantly shifting its coloration this way and that.

Stone, her society's Lictor of Magic, had almost

single-handedly saved the rest of the campus. What he hadn't killed, the campus security unit did. This she knew because she too had counted the enemy dead. Stone's telltales had been the easiest to spot— decapitations, torso guttings, missing limbs, atrocious wounds. By her own count, Stone had claimed close to eighty CMES troopers and, purportedly, three helicopter transports. Apparently, the fourth just managed to escape him. Stone, she decided there and then, was a one-man wrecking crew. But, really, she already knew that. What he had done to four CMES squads in the Santa Fe National Forest was proof enough.

She also knew for a fact that this bold attack on the Academy, CMES' second such foray, was only the latest escalation in their ongoing war. Soon, there would be an outcry for revenge. Stone would surely want a piece of that action, and the war would grind on and ratchet up in an ever-rising tempo of destruction and mayhem.

I will have to tamp down the initial primal urge for vengeance. Our response must be measured, in kind, and appropriate. Otherwise, we will descend to their level of depravity.

Then an icy chill ran up her spine.

But Betsy, where will that response ultimately lead?

Taking a deep breath to calm herself, the TIIIS president caught the sweetness of death all around her, mixed in with the truly rank and putrid. She scanned her surroundings and noted for the first time the flattened and melting snow, the many patches of rusty, coagulated red where her colleagues and friends once lay. The black uniformed bodies of the CMES assault troops that wallowed in their own private pools. Towering over these fragile organic remains sat one inert helicopter transport and the strewn and twisted wreckage of two others that littered a once bucolic campus.

Finally, Silver Moon's eyes settled upon the blackened chapel itself. In the bright sunshine its lone buttress looked like a charred brontosaurus rib leaning up against a slivered wall fragment.

"Excuse me, Madam President."

Startled by his sudden appearance, Silver Moon turned to her assistant, Mr. Malcolm Porter.

"What do you propose we do with the remains of the CMES personnel?"

"Strip their weaponry and send it all to the armory. Have a mass grave dug, at the edge of the tree line over there," she indicated with her chin, "and burn them. Burn them all."

This directive earned a frown from the impeccably dressed man.

Silver Moon saw his disapproval. With her hands on hips, she quietly said, "Mr. Porter. Would you prefer I FedEx them all to a certain Rome address?"

"Oh no, Madam President."

"Good. Now, have our people been properly attended to?"

"Oh yes, Madam President. All the wounded are in the infirmary. Many of the dead have been claimed by their next of kin, but nineteen do not have … ah … a place to go."

After a moment of thought, Silver Moon glanced back over at the chapel and smiled for the first time that morning. "The foundation of our ruined chapel will become their cenotaph. Raise nineteen pavement stones, and prepare each for burial. A campus-wide funeral service will take place in three days. Thereafter, I want their names properly inscribed."

"Very good, Madam President. But what of the rest of the … debris?"

"After the funeral, I want all the unexploded ordinance cleared, the intact helicopter moved to our hanger, and this campus restored to its pristine condition, with one exception." She pointed, "That chapel is not to be restored in any manner. It is to remain as a monument and reminder to all."

*   *   *

I never liked funerals. I had participated in far too many of them in Iraq. But at least those memorials had been relatively brief, intensely emotional remembrances of one to eight heroic soldiers at a time—not seventy-three civilians.

I stood at attention dressed in my black suit throughout the reading of the names. Most I did not know. I probably would have recognized their faces, but I failed miserably at putting a name to a face.

But not all.

I lost Mr. Theodore Good, my favorite teacher of demonology, colleague in ancient languages, and source of good advice. My last memory of him was at the Pressure Cooker. He had been much relieved after I had destroyed an especially cunning demon, which he had accidentally conjured while translating an obscure text.

I lost also Mr. Gregory Loomis, the society's

master armorer, who constructed my UCS, crafted my Bone Sword, and initiated me into the way of the sword. I will sorely miss his thick Scottish brogue, dry humor, quick turn of phrase, and his goading at the pell.

On the other hand, a handful was counted among the living. They had sustained injuries, several severely, due to the assault.

Among them was Mr. Henri Dexter, who without question is the society's master of lethal offensive and defensive magic. Mr. Dexter, while seated within the Chapel, had sensed the attack at the last moment. Spreading his arms out wide, he had saved himself and two others within a protective bubble of magic. In the process, he endured unspeakable burns to his back. While he will recover, many skin grafts will be necessary.

My young friend with the IT and Security Department, Mr. Joshua Remington, sustained multiple gunshot wounds, yet soldiered on in the defense of the Academy, its students, and staff. Many of his department, however, had not been so lucky. He's young. He'll mend.

My mind wandered and my eyes filled with tears of thanksgiving. Mr. Henry and Peter Glass had not been on campus during the raid. Neither had President Silver Moon and countless others. Best of all, my Mel was back in San Francisco, safe and sound.

It was then I heard President Silver Moon speaking words meant to heal and soothe. But for me, they were a clarion call to action.

*   *   *

Following what came to be known as the Christmas

Eve Massacre, TIIIS resources began appearing at the Academy to take up the slack. One of those many was none other than Mr. Henry, whose presence I truly appreciated.

"Bloody business this," he whispered into my chest upon greeting one another.

Looking me in the eye past his bushy white eyebrows, he asked, "How bad was it?"

"A nasty night fight. Very ancient in character. Very close, personal. What I always imaged the last engagement at the Battle of Thermopylae might have been like."

"Bloody?"

A simple head nod.

"Used your sword?"

Another nod.

"Damn. I wish I'd been there. Maybe I could've saved Good. Then again, maybe not."

He changed the subject.

"How's that Professor Makris, J.J.?"

A smile must have creased my face, because his eyes twinkled.

"She's just wonderful, Mr. Henry."

"Does she know what's she's getting into?"

"Oh, yeah. Mel has even committed to spending the summer here for offensive and defensive training in lethal magic."

"You don't say ... that sounds like she's serious. But are you?"

"Yes, sir. I figure we'll make a formidable pair."

"I'll just bet."

*　　*　　*

Mel. My God, where do I begin? Professor Melaina Makris, my Mel, has more facets to her than a fancy cut Belgium diamond.

Let me start with the basics: born an Alexandrian Egyptian in 1970, Coptic Christian, fluent in Arabic, French, and English, the offspring of two powerful sensitives, educated at Oxford and the University of Chicago, now a full professor at Berkeley in their Ancient Near Eastern Languages Department.

Exotic, if not stunning in appearance, Melaina represented a mix of Egyptian and Greek. Her honeyed visage possessed a narrow long nose, high cheekbones, and full lips. Her shiny jet-black hair hid her large-lobbed ears and framed her deep brown, almond-shaped eyes, which were chock full of glinting intelligence. Lean and willowy of build, she stood five foot nine with delicate hands notable for their long, artistic, almost spidery fingers.

She was one of the white witches in attendance at my first academic presentation in San Francisco. Because of that paper, she later sought me out at the University of Pennsylvania, where my academic advisor, Peter Glass, introduced us. That "chance" meeting led to lunch, which triggered an intriguing and surprisingly frank shop talk discussion, after which I left the Greasy Onion with my head in a spin. She had pursued her academic career early in life, while I had enlisted in the U.S. Marines. Yet, here we were, discussing magic from two very different points of view. As the carrier of the First Soul, I was practically born to it, while she only realized her potential after finding and translating her family's book of spells.

Frankly, I didn't think much about the social

aspects of that lunch. She was an older full professor at a big school and I was an awed, focused, heads-down studying undergrad. But the academic upside was formidable, because Peter Glass headed up a special research group dedicated to magic in the ancient Near East. Professor Makris was a part of that inner group. I was studying and translating demonic Sumerian tablets at PU. So, I figured that if I played my cards right I too might become a member of this select group.

That all changed, however, when Professor Makris presented me with a protective amulet to wear. Not thinking much of the little mummiform object on a leather thong, I considered the present a good luck charm and nothing more. Stupid me.

During a serious paranormal standoff between the evil Charles Smithers and his twin brother, the former president of TIIIS, Peter Smithers, I got roughed up quite a bit. Here's the kicker—so did Professor Makris who had been wearing the amulet's identical twin. The black eye and bruises that I got were shared with her. The amulet's reciprocal nature I hadn't known about.

Apparently, when Professor Makris experienced these injuries, she then understood why the construction of this particular amulet had been included in her family's spell book. It was meant to be worn by family members. In essence, the amulets so crafted, shared and, therefore, halved the effect of any magic or physical harm that may befall its wearers. It was only later that she rather sheepishly admitted what had happened, but only after sharing a gunshot wound to her upper arm. As a result, the good professor eventually took off her amulet to prevent this sort of reciprocity from occurring again.

After I graduated from PU and began in earnest my duties as TIIIS' Lictor of Magic, my interest in Professor Makris again shifted. What held me back was a well-grounded fear that someone would harm her for just being my friend. That had already been tried twice with my parents. But the First Soul's counsel slowly turned this reluctant social dinosaur, and I began to seriously accept the idea that Mel understood the dangers involved.

What nearly broke it for me was Mel's surprise visitation one evening as an astral projection and the concern about me that she shared. I almost balked, but my spiritual companion, the First Soul, did point out that she, once again, had reached out to me and what on earth was I waiting for.

But it was Mel's invitation to give a paper on a panel devoted to ancient Near Eastern magic at the University of Chicago's Oriental Institute, finally kicked down the door. Even then, I surrendered to her charms only on the condition that she must take some offensive and defensive magical courses at the Old Oaks Academy. To this she agreed.

At that point, was I whipped? Yes, I can now admit it freely. Besides, when you confide with your parents that you have met a wonderful lady, well, that about says it all.

Chapter 2
Post-Op Assessment

Sitting in his temporary office off of Times Square, a modest hotel room on the thirty-first floor, William DeSalvo, the new assistant regional director of CMES North America, heard his laptop *ping* at 8:16 in the morning. Word finally arrived from his region's head of Communications and Security—the post-action report on the assault of the TIIIS academy in Pennsylvania.

Anxiously, DeSalvo read its terse contents, reached over, and gulped down his coffee, dregs and all. He then threw the empty mug viciously against the opposite wall, making yet another impression in the wallboard, all within a tight grouping. Several deep breaths helped, but it didn't calm the Roman. That the coffee mug's handle now impaled the wall somehow did.

STONE! That son-of-a-bitch did it again!

DeSalvo paused and looked away from his laptop's screen in disbelief.

How do you lose so many on a surprise attack?
How is that possible?
Do I have a security leak?

His mind reeled as he juggled the possibilities, searching for an explanation for this disastrous failure. He masochistically reread what had so vexed him.

The initial target was neutralized with an estimated kill rate of one hundred percent. Our tactical mistake was landing. Someone, or something, attacked our ground troops and helicopters. The return of Marauder Two, which took off early, leaving behind some assets, prevented the operation from becoming a complete loss.

Mio Dio.

DeSalvo rubbed at his clean-shaven chin in thought. *Only one person could have done this—Stone. He did something like this before in the mountains of New Mexico. The oracle Valeria Costa specifically warned me about him.*

Far more to the point, DeSalvo realized that his first foray against TIIIS came at a dear cost. Indeed, he had injured the enemy. TIIIS personnel had fallen. *But at this rate, how far would the blood-letting go? Until both sides are bled dry?*

DeSalvo sat back and steepled his fingers in thought. His brow wrinkled under curly hair that was going gray by the minute. *The key to TIIIS' new-found bellicosity and effectiveness centers on Stone. How do I get to Stone?*

He punched several buttons on his desk phone.

"Mr. Kiel. I need you immediately." Hanging up, *I need to speak again with* Signora *Costa as well.*

Several moments later, DeSalvo heard a knock on his hotel room's door.

"Enter."

A fit man in his fifties did so while carefully avoiding the shattered remains of a coffee mug on the carpet.

"Sit," the Roman pointed to the only chair. The man in the dark suit and tie did.

"Give me your assessment of Jonathan Joseph Stone's weaknesses."

After a few moments, the ex-government spook and operations officer thoughtfully began. "Devout

Christian and Southern Baptist. Moral to a fault. An idealist. Unmarried. He has no known social interests. His parents are still alive, but are nowhere to be found; TIIIS has seen to that. In short, he's got none."

"How can a moral idealist be so brutally effective on the battlefield?"

"He was a U.S. Marine." Kiel gestured with open hands. "Marine doctrine ingrains certain bloodthirsty qualities, while managing to preserve the conscience. The use of derogative names de-humanizes the enemy, which makes them easier to kill. In Stone's case, demons and the demon-possessed are no-brainers. His religious upbringing sees to that. Since he can see auras, and understands what auras reveal about a full human, he can readily pass judgment on them with a clear conscience."

"Mr. Kiel, your new priority is to find me a weakness."

"Yes, sir."

*　　*　　*

Several days later, DeSalvo flew to Italy, rented a bright red Guilia, and took a short drive into the Roman foothills. In a quaint family restaurant on a quiet side street in Tivoli, DeSalvo sat down with the most powerful oracle alive.

"*Signora* Costa, what a pleasure it is to see you again," DeSalvo murmured in his native Italian to the stunning middle-aged woman of ancient heritage and frightening ability.

DeSalvo, troubled, got right down to business.

"*Signora* Costa, I come again seeking your wisdom about a matter that we have already discussed."

"Ah, *Signore* DeSalvo. You must be referring to the *l'umo potente,* that American called Stone. What has he been up to lately?" She leaned forward against the white linen tablecloth with genuine interest. Her perfume scented the moment.

"He menaces our Gathering."

"Oh, that. *Sí,* that is true," she said with a slight smile and nod. "Has he done something exceptional recently to heighten your undying hatred?"

"The loss of too many of our best troops."

"Oh, so he has been busy," she commented, again with that subtle smile, and followed with a sip of red wine. She twirled the hand-blown glass in the candlelight examining the legs of alcohol on the glass's barrel. Finished, the oracle carefully placed the glass back down on the white linen.

"Well, *Signore*, the last time we spoke I told you Stone would become something more *if* he ever came into contact with the ley line called the Silver Nile. Do you remember that?"

"Sí."

The waiter arrived with a linen-covered basket of freshly-baked bread and a plate pooled in olive oil generously sprinkled with herbs. After he left, she leaned in again, her perfume wafting.

"Well, he has. He's now part of the most powerful ley line of the American Southwest. As a consequence, anything you tell me about the man, I will believe."

Silence.

The waiter returned to take their order.

"Richardo. Two daily specials, please."

The waiter made a notation on his pad, silently nodded, and left.

The assistant regional director now leaned across the table and quietly said, "So, *signora*, how can I get to him, if I can't kill him?"

Looking into her half full glass of red, the oracle cocked her head to one side. "Sadly, you can do very little, directly." Her eyes flashed. "However, I can suggest several indirect possibilities."

*   *   *

Not by chance, Tivoli was only some twenty miles from CMES' central headquarters north of Rome. Per his agreement with Feng Bai, the newly appointed chairman of CMES, DeSalvo owed the man a progress report on Stone and what was being done about him. The assistant director wanted to tell his boss face-to-face not only the grim news of the disastrous raid, but also to offer a potential solution.

The Rome center consisted of a villa that stood atop a hillock of limestone and barren, lifeless sand. When seen from the air, its faded red tiled roof surrounded a parched gravel and terrazzo enclosure with deeply shadowed porticos. This desolate façade fronted a myriad of underground chambers that honeycombed the bedrock of this stoutly-defended outcrop.

Stark and forbidding, this was the home of CMES, with a membership that reverently referred to this hallowed ground as *Romae matrem*, "Mother Rome," since its relocation there in 30 BC after the fall of Ptolemaic Egypt to Augustus' legions.

DeSalvo met with Feng Bai within a newly renovated high-ceilinged chamber, an airy space which was once a grand dining room. Transformed to suit

Feng Bai's Hong Kong tastes, his office was a serene island of silk pastel carpeting centered on an inlaid wooden floor. A low desk and cushioned furniture made of fragrant teak woods completed it. Long removed were the ostentatiously gilded high baroque appointments from the previous administration. DeSalvo intimately knew all about this, for he had, as the former chairman's assistant, been in charge of that administrative transition.

Still, upon entering the chairman's office area, DeSalvo sensed a tension in the air he would have to somehow relieve. If he didn't, he knew he would leave as a dead man.

Standing in his socks at the leading edge of the luxuriant carpeting, DeSalvo waited for the chairman's acknowledgement before entering his space. He knew Feng Bai had heard his approach, but had continued on with his writing nonetheless. Finally, the man put down his pen, raised his bald head, and signaled the Italian to approach.

Still DeSalvo stood patiently, awaiting the invitation to sit. Feng Bai's eyes softened ever so slightly at his guest's careful deference, his appreciation of place, especially given the precarious nature of his situation. Feng Bai nodded toward a cushion. His subordinate sat.

After a few moments, a deep sigh came from the chairman.

"*Signore* DeSalvo," the chairman began in flawless high Italian, "my ears have heard some distressing news."

Feng Bai, a kinesic empath and telepath, mastered languages with ease and enjoyed unnerving many by addressing them in their native tongue. Still, the man had his favorites—Cantonese, Mandarin, and Thai in the East, and Spanish and Italian in the West, based purely on their tonal qualities. The many Germanic and Slavic tongues he spoke as well, but he found their guttural sounds distasteful. No one knew what his preferences were on the many Arabic dialects, even though he could seamlessly speak them.

Ah, DeSalvo thought, *I see that my superior in New York, El-Najjar, has taken the opportunity to sarcastically sing my praises.*

"Chairman, I am burdened with far worse news."

This caused the chairman's eyebrows to raise, his round face to pale.

"Speak."

"Mr. Chairman, J.J. Stone, the TIIIS Lictor of Magic, has come into contact with a powerful North American ley line called the Silver Nile. The man has evolved, and my assault teams blundered directly into him. Prior to the raid, we did not know of this development."

At this turn of events, the chairman sat back and slitted his eyes. "Tell me more."

"Yesterday, I took the initiative and was informed of this information by *Signora* Valeria Costa, the former oracle of the Presto *familigia.* Just what Stone's capabilities are, at this point, no one knows. Frankly, sir, I would counsel that we should henceforth expect the worst."

Again, Feng Bai's eyebrows rose, causing wrinkles to form high up his scalp.

"I am very familiar with *Signora* Costa's flawless reputation and I commend you for consulting with her.

But when you say, 'expect the worst,' what precisely do you mean?"

"*Signora* Costa has called Stone an *l'umo potente*. While not a precise term, it is evocative of the man's power and potential. Additionally, I discussed with the oracle a possible means of injuring him."

"And ..."

"She advised me to systematically and graphically remove all of his friends and relatives. She further suggested that such a course of action would eventually drive him mad with grief, perhaps even to suicide."

Several moments passed as Feng Bai stared holes through DeSalvo's head, who somehow remained resolute and cool.

Finally. "Is this not the same man who killed our security forces somewhere in the American West?"

"*Sí*, Mr. Chairman."

"And Stone, now enhanced, has killed many more of our brethren?"

"*Sí*, Mr. Chairman."

The chairman's fingers began drumming rhythmically on his desk's green leather writing pad.

"First, I find *Signora* Costa's recommendations overly hopeful and ludicrously weak. If anything, if any harm befell Stone's friends and family, I would fear the man's vengeance long before his suicidal grief. Stone is a soldier, a warrior, a bannerman, first and foremost."

"Second, is there any possibility that the man might become one of us?"

DeSalvo had never before entertained that audacious thought, and he even dared to say so.

"Every man has his price, *Signore* DeSalvo." Feng Bai emphasized with a raised thick finger. "Find out

Stone's.

"Finally, *Signore* DeSalvo," Feng Bai's eyes hardened, "you are a cultured man. I have faith in you. Otherwise, you would be dead."

CHAPTER 3
The Thirty-First Floor

Times of high stress or grief motivate people. I experienced this all too often while in the military. So when an old acquaintance called me up, I wasn't really all that surprised.

"Is that you, Mr. Stone?" a tentative male voice asked.

"Yes, it is."

"Mr. Stone, this is Alex Grimes, we met a while back during a traffic stop on the New Jersey Turnpike. I was driving a bright yellow Ferrari Spider. Remember that?"

On the other end of the line was Gordi Meneer, a former CMES researcher and freelance news journalist, but now with a new identity—Alex Grimes.

"Oh, you bet I do." I answered having finally put two and two together. "So how's the Wild West working out for you, Mr. Grimes?"

"Just wonderful." I could hear the crinkle of his smile in his voice.

"So what can I do for you, Mr. Grimes?"

In a conspiratorial tone, "Well, just yesterday, right out-of-the-blue, I was visiting the Georgia O'Keefe Museum in Santa Fe over on Johnson Street, when I ran into an old friend of mine. What are the odds? Well, she was bitching a blue streak about the poor morale in her finance department to the point she quit her job. She also told me where her former employer is located. It turns out that they're all crammed in like sardines onto the thirty-first floor of a hotel overlooking Times

Square. Needless to say, I figured that you would appreciate knowing that."

"Indeed, I would." Stone said juggling his smart phone against his right ear. "I have my pen ready. What's the address?"

Later, after I had finished shooting the breeze with Grimes, I was back on the phone.

"May I speak with President Silver Moon?" I said to an unfamiliar male voice.

"And who's this?"

"Sir, my name is J.J. Stone."

"Sorry, Mr. Stone. I'm new at this post. One moment please."

After a brief pause, a connection was made.

"What can I do for you, Mr. Stone?" President Silver Moon said in her crisp, business-like way.

"Madam President, I have acquired the address of the temporary CMES North American headquarters."

"You don't say."

"Ma'am, what do you want me to do with this information?"

"I will leave that up to you, Lictor of Magic. Rely on your common sense and keep me in the loop."

"Will do, Madam President."

*　　*　　*

I needed to pull my team together who had, in the past, brimmed full of creative ideas. So I asked Peter Glass and Mr. Henry to join me at the Academy for the weekend. They agreed—eagerly I might add, because not being stupid, they had an idea of what might be on the agenda.

We gathered at the Acorn, the Academy's pub in

the basement of Old Main. Here, low ceilings, lower lighting, intimate nooks and crannies, wooden beams and woodwork long etched with names and loves, wonderful food, and even better beer all reigned supreme.

The wizened Fourth-Class Adept, Mr. Henry, as usual, brought his thirst. Smacking his lips following a long draught, he began the proceedings. "J.J., what's got you all hot and bothered now?" he stated with a dirty grin dripping with conspiratorial anticipation.

"Do you remember a certain yellow Ferrari that we pulled over on the Jersey Turnpike?"

"How couldn't I? That thing was an automotive wet dream."

"Well, I got a call yesterday from its owner, Mr. Meneer, who is now Mr. Grimes courtesy of our security department, and he passed along the location of the temporary CMES North American headquarters in Manhattan."

"You don't say," Mr. Henry said with another big grin.

"And gentlemen, President Silver Moon has given me a green light to use that information as I please. Hence today's topic. We did a damn good job of planning and executing the removal of Presto. Now, what should we do about their temporary digs?"

Peter Glass adjusted his new wire-rimmed glasses and frowned over his pint. "Just how far do you want to go with this, J.J.? Do you intend a biblical one-for-one exchange? Exact direct retribution for the Christmas Eve Massacre?"

"Our president requested that I use my common sense in planning this op, which I intend to do. But no,

Peter, my thought is not to go ape, but instead to simply unnerve CMES with a feat of sheer audacity."

"What do you have in mind, J.J.?" Mr. Henry asked.

"Imagine for one moment how CMES would react if we *again* plundered their HQ like we did several months ago, but this time we abduct their new regional director. Once in our hands, we squeeze him dry of intel, and when we're finished, we deposit him at the front door of the hotel we kidnapped him from. A quick in and out, with little or no bloodshed, but with a big message sent: You're powerless to stop us."

"I really like the minimal bloodshed angle," Peter admitted. "What you describe sounds more like an elaborate prank. The more we make it look easy, the more it will hurt. Do we want to leave a calling card? Just to grind it in?"

"No, whatever we do has to be as sanitary as possible," I said. "Let's create some doubt and confusion within their operations and security personnel."

"Dazed and confused, I really like that. Do I get to interrogate their new RD?" Mr. Henry wanted to know.

And before we knew it, we were off to the races, brain-storming and scheming. Our table fast became a forest of empty beer bottles.

"We'll need some recon, J.J., to get a feel for the place, don't you think?" Mr. Henry said rubbing his hands together and glancing over at Peter.

"My thoughts exactly. What do you say, Peter? Up for some good old fashioned astral projection recon?"

Peter smiled beneath his mop of salt and pepper curls. "I would love to."

*   *   *

I personally experienced in Somalia and Iraq just how any planned action can fall apart, come undone, or go seriously sideways at the most inopportune moment. In fact, throughout military history, uncertainty had become so axiomatic that terms like SNAFU and FUBAR said it all.

My battlefield experience told me that magical confrontations had to behave the same way, since the paranormal, by definition, presented more variables, more unknowns. Once an aggressive undertaking was put into motion, the opportunity for those plans to unravel became extreme.

With these considerations in mind, our assault on the thirty-first floor began at six pm, on a Saturday, because my planning team wanted to keep civilian casualties to a minimum. But since preparations for the raid began the day before, CMES would have, at least potentially, more than enough opportunity to make things go terribly wrong.

Trouble nonetheless began, not with CMES, but rather with the hotel's management, who could only provide us five of the eight rooms needed on the thirty-second floor. Our plan specified that these upstairs rooms were to be evenly spaced on the hotel's square floor plan, two for each of its four sides. The actual distribution was decidedly lopsided leaving one side completely uncovered. Regardless, we went forward.

*   *   *

On the Friday before, Bill and Sue checked into the fancy hotel on Times Square. Posing as newlyweds, they were all giggles. But once they reached their passion-pit on the thirty-second floor, they flipped over the room's bedding to reveal the carpeted floor surface beneath, complete with dust-bunnies. From her luggage wheelie, Sue handed out the safety goggles, removed a high-torque, low-speed power drill, and loaded up in its chuck a long, half-inch masonry bit.

Meanwhile, Bill busied himself with a magnetic rebar detection device the size of his palm. The gadget blinked a red light whenever it passed over a metallic object. After a few swipes, Bill tore off two pieces of blue masking tape and made an X on the carpeting.

"Here you go, Sue. Go slow and I'll cover you."

Slowly she began turning the drill bit into the fire resistant concrete slab that divided the two floors. Bill figured that it would take them about an hour before they reached their initial ten inch bore—one to two inches short of breakthrough.

During the drilling process, Bill removed a portable vacuum cleaner from his luggage wheelie. With it he vacuumed the floor in an attempt to cover any sound or vibration from Sue's industry, and in the process, cleaned up any evidence of their handiwork and all those dust-bunnies.

A little over an hour later, and with their drill and vacuum all repacked, the team of Bill, Sue, and the three other TIIIS couples now sat back and waited for their appointed moment.

Unfortunately for the four couple-teams, the subtle rumble from one of their drills had been heard on the floor below. A quick call from the CMES Security Department to the hotel's management confirmed that no construction-oriented work had been scheduled for the thirty-second floor.

As a consequence, the North American region's armorer, Mitzi Randolph, posted a red flag warning, as the assistant regional director, Mr. William DeSalvo, was out-of-town. In his absence, the responsibility for their operational security temporarily fell to her. Now with their security cordon bow-string tight, no threat appeared. Hours dragged on and still nothing. After ten hours, Randolph eased the alert status, mindful of the strain, and much to everyone's relief. The detected mystery rumble was all but forgotten.

Mitzi Randolph, nonetheless, remained worried because while the assistant regional director was overseas, she backed him up. Always had, always would. The two shared a bond that went way back. As for Randolph, she was a smallish, almost mousey woman of indeterminate age, with brown hair and eyes, a lean build, and about five-four. In essence, a face easily lost in a crowd, but a highly intelligent one.

Since Randolph was the region's new armorer and DeSalvo's long-recognized assistant, rumor said there had to be far more to Randolph than met the eye. For one thing, her oddly accented English grated on the nerves like fingernails on a blackboard. For another, she had a stiff, formal demeanor, which meant the armorer rarely smiled.

*   *   *

Bright and early on the day of the assault, a Saturday morning, four TIIIS agents posing as hotel HVAC engineers began their inspection of the ventilation systems for the thirty-first floor. These they accessed through a maze of narrow, walled passageways that serviced every room's plumbing and electrical. Almost one fourth of the hotel's footprint had been devoted to such service passages.

Standing before the HVAC schematic that had been posted on the back of the access passage's door, the fingers of the four technicians traced and confirmed where they should go.

"Joey, this section is going to be a tough squeeze for you," one quipped. "You gotta' start laying off the pasta."

With their inspection completed by noon, the four pseudo-HVAC engineers did what all such workers do, they went to lunch. Joey was predictably ravenous. When they returned, however, each member of the foursome carried a dark duffle bag and wheeled between them four large, high-pressure gas cylinders that looked like welding tanks. Once they got back into position within the access passages of the thirty-first floor, they too waited for their appointed time.

The welding tanks contained a sleeping gas called Penthrane. A volatile gas, when introduced into an environment, it readily vaporized. Pleasant smelling, Penthrane fit this assault's non-lethal requirements and presented few medical risks.

Remarkably, all of these activities remained transparent to the CMES staff and their security personnel.

*   *   *

That Saturday, at 5:40 pm, the four TIIIS HVAC engineers closed and taped off the exhaust ducts on the thirty-first floor while setting its atmosphere to recirculate. Donning gas masks from their duffle bags, they vented the four high pressure tanks into the thirty-first floor's intakes. The Penthrane began to flow. While the egg-heads had run the numbers, doubt still remained as to whether the four large tanks would be sufficient to knock out the floor. Working in their favor were the floor's sealed windows and emergency exits. The borders of the five elevator doors, however, leaked like sieves.

*　　*　　*

Twenty minutes later, a steady flow of delivery personnel began showing up before the hotel's central stack of twelve elevators—parcel post, pizza, donuts, telephone technicians, a florist—twenty in all. All headed for the thirty-first floor. Each waited to take a different elevator.

A few minutes later, two FDNY first responders with a gurney showed up. When a hotel staffer made a point to help, one said, "Naw, not necessary. The call came from the thirty-first floor. The guy's got a known heart condition. Probably too many donuts. We got it handled. But thanks for the offer to assist."

Excepting the first responders, all of this activity went unnoticed in the usual hubbub of the Saturday evening hotel guest traffic.

*　　*　　*

At 6:00 pm, Bill, with a sweating brow, swung a heavy hammer and drove a quarter inch steel bar through the remaining structural concrete with a bang.

"Shit! That was loud enough to wake the dead!" Sue hissed.

"Yeah. It was," he agreed.

Her partner's swing resulted a neat conical hole in the ceiling of the thirty-first floor. Removing the steel bar, Sue quickly inserted a live Wi-Fi jamming antenna that extended four inches into the room. Bill then filled the aperture with expanding foam on the thirty-second floor side to prevent any gas leakage. By 6:01, the five couples crossed their fingers hoping that the Wi-Fi on the thirty-first floor had been fully suppressed to the outside world.

*   *   *

Those hopes were dashed when two CMES North American security staff heard a distinctive ping as a chunk of the ceiling flew down at them. Looking up they now saw a black antennae pigtail hanging down from above their heads.

"What the fuck is that?" one immediately blurted out.

"Dunno. Looks kinda like a piece of black licorice. Yeah, you know, like a Twizzler that you get at the movies. Better call it in to Randolph, Craig."

Craig did, and then the pair collapsed while in mid-sentence as they were overcome by the Penthrane. Their call, however, had not gone unheeded, for while most were already fast asleep, Mitzi Randolph remained bright-eyed and bushy-tailed.

"Craig. Come in, Craig. Damn it! Were under attack again!"

Randolph tried to call for backup, but discovered that she couldn't. Looking down at her device, she saw that there were neither cell signal bars nor Wi-Fi.

"Shit! We're being jammed!"

*   *   *

At 5:57 pm, Andy Green, former senior IT manager, and newly promoted CMES North America Security and Communications Manager, luxuriated in a hot shower. In fact, the entire bathroom of his hotel room took on the appearance of a steam bath.

Damn I need this, Green thought as the hot stream pounded the back of his neck.

We lose that entire detachment in the New Mexican Mountains. Then our headquarters floods out. I get handcuffed and interrogated by a blue-eyed security Nazi wearing SWAT gear. Our regional director is murdered the very same night. What the hell is this world coming to?

Bam! Regime change, and that damn rehiring process. All those interviews. You'd think that I had done something wrong. Now at long last, my promotion comes, but with a ton more stress.

Not good. Not good at all. I'm outta here. Things are looking pretty shaky. But not before tonight, and my hot date with that luscious Cuban in finance. Then I'll walk away a satisfied man and never look back.

*   *   *

I arrived first on the thirty-first floor. You would have to be deaf, dumb, and blind not to sense the oppressive weight of the magical defenses—and that was before the elevator doors opened. When they did, the sensation felt like breathing in syrup. We fully expected to find the same at the floor's emergency exits. In fact, Peter's astral visit several hours before confirmed it. Based upon what we learned from the raid on CMES' Fifth

Avenue property, their magical defenses would not trigger if someone did not cast any magic. At least that was what the experts had to say.

Dressed as a brown uniformed parcel postman, with my UCS underneath fitting like a second skin, I carried two boxes. One had held my gas mask, which I now had on. In the other, I had my X-26 Tazer with two spare electrical cartridges.

As the elevator door opened, I remained back in the cab, partially hidden behind the right side panel, and it was good that I did. Apparently, the look of my gas mask was not exactly a welcome fashion statement.

BRRP ... BRRP went a machine pistol.

A suppressed round flung me back, while the weapon continued to stitch the cab's back wall of shiny brushed stainless with punctures. Meanwhile, the CMES security guard—who had shot me from behind a make-shift security barrier of room desks fronted by door panels—collapsed due to the sleeping gas. His partner, already affected, had fallen face first into a half-empty box of chocolate cake doughnuts with toasted coconut sprinkles. Two other guards were also out cold behind the check-point.

Sitting on my butt, I looked down and saw that my UCS was intact—*Thank God!*—but my left shoulder hurt like hell. It hurt to even breathe. I knew, at best, I was heavily bruised, but my past experience with gunshot impacts in Iraq suggested damaged cartilage. With my left arm numbed silly, I grabbed the railing with my right, and, wincing, grunted, pulling myself up. Finally exiting the cab, my left arm just hung there, limp, buzzing, tingling, and screaming at me all at the same time. *Oh, for joy. What a way to start an op!*

Once the next elevator arrived with five more of the assault team, we disarmed the security guards, disassembled their weapons, and cuffed them where they sat or fell. We even left the one guy with his doughnuts. By now my arm began to respond, but continued on with its god-awful screaming.

Only then did we begin our sweep through the floor, heading off in a clockwise direction. Half way down the first hallway, lay several other collapsed security guards. We extended them the same courtesies as we did the guards at the elevators.

*　　*　　*

The teams continued to arrive, and silently went about their assignments. Our opposition appeared to be all down for the count. It seemed the eggheads had gotten their calculations right on the gas.

The techies scrounged whatever computer data they could. Going from room to room, they gathered laptops and smart phones, and loaded up the boxes we had brought up. Meanwhile, we trussed up all the security types, who numbered twenty in all. We found only four civilians and the regional director, a low count, probably because it was a Saturday evening.

On my sweep I entered room 3102, and I opened its bathroom door. And there, on full display in his birthday suit, stood this skinny guy shaving in a cloud of hot shower steam.

I laughed into my gas mask at his look of complete surprise.

"Time to get dressed buddy. I'm not room service."

Every op has such moments of incongruity. The guy with shaving cream on his face hurriedly got dressed, but didn't get sleepy. I couldn't figure it out until Stephenson caught up to me, looked in, laughed at the scene, and said, "All clear, Stone. You can take off your mask."

Then the skinny guy gave me a shocked look. "You're Stone? The guy from New Mexico?"

I nodded, "Yeah. What of it?"

"You're our worst nightmare."

"Where did you hear that?"

"I was the guy you talked to on the sat phone."

"You don't say?"

"Please don't kill me!"

"Well, today's your lucky day. Stephenson," I called into the hallway, "get back here, pronto."

A rush of steps later and the TIIIS security agent returned. "What's up?"

"Take this guy downstairs. If he makes one false move, kill him." I said with an unseen wink.

"Understood. What's your name, buddy?"

"Green, Andrew Matthew Green."

"Well, Mr. Green, follow me."

*   *   *

I never saw the regional director as the first responders had evacuated him on the gurney sometime during the first ten minutes of the raid.

At fifteen minutes into the op, we called it quits. Our evacuation plan called for a buddy system, two-by-two evacuation in separate elevators, each with a box loaded down with plunder. We were all gathered at the floor's lobby, ready to split, when all hell broke loose.

Soul Carrier, look out! The First Soul screamed into my inner ear.

All clustered together in the elevator lobby, we made for easy targets who could not maneuver without injuring one of our own. I heard the awful sounds of breaking bones and the screams of pain.

Whirling around, I saw it, just as two elevators arrived—a short, hairy, ape-like thing swinging two nasty looking clubs etched with glyphs. With large yellow eyes it paused in its carnage to stare at me.

With four men down, and more sure to come, I screamed, "Get in the elevators! This one's mine!"

Not thinking, I rushed the thing. Its mind was blocked, but its widening yellow eyes told me that it recognized me. And when its drooling mouth filled with dagger-like teeth smiled and said, "Stone." That confirmed it.

Not daring to use any of my offensive magic within the heavily warded lobby, I instead discharged my Tazer into the creature's face. One dart penetrated each of the creature's cheeks. This caused an enraged and echoing shriek that seemed to pressurize my ears. I quickly slapped in another battery and zapped the creature again. It seemed to stiffen.

Dropping its wooden clubs, the hairy ape-like thing fell to its knees as it struggled to pull out the Tazer darts from its face. Silver-coated, the darts delivered their electrical shock, but also poisoned their entry wounds, temporarily incapacitating demon-kind. While it was distracted, I swung hard with my right fist and connected with a meaty *thud* against its jaw, which dislocated grotesquely. I knew that I connected because its big yellow eyes rolled back, and body collapsed in an unconscious heap.

What the hell was that! I said to my disembodied

tenant.

A very dangerous body-morph, Soul Carrier. Not a shape-shifter. This one retains its full adept intellect, while it changes into a specific form, instead of many.

That was when the third elevator arrived. The four remaining team members jumped in. With my shoulder still hurting like hell, I staggered into it, and only breathed a sigh of relief once the cab began to descend.

"That was damn close," I gasped out.

"What the hell was that?" Bob Jacobsen asked, also in a brown parcel post uniform.

"Not sure. Maybe some kind of shifter. Definitely demon-possessed. Its aura was an inky black. What's the status of the injured?"

"Already en route to a friendly hospital," Shirley Smithson said in her florist outfit, "The one that the plan called for."

"Good."

"How about you? I can tell that you're hurting something fierce." Jacobsen observed.

"Shoulder, maybe cartilage. We were damn lucky."

"No shit." Smithson agreed.

While the raid was underway, the four Wi-Fi couples pulled up their antennae, refilled in their bore holes with foam, and replaced their bedding, all nice and neat. The HVAC engineers, having restarted the floor's exhaust vents, had already left with their tanks and gear, no one the wiser.

As hoped, we reaped another bonanza of CMES financial and human resource data. When compared with the first haul, the tech-heads discovered many new links and confirmed established ones, much to the glee of those who live for such things.

The regional director, a fellow called Mukhtar El-Najjar, after several hours, sang like a bird, and in the process—or so I'm told—basically outted the entire CMES upper echelon in lurid detail. Another intelligence windfall. But the best part—when we finished with him, we left him on the curb of the very hotel we borrowed him from, in his disheveled clothing. Talk about being reduced to carrion for the vultures.

The real prize, however, remained Andy Green. TIIIS now had its hands on a CMES North America Security and Communications manager who could answer our technical and operational questions. On top of that, Green turned out to be a likeable sort, who even knew Gordon Meneer, aka Alex Grimes. Small world.

*   *   *

Mitzi Randolph awoke to a pounding headache and a throbbing jaw. Naked, she slowly took inventory of her overall condition, while she painfully levered herself up to a sitting position. Unconsciously, she had gritted her teeth, which sent another wave of nausea through her. Touching the highly sensitive right side of her face, she barely recognized it from all the swelling. Feeling the two ulcerous and weeping holes in her cheeks reminded her of who had given them to her.

When Randolph had been rendered unconscious, her form naturally reverted back to its usual human appearance. In the process, her jaw had realigned, but the injured region still needed nature's own mending.

Randolph's mind raced. Her first priority was to assess the damage. Next, was to contact DeSalvo. Only then would she care for herself.

*   *   *

The CMES chairman sat with William DeSalvo over lunch. The man graciously chose to deliver his monthly status report in person at the Roman enclave.

"*Signore* DeSalvo," Feng Bai queried in flawless patrician Italian, "how is Manhattan?"

"I have just received a communication from my assistant. The news is not good. The temporary headquarters has been raided … by TIIIS."

"TIIIS! Again? How?"

"My assistant, *Signora* Randolph, whom I left in charge of the facility's security, positively identified Stone at the scene. In fact, she engaged him, and failed to kill him.

"As to how the facility fell, Randolph said they had been gassed. Only she was able to fight back."

"How was that possible?"

"*Signora* Randolph … how can I say this … possesses a very special physiology that is immune to sleeping gas … among other things."

"I see. But what is the status of Manhattan?"

"Our computer data was plundered. Our regional director was taken as well."

For the first time in a long time, Feng Bai felt a chill on the back of his neck.

What's with the North American region? Feng Bai asked himself, while shaking his head.

More importantly, who will be the right person to fill its regional directorship?

Feng Bai's chill intensified. *How can TIIIS repeatedly do this, and with such apparent ease?*

Feng Bai then made his decision.

"*Signore* DeSalvo, you are to be my new regional director of North America. Sadly, your predecessor was not up to the task. Because of that, I have lost face."

At the sudden announcement, DeSalvo dared not to move, much less blink.

"As the new regional director of North America, I expect two things. First, the full restoration of our Fifth Avenue property. And second, a permanent solution for Stone."

Feng Bai then leaned forward over his lunch and locked eyes.

"*Signore* DeSalvo, let me be absolutely clear: I want Stone dead. I do not care how. I do not care the cost."

Throughout that brief pronouncement, to an outsider, the chairman's face would have appeared neutral, as if he had been describing a carry-out order of spicy ramen noodles.

But from DeSalvo's practiced point-of-view, never before had he seen this man's emotions surface so forcefully. His usually sublime countenance now radiated the snapping crackle of pure anger and frustration.

"Understood, *signore*," he said as a bead of nervous sweat formed at his hairline.

*   *   *

"My most beloved one," the Devourer of Souls keened from the abyss of the Dark Realm into the mind of Mitzi Randolph. "You have been cruelly injured by the most hateful of beings. Yes, it was the Lictor of Magic who did this to you, but he is controlled like a puppet by the First Soul of Creation. That, my dearest, is our greatest foe. And to defeat both, you will require far greater power, and this I will gladly provide thee."

So was put into motion the devious plan of the Devourer of Souls.

CHAPTER 4
Grand Opening

Unlike El-Najjar, DeSalvo's stint as the former CMES chairman's assistant had seasoned him well, exposed him to CMES' staggering human intelligence— HUMINT—capacity and its technical resources. Even with the recent scandal of the twenty-two within the U.S. Congress, DeSalvo saw that as only a temporary hiccup. Replacements would be found. Politicians loved power and money and DeSalvo had access to both.

El-Najjar had blundered into thinking the floor of a Manhattan hotel could be transformed into a fortress. He should have known better, especially since Baghdad's Green Zone had been his home for most of his life. Yes, DeSalvo recognized this represented El-Najjar's first foray into the rarified atmosphere of CMES leadership. As such, he unconsciously cut his former superior some slack, even to the point of pitying the man.

What a way to go. To be dumped like so much garbage in the street.

That's why, when DeSalvo took over, he had moved CMES North America's headquarters out of Manhattan and into a secluded Westchester estate. Here, his security staff enjoyed spacious fields of observation, a tall stone wall, and a single entrance gate. Further defensive preparations were in the works. Best of all, Mitzi Randolph was seeing to them.

The newly appointed regional director heard a knock on his office's door jam. There, standing at the threshold, stood the still hideously black and blue Mitzi.

He waved his assistant in and pointed to the lone chair of the austerely decorated room. She sat with her hands folded on her dark pant suit.

"Mitzi, what can I do for you?" DeSalvo asked while staring directly into her pain-faded brown eyes, purposely ignoring the two festering wounds on her cheeks.

"I wish to report that the electronic security improvements to our estate's grounds have been installed and tested. As for our own … defenses, they will be completed within a few days."

"Excellent. Is there anything else?"

"I want a shot at Stone."

"You'll get one, Mitzi. I promise."

*　　*　　*

Early on, the new regional director of North America, DeSalvo, had met with all the principal contractors involved in the renovation of the flooded out headquarters building. In no uncertain terms, he held them all to their schedules. In fact, DeSalvo established a generous bonus scale for the building's completion ahead of schedule, and at the same time outlined serious penalties for any overruns.

With carrot and stick established, the North American headquarters building was completed early. Its grand opening now stood before him. But that stunning signature event paled in the mind of DeSalvo, who so dearly wanted to turn his attention to the ultimate source of his organization's considerable ire— the man who had ruined the forty-one-story Fifth Avenue address in the first place.

Yes, the Vatican had been involved, DeSalvo

conceded. Of that there was no question. The expert testimony of a spell whisperer proved that connection. But to everyone's surprise within CMES' hierarchy, TIIIS had played an even greater role. Based upon several pieces of circumstantial evidence and the testimony of a defector, so had its Lictor of Magic.

Down deep, the Italian wanted to capture Stone, break him, and then make an object lesson of his displayed remains. But this was not about what he wanted, but rather his chairman's most recent direct order to eliminate him at any cost.

On DeSalvo's desk blotter rested the man's dossier, which grew in thickness with every exploit. It was first assembled decades before by the late Regional Director Alexander and updated by the late Chairman Presto. DeSalvo himself had tweaked it.

He whispered to himself as he patted the thick folder, "Indeed it's time that Mitzi sunk her teeth into something meaty. I'm quite sure that Chairman Feng Bai wouldn't mind."

That decided, he reached for his phone to address another matter.

"Ms. Goodson. Hello, this is William DeSalvo. How are you today?

"Just fine, Mr. DeSalvo," the husky feminine voice answered. "I was hoping to hear from you."

"Do you remember our discussions about our club's membership drive and grand opening? Well, we now have firm a date: thirty days from today. I am authorizing you to go ahead and launch the campaign that we agreed upon."

"We are ready, Mr. DeSalvo." A confident Goodson said. "Do you want full saturation?"

"Excellent. Begin tomorrow. And yes, I want full media saturation. Goodbye, Ms. Goodson."

For the first time that day, DeSalvo smiled. *THIS is going to be apoplectic.*

It is fair to say that marketing makes the world go round, and DeSalvo knew he found a keeper in Shelley Goodson. When he offered her control of the whole enchilada—a blitz promo in print, social media, radio, and cable TV, she had bit, and bit hard. On top of that, her edgy and gifted team needed just two months to create all of their eye-popping creatives he paid for upfront. Truth be told, it wasn't all that hard. After all, the product was the stuff of pure fantasy—an exclusive Manhattan social club and spa devoted to skills training in witchcraft and wizardry.

Now, in DeSalvo's mind, it was just a matter of timed execution and the canny release of further teaser-material, all to create a brilliant, Fifth Avenue, media sensation.

"*Wicked*, eat your heart out!" he said.

*　　*　　*

Gala Grand Opening

The Gathering opened its Fifth Avenue doors yesterday. This high-end social club and spa caters to paranormals—or those who think they are. The lavish red carpet festivities were invitation-only.

The newly renovated property has consumed the Manhattan building trades for the past fourteen months. "No limit" became the watch word for this tastefully appointed, if elitist, establishment.

Membership provides valet parking, concierge

services, meals 24/7, hotel room, a mesmerizing list of personal amenities, and paranormal training. Access to this sybaritic experience is granted via a chipped, carbon-fiber membership card, complete with holographic image.

Want to become a member? Expect a stratospheric initiation charge and monthly service fees higher than any country club in the Hamptons.

(*The New York News*, Op Ed Section, A1)

"So," DeSalvo asked from the head of his boardroom's conference table, "how goes our membership drive?"

Jennifer Sauerbrünn, the club's statuesque blond Director of Membership, gushed, "Through the roof, Mr. DeSalvo. I predict that we will have to tighten our membership requirements. Otherwise, we will be in danger of diluting the occult talent of the Gathering."

"An interesting problem to have, but I am quite sure you will somehow manage." DeSalvo replied with a smile only for her. Sauerbrünn's response was a deep blush, while she wetted her lips.

"Finance. How are we doing?"

Vince Spence, the CFO of CMES North America, unconsciously spoke with his hands and exceptionally long fingers, which formed elaborate gestures as he quite literally manipulated his ledgers in the air. "Pre-sales' figures, $2.19 million. Opening day sales, $1.7 million. Our first week of business, not including opening day, another $3 million. These figures do not include our former CMES memberships, who took advantage of our generous special offer."

"How many members did we retain, Ms.

Sauerbrünn?" the chairman asked.

"Seventy-two out of seventy-three for Manhattan. 399 out of 430 state-wide. Only Andrew Green, our former Security and Communications Manager, has not re-upped since the break-in at our temporary office on Times Square. In fact, he has gone missing since that event. Mr. DeSalvo, I find it … suspicious."

"Why?"

"Because Green's aura was all wrong, in spite of his recent promotion. He remained a dissatisfied man. Either he's dead, or, far more worrisome, may have betrayed us."

"I see. Get with security and look into that. We can ill afford to have former employees running around loose and giving away our state secrets, now can we?

"Out of curiosity, how many new members have we attracted to our Gathering, meaning specifically, CMES?"

"Fifty-three. Many are foreign nationals."

"Nice.

"Back to finance. Based on the numbers you quoted, Mr. Spence, what do you project as our annual gross?"

Spence closed his eyes while his fingers caressed the air before him, and ten seconds later, by DeSalvo's own reckoning, Spence responded, "For this quarter, $21 million; for the year, close to $100 million. After our initial surge, I expect at least a ten percent drop off before we settle out."

To this news, DeSalvo grunted with satisfaction. In the meantime, he noted that Spence's forecasted decline had caused Sauerbrünn's back to straighten, her demeanor to bristle—a sure sign of turf issues.

Turning toward another sector of the table, he asked, "Advertising. How is the spin, the juice, doing?"

Constance Goodman, a thirty-something brunette who had somehow remained her own woman in charge of her own ad agency, said, "Mr. DeSalvo, your club's logo is everywhere; word of it is on everyone's lips. Daily hits on social media alone, since day one, have not fallen below a half-million. We have saturated cable and satellite television with your commercials. Mr. DeSalvo, you command an international juggernaut."

In acknowledgement, DeSalvo nodded in Goodman's direction.

"Any security issues?"

Gregory Anderson was a powerfully built black man with a no-nonsense demeanor. "Counterfeit membership cards have already begun springing up. Four were confiscated yesterday when they attempted to gain access. It seems, at least on the street, that our cards are the thing to have. Other than that, we've been air tight."

"Thank you, Mr. Anderson. So our membership cards are all the rage. What a pity."

Shifting gears, DeSalvo added, "Anderson, be sure to get together with Sauerbrünn about this Green character. He occupied a sensitive post. You have full authorization on background and surveillance."

"Yes, sir. Right away, sir."

To all of this good news, DeSalvo internally beamed. Within perhaps five years, the cost of the building's restoration should be behind them. After another, the entire operation would be financially deep in the black. Best of all, he was doing his job promoting CMES in the most audaciously and public of ways.

Suddenly, a thought occurred to him. DeSalvo saw himself as a twenty-first century Hugh Hefner, the very architect of the sexual revolution, free love, and the Playboy mansion phenomenon. In order to achieve that kind of impact, DeSalvo knew this Manhattan flagship facility represented just the tip of an iceberg. Las Vegas was next, a bastion to be built in the center of the enemy heartland, and near a ley line to boot. And his lawyers were jockeying for a prime Madison Avenue property in Chicago. And after that, who knew?

But most satisfying to DeSalvo was the impregnable nature of his facility. The Gathering was just a club, a legitimate business. As a twenty-four hour, three hundred and sixty-five day a year private club full of innocents, who would dare attack it? Yes, upgraded magical protections had been installed—especially on the roof—and yes there were four internally camouflaged floors, designated CMES-only, which were off limits to the general membership. Yet, DeSalvo knew that its very presence would vex those he was trying so hard to smoke out. He knew at some point, they would again show themselves. When that day arrived he would be ready, as he was that very moment.

After the board meeting, DeSalvo retired to his private office suite. He relished his club's many initial successes, but then his phone rang.

"Mr. DeSalvo. Chairman Feng Bai is on line three."

"Thank you, Charlene."

Punching the three button on his encrypted phone's base, DeSalvo looked up at his office wall with all the international clock faces and said, "Good morning, Mr.

Chairman. I trust that your day began well."

"Indeed it has, Mr. DeSalvo. I have just received an update on the reinvention of your Manhattan headquarters. You have been most imaginative."

Not really knowing what Feng Bai meant by "imaginative," DeSalvo chose to flat-out ignore it, and instead dispassionately stated the financial and membership facts.

"Very good, Mr. DeSalvo. Most promising indeed, and after only one week. But what of your missing employee, Andrew Green?"

At the mention of Green, DeSalvo's pulse elevated, but he quickly recovered.

"Sir, I have authorized a full background check and security sweep on Mr. Green and his whereabouts."

"Very good, Mr. DeSalvo. I am looking forward to reading your monthly report. Good day, sir."

DeSalvo hung up the phone. Feng Bai's mention of Green floored him. It revealed so many things; could be read so many ways. On the one hand, the chairman told him a member of his executive board was in his pocket chirping like a little bird. On the other, his chairman's call represented a raw flexing of influence that heightened his caution and quelled any overconfidence. Feng Bai was far more intelligent than Presto had ever been. As far as DeSalvo was concerned, that phone call was a sobering reminder that success could be fleeting.

CHAPTER 5
The Oracle's Overture

DeSalvo, still stunned by Feng Bai's knowledge of Andrew Green's status, had his train of thought shattered again by his receptionist, Charlene.

"Mr. DeSalvo. You have another overseas call on line two. The caller would not identify herself, but was most insistent."

"Thank you, Charlene. I'll take it."

"DeSalvo."

"*Signore* DeSalvo, I sense that your day has been a a horse ride. Is that not so?" purred the Italian voice.

"You are most perceptive." DeSalvo replied in his native tongue. "Indeed it has, *Signora* Costa. What a pleasure it is to again hear your voice …" Glancing at his collection of clocks on the wall, he smoothly added, "… and how is the weather on this Roman afternoon?"

"Glorious, simply glorious, *signore*. However, I did not call to discuss such pleasantries. I wish to invite you to my family's restaurant for dinner. What does your calendar look like?"

DeSalvo's mind staggered. Such an invitation was not the usual, especially from an oracle like *Signora* Costa. He instantly decided.

"That is most generous of you, *signora*. I can be in Tivoli in two days' time. Would that be agreeable?"

"That would be agreeable, *signore*," Costa echoed with pleasure. "Dinner will be at nine. *Ciao*."

DeSalvo hung up the phone and sat back into his cocoon-like office chair.

What just happened?

*   *   *

Valeria Costa's family restaurant had been part of the economic fabric of Tivoli since before the First World War. Once during that period, a Michelin representative had stumbled into its cozy confines and had rated it at three stars, but the family had purposely held back, not wishing the unwanted notoriety. They were content, instead, to allow the ancient town's other restaurateurs the gustatory glory. This self-effacing deference was noted within the tight community, appreciated, and the family's wine was subsequently adopted by several kitchens as a result.

Prior to that, the Costa family had only sold its wine at the Via Scuole Rurali address. For how long? Centuries. It is said that the family made its first fortune by providing the common table wine for a long line of vacationing Roman pontiffs. Today, if one can acquire a bottle, their reds consistently rate in the high nineties. None is exported beyond the province.

*   *   *

DeSalvo's curiosity caused him to arrive five minutes early. Or was it his stomach's anticipation of an exquisite meal? Split on which ruled him at the moment, he instead smiled and surrendered. He ducked under the heavy wooden lintel and entered a meagerly lit atmosphere of elegantly appointed tables and indescribably delicious aromas. His stomach churned. Yes, he decided. While very curious, his gut had won the day.

All the tables at that hour were full of patrons, their conversations subdued. In the far corner sat an attractive middle-aged woman with flowing dark hair. He made for her and en route was acknowledged by a raised glass of red wine.

"*Signore* DeSalvo. You're early. Could it be that you are hungry?"

Smiling, "*Signora* Costa, indeed I am, but this evening it is you who is a feast for the eyes."

Costa enjoyed this clever compliment.

She poured her guest a generous glass and then lifted hers.

"*Signore* DeSalvo, welcome again to my family's restaurant, and thank you for fitting me into your busy schedule. Here is to the future."

They sipped at their wines, locking eyes.

"*Signora*, what do you have on your mind?"

"An alliance, *Signore* DeSalvo. I am an oracle without a patron."

The regional director of North America put down his wine and sat back in order to take stock.

Costa leaned forward on her elbows, peered back over the edge of her wine glass, and waited with expectation.

"I am most flattered, *signora*. Why?"

"Because you are highly intelligent, someone who I admire, and, I suspect, someone with a future."

"Currently, I could use your advice." DeSalvo admitted. "It is true that I am juggling several balls at the moment."

"Allow me, *signore*, to guess—the launch of your new enterprise and a directive from on high to deal with a certain *l'umo potente*."

Now it was DeSalvo's turn to blush.

"You are most astute, *signora*. In many ways, the

'launch' as you say, is proceeding quite well. But that *l'umo potente* does indeed remain problematic."

"We have discussed him and a feasible solution for him before. What has changed?"

"I have been ordered to pursue a different path, *signora*."

"Really ..." the oracle murmured with a tilt to her head.

"He is quite a specimen, *signore*. Do you wish me to deal with him?"

"Would that be wise?"

"Probably not. But it *is* a viable option. Around women, he seems quite gullible, almost child-like."

"Interesting observation. But for the moment, let us return to your first offer before we consider the second. It is one I would embrace. How do we ... formalize such an alliance?"

"With your signature."

"In blood?"

"No, *signore*. Don't be so melodramatic. The contract, while quite ancient, is also blessedly devoid of juristic nonsense. Can you read Latin?"

He nodded, which caused Costa to genuinely smile with pleasure. She leaned over and retrieved a large cardboard mailing tube. From it, she carefully extracted a rolled parchment wrapped in white silk. With both hands, she presented the curiously scented document like a fragile gift.

Now holding it, "May I unroll it?"

"Gently, *signore*."

DeSalvo did so, slowly. What he saw he couldn't believe. Indeed, it was a contract, written in the old style grammar and legalistic format that he remembered from an old university class devoted to ancient Roman law. Brief and succinct, the liabilities and responsibilities of both parties were clearly specified in only four paragraphs—the statement of purpose, the provider of services, the buyer of said services, and the indemnity clause. All followed by a long list of signatures that took up most of the document's space. With too many to count, DeSalvo estimated that before him were over sixteen centuries of signatories. He noted at least five different lettering styles. The last he easily recognized, as he had forged it many times— Giovanni Presto.

Truly awed, DeSalvo reached into his suit coat, removed his fountain pen, ever so carefully signed his name, and blew on it to dry the ink.

After carefully rolling up the parchment and placing it within its silken sheath, DeSalvo handed it back to the oracle, who immediately slipped it back into the cardboard cylinder.

"And now *signora*, I am curious, how do you propose to deal with this gullible child?"

CHAPTER 6
The New Chapel

Two people huddled before the burned skeletal remains of the Old Oaks Academy chapel. Deep in conversation with heads together, nearly touching, they ignored the cold. The blond, bearded, tall one was lean and wore a bright blue down ski coat, faded jeans, and work boots. The other stood only to his shoulder, her long black hair hung in a tight ponytail with turquoise ornaments that glinted in the frosty sunshine.

"Professor Humphreys, what you propose I truly welcome. How did you know I wanted to build a new chapel?" President Silver Moon said.

"Frankly, Madam President, the need wasn't exactly a state secret. In my plans for the new chapel I've added a crypt for the unclaimed nineteen."

That detail sold it for the president. "How will this crypt be constructed?"

"It won't be, Madam President. Instead, it will be hewn out of the native limestone bedrock. I have already taken the liberty to discuss the matter with the Brood Mistress of the *Argenti*. For a small sum, her brood will provide what we need."

Forgetting herself in the rush of detail, the president asked, "When can we begin?"

"Madam President, we have already begun with this discussion. But specifically, and with your blessing, in the early spring, just after the snow disappears. The *Argenti* hate the stuff."

* * *

True to Humphreys' schedule, on March 15th, his student surveyors began their careful work, aided by the many advances in single station, laser technology. Their challenge was to lay out the new chapel's foundation right next to the old without endangering it. The plan called for an overarching, porch-like roof of aluminum and glass that would enclose the relic, making the two edifices one.

The curious came and went, but two witnesses remained, who felt their presence during the snapping-of-the-line proceedings would somehow ratify the project. I was one of those hangers-on, who found the entire process fascinating, if not a sacred act. Critical was the delineation of the future crypt, which took several hours of care. By the mid-afternoon of day one, with all the lines established and flags in position, the *Argenti* got to work.

I sat on the sidelines just watching, taking in all the proceedings. Professor Humphreys, finished with his management of the survey, sauntered over and joined me.

"Well, Mr. Stone, what is about to happen I think you will find quite interesting," the professor hinted.

One moment the heavily trodden ground was quiet and abandoned as the survey lines' many florescent flags waved in a gentle breeze. The very next, the *Argenti* brood arrived quite literally out of thin air, and suddenly, the new chapel's foundation was overrun with scurrying silver and tan streaks running every which way. I smiled, being reminded of a Chinese fire drill, but far more frenetic.

"That's the brood mistress," the good professor said as he pointed her out in the midst of this maelstrom. How, I don't know. "You'll excuse me for a moment."

Humphreys got up and crossed over into the survey area, bent down on one knee, and began a conversation with the brood mistress, pointing this way and that. Then he rejoined me at my place of observation.

Thereafter, in the course of an hour, I witnessed the clearance of the soil overburden from the entire foundation down to its uneven bedrock—some three feet deep on average. The spoil was neatly piled nearby as if by magic. Then, just as suddenly, all the *Argenti* disappeared, except for the brood mistress, who came over to visit us.

"Honorable Rasha." I said. "What have I just witnessed?"

Surprised by my comment, the brood mistress looked at me, tilted her head, and then nodded to herself as if the question needed a reply.

"Noble Lictor of Magic. The *Argenti* must pause often in our labors to replenish our fluids and groom ourselves. We love water and my brood is currently enjoying it." Then she added with an offhanded shrug, "It is the way of things."

The brood mistress then addressed my companion.

"Honorable Professor Humphreys, where do you wish the crypt's entrance to begin?"

Then it hit me. The florescent stakes, orange construction tape, and flagged lines meant nothing to her. They were for *us*.

Professor Humphreys seemed to understand this, because he stepped over the surveyor lines and showed the Brood Mistress within the staked out foundation where the crypt's descending passage was to begin.

"I wish your brood to begin here," he said as he went to his knees and carefully marked out a rectangle on the bare rock with a black marker. "Make the entrance a rectangle like this, oriented in this direction," he indicated with parallel and outstretched arms, "that would be easy for someone like Mr. Stone over there to enter without hitting his head."

"Honorable Professor Humphreys, do you wish a gentle ramp or a staircase?" She queried.

"A staircase will do nicely."

The brood mistress, a chipmunk-like creature that stood almost six inches high, now surveyed the scene. She, for her part, cocked her head this way and that, with her eyes, looking here and there, quite clearly surveying.

Finished, she asked, "Noble Lictor of Magic, please stand so that I may measure you."

So I did, while she walked around me, penguin-like, on her two hind legs.

"Thank you, Noble Lictor of Magic. I now have my marks." Then she said, "Honorable Professor Humphreys, how deep do you wish the passage?"

"Deep enough to provide the crypt with a bedrock roof three feet thick,"

She just nodded again, paused in thought, and disappeared right before our eyes. I guessed, probably to refresh herself.

I sat down again with Professor Humphreys, and waited for the *Argenti* to reappear. When they did, some fifteen minutes later, I could see there must be about three hundred of them. Working as one—just watching them, their organization, their industry, mesmerized me—they tore into the bedrock that the architect had marked out.

From my vantage point, as if by magic, the limestone bedrock within the outlined rectangle began to disappear.

So that's how they do it! I realized. *They don't walk anything anywhere. They just move it really fast somehow.*

"Ah, Professor Humphreys, how do they do that?"

"You mean their ability to translocate?"

Thereafter, like a kid at his first baseball game, I was torn as to where to sit, because I couldn't keep still. *Should I watch the digging? Or, should I marvel at the ever-growing mound of soil?* In the end, the amazing excavation of the crypt's entrance won out.

So picture this: Me sitting cross-legged with my elbows on my knees on an upslope edge of the surveyor's foundation markers. My eyes recorded what looked like a buzz saw tearing into the bedrock, but with no dangerous flying debris or clouds of dust—just the ever-constant disappearance of rock within that rectangle. So precise were the *Argenti* that the ink from the master architect's own marker was partially shaved away here and there. I know. I eyeballed it.

During a work stoppage, the brood mistress again visited us. At her approach, seated as I was, I bowed my head to the creature before me. This time it was Humphreys who spoke.

"Honorable Brood Mistress, the labors of your brood I find most remarkable. Kindly excuse me, however, as I have other preparations to attend to." And with that, Humphreys stood up, bowed deeply, and withdrew.

The brood mistress turned to me as if she expected

me to say something. After an embarrassing moment, I found my tongue.

"My apologies, Honorable Brood Mistress, for not knowing of your ways. Can you teach me about them? I can assure you that I am a ready listener, and a good student."

To my request, the brood mistress' eyes widened. Then she bowed her head in assent.

"Thank you, Honorable Brood Mistress. I would be most honored to learn of your ways."

To that, the brood mistress actually shied her head to one side.

"As a tribute to your brood's industry, I wish to make a gift." With that said, I removed the small backpack that I wore and placed it in my lap.

Opening it, I said, "I am told (thank you, Mr. Good!) the *Argenti*, next to silver, prize dark chocolate with almonds the most."

I carefully placed before the brood mistress six packages of mini chocolate bars, some three hundred individually wrapped silver foil chunks. Seeing this, the brood mistress betrayed herself as she took two steps back with an open mouth of surprise.

"Oh, Noble Lictor of Magic, this is not necessary. It is not part of the original bargain," she said as she gazed drunkenly upon the vast boon.

"Honorable Brood Mistress, I believe that a lasting relationship sometimes begins with a simple gift."

I got up, announced that I would return the next day to observe their labors, and turned to leave. Several steps away, I peeked over my right shoulder. Both the brood mistress and all the chocolate had disappeared!

The next day I arrived early at the excavation site,

only to find the brood mistress waiting for me. Bowing low, I said, "Good morning, Honorable Brood Mistress of the *Argenti*."

Bowing her head, she said with warmth, "Good day to you as well, Noble Lictor of Magic. Please sit, and be at ease."

I sat down as before, cross-legged, and leaning forward.

"Noble Lictor of Magic," She began with her head held high. "We, the *Argenti*, wish to thank you for your most generous gift. And I have considered your request for instruction in our ways. I believe that I can fulfill that request." Her voice trilled with pride.

Delighted, I bowed my head low and murmured, "Thank you, Honorable Brood Mistress. You may begin."

"Firstly," she began, "all *Argenti* live where there is a nearby spring. It is vital to our needs and community.

"Secondly, we hoard silver and consume it with our food. This is why our teeth and claws shine so brightly. And why demons and demon-kind fear us so.

"Thirdly, we *Argenti* prefer to live in oak forests, for that is where our old broods first resided. I believe that you call it Central Europe.

"Noble Lictor of Magic, what else might you wish to learn of our ways?"

"I want to learn how to translocate."

CHAPTER 7
Translocation 101

I returned to the *Argenti* excavation the next day, plopped myself down once again on the now long trampled margin, and soon enough fell into a conversation with the brood mistress.

"Noble Lictor of Magic, since we will be working together on this quest of yours, we must be honest with one another, as one is with family. As a way to initiate this relationship, I henceforth wish you to call me Rasha. It is my birth name, and one that is only used amongst family and relations."

To this, I bowed my head and said, "It would be my pleasure, Honorable Rasha." And sensing the need for diplomatic parallelism, I returned, "And henceforth, Honorable Rasha, you may call me J.J., my human nickname, used only by my family and close friends. It is far easier to say than my long birth name of Jonathan Joseph."

"So be it, Noble J.J. Let's us begin."

I saw that the curl of her tail signaled pleasure at our exchange. But to my surprise, Rasha's tail suddenly straightened. She frowned and crossed her tiny arms across her furry, silver chest. Seeing this development, I waited.

Finally, she spoke. "Noble J.J., I am told that virtually anything that can be imagined can come to be. Our ability to move without moving is taught to our young from the beginning. It is a long and ingrained process. I do not know, however, whether a being as large as you, has ever learned to do so."

"Okay, I see your point, Honorable Rasha. But how are your young trained in the first place?"

Twisting up her face in embarrassment, Rasha turned her head this way and that before she provided me with an answer.

"We initially associate the skill with bodily elimination. As a young one feels the urge to purge, that necessity is linked to moving without moving beyond the brood's nest. It is a hygienic issue. As a consequence, the skill early on is associated with a young one's control of its physiology, from which it earns social acceptance."

"Surely," I argued, "there must be some sense of focus, some physiological triggering mechanism that can be learned … taught."

"No, Noble J.J., the act of moving without moving becomes entirely instinctual. Your challenge is to imagine yourself needing, at a primal level, to move a small distance. I do not know how to translate this feeling to you. You must discover it yourself."

On this flimsy basis, I began my experimentation with translocation. I sat and imagined myself several feet to the right. That didn't work. I tried to imagine the deep-seated urge to urinate, but could only do so once I successfully translocated. That didn't work either.

I was missing something obvious, maybe something even simple. So I kept working at it, all day in fact, without any result. Then it hit me. Push and release. That mantra John Running Deer had drilled into me way back during my early hand-to-hand defensive training. The mental exercise was similar to holding one's bowels and bladder, and then the relaxation of their purge. It was like tensing my lower gut, squeezing, and then releasing with an audible grunt. So I tried it, got really dizzy, and for good reason. I had spun myself around four times!

While I was struggling with this new "project," the laboring *Argenti* brood watched me. They somehow sensed my failing efforts and found it amusing. But when I had finally performed my "spin move" near day's end, a noisy chatter erupted as the *Argenti* had cheered my first successful attempt.

"Quite well done, Noble J.J.," Rasha commented. "But if you can imagine yourself leaning forward, perhaps next time you will actually move somewhere without moving," she finished with a wry smile.

For the next several days, I learned to "lean" toward where I wanted to go during my "push and release" exercises. I realized the sensation of leaning was itself a mental command, and so I tried it that way, and discovered a far greater level of success.

By day four, I was zipping about the construction site, a virtual blur. While I most certainly was not ready for blind map coordinate translocation, I had become sufficiently proficient with my line of sight movement. Soon I was gobbling up fifty, sixty yards in one translocation. I also realized how handy this newfound trick would have been in that New Mexican pine valley, or, for that matter, during last Christmas Eve. Zipping around, sniping, zipping again, slashing with the Bone Sword, it sure beat bellying crawling from place to place or sprinting to the next helicopter.

This new skill also reminded me of swimming across a river, where every so often, you had to stop, look up to orient yourself, before you could proceed again in the direction desired. Needless to say, this required practice, and while the *Argenti* performed their excavation miracles, I practiced my own.

CHAPTER 8
R.I.P. Mr. Good

Early on in life, I learned to stay busy and work ahead, as unexpected surprises do happen and emergencies always arise. A classic example of this "life happens" phenomenon was my hurried evacuation from Philly on that November day. I had all of my critical gear in my scoot-and-scram duffle bag when I grabbed my computer and drove my red Colorado truck to the Academy. Only moments later, several CMES goons blew up my dorm.

Now billeted at the Academy, I finished up the edit on my MA. Mr. Good, my on-campus a thesis reader, helped me immensely. Eventually satisfied, I submitted the work with a cover letter to the publisher's website that Peter Glass, my thesis director at the University of Pennsylvania, had strongly suggested.

Now here is where things got a bit tricky. In order to submit my materials, I had to go to the public library in Latrobe to transmit the files. I did so only once, and left detailed instructions for the submission's editor to contact me via one of my throw-away smart phones.

Three weeks later I got a call. Sam Dempsey, my editorial contact, liked my manuscript and wanted to include it in their series on ancient magic. Dempsey said that he'd give me a call if there were any issues.

*　　*　　*

Prior to the Christmas Eve Massacre, I regularly visited Mr. Good, who was also the Academy's resident expert on ancient magical texts. This fine scholar labored over *The Book of Spells* that I had "recovered" during the first raid on CMES' North American headquarters in Manhattan. And in case you haven't noticed, he co-edited the translation of *The Knot of Eternity* with Gregory L. Love, and wrote a commentary on that oftentimes inscrutable work. When it came to ancient languages, Mr. Good was simply better. And to have the man as my thesis reader made it only better as well. As an academic courtesy, I had my publisher send Mr. Good a pre-publication review copy of my thesis for his personal library.

Visiting his office was always a treat. Entering the Meyers building was like visiting the European Dark Ages with its massively thick Romanesque architecture and narrow, arrow-slit windows. Just getting to the second floor required a steep climb up a tightly twisting, easily defensible, stone staircase.

Mr. Good could always, somehow, sense my approach, for before I had even a chance to knock on his door frame, he would warmly greet me with, "Enter, J.J. I have been expecting you." How he did it, I was never quite sure, so it became a game. I shielded my thoughts well before entering Meyers, and still the man could sleuth me out!

His office was downright cramped, more a rough stone walled broom closet than anything else. But that was his way. The gifted linguist preferred closed in, uncluttered, monkish surroundings.

For today's visit, however, that certainly was not the case, as everywhere books were stacked high upon the floor all around his desk. His desk's top was similarly crenellated with just enough space for several sheets of paper. In truth, all I could see of the man was his balding head and ever radiant smile.

Seeing my shocked face, Mr. Good just smiled and said, "Have a chair. As you can see, I'm up to my eyeballs."

Without skipping a beat, he went on, "And thank you again for that advanced copy of your thesis. It's so full of insights and novel conclusions and its indices are an absolute lifesaver. I have already used them twice today. I'm quite convinced that it will become a cornerstone publication among certain academic circles. I think the general paranormal community will snap it up as well."

"Why?" I asked.

"Because J.J., you're writing style, your voice, is so clear and matter-of-fact. In this dusty field, it's like a breath of fresh air."

I felt a warm blush spread across my face that I hadn't gotten since Adam Gibson found me teaching myself Sumerian in the Willis Library. "Thank you for those kind words. I guess we'll just have to see."

"Now, regarding *The Book of Spells*, I have done a careful comparison of the incantations contained within with those in your two articles and thesis. And guess what? Fully twenty-five percent of them are not only Sumerian, but are, practically speaking, word-for-word copies, which, most wisely, you edited for public consumption. As a result, *The Book of Spells* proves one of your thesis' conclusions. To wit: that there must have been a thriving trade in seriously dark spells way back when, and, apparently, the sellers were not all that particular to whom they sold them."

My thoughts exactly, and I said so. "In fact, Mr.

Good, since the Dark One began collecting his spells during the Venetian Renaissance, it only emphasizes the wide dispersion and longevity of these spells. In some ways, that fact alone is quite frightening in and of itself. I'm just amazed that we haven't detected evidence of trouble earlier in history."

To this, Mr. Good, sat there thinking, brow furrowed, clearly deep in thought. Then, "'Longevity,' yes, that is precisely the issue, their preservation and transmission over the intervening centuries, if not millennia. It's well understood that papyri undergoes a natural burn, a process of fibrous deterioration over time that requires their copying. That, however, is not the case for fired clay tablets. They, like any fired ceramic, persist far longer. Nonetheless, the trade in illicit magic must have been brisk and supported by a clientele who could pay for it.

"As for the historical record, I'm afraid that if we began looking for evidence for the use of dark magic, we might be surprised. Just off the top of my head, the outbreak of the European Black Plague of the fourteen hundred's might have been such a result. After all, it did begin in Venice, the home town of the Dark One.

"That suggests to me, that perhaps CMES actually might have been involved in the tamping down of some of these magical outbreaks before things got out of hand."

"What, CMES doing the right thing?" I said with surprise.

"Why not, if it wasn't in their own best interest? Besides, consider the issue of competition. Do you really think CMES would foster it?"

After that heady discussion with Mr. Good, my

head was in a spin with all the possibilities about where history might have been directly or indirectly affected by dark magic.

Damn, I miss that man.

CHAPTER 9
Summer Course in Spell Casting

Being a self-made Alexandrian white witch is one thing, but being able to wield lethal magic at a moment's notice is quite another. Such craft called for alacrity, a good memory, and the common sense to control one's intensity during the heat of an engagement. Otherwise, as my tutor, *Monsieur* Dexter, always reminded me, "*Madamoiselle* Melaina. Why use a sledgehammer, when a fingertip will do?"

I took my long summer break from the university to reside at the Old Oaks Academy in order to immerse myself in defensive and offensive magic per my promise to J.J. I found the daily grind of one-hour sessions with *Monsieur* Dexter to be mentally strenuous and physically intense, bruising, and sometimes even brutal. I now know why J.J. insisted on this training. He was absolutely right. I had simply no idea. I needed game.

Ah, J.J.

I have to admit, his presence on campus drew me here. I shamelessly admit it. Using the excuse of my intensive training made that decision easy.

Nearly every day I see him, while he watches over the new chapel's construction, all the while putting himself through God knows what in order to master that arcane ability of translocation. *Monsieur* Dexter, still recovering from his grievous burns from the Christmas Eve Massacre, has quietly praised J.J. for his efforts to master an ability that the *Argenti* had made their trademark.

Whenever I see that Marine's infectious grin, my heart jumps. His energetic enthusiasm suddenly appears whenever he completes a new feat, or while he explains an ambitious plan. His sheer energy and force of will I find breathtaking.

But enough about J.J., back to my training. I met with my instructor, *Monsieur* Dexter, every morning, Monday through Friday, in his office precisely at nine. Located on Old Main's third floor, it was the last door in the building's southwestern corner. Whenever I knocked on that old wooden portal, I heard from within, *"Entrez."* Frankly, it reminded me of my childhood days in Alexandria and my visits to the French Archaeological Mission's headquarters. No matter how lightly I treaded, or which path I would select, his office's wooden floor betrayed me.

I must admit that I have a special place in my heart for *Monsieur* Dexter. For a man past his prime, perhaps in his mid-fifties, he had shown extraordinary courage and sacrifice during the Christmas Eve Massacre. That heroic act had taxed his system. Since I had seen him last, he had lost weight, making his large Gallic nose, thin lips, and concave cheeks even more so. There was that noticeable shrug to his injured shoulders and back. Outwardly, he had that stock vampiric look, if such things ever existed. But to me his smoothly shaven continence, sheer will, and unflagging desire to teach made him my Achilles.

In truth, *Monsieur* Dexter matched his eighteenth-century surroundings and period correct furniture—the floor to ceiling bookshelves, their attendant wheeled wrought-iron ladder, Louis XIV desk, seminary book stand, and a massively gilded, throne-like visitor's chair. These trappings he juxtaposed against several Neolithic, rock-hewn monuments of unknown providence and purpose.

Naturally, we conducted our sessions in French, which began with an observation from the previous day's lesson, or, a common pleasantry. This last was required because oftentimes our sessions would end in emotionally charged words. Still and all, it was understood that *rigueur suffisante* was required if I was ever to succeed at standing by J.J.'s side.

"*Madamoiselle* Melaina. To date, your mastery of the spells is excellent, but the force behind your words is lacking. Must I always goad you or prick your finger?

"Must I remind you again that words are just a focusing tool, like the lens of a microscope? What you must grasp is that emotion cannot solely drive your castings. Emotion saps one's energy; a resource that must be carefully managed. But your *will* does not. Your *will*, *mademoiselle*, must be developed, tempered, and strengthened into a formidable tool.

"Have I made myself clear?"

I nodded.

Monsieur Dexter then stood up from behind his desk, removed his suit coat, cravat, and to my surprise, even his cufflinks and dress shirt. Standing tall before me was the pale and hairless torso of a gaunt man.

"*Mademoiselle*," he commanded, "this"—while gesturing to himself—"is what emotion brings to magic: weakness."

He then turned and showed me his ruined back, a painful looking patchwork of healing skin grafts from the burns he suffered during the Christmas Eve

Massacre. Here and there I saw scabbing and oozing plasma along their many imperfect borders.

Monsieur Dexter then pointed to his back. "And this, *mademoiselle*, is what *will* can do."

As my tutor dressed himself I noticed the many dried blotches of blood on his dress shirt and realized that he must be in considerable pain. And yet he soldiered on to teach me his craft.

Did I feel shame? Deeply. Did I silently vow to reapply myself? Most certainly.

Now fully dressed and seated again, *Monsieur* Dexter looked at me, and my tears, with hard and penetrating eyes said, *"Bon ... en garde!"*

* * *

"*Madame* Melaina, this session was your best effort to date. Your limits were stretched. And today, we have established you do indeed have a will." A heavily sweating *Monsieur* Dexter gasped out.

Meanwhile, the Alexandrian noted her linguistic promotion from young lady to woman. On some subliminal level, she must have passed a test, reached some threshold. Maybe had even gritted out some new-found respect?

Dexter's unfocused eyes suddenly hardened. "*Madame*, have you ever killed?"

Ashamed, I admitted that I had, of a CMES physician who had murdered my mother.

"How did you do it?" Dexter pushed.

"With magic."

A moment passed.

"With far more than just that my dear," Dexter said as he carefully sat back into his chair.

"We have also established you have a serious disadvantage. Your mind is transparent." Dexter observed. "You cannot block your thoughts. While your defensive magic is improving, your offensive attempts I could easily block, even though they were appropriately placed."

"Is mind control hard?" I foolishly asked.

"*No, Madame*. It is necessary."

"I will teach you. We will begin tomorrow.

"In preparation, you now have an assignment. An effective mind block is an image or abstraction that one hides behind like a Greek hoplite shield of old. Not just any convenient icon will do. It must be something you can embrace with all of your being, yet to an outsider must appear confusing or mysterious. *Madame* Melaina, your symbol must attract your attacker's curiosity and confound him just long enough for you to strike back with a telling blow.

"Until tomorrow, *Au revoir*."

CHAPTER 10
The Crypt

By week two the entrance to the crypt, its stairwell, and chamber had been completed. The crypt's narrow floor now held nineteen perfect rectangular trenches, all precisely cut by the *Argenti*. Meanwhile, my line-of-sight translocation skills had become *almost* second nature.

A few words are necessary regarding the quality of the *Argenti*'s work. Somehow, someway, these master excavators produced an entrance passage and chamber with smoothed wall and ceiling surfaces that reflected like a mirror. How they did it, I haven't a clue. With the addition of minimal lighting anyone's claustrophobia would vanish in an instant. Meanwhile, the staircase and floor surfaces were prepared with a uniformly pebbled texture that easily gripped one's shoes. Throughout, all dimensions were spot on and square. I even assisted Professor Humphreys in their measurement—an act that was more ceremonial than qualitative.

As for the nineteen sepulchers, each was provided with grooved edges, precise to the millimeter, ready for their marble slabs. Humphreys confided to me that the marble quarry could not guarantee that nineteen slabs would properly fit, so he had entered into a second contract with the Brood Mistress for her kin to finish dress each.

While speaking of grand productions, at the conclusion of the *Argenti*'s excavation project, Professor Humphreys presented the Brood Mistress, per their agreement, with two ingots of fine silver, each weighing approximately a kilo, or forty measures by the *Argenti* reckoning. This presentation I observed, as with all things *Argenti*, was performed with the utmost seriousness and ritual.

*   *   *

Once the marble slabs had been fitted and inscribed with the names of the nineteen, their ceremonial transfer took place with solemn decorum. Only then, once finally interred, did the construction of the above ground portion of the new chapel proceed, following strictly to the design of the former, literally above the watchful eyes of the nineteen.

CHAPTER 11
The Portent

Valeria Costa doted over her roses. Starting in the early spring she would don her gloves, her mother's old rubber knee pads, and begin her daily visitations to weed out this, prune that, water, and fertilize. The flowers benefited, but Valeria did, too, for during their ceaseless care she was enjoyed a brief respite from the harsh realities of the paranormal world.

But this day, those realities intruded upon Valeria's peace of mind. While watering her roses with a large galvanized can, the water in mid-pour became a bright bloody red color.

A portent has arrived! Valeria recognized. *I must get to the grotto!*

Dropping the watering can, Valeria ran like the wind.

She entered into the darkened family chapel, constructed of native stone and crudely dressed. The only light came from a brazier that cradled the original Eternal Flame of Rome, which flickered out its light through a battered bronze grating; its oaken smoke scented the air. To Valeria's left, a polished silver basin rested upon a short Corinthian-styled pedestal. Gripping its sides, she prayed to its clear waters.

I, Valeria, call upon Thou, oh ancient one.

I, Valeria, devoted high priestess of Vesta, seek a vision.

I, Valeria, spiritual daughter of Coelia Concordia, *Vergio Vestalis Maxima*, command you to do so.

I, Valeria, keeper of the most sacred flame of Rome, command you to do so *now*!

The basin's crystalline waters stirred, darkened, and then presented the image of a man appearing, disappearing, and reappearing in different locations around a ruined stone foundation. The waters briefly settled, then reformed around the image of what looked like a ground squirrel, but one with shiny teeth and claws of silver, who clearly was instructing the man. The waters settled and cleared. The portent ended.

Valeria's brows first wrinkled in thought, her eyes then widened in revelation, and she clapped her hands over her mouth in understanding.

Stone can now translocate like an Argentus!

Stunned, the oracle drunkenly shuffled out of the grotto's darkness and returned to the bright morning sunlight of her rose garden. While bees buzzed about, she contemplated the ramifications of what she had just seen. She thought about how to frame the significance of this new development for her new patron.

He won't believe me. Valeria thought as she finished her watering. *I must convince him nonetheless.*

* * *

A heavily encrypted e-mail arrived at DeSalvo's laptop in his Manhattan office. One look at the address told him its origin and of its importance. Once opened, he read, and then reread it again.

This cannot be true. If it is, this means serious trouble. Something that I cannot hold back. Feng Bai must be informed. Somehow, I have to confirm this before I do.

CHAPTER 12
Paul Kiel

Mr. Paul Kiel, a senior intelligence asset of the North American regional director, inwardly smiled at his boss' request. *It's about time,* thought the former executive of a Washington Beltway alphabet soup agency. Kiel took pride in his ability to anticipate a superior's needs.

That remarkable skill, however, was a two-edged sword. Kiel's preference to undersell and over-deliver had gotten him into trouble by out-performing Beltway institutional favorites. His current employment with CMES North America was the direct result of such a predicament.

Kiel had had Stone's file on the back burner simmering for several months, ever since his damaging exploits against CMES' daring, if not blasphemous, Christmas Eve airborne assault on their Academy. Thereafter, the man had practically fallen off the face of the earth. Kiel well-recognized Stone could be practically anywhere.

How odd. The former intelligence analyst thought. *The man is like a nuclear submarine—periscope up, periscope down. He effortlessly goes off the grid and suddenly resurfaces in the most tantalizing of ways with a* New York Times *bestseller on a provocative subject—demonology in the ancient Near East. Then, after Christmas Eve,* poof, *he disappears again.*

Kiel frowned in thought, and his eyes carelessly settled on his own thumb-worn copy of Stone's book, *Curses and Demons: Dark Magic from Ancient*

Mesopotamia. Its paperback spine was heavily creased from use. It's printed title barely readable.

I'm missing something. Stone's a bright guy.

More deep thinking.

His forthright presentation of the material has even spilled over from the academic world into the public domain. He's now "a must read" among normals and paranormals alike. Stone would be a sure-fire talk show celebrity. But no, he's chosen the shy route without a public face or voice. Was that his intentional choice or his publisher's marketing angle?

And what an odd publisher he hooked up with. They offered zero personal information and couldn't locate him either. Our hack of their accounting system proved a total bust, as all of their authors' names have been reduced to random ciphers. Clearly, they have an antiquated, perhaps even manual, system, but one that must curry the favor of their clientele, who are quite an odd bunch in and of themselves.

Before the Christmas Eve Raid his only in-the-flesh appearance was based on a dicey second-hand report from that special congressional investigative hearing of the infamous twenty-two. Some nonsense about a blinding light, ectoplasm, maybe even an exorcism.

If true, that's confirmation he's TIIIS' Lictor of Magic, which nicely dovetails with what the South African defector told us. That would explain why TIIIS is actively counter-punching, something, I am told, that they institutionally have never, ever done before.

Kiel went over yet again Stone's background, studied his Marine photo, smiled, and slammed the file closed with conviction.

TIIIS has a for real combat veteran for their Lictor

of Magic—a guy who just so happens to be an expert on ancient demonology. That First Soul business is just icing on the cake. Now it all makes sense. He's using technology that cannot be as readily tracked instead of magic. Get in, get out, with as little evidence left behind as possible. Use misdirection and disinformation. All, standard, military psy-ops doctrine.

I wonder what DeSalvo would think of this analysis?

*   *   *

"I'm sorry," Stone declared to his president, "but we should do something to CMES, something that will hurt them. I'm not talking about biblical retribution, no overt reduction to their numbers, but instead something that will harm them institutionally. We've got to get into their heads and begin messing with them."

President Betsy Silver Moon was intrigued. Never before had her society's martial Lictor of Magic so passionately expressed what amounted to a non-violent action.

"What do you have in mind, Mr. Stone?"

"I want to plant a question mark in their thinking, and here's how I want to do it."

*   *   *

"Mr. Kiel?"

"This is Kiel."

"Mr. Kiel, I'm Kelly Post with Internet security."

"What's up?"

"I have activity in Pennsylvania that I think involves Stone."

"Send it over, immediately. And, thank you."

"You're welcome, Mr. Kiel," the timid voice said, happy to be off the line.

Well, if manna didn't fall down from heaven! Kiel groaned with anticipatory excitement.

Moments later, he was right.

Would you just look at THIS. Stone must be throwing a barbeque party tomorrow evening. He even used his credit card to set it up. Hello, Mr. Stone. What an opportunity for some pay back!

He reached for his phone.

Kiel arrived at his boss' office five minutes later and then cooled his heels for another three. Being ushered into DeSalvo's office represented a psychological treat for the former company man. The regional director was not about appearances, but results. His office was sterile, functional, but technologically leading edge. It wasn't a throne room. The only flaw to this picture hung on the wall—a magnificently framed six by three foot black and white photograph. A white-haired Enzo Ferrari in sunglasses cheered in raised armed jubilation, while his victorious F1 car blurred by.

"Mr. Kiel, what do you have for me?" said DeSalvo, all business.

"Sir, Stone has for several months eluded us. That is, until today."

That news got his boss' attention, making him lean forward.

"Today, our Internet Security office reported that Stone used his credit card in a western Pennsylvania location near the TIIIS Old Oaks Academy. The purchase was for the catering of a celebration that will take place in two days. Sir, what do you wish me to do with this intel?"

DeSalvo weighed the information. Kiel could tell because his penetrating eyes turned distant and far away.

Then he pinched his lower lip and grunted.

"Mr. Kiel, Stone is very special, very dangerously special. This intercept is much like the one he used to set up the massacre of thirty-six of our security force in New Mexico. Is there any way that you can corroborate this intercept? You Americans have that marvelous saying, 'Fool me once, shame on you, but fool me twice?' No, sir, I will not authorize any action until you come up with supporting evidence. Hell, for all we know that credit card could have been stolen, cloned, and only now used by some third party."

The security expert couldn't disagree with his boss. In fact, he found himself completely agreeing with him. We needed more data, pure and simple, before any decisive action could be made.

*   *   *

"Is this Kelly Post?"

"This is she."

"Ms. Post, this is Paul Kiel."

"Ah … what can I do for you, sir?" the timid voice faltered.

"Ms. Post, that intercept you told me about today I shared with Mr. DeSalvo. He's quite interested in it."

Gulp!

"Now, what he wants you to do is corroborate the content of that intercept. Find a way to verify it."

"Mr. Kiel, right off the top of my head, I can't think of any way to do that, but if you give me, maybe an hour, perhaps I can come up with something."

"You have that hour. Don't disappoint us."

Kelly Post felt as if the entire weight of the world had been placed on her shoulders.

What am I going to do? She furiously thought.

Then it hit her and Kelly's fingers began furiously keying.

Forty-eight minutes later, Kiel's phone rang.

"Kiel, here."

"Mr. Kiel, this is Kelly Post from Internet Security. I have your confirmation, sir."

Pleased, Kiel couldn't help but smile while he asked. "What's your confirmation?"

"Well, my niece just got married and I had to call and call to make all the arrangements, and that's when I thought that I'd do the same in this case. I researched the establishment where the celebration is to take place and I called them. I asked if I could make a reservation for ten on the same day as Stone's party. The kind lady said that their kitchen could not help me as there was already one scheduled for that evening."

"So you spoke with the restaurant owner directly?"

"No, sir, just someone named Yolanda, who works there."

"Ah-ha. Did you happen to get a name on that other reservation?"

"Yes, I did, sir. She referred to it as the 'Stone party of eight.'"

"I see. Well done."

CHAPTER 13
The Barbecue Palace

When Kiel informed DeSalvo of the latest evidence on the Stone party, he received authorization to send three squads to Pennsylvania. To Kiel's surprise, DeSalvo also included in that deployment the region's armorer, Mitzi Randolph. Apparently, the opportunity to nail Stone once and for all had arrived.

What had been left unsaid during all of this were the repercussions of another failure. Still Kiel lived for such decisive decision-making. It made him feel alive and on the bleeding edge, which ironically could well be the case.

Around nine that night, a private jet took off from Newark International Airport. The airframe contained eighteen of CMES' finest security personnel, full humans, not directionless goons. All had seen action in the Middle East and Afghanistan. All were highly motivated to get payback for their lost team members during the Christmas Eve Raid and in the mountains of New Mexico.

While Randolph knew them and had provided each with custom adjustments to their weapons, she wasn't considered military, much less one of the boys. Randolph, for her part, frankly preferred it that way, leaving little room for misunderstanding. The armorer nevertheless knew her inclusion on this op was because of her solid working relationship with DeSalvo. She wouldn't be there if she wasn't battle-hardened in the paranormal sense, and her mastery unquestioned in ancient, medieval, and modern weaponry. Then there were those other skills of hers, things that made humans squeamish.

After landing at Latrobe's Arnold Palmer Regional Airport, a private bus shuttled the CMES assault team to a hotel where they hydrated and crashed. The next morning, bright and early, as a group, they went on a three-mile run. Randolph, who had followed the team, did so effortlessly without breaking a sweat. After a hearty breakfast, all showered and were told to chill, as their commander wanted them at their absolute peak for that evening's party crashing.

Under no circumstances did Thomas, the CMES commander, want to have the blood of more good men on his conscience. As a further incentive, as if the commander needed one, Kiel had told him that what happened in December was not to be repeated.

Thomas' opinion of Randolph's surprise inclusion in his op, however, ran the gamut from a distraction to a potentially valuable wild card. Frankly, the woman gave him the creeps.

*   *   *

At three pm, Stone and a contingent of TIIIS security drove north from the Academy to the Barbecue Palace, a quaint and rustic establishment southeast of Latrobe. They parked their nine vehicles in its dusty parking lot, retreated into the dense brush across the two-lane road opposite, and settled in like ghosts.

On one end of the Palace, its brick smoker's chimney belched out its seductive aromas. Just being near the place, the deliciousness filled the air, effectively dilating pupils and filling mouths with saliva. Well-fed in advance, every stomach of the hidden TIIIS force groaned, nonetheless.

Within the Palace, a wide open and wooden pillared barn space, two long tables occupied its center, arranged end-to-end, covered with red and white checkered tablecloths, plates, handmade cloth napkins, silverware, and condiments. At one end on the floor sat a massive Yeti cooler filled to the brim with ice and bottled beer.

*　　*　　*

At 6:00 pm a tourist bus arrived loaded up with serious looking men, each with a large duffle bag, and a slight woman. The bus driver had been told that they were crashing a private party and that they were delivering the party favors. The driver, at seeing them, feared for his life and recited a silent prayer.

The bus driver arrived at the address given him. The barbecue joint, a converted barn, the driver and his family had eaten at two months prior. In the lot, nine vehicles were parked—one a red pickup truck with white Texas plates. Randolph noted this through the bus' window with a toothy smile.

Even from within the bus, the rich smell of roasting meats permeated the air. Each found their mouth watering. When the bus door opened, the scent only intensified. Unconsciously, as if struck by an aromatic tidal wave, a few stomachs growled in anticipation as no one had eaten since noon, as no one wanted to be sluggish. Everyone wanted to be as sharp as humanly possible. Randolph, in this regard, had them all beat.

The CMES assault team, now dressed in black jumpsuits and ski masks, exited the bus carrying assault shotguns. Randolph just carried two wooden clubs the size of heavy baseball bats. Wordlessly, they efficiently spread out and surrounded the structure. The bus driver thought, *Some party favors these guys are. And what's with the woman and the bats?*

"Execute," the commander said into his stalk mic. They entered through the front entrance and back service door in close order, single-file. The assault team found the restaurant deserted. Unconsciously, they gravitated around the central table. A cold, sweating, and open beer bottle had been placed before each table setting. Four loaded serving trays of freshly sliced barbecue adorned the long, groaning board, which had eerily been set for twenty—their exact number.

The team's commander did not like the look of their situation, not one bit, but then saw a sealed envelope at the lone setting at the table's head. Curious, the commander carefully looked for a trip line or some kind of nasty triggering mechanism. Seeing none, he quickly plucked the envelope off its plate, savagely tore it open, and read:

CMES Team Lead:

I thought I would throw a party for you and your team.

The grill is full. The sides are in the kitchen on the stove. More beer is in the kitchen fridge.

Enjoy.

J.J. Stone

"The balls!" the CMES commander whispered. Then the entire team went down as one with a clatter as the fast-acting sleeping gas took them all. Its pleasant, signature smell had been totally masked by the barbecue.

Only Randolph remained standing with a club in each hand. She smiled, quickly unzipped her black assault suit, and transformed into her hairy, ape-like form of ropey muscles. Her eyes, now yellow orbs, could see in the dark.

Randolph moved quickly, found the room's electrical mains, and turned off the interior lighting. Now enveloped in gloom, she backed into a corner near the entranceway. Focusing her energy, she powered up her clubs until their hieroglyphs glowed subtly. Randolph squatted down to make herself small. She wore a hideously drooling smile.

*   *   *

I watched as my CMES counterparts spread out to envelope the Palace.

Their movements are way too smooth and coordinated to be goons. These guys must be full humans which their auras confirm. But isn't that the same woman I encountered with the clubs? Oh, I get it. Her aura is all wrong. Must be some kind of dark adept. They're hedging their bets by bringing in a heavy hitter. Yet another escalation.

After waiting a good twenty minutes in order to allow for the gas to take effect, we began our approach on the Palace from our positions across the road. Through our combat radios, I informed my team to be on the lookout for the added threat.

But first on our list, we secured the bus driver, who wisely didn't put up a fuss. Besides, it turned out he was a local, who was more than happy to cooperate, so we let him leave with his bus.

Next, we surrounded the Palace. My guys all wore full battle armor and riot helmets with gas masks. They carried Tazer rifles armed with silver-coated electrodes. I, however, had none of that. I wore my urban combat suit and was armed with my 9mm and Bone Sword. My argument—someone just might need to have the last word.

As soon as we entered the darkened building, I knew something was amiss. I reached up to my UCS' head gear and turned on my night vision. Moving forward carefully in the sparkly green gloom, my team began tripping over several sleeping forms, which caused some consternation.

"I'll find the lights." I loudly announced. "Stay where you are."

Careful, Soul Carrier. There is evil in this building, the First Soul whispered into my ear.

No shit. I saw her enter.

Looking around, I saw on one wall that the electrical breaker box's door was open. I took one step toward it and at that precise moment, out of the shadows, a deafening inhuman battle cry sounded. I glanced around and saw nothing, but my dark-blind team was under attack. Their screams of pain said so. I thumbed my head gear again, switching from night vision to infrared.

What I saw was a field of stationary upright thermals, my team, getting mowed down by one intensely bright one that was swinging two glowing clubs. At their impact, a fountain of thermal energy washed over their targets, practically electrocuting them, not to mention the blunt trauma of the blows. The air filled with a numbing static charge and the smell of burnt body armor and flesh.

I espy the signature of dark energy, the First Soul whispered. *This hellion is connected to a nefarious ley line. Use care, Soul Carrier, and beware of its cudgels.*

As I saw it, the space was too cramped to fully swing my sword, so I ducked down behind the dinner table and grabbed a Tazer rifle from one of the fallen. With five men down already, I aimed, fired, and scored against our attacker.

The scream that resulted within that confined space was indescribable and threatened to plug my ears from its overpressure. I was amazed that the roof hadn't lifted off, but the antagonized bright thermal continued to thrash about, and in the process, took out several more of my team. Frustrated, I drew my Bone Sword, waited in a crouch for an opening, and in mid-translocation, swung a tight arc with all my might. I cleaved right through one of the adept's clubs, shattering it. That experience jarred me to the core like no sturdy pell ever could. Fortunately, the Bone Sword continued on and severed in two, the bright form below its shoulders. That abruptly silenced the screaming rage with a ringing echo.

Finally, turning on the lights, I glanced about the carnage and called out, "Call in the medics. We have people down."

* * *

Deep within the Dark Realm, that place where all souls must first go to decide their fate, its hideous master stirred with extreme irritation. Yet another dark one had fallen to the silver impregnated sword of the Lictor of Magic.

"Oh, how I hate thee." It hissed.

"And I so enjoy your vexation," retorted the First Soul.

"You! You! You foul excuse of a soul. How dare you address me so! You coward, who has never dared to descend into my kingdom!" the Devourer spat.

"Eventually, I will. But by the time I do, you will have long expired."

"Beware, First Soul," the Devourer of Souls sneered, "A storm is coming. A storm of my very creation! You will not withstand it."

The First Soul laughed in derision and shouted back, "You are mistaken vile slime. I *am* the Storm."

* * *

After the medics evacuated our injured, we hauled out the bound and disarmed CMES personnel, placed them in our transport, and took them back to the Academy for holding and interrogation. The naked and severed woman went into a sealed body bag. Her gore had taken some time to clean up. As for the Barbecue Palace, only five chairs needed to be replaced. Sadly, all that food had to be discarded. What a waste.

My typical after-action reaction kicked in right on time as soon as we made it back to the Academy—nausea, migraine, and fatigue. But before I transformed myself into a bawling infant, I took note of the Bone Sword's blade. Where it had cut through the demon's club, there was now a nasty blackened streak across it that seemed to be growing by the moment.

*   *   *

"There are several ways we can do this, Commander," I said as I looked into the CMES leader's face through the red eye of a remote video camera.

"One option is that you and your team disappear. That option I would prefer to leave as a last resort. The other option is that I turn you guys loose. That option I would prefer, but to make that happen, I need certain assurances," I offered via an overhead speaker and voice scrambler. "So, Commander, which will it be?"

"What kinds of assurances?"

"That you leave Pennsylvania peacefully and that you tell whoever you work for that this state and the state of New Mexico are off limits."

"You know damn well that I cannot make promises like that!"

"No shit, Commander!" I said with my very best Marine command voice. "I said 'tell whoever you work for' that the states of Pennsylvania and New Mexico are off limits. That is what I said. I damn well know that you can't make a promise like that. Think of it this way, Commander, you're the messenger. Just deliver the damn message to your boss. That's all I want."

"What about our gear and weapons?" The CMES commander pressed.

"Confiscated."

Grumble. Then, "What about Randolph?"

"The woman?"

"Yeah, you could say that."

"Dead."

A grunt. "Okay, whoever you are. You have yourself a deal."

*   *   *

Kiel was in shock after the safe return of his men, minus Randolph. Never before had someone co-opted one of his own, much less an entire team. More importantly, his team's ambush had been brilliantly executed—even when accompanied by an experienced shape-shifting warrior.

That caused Kiel's mind to wonder about what had taken out Randolph. Was it the same entity that so ruined their Christmas Eve Raid? Kiel, frankly, had a hard time imagining that Stone could be the common denominator in these two events. While possible, he couldn't accept the likelihood.

But he had far bigger issues with his own security department's ability to vet information. After all, this was the second time that a credit card with Stone's name on it had fooled them into deploying a team. The first instance was that total disaster with thirty-six killed in New Mexico. This time, nineteen were spared. Perhaps, there was a better way of digitally tracking someone other than by following their purchasing behavior, but he didn't know what that was.

That left only HUMINT that could be deployed on the ground. They were far harder to fool, more reliable, and intellectually flexible. The problem with HUMINT was the factor of time. The best were moles, who had burrowed into the fabric of a community over a period of years, thereby gaining trust and access to sensitive resources. The friendly mail carrier, the knowledgeable bookstore owner, the reliable milk man, you name it, they all made great intelligence resources.

Within the United States, Kiel knew well enough

the demographics of CMES' membership, which tended to gather solely in big coastal cities or Washington, DC. That left the vast American interior as a vast untapped reservoir.

But in places like Pennsylvania and New Mexico it was extremely difficult to recruit intelligence sources. While marginally possible in western Pennsylvania, in New Mexico it was downright impossible due in large part because of its Native American population and the presence of the Silver Nile ley line. Native Americans, in the main, natural sensitives, can practically smell a dark paranormal from across a crowded room. The Silver Nile ley line, that powerful paranormal conduit of raw power, invigorated these Native American sensitives to a frightening extent, making them even more powerful and adroit at weeding out CMES operatives.

Perhaps, Kiel considered, *we* should *consider these two states off limits—at least for now?*

CHAPTER 14
How to Address a Blight

President Silver Moon sat in her temporary office at the Academy and took note with considerable dread how entrenched into the culture of central Manhattan the Gathering club and spa had become. For her, such an institution left a bad taste in her mouth, like sampling a wine gone bad without a couth receptacle to expel it.

This makes a complete mockery of civilization and openly flaunts any reasonable code of ethical standards, she silently railed.

"Madam President," J.J. Stone said shattering her train of thought, "consider also that building's close proximity to two hallowed Christian places of worship—St. Thomas's Episcopal Church and St. Patrick's Cathedral."

Silver Moon blinked at the comment from her society's Lictor of Magic. *He read my mind. Am I getting that sloppy? Or, since his evolution, has he become that powerful?*

"You're absolutely correct, Mr. Stone. This time CMES has gone too far. Clearly they have decided that being the globe's foremost dark paranormal enclave is not enough. They now boldly market themselves, daring anyone to oppose them. The result: the ignorant clamor to them, like children turned loose in a candy store with fistfuls of money."

What truly stunned the president was the sheer cunning behind the entire enterprise. Someone with foresight had dreamed this one up, and that worried her. That brilliant someone calculated rightly that the

Gathering would be immune to frontal attack. With so many civilians filling its confines around the clock, any aggressive act might involve innocents. Furthermore, that diabolical someone realized that if CMES' true character was correctly marketed, it would sell.

Sybaritic indeed!

Ultimately, that meant an increase in its membership and, with that, influence.

"Mr. Stone, we must somehow deal with this development. If we don't, this cancer, this blight, will spread, and spread swiftly."

Right there and then, she decided the Gathering had to be brought low, somehow, someway, before clones of it dotted the U.S. landscape like so many exclusive athletic facilities. And that, President Silver Moon's instincts told her, would surely be the case.

* * *

With Mr. Good and the Academy's armorer Mr. Loomis dead, I didn't know who to ask about the black crud that was slowly growing on my Bone Sword like mold. That all changed when I mentioned the issue at lunch with *Monsieur* Dexter, my mentor in defensive and offensive lethal magic.

"*Monsieur* Stone, I have a suspicion," he said with an upraised finger, "but first I must hear a full account of your engagement with that woman, every nuance."

This I readily did, and during my narration Mr. Dexter's eyebrows several times rose and fell like window blinds. When I had finished, he simply said, "Let us go to my office."

Once seated in his palatial visitor's chair, Mr. Dexter opened a side drawer of his desk, removed a flat, green, rectangular box, extracted two pristine white cylinders, and placed them in the center of his red leather desk pad.

"*Monsieur* Stone. Do you know what these are?"

I shook my head in negation.

"Not long ago, these were important instruments of education. These pieces of chalk wrote on blackboards assignments and provided knowledge. Today, sadly they are long forgotten tools of the trade. But for you, *monsieur*, they will restore the integrity of your sword's blade."

Delicately picking up one piece, the Frenchman continued. "Rub this against the dark smudge. Do so in one direction only. Do not saw it back and forth. Work slowly and the 'crud' that you so colorfully described will begin to flake off. Use one piece only for each side of the blade. Do not mix them. And above all, be careful, as these sticks break very easily."

Gently placing the stick back down on the desk's red writing pad, they took on the look of two white slashes of color.

"*Monsieur* Stone, while I give you a corrective for your sword's blight, I can also offer an explanation for it. Consider what was involved—the Randolph woman's use of dark ley line energy to empower her clubs, your translocation, and the innate charge of your sword. It is my belief that a momentary rift between the Mortal and Dark Realms occurred when you cleaved her charged club. The path of its destruction marred your blade with that which is not of this world. Unlike ectoplasm which rapidly disintegrates in the Mortal Realm, this is something different. This represents an unnatural foothold of the Dark Realm in ours. Care for your blade immediately, before it is devoured and spreads elsewhere."

Again, picking up a piece of chalk, my teacher paused while he held it before my eyes, "*Monsieur*, this ordinary looking object is manufactured from the long dead and refined remains of minute sea creatures. It is in its very essence the bones of Nature. It is anathema to your sword's blight."

Again, another one of Mr. Dexter's long pauses as he examined his hands.

"*Monsieur* Stone, might I suggest that in the future you consider not repeating these unfortunate conditions. Another instance of this unnatural blight might not be so easily mended."

* * *

A hiss of frustration exploded forth from the Devourer of Souls, the Master of the Dark Realm. Its attempt at the destruction of the Soul Carrier's sword had been thwarted. The sacrifice of a dark adept wasted. It had to devise another way.

* * *

"Mr. Remington, I've got an idea that I would like to run by you," J.J. said to Josh Remington, while visiting the IT and Security Department at the Academy.

"What do you have in mind?" the eager staffer asked.

"Can we set up four video cameras to record the thermal imagery of the Gathering building's four sides, twenty-four/seven?"

"Sure, Mr. Stone, that's very doable. What are you

looking for?"

"A very reliable source told me that four floors of the Gathering building are off limits to the general membership. I found that intriguing. So, I figure that if we record, say, two weeks of activity, that those off-limit floors will stick out like a sore thumb."

"When do you want to start this experiment?"

"As soon as possible. I happen to know that President Silver Moon is quite vexed about this Fifth Avenue sensation and would love to shut it down. Let's give her some intel that she can act upon."

*   *   *

Several weeks later, Josh provided me with the results from the infrared observations.

"President Silver Moon," I said into the receiver, "I have some information that you might want to consider."

"I'm listening, Mr. Stone."

"Over the past several weeks, I asked our IT and Security Department to video the CMES North American building with an array of infrared cameras. I asked them to do so, on a tip that the building had four special floors that were off limits to their usual clientele."

"How intriguing ..." the president said.

"I figured that anything made off limits would be of interest to us and of vital importance for the building's management and administration."

"That would be the obvious conclusion, Mr. Stone. What did the cameras reveal?" the intrigued president asked.

"Four contiguous levels situated at the structure's

center.

"Madam President, how do you wish me to proceed?"

"Mr. Stone, as you always have. Think outside the box and do us proud."

*   *   *

If I was planning an assault on a heavily defended military objective, reliable information would be key. When it came to the newly refurbished CMES North American headquarters building, no one had such intel within TIIIS. For all practical purposes, the Gathering property represented an intelligence black hole, not to mention one with rigorously updated defenses. It would require someone on the inside to acquire the needed details. In short, I needed a volunteer to penetrate this bastion, but the first person who came to mind was a dear friend.

So I called up my paranormal mentor, Mr. Henry, and suggested that we have lunch the next day. When we were both in Philly, our dive of choice had been the Greasy Onion. This establishment possessed historic atmosphere, near endless beer choices, and simply dynamite bar food. At the Academy, however, there was only the Acorn, nice, but not as seedy. Nevertheless, after four pints Mr. Henry wore a Cheshire grin and judged the place as "acceptable." Neither of us could bring ourselves to say it, we both dearly missed our old Philly pub with its worn-in grudge and bowling alley of a bar. The Acorn, however, was far more secure.

"What's up?" he asked.

"We have lots to discuss," I said with a serious

look on my face. I had purposely selected a table off in a corner.

"Such as?"

"The second raid in Manhattan was a real plum. I wish you could have had a hand in it. As it was, there were injuries."

"Yeah, I heard." He said glumly.

"The ambush over at the Barbecue Palace, while it got our message across, didn't turn out as well as I had planned—more injuries again, but, fortunately no casualties."

"J.J., that's war my friend. Stuff and people get broken, or worse. But I would have given anything to have seen the look on that CMES commander's face after he read your love letter," the Fourth-Class adept admitted over the rim of his pint.

After a long pull of his dark stout, he continued, "What's bugging you, J.J?"

"Mr. Henry, I seek your wisdom."

That raised the man's snowy white eyebrows. "Oh?"

"Yep. I have been authorized by our dear president to come up with an imaginative solution to shut down the Gathering."

Now wolfishly grinning from ear-to-ear, "You don't say."

*   *   *

Early on I thought it wise to send Melaina an autographed copy of my book, *Curses and Demons*, as an academic courtesy. That act on my part helped with our friendship, which today, has matured into something I consider something more. But now what I had to ask her required us to meet face-to-face. In my mind, there was no other way. So we met at a neutral site, a quiet and out-of-the-way place.

When I arrived at the Luxor Las Vegas, I found my Alexandrian witch already at the bar with her strong chin perched in her palm, a partially finished drink before her. Apparently deep in thought, she was content to allow it to evaporate.

Glancing at my watch, I asked, "Am I late?"

"Not at all, J.J. I was just anxious to see you."

"You don't say … "

"By the way, I finished your book on the flight in. I'm quite impressed." She grinned.

"Thanks."

"You're most welcome. Now, as to why I was so anxious to see you." She paused. "I haven't been as frank as I should have been about my past. Honestly, at first I wasn't sure about a lot of things, but now I'm all squared away, especially given what has happened recently in New York."

"What do you mean?" I said with a cocked head.

"The opening of that abomination, the Gathering. The brazen gall of it vexes me to the core," she murmured out with considerable heat.

That reaction surprised me and I wondered why.

"You probably don't know this, Mel," I interjected, "but the scuttlebutt says that the next one will be built right here in Vegas."

At that I got a flat, stony look, and a curt, "I'm not surprised. But to get back to what I was saying, I was not as forthcoming as I should have been with you. CMES made me an orphan at the age of eighteen."

"What?"

"Yes, you heard me correctly. Both my father and mother were killed by their agents."

I just sat there bug-eyed and speechless at this revelation, while my drink now sat untouched.

"J.J., I'm a Coptic Christian. In Egypt that means my family was part of a very close-knit minority community within a hostile Islamic culture. Never forget that. My father, while the boyhood friend of President Anwar Sadat, and perhaps his closest confidant, survived an assassination attempt that unfortunately claimed the life of our beloved president. Two years later, a powerful dark wizard, known only as the Dark One, conjured an awful spell that claimed my father. My mother was a housewife, social worker, and the last white witch of her family's ancestral line. She was murdered during a botched surgery by a CMES physician, through sheer carelessness, and neglect."

Holy shit!

"Then, eight years later, I took care of that animal myself."

My eyes were the size of dinner plates at her mention of the Dark One, but her taking care of her mother's murderer shook me to the core. Throughout, her narrative was quite frightening in its matter-of-fact tone. As for her aura, that she couldn't hide. It blazed brightly because of her heightened emotional state.

"But there is more."

More ... there's more*? How can that be? She just said that she murdered someone.*

"I wish to exact vengeance."

"Are you absolutely sure? 'Vengeance is mine, I will repay, says the Lord.' Besides, isn't the physician already dead?"

"Yes, J.J., *he* most surely is, but I wish to hurt CMES in a way that is crippling, memorable."

"If that's the case, then I have something to share with you."

I laid out the plan that Mr. Henry and I had cooked up. Listening carefully, Mel surgically punched several holes in it, but to her credit, she offered several sensible solutions. In short, we thrashed the hell out of the plan, at the end of which, I asked.

"Mel, are you absolute sure that you want to do this?"

"Without question."

CHAPTER 15
Secret Plans & Hidden Crimes

While it had only been a year and a half, it seemed like an eternity since I last spoke with Father Jerome Flanagan, the diocesan assistant of the late Cardinal Garibaldi.

"Good afternoon, Father. This is J.J. Stone."

After a distinct pause, "Mr. Stone, please give me your number and I will call you back."

So I did.

Thirty seconds later my cheapo throw-away cell started ringing.

"This is Stone."

"Ah, Mr. Stone, it's good to hear from you. I apologize for all the cloak and dagger, but I had to be sure. By the way, is this an encrypted line."

"Encrypted? No, it isn't. It's a temporary, discardable device."

"I see. That is acceptable. Ever since the murder of the cardinal, the Vatican insists on encryption, especially since our neighbor to the northwest has become so, flamboyant. What can I do for you?"

"Father Flanagan, is there any way you can get your hands on the architectural plans of your 'flamboyant' neighbor?"

"Actually, Mr. Stone, divine Providence has just smiled upon you. The plans you refer to exist in two versions. Those approved by the city and state inspectors, and those which were the actual plans. The latter I have just come into possession of."

"You're kidding!"

"Not in the least. In fact, these working plans were delivered to me as, let's just say, an act of contrition."

"What?"

Smiling into the phone, "Mr. Stone, in New York *nearly* everything is negotiable, and in some cases, even absolvable. Guilt, followed by regret, is an extremely powerful cocktail, Mr. Stone.

"But as to the actual architectural plans, they are quite extensive, and in particular, are extremely detailed regarding a specific center section of the building in question. And here's why: Sixty-three murders took place after the central section's completion."

That news stunned me silent.

"Are you still there, Mr. Stone?"

"Yes, Father, I'm still here."

"Mr. Stone, are you familiar with the tale that pharaoh's workmen were massacred following the completion of his tomb? Well, it seems that here, in Midtown Manhattan, that security measure was thoroughly embraced."

"I haven't heard anything about this in the media." I stammered out.

"Nor will you ever," the cleric said. "The authorities don't know about it. Currently, I am gathering evidence, and when I have a sufficient amount that I believe will stick, then I will go to the NYPD."

"Sixty-three? What did they do wrong?"

"Absolutely nothing, Mr. Stone. The sixty-three were just hungry young Teamsters, working their tails off at triple pay. Their only crime was that they were single and without families to take note their disappearance. However, quite a few colleagues did notice, put two and two together, and several of them came to me, individually, to express their concerns. Apparently, a special cleaning service came in and dealt with the evidence."

"How can I get a copy of these plans, Father?"

"Again, I found in Cardinal Garibaldi's Rolodex the Pennsylvania address to the Old Oaks Academy. Associated with it was the name P.E.I. Smithers. Does either name ring a bell with you?"

"Indeed, they do, Father."

"Well, I sent the plans to that name and address yesterday."

I couldn't breathe.

"Mr. Stone, are you still on the line?"

"Barely, Father, just barely."

CHAPTER 16
Remoras

"Donaldson, here."

"Hello, sir. This is J.J. Stone. Josh Remington of IT and Security suggested that I call you. How are you today?" I cheerfully asked with a heart full of hope.

"Ah, Mr. Stone, 'tis truly an honor to be speaking with you, sir," the thick brogue answered. "Josh gave me a heads up that you mightn' be callin'."

"Did Josh explain what I had in mind?"

"He did indeed, sir. And we just might be in for a bit o' luck. You see, several of our people were involved in the refurbishment of that building. Two in particular were IT types who left behind several items that may offer some answers to your questions."

"May I speak to one of them?"

A long pause.

"Ah, I'm a very sorry, but the two people of interest have turned up missing. In-house, there's lots of concern for them, but try as we might, we've no clue what may have become of them."

Holy shit! Two of our own were among the sixty-three that disappeared!

"Are they the only two TIIIS agents that have turned up missing, who worked on that building?"

"That's a question I canna' answer. All I know is that two of my staff—fine young gentlemen they were—have vanished from the face of the earth. That's all I can say."

"So what can you tell me?"

"It's like this. Do you know what a remora is?"

"Yeah, it's a scavenger fish that attaches itself to a shark."

"That's correct, but in IT a remora is a piece of hardware, very specialized hardware mind you, which remains dormant until needed."

"Kind of like a mole in spy stories?"

"Ah, exactly, Mr. Stone. You've really put your finger on it. You see my two laddies were installing remoras throughout that building's IT system. Hazardous work that was. If they had been discovered, God knows what might have happened to them. And now that they both have turned up missing, you can probably understand why I am so concerned about them."

"What can these remoras do?"

"Just like a real remora, they attach to their host and just sit there all nice and quiet until we need them. They have their own power supply—a wee battery actually—and we can individually fire them up or shut them down using Wi-Fi. As you can imagine, being battery powered, once activated, they have a limited life span."

"How many remoras did your people install?"

"That, I really don't know. The boys went out with thirty. They reported in having installed a total of sixteen before they disappeared."

"Sixteen out of thirty."

"That's correct. And sixteen's a lot if you think about it. The only fly in the ointment is that we don't where they were placed and whether they were ever discovered by CMES."

"Have you tried to fire one up, Mr. Donaldson?"

"No, I haven't, sir. And I will not until someone

authorizes me to do so. To waste even just one on a foolish snipe-hunt would be a crime. Even more so as two of my best are probably missing because of them."

"Who authorized their install?"

Pause.

"That was President Silver Moon's call."

"Why?"

"Because a remora is a solid hardware hack—the very best kind."

I closed my eyes at the magnitude of my ignorance and the immense opportunity that just one operational remora would bring.

"Now, I fully understand, Mr. Donaldson. Thank you for your time."

CHAPTER 17
Deep Cover

Melaina initiated her part of the grand plan when she e-mailed a colleague at the Metropolitan Museum of Art. It was a chatty affair, wherein Mel expressed her desire to undertake a year of sabbatical research within the museum's papyrus collection. The e-mail's response was positive and encouraging, even to the point of discussing apartment rentals that the museum had for visiting scholars such as she.

That hurdle overcome, the Alexandrian told her departmental chairperson of her research plans for the next two semesters, and, again, received a green light if Mel could find a temporary replacement. Thinking quickly, she suggested one of her advanced graduate assistants. Her chair was delighted.

The last item, and the trickiest, was the crafting of a letter to the Gathering itself, requesting membership information and a personal tour of the facility. Composing the inquiry was child's play. What wasn't, involved the application of sufficient enchantment within a layered spell. In essence, Mel leveraged her magical credentials so that her requests would be granted. The onerous cost of membership, TIIIS would provide.

*　　*　　*

Jenny Sauerbrünn, a tactile hypersensitive adept, could run her hand over a book and not only absorb its content, but could sense from its words the very character of its author. Foreplay and sex in her world possessed an intensity that was beyond electric, verging more on the transcendental. As a consequence, her bedding and clothing were silks, her towels fine Egyptian cottons. Under no circumstance, and no matter how fine the quality, could the woman endure clothing made of wool or wool blends. She described such fabrics as razor wire and her skin reacted in kind with hive-like blotches. Scratchy facial hair similarly had absolutely no place in her universe.

When Sauerbrünn held Professor M. Makris' fine linen envelope it literally vibrated. Intrigued, one practiced slash of her letter opener exposed her to an exotic world. The crisply folded parchment, when opened, hit her like a dry desert breeze perfumed with the heady scent of jasmine blossoms. The strong calligraphic handwriting flowed across the page like the sinuous movements of a serpent. Caressing the letter's surface with her finger tips caused her eyes to widen in absolute wonder. Unconsciously, she shifted her hips in arousal. She could see Makris' innate beauty and was awed by her high intellect. While the letter's actual words were skillfully composed, subtly empowered, the intoxicating magical layering told the story of a witch wishing to become more, desiring to bloom, like jasmine in the spring.

Sauerbrünn, now nearing full flush, carefully and delicately put the letter aside, sat back in her office chair, stared at it, and openly, lustfully, fantasized about its maker.

What a candidate, she breathed huskily. *Where have you been all my life?*

*   *   *

Three months later Mel arrived in Manhattan. True in all ways, her colleague at the MMA had cleared a path through the museum's administration, secured for her a research carrel, and came up with a modestly furnished apartment only four blocks away on Third Street. The tenth floor flat had a balcony that faced the museum and the lush rectangle of Central Park behind it.

The following day Mel purposely slept in late in an effort to defeat her Pacific Coast jet lag. After a quick cup of instant coffee, for that was all that her Spartan kitchen contained, she very carefully dressed and made a point to add some of her mother's jewelry. After all, today began her personal assault on an institution that she considered the epitome of pure and unadulterated evil. A soldier did not enter battle without a shield.

The Alexandrian witch looked stunning as she stood at the curb. After a few moments, she hailed a yellow cab and wordlessly presented her cabbie with her destination's address written on a slip of enchanted paper. At its touch, his brown eyes widened, he nodded simply, and drove.

Fifteen minutes later, she arrived at the Fifth Avenue address. Uncharacteristically, the cabbie got out, held the door open for her, and received a generous tip.

"Shukraan," she breathed in her native Egyptian Arabic.

"Barak allah fik," he returned with a bow of his head.

The building itself was unremarkable, clad as it was in gray aluminum. But its heavily logoed entrance caught the eye, being dominated by exquisitely designed bronze-colored Celtic knots that looked like blooming chrysanthemums. The symbol, however, hit Mel like a slap in the face, because when she squinted, an inverted five-pointed star nestled within the complex pattern.

Nowhere did the words the Gathering, appear. Instead, management chose to emblazon the knotted logo on each of the automatic revolving doors and flanking double-sided delivery doors.

Having passed through the revolving entrance, the white witch briefly hovered her hand over the logo before her and felt the distinctive warmth of defensive magic. Now within, Mel stopped to take in the long and narrow lobby. Before her, the reception area's black slate flooring passed the reception desk to the left and continued on toward two banks of five elevators. The same black surface then continued on to cover the wall opposite to the ceiling with five vertically arranged logos. Reception hid behind a long, black, and monolithic marble desk, which was decorated with five bronze logos arranged horizontally beneath its counter surface. But the overpowering branding did not end there, for on the opposite wall, facing reception, were another five logos. Then there was the black slate flooring itself, dominating the center with one bronze inlaid logo almost six feet in diameter.

Out of curiosity, Mel passed her foot over the floor logo and sensed again an all too familiar warmth emanating from it. As she stepped into to the reception area proper, the Alexandrian quickly glanced around and noted all the lines of intersection that the logos made and came to one clear-cut conclusion—total magical containment.

"How may I assist you?" an extremely cool and aloof male receptionist asked, who was dressed in a severe black uniform that emphasized his taut build and made his pale complexion ever more so.

Try as he might, Mel could tell that he disapproved of her brilliant turquoise and gold cotton peasant dress. His brass name badge said Brett.

"Why, yes, thank you … Brett. I have an appointment with Ms. Sauerbrünn. Would you be so kind and inform her that I have arrived?"

At the mention of her name the Alexandrian saw that his eyes had fractionally dilated. "I will be happy to inform Director Sauerbrünn of your arrival, Ms. …?"

"*Professor* Makris."

"Ah, thank you, Professor Machrees."

Mel ground her teeth at his butchered attempt. But it did emphasize his distraction, so she pleasantly smiled back.

Moments later, another male appeared wearing the same black uniform, a virtual clone of Brett, but this time badged as Todd. He carried a touch pad, greeted Mel, and requested identification. Once provided, he lightly tipped and tapped at his pad, pressed ENTER, and smiled at the result. "Kindly follow me, Professor." Wisely, this one had avoided vocalizing her name.

Todd led the Alexandrian witch to the left bank of elevators, where she stood before a door with a logo. Being playful, she casually passed her hand low over it and again distinctly felt that warming sensation.

Todd, seeing this, asked. "Is something wrong, Professor?"

"Oh, no, not at all." Mel airily answered with a

wave, "I am just overwhelmed at the fine workmanship of all of these beautiful bronze castings."

The elevator arrived and the pair entered. Mel got her first look at the elevator's bank of buttons—one through forty-one. Her escort, however, pressed none of these. Instead, he inserted a key into a brass lock fitting with four notched positions. When he turned it, he selected the second notch, and with that, the elevator began its vertical journey, but only for a while.

"Professor, kindly take hold of the bar." Todd said solicitously.

Mel did, and it was good that Todd had warned her, for the elevator came to a halt and then shifted its weight horizontally to the left for several moments. The sensation from this unexpected motion felt so odd that Mel remarked, "Did we just go sideways?"

"Yes, Professor, we did indeed." Todd answered with a smug smile.

Coming again to a halt, the doors opened to a small reception area. This one was decorated virtually identical to the street level entrance, down to the five logos facing the elevator bank. Stepping out of the cab, Mel experienced a heavy psychic overpressure that seemed to clog her ear canals. Unconsciously, she worked her jaw, but it didn't help.

Todd noted the professor's reaction.

Behind the long receptionist desk sat three powerful looking individuals. These "receptionists," dressed in tactical black jumpsuits, wore radio microphones attached to their left shoulders. Mel highly suspected that, out-of-sight, they were heavily armed as well. But what truly troubled her were the auras of the two on the left—utterly black. Other than her tactile registers of magical defenses, this was Mel's first positive evidence of what CMES truly was—two demon-possessed individuals. Inwardly, she struggled with whether to hate or pity them.

While Mel was deciding, Todd approached the reception desk and leaned over to the guard on the far right, the one with only a muddy brown aura. He said something to him, received a nod, and a door opposite clicked open. As Mel and Todd passed through it, the massive overpressure vanished so suddenly that the Alexandrian staggered slightly from the change. This, too, Todd noted with interest.

Thoughtfully catching his guest by the elbow to steady her, Todd said, "Sorry about that, Professor. It's just the building's security. Would you please follow me?" He said as they began walking down a long, carpeted aisle surrounded on both sides with low-walled cubes filled with worker bees.

Remarkably, Mel saw that not one person looked up in curiosity as the pair passed by them, which she found extremely telling, as in positively odd.

At the end of the nearly two hundred-foot-long aisle, they arrived at an alcove with a private secretary sitting behind a cherry-wood desk. Beyond him, stood a massive set of double wooden doors, also in that same, gorgeous, hand-rubbed cherry.

"Jonathan, this is Director Sauerbrünn's two o'clock, Professor Makris." He introduced.

Todd, having pronounced her name correctly, then turned, and left without a smile much less a word.

"More strangeness," Mel whispered as Jonathan picked up the phone to announce her.

CHAPTER 18
Gainsworthy

"Mr. Jeremy Gainsworthy, my name is Paul Kiel. I work for Mr. William DeSalvo, the regional director of the Gatherings' North American region."

After a moment of thought to process the many possible implications and nuances of what the caller stated, Gainsworthy responded. "Thank you, Mr. Kiel, for calling. What can I do for you?" His dripping British solicitousness politely asked.

"Your services have been requested by the regional director."

"I see. Precisely what services does the regional director of North America require?"

"I know you typically prefer to work alone, however, the target involved requires something more. I see that in the past you have collaborated with an Assyrian griffin. This undertaking will again require such a collaboration."

Me and *an Assyrian griffin*, the veteran wizard, assassin, and paranormal champion considered. *The last time that I used such a force of Nature, I was working my way through a long list of non-aligned rogue diplomats. Bloody business that was, but extremely lucrative.*

"Mr. Gainsworthy. Are you still on the line?" Kiel inquired into the silent phone.

"Excuse me. I was just thinking. So, what's the target?"

"The TIIIS Lictor of Magic, a man named Jonathan Joseph Stone."

Gainsworthy knew well who Stone was. *I'm being contracted to take on my counterpart ... a former Marine ... a published scholar in ancient demonology ... and the carrier of the First Soul of Creation. What a delicious opportunity to pit myself against a true equal. Once I defeat him, no one would dare to ever oppose me again!*

Gainsworthy decided to play dumb just to see what this guy on the line really knew about this most worthy opponent. "Mr. Kiel, what do you know about this man?"

"Frankly, the man is a cold-blooded killer, who has claimed way too many of our security personnel. The regional director wants him dead."

That frank answer was not the one that I expected ... but then again, Jeremy old boy, this is CMES after all. They need a wet job done, pure and simple, with little concern for the contractor performing the service.

"Bottom line—you are contracting me and one Assyrian griffin to remove this TIIIS enforcer?"

"Precisely."

"Are you aware of my usual rate for such a contract?"

"I am."

"Given the target specified, my fee will have to be quintupled."

Silence.

Then.

"Agreed. The paperwork will be sent via the usual means. Good day."

"One moment, Mr. Kiel. I require one other thing."

"What might that be?"

"I require a copy of your security file on Stone, the

file that your regional director has access to."

Pause.

"Agreed. That too will be sent via the usual means. Good day." The phone connection ended.

My God, they must be desperate! No haggling whatsoever.

Then surfaced a nagging inner voice. *Now what have you gotten yourself into this time, Jeremy old boy?*

* * *

Where to begin? Perhaps from the beginning would be best.

In 1980 Jeremy Matthew Gainsworthy was born to Anglican missionaries who spent nearly their entire professional lives in the wilds of Central Africa. Geoffrey Gainsworthy was a dentist and Catherine a physician. Together, the villagers worshipped them, since they unswervingly made their lives better, while they taught and shared everything they could.

Over time this openness earned the pair the grudging trust and respect of the local shamans, who in turn taught them their skills, shared their jungle medicines and drugs, and their knowledge of powerful demons. It was never a question of who knew more, just "what can we do together, side-by-side, to help an ailing human being." Modern medicine and dentistry provided answers to the how. Shamanism answered the what.

Within this cultural miasma young Jeremy grew up at the cusp of where Western science, African folk lore, and magic became one. Conversant like his parents, in the local Bantu and Khoisan African tongues, the boy naturally absorbed an immense amount of raw science, colorful tribal lore, and yes, magic.

Brown-haired and -eyed, lanky, and hard-muscled from running and hunting with his peers, young Jeremy often asked his parents which was stronger, belief or medicine. Their answers did not excite the lad, because they led to the questions that all societies ask: Did God exist? Was He merciful? Did He care for those less fortunate? While raised an Anglican, Jeremy, because of his environmental immersion, was well aware of the many jungle spirits, some beneficial, some not.

At an early age, Jeremy did not so much see things as sensed them. It was only later that he became aware of the jungle's many spectra of colors, and the colorful auras that animals and men wore. With hard-earned experience, he learned early on to anticipate an opponent's or animal's next move. At the same time Jeremy learned the ways of the spear and bow, as well as the family's ancient Mauser Karabiner 98k rifle, which his father Geoffrey had acquired in payment for two gold teeth.

While his mates would run around buck naked through the bush, Jeremy's parents insisted that he wear cargo shorts. Trying to fit in, he baked his skin into a deep, dark brown, but failed to imitate his blue-black boyhood friends, who teased the skinny brown boy.

Things changed for Jeremy when puberty arrived. His friends were initiated as full men into their tribes, underwent rituals, and ceremonies that Jeremy could not take part in. It was a difficult time for the home-schooled man-child, and also one of sadness, as his parents prepared to send him off to England for a proper education.

Before his departure, tragedy struck in the night.

Four rogue lions broke into his parent's house, brutally killing them, seemingly for sport. Enraged beyond all belief, Jeremy forgot himself and slew one with a clean spear throw down its throat that skewered the beast's heart. Then he killed another with two well-placed arrows that perforated its lungs, causing it to cough up gouts of blood, which eventually choked it to death. Now emboldened and sensing a strength he never knew he possessed, Jeremy stalked the third animal and slit its throat with the household machete before the cat even knew what had happened. As for the fourth, it wisely ran off in fear for its life.

These martial deeds did not go unnoticed by his neighbors. For Jeremy, in his tightly focused and frenzied overdrive, had claimed three adult lions, a feat never before heard of in the region, much less by one so young. As a consequence, the four local shamans took Jeremy deep into the jungle, and after undergoing the proper rites, rituals, and scarification of his biceps, they declared Jeremy officially a man, and a full tribal member adopted by his best friend's family. His circumcision was not deemed necessary as it had been already performed at birth.

Nonetheless, and with great sorrow on his part, Jeremy followed through on his natural parent's wishes and departed, albeit late, for the British Isles. Once in England, the orphaned young man was placed under the guardianship of a kindly aunt and uncle, who enrolled Jeremy in preparatory school. There he was initially considered something of an exotic urchin and occasional hellion. But soon enough university beckoned and, at Cambridge's Trinity College, Jeremy finally found himself. His subjects weren't the dentistry or medicine of his mother and father, but rather cultural anthropology and psychology.

Now squarely in his element, Jeremy pieced together from his lectures a meaningful path that he knew worked from his childhood. Yes, some of the modern claptrap made sense, but just as much was utter nonsense. Then, in a moment of Providence, Jeremy ran into a clutch of students similar in their disposition—psychically sensitive, empathic, telepathic, and gifted in ways that few could understand. It was as if the young man had returned to Central Africa, back to Nature, roaming the jungle feeling and thinking free. He stretched his psychic musculature and found new limits.

In time this pack of five caught the attention of a local paranormal group. As one, they had joined to enhance their innate skills and abilities. But the five quickly discovered that this association was a flimflam sham that catered to the overblown egos of stylish wannabes. Thoroughly disgusted, the Pentangle, as they called themselves, moved on in search of substance.

One day while ruminating over their collective futures at the Maypole public house—their whimsical favorite—a tall fellow wearing a finely tailored three-piece suit approached them.

"Gentlemen," the man with a black ponytail announced to the table, "may I buy a round and join you for a moment?"

Plainly surprised at being referred to as "gentlemen," an offer of pints all around clearly was not to be ignored.

"Take a seat guv'nor," Winston, who hailed from a middle class neighborhood of London, declared with a flourish. "We're all ears."

The well-turned-out man with gold cufflinks sat, signaled to the bartender with a circling forefinger for a round, received a nod of acknowledgment, and forthwith said: "Am I correct to understand that I am in the presence of the Pentangle?"

Five guarded nods.

"Am I also correct in assuming you are looking for, let us say, assistance with your extracurricular studies?"

"Might," a dark curly headed Paul curtly piped over his pint.

"Wonderful. Then take note. Tomorrow night a seminar will be held that you five will want to attend. Coat and tie, proper shoes and all that. The presentation will start promptly at seven."

"Where?" the ginger-haired Philip eagerly queried.

"The Allhusen Room. Take the South Staircase. It's at the first flight. You cannot miss it."

"And you are?" Jeremy, ever the quiet one, wanted to know.

"Oh, yes, so sorry. I am Philip Meyers, the head of recruiting for our local Gathering of the *Consilium magorum et sagarum.*" Noting five blank looks, he then added, "The Council of Magicians and Witches."

"The Council of Magicians and Witches?" a wide-eyed Angus repeated in disbelief tinged with derision.

"Indeed, gentlemen." Meyers leaned in conspiratorially, "and we've been in existence longer than Britain. Come to the seminar tomorrow evening. I guarantee that you will not be as disappointed as you were with those paranormal research hacks."

And then Meyers left without once touching his pint.

"Odd duck, that," Philip offered.

"How old did he look to you?" Angus queried.

"Mid-thirties," Paul guessed.

"Yeah, has to be." Winston allowed. "No old guv'nor would wear a pony tail."

"What about you, Jeremy? Whatcha think of his offer?" Philip asked.

"That it's one we had better check out."

Filled with bundles of misgivings, but curious nonetheless, the Pentangle showed up at the Allhausen ten minutes early, only to find there were only five seats left in the tightly packed seminar room. At the head of the long central table stood Philip Meyers, who seemed to visibly brighten at their arrival.

"Well, gentlemen, welcome, and thank you for considering my organization's invitation. This evening we are honored to entertain Mr. Oliver Paine. Mr. Paine is a longtime member of our local Gathering, who hails from Carlisle. Among some circles, Mr. Paine is considered, outright, a wizard pure and simple. He is here today to speak to you."

Paine's visage was that of a gnarled oak tree, deeply weathered, craggy, with prominent and bushy gray eyebrows that overshadowed glacial blue eyes that flanked a distinctly Roman nose. His long, gray hair possessed a randomness that suggested it was arranged by the wind. He wore a brown tweed three-piece suit that looked slept in. Levering himself up off of his chair, Paine had the distinct look of a short, but broadly-shouldered, troll. He took a moment to take in the expectant faces before him.

Finished, Paine pointed directly at Jeremy and said with a gravelly voice. "Three lions slain. I have never before met anyone who has done that before … much less lived. Such bravery, strength, and skill. I am honored to be in your presence, sir."

The entire room hushed, and turned as one to follow Paine's thick and callused finger. Jeremy, sat in wide-eyed shock, blushed brightly, but said not a word, as even the members of the Pentangle did not know of his extraordinary boyhood achievement.

"I suspect," Paine continued as if reading from a theatrical script, "Mr. Gainsworthy, that during that ordeal your mind and body acted as one. Like a finely-honed weapon. That your blood boiled with purpose. Those rogue lions, after all, had just claimed your beloved parents. Isn't that so, Mr. Gainsworthy?"

Jeremy numbly nodded in acknowledgement at the awful memory. A lone tear escaped and ran down his cheek.

Paine, now standing fully erect, continued.

"Mr. Gainsworthy, you didn't run away or hide in the face of such danger. Instead, you stared down death itself, and then acted, *decisively*!" Paine said as he smashed his meaty fist against the seminar table in emphasis, sending a tremor through its wood.

"Mr. Gainsworthy. I value these qualities in a man, for it establishes, beyond all doubt, his true measure. As a consequence, I would be proud to be your paranormal mentor," the wizard concluded with a whisper and sat down.

CHAPTER 19
The Job

"If you know the enemy and know yourself, you
need not fear the result of a hundred battles.

If you know yourself but not the enemy, for every
victory gained you will also suffer a defeat.

If you know neither the enemy nor yourself, you
will succumb in every battle." —Sun Tzu

For Gainsworthy, when he reread the quote, the second
stanza was the important one. He knew this Stone by
rumor only, and so he set off to address that. His
target's security file was a thick one, being made up
mostly of the man's publications. Methodical, the
paranormal champion and assassin began with the co-
authored piece, a fascinating work about a Sumerian
soul container written with a surprisingly forthright
style.

*I wonder if Stone actually experienced that? For
some reason, I wouldn't be surprised in the least.*

The next publication, too, contained many first-
hand insights into ancient curses and demon-
summoning tablets. Once again, the clarity and logic of
the man's mind clearly showed through.

More personal experiences, Mr. Stone?

With his intellectual palette now whetted,
Gainsworthy dived into Stone's book, *Curses and
Demons*. Once again, in the most approachable, matter-
of-fact narrative, the author explained and placed into
context the supernatural mindset of the ancient

Mesopotamians. Quite often, the assassin caught himself chuckling as if Stone was writing purely for his own benefit with the occasional insertion of insider paranormal knowledge. Again, Gainsworthy found himself impressed by the achievement, noting the logical analysis and well-marshaled arguments.

This Stone possesses a formidable intellect.

Now moving on to the rest of his security jacket, here Gainsworthy read about Stone's military background, with his many citations for bravery, heroism, and his wounds. His early graduation, *cum laude*, from a well-respected East Coast U.S. university came as no surprise.

His operational actions against CMES intrigued the man as the Gathering grouped them under the rubrics of confirmed, probable, and possible.

Clearly, in a very brief time, this man is already considered a legend by his most bitter enemy.

Much of this breakdown, Gainsworthy read on, was made possible by information provided by a TIIIS defector, which caught his discerning eye.

I have never before heard of a TIIIS defector. Plenty from CMES, but never from them ... What was his problem?

Gainsworthy, now thoroughly engrossed, read through the man's exploits over the past two years.

To the assassin, the man seemed to be everywhere, and was extremely well-connected with the Roman Church, even though he was raised a Southern Baptist. Bottom line: Stone routinely destroyed demons and exorcised the possessed without skipping a beat. Then returned fully human captives with barely a scratch.

"New Mexico and Pennsylvania is off-limits," one

returned commander relayed to CMES Operations. What stones!

Mitzi Randolph had disappeared after the most recent engagement and was presumed dead. That raised Gainsworthy's eyebrows. *She was formidable.*

Once Gainsworthy had fully digested the personnel jacket of one Jonathan Joseph Stone, the paranormal champion concluded that CMES' North American leadership doubted the capability of its operational department. Surely Stone's return of their troops must have subliminally planted a seed, that while TIIIS might be many things, its chief enforcer was merciful. Gainsworthy knew first hand that CMES' operational doctrine was anything but merciful. Furthermore, CMES was not used to losing, ever, much less multiple times.

So that's it. CMES is experiencing a crisis of confidence within its ranks. The old psychology major realized. Now his hire made sense.

So, Jeremy old boy, we have before us a man who is carrying the First Soul of Creation. Okay, fine.

Second, all attempts on his person during his childhood failed. Now why is that? Both Shapiro and the Weasel were top-notch professionals.

Third, he's a man of intellect, a deep thinker, a man interested in ancient demonology who stole the Dark One's Book of Spells. Now that's really fascinating. What a coup that must have been for TIIIS, and according to that CMES mole, apparently for the Vatican as well.

Fourth, his assault on the North American headquarters, now the Gathering building, reveals a sophisticated strategic and tactical mind, which prefers technology over magic. And then there is a moralistic tendency to do wholesale destruction without excessive harm.

What a package for TIIIS ...

... The advantages that I possess are time and place. While Stone clearly is a deep thinker, if I can catch him off guard, then I will have my chance.

A sudden ambush it will be, then.

*   *   *

It was lunch time on a Wednesday. Mr. Henry, while sipping a beer with me, suddenly went quiet as his eyes dilated far beyond the normal. The seasoned Fourth-Level Adept, while visiting the Academy, seemed to experience frequent and heightened psychic episodes. This, clearly, was one of them.

"J.J.," he whispered, "you wouldn't believe what I just saw."

"What did you see?" I said with genuine concern on my face.

"I saw you, son, in a fight for your life, in, of all places, the Academy's parking lot—the one near your dorm. You had your hands full with a wizard, and of all things, an Assyrian griffin. Your little red truck gets trashed."

"When, Mr. Henry? When?"

Now shaking his white-haired head in dismay. "I don't know, son. But it felt real soon. You better start wearing that fancy combat suit of yours to bed regular like. You're gonna need it."

As a consequence, I did that very evening.

That same Wednesday, around four o'clock in the afternoon, I got a call from Melaina. She was all shaken up. I could clearly hear the trembling in her voice.

"J.J., I'm sorry for bothering you, but I just had to call you straight away."

"What's wrong, Mel?"

"You're in deep trouble, J.J. I was working in my office at the MMA and got this really spooky feeling about tomorrow."

"Such as?"

"You're going to be attacked around 10:45 tomorrow morning. I don't know where or how, but that time came through quite clearly. Someone or something is coming for you, cowboy. Be alert, and, what is it that you Americans like to say? 'Be sure to keep your eyes peeled.'"

*   *   *

Mel was so disturbed by her vision about J.J. that she immediately packed up all her things and left for the day. Somehow, someway she had to protect him and Mel knew she had options back at her Manhattan flat.

Sitting at the kitchen table, the native of Alexandria opened her mother's book of spells and began to drift among them—a love potion, how to prevent bread from going stale, another love potion, fashioning a seeing spoon, how to prevent spiders and scorpions from stinging newborns … she flipped back to the page about the fashioning of a seeing spoon.

Yes! Yes, this is what I want! Mel thought with excited hope as she eagerly read about how to first fashion a seeing spoon, and then how to enchant it to do her bidding.

I know, I'll go back to the MET. In the conservator's laboratory, I saw a Dremel Tool that I can easily bore a hole through the bowl of the spoon to see through!

Fortunately, after that, the spell wouldn't take long to prepare and execute, and best of all, just last week on a whim, she had bought several large wooden stirring spoons that were perfect for the task.

Once fashioned, Mel intended to watch over J.J. at the appointed time stipulated in her vision. Then, granted through the magical artifice, she would know how and when to assist that hunky Marine.

*　　*　　*

That same Wednesday evening, while Mel prepared her seeing spoon, Jeremy Gainsworthy went over his checklist: favorite African machete and sheath, blade freshly sharpened and coated in curare; three throwing spears, their long and narrow blades carefully honed and dipped in, yes curare; and his leather pouch with enchanted thumb ring crafted from the last tail vertebra of an Assyrian griffin-demon; blood coagulant powder; two small rolls of surgical tape and gauze; a granola bar; and a Swiss Army knife. While Jeremy preferred wearing his silk business suit for such encounters, he instead opted to go bare-chested in a loincloth made from the skin of the fourth lion that had mauled his parents. If you asked him why, he couldn't tell you, except that it felt appropriate. For a touch of flash, he finished off his preparations with bright, neon yellow Nike cross-trainers. They would do nicely.

That might not seem like a lot for a veteran paranormal champion and wizard-assassin, but Gainsworthy believed in simplicity, things that wouldn't jam, like a gun mechanism. Fearless and supremely confident, the man was aggressive to the extreme and cunning in the use of his environment and what might be at hand. Once conjured, the demon Assyrian griffin he controlled with his left hand thumb ring would attack whoever or whatever his master commanded. His natural physical gifts of speed and stamina he had maintained since his time in Africa as a youth. This alone allowed Gainsworthy to go into a metabolic overdrive for brief periods that produced Olympic-level speed and extraordinary accuracy, but at a cost.

On top of that, he could easily perceive the auras of animals and men. While not fully telepathic, he could guess what his prey might do in the short term. When in a tough situation, Gainsworthy could generate bolts of psychic energy, but again at a serious cost, unless his bare feet were in contact with the ground where he could shamelessly tap into a ley line. Above all, Gainsworthy was a realist, who knew when to back off and retreat, in order to fight another day. But such instances, in his experience, were few and far between.

The man did have his weaknesses. He liked to take his time with the hunt, the stalk of his prey. That desire sometimes led to overly clever, verging on cute, ploys and strategies, which occasionally backfired.

Tomorrow, he vowed, he would be careful. This Stone was battle-tested and his paranormal abilities were largely unknown. The only details reported in his security file were his blinding speed and the inability to track him easily. Those alone, Gainsworthy knew, could be due to any number of reasons. Only a face-to-face with the man could provide him with the answers he needed.

*   *   *

On Wednesday evening, I sat in my dorm room going over what I needed to do. I even made a list. Glancing over at my Mk. III UCS that was lying over the back of my easy chair, I had to look closely just to see it as it blended into the brown leather so well. Then, in a frank moment of truth, I finally admitted to myself.

I've been warned—twice, by both Mr. Henry and Mel. One with a location, the other with a time. So big guy, just think of this as an important test. Yes, you have butterflies, big time. Who wouldn't? But at least you know that this is coming.

Then a memory of Mr. Dexter's training snapped into view, one which seemed most appropriate.

"*Monsieur* Stone, there will come a time when you will come up against a formidable foe. This will not be a chance encounter. Rarely are the truly important ones.

"*Non, mon ami.* This encounter will be planned, if not orchestrated, to occur. You will be given fair warning. The more warning received, the graver the threat.

"When this happens, *Monsieur* Stone, remember to make your movements subtle. A deft flick of your head to direct a draught of energy is far better than a dramatic Hollywood thrust of your arm. That, *monsieur*, is a pure waste of energy and potential opportunity.

"Always remember—keep your movements subtle, focus, and conserve your energy. If you survive, afterwards be prepared to experience an exhaustion which you cannot imagine. You will be coming off an adrenaline high like no other. As you well know, the transformers of urban power grids heat up as they dole out their electricity. This is precisely what happens to you when you exhaust your reserves and tap into the power of a ley line.

"And finally, *mon ami*, strike first, quickly, and give no quarter, whatsoever. To play with your opponent is not only a needless waste of energy, it is extremely stupid, and *above all*, dangerous."

The next morning I would eat light and hydrate heavy, just as I used to do before going into battle. The game-meal ritual would help to settle me down because of its familiarity. Sportscasters and pundits often remark that this is all about superstition. What hogwash! It's all about settling down with something known prior to taking on the unknown.

Nervous, I went to bed suited up with the UCS just in case, with my Bone Sword within easy reach. Only my UCS boots stuck out, which at first glance made me look like I was floating on air with no feet.

I decided to wear a raincoat tomorrow.

CHAPTER 20
Engaging Tigers

When I got up around six, I reparked Old Faithful off to one side of the half-filled dorm parking lot. I figured that we'd need some room.

I messed around my room, doing this and doing that. Then I glanced up at my wall clock. It said 10:42.

Game time.

I walked out the door and toward my pickup. It was a pretty Pennsylvania morning. Here I was in the parking lot all by my lonesome, during the third class session, and I was missing a lecture on magical potions.

Those thoughts didn't last long.

Zero seconds. The First Soul screamed into my inner ear to get the hell out of the way. Being agreeable to its strong suggestion, I translocated fifty feet to my right.

A moment later, in the exact spot where I had been, a ton of Assyrian griffin cratered the asphalt pavement! Its yellow-scaled forearms and sickle-shaped talons dug deep furrows into the lot's old tarmac. Its heavily clawed and leonine rear legs did the same. The tips of the demon's outstretched golden wings brushed the ground upon the fierce force of the impact. The griffin's head, that of a golden eagle on a longish neck, bent low as well. Its bone-colored beak, the size of a trash can, reflexively snapped at the empty space where my torso once was. With a tawny-colored lion's body almost ten feet long, the damn thing looked like a creature straight from the walls of Nineveh! Well, it was, and I recognized it.

Four-tenths of a second later. Things got interesting. As the griffin's body rebounded from its initial pounce, I saw that the damn thing stood nearly eight feet tall at the shoulder.

Then approached this bare-chested guy about sixty feet away, wearing nothing but a furry loincloth and neon yellow Nike sneakers! I kid you not! What made him so remarkable were the three light spears he was casually carrying in his right hand, which just by the look of them shrieked poison. And then there were all of those scars on his upper arms which were toned a bloody red.

At that point I dumped my raincoat and pulled my hood and facemask into position. I was now nearly invisible.

Loincloth Man had a small leather pouch around his neck, while he carried what looked like a scabbard across his back. Meanwhile, I saw him fingering a large, whitish ring on his left thumb with the meat of his forefinger. The griffin-demon responded by leaping at me again.

Royally pissed off at missing me on its first attack, it sprung at me with its talons spread wide. At the same time it let loose a psychic screech that was probably designed to immobilize me by sheer fear. It almost did.

Another tenth of a second later, seeing the griffin-demon react caused two things to occur to me. The griffin-demon was telepathic and I could move in ways that it wouldn't expect. So I broadcast telepathically that I was pissed off and wasn't moving; I was going to make a stand. And second, I translocated fifty feet behind the approach of Loincloth Man.

Well, my ploy faked out Polly-Wants-a-Cracker

into missing me again, as it cratered heavily into the asphalt, again, on that bright and shining morning.

My new location behind the bare-chested Loincloth Man bought me a moment, but not much. He had his spears up at the ready, but now realized he didn't have a target.

Somehow, someway, the demon-griffin located me behind its master, and leapt again heedless of Loincloth Man directly in front of me. Incidentally, from this point-of-view I could see Loincloth Man wore a long and swinging lion's tail attached to his getup.

Loincloth Man, not understanding what his directed demon-griffin was doing, saw a threat and hurled all three of his spears as one into the onrushing chest of the griffin. They stunned it, but in no way halted its progress. That spear cast, by the way, was a thing of beauty, Loincloth Man did it with such a fluid and effortless motion.

A moment later, Polly-Wants-a-Cracker blundered past Loincloth Man, shouldering him aside, while it continued to charge, but slowed somewhat by the deeply buried spear shafts.

I, in a two-handed Weaver stance, fired off a double-tap at the back of Loincloth Man's left hand just as he was body-checked to the side. The 147 gram hollow point rounds flew true and utterly ruined his hand, and smashed the large white thumb ring into several pieces in the process.

I again screamed telepathically my intent to hold my ground, and instead translocated to my right another fifty feet, cutting the move way too close as I literally felt the griffin's fore-talons clawed through the air.

Once again Polly-Wants-a-Cracker missed me. It

cratered the parking lot yet again, and immediately began its muscular rebound with its head on a swivel, looking for me.

As for Loincloth Man, he somehow spotted me to his right, and while ignoring his shattered and bleeding left hand, advanced, and drew with his right hand a large weapon from the scabbard on his back.

Out of nowhere, a large bubble of moisture formed around the demon-griffin's body. Shaking its head this way and that in utter confusion, its vision clouded, while water droplets formed over its magnificently feathered wings and lion's body. It shook, rippled its fur, and spasmed in agony at the sudden contact with moisture.

At the threatening approach of Loincloth Man, I subtly flicked my head in his direction with a powerful cast of *Monsieur* Dexter's offensive magic.

The cast's impact on the man's bare solar plexus was telling, for not only did it stop him dead in his tracks, it threw him backward, cracking his head several times on the tarmac, knocking him senseless. He skidded on his back, and though partially on his scabbard, still seriously abrading the skin and muscle covering his left shoulder blade, motorcycle style. His broken body finally came to rest in a tumbled, unmoving mound against a cement curbing.

Then, the moisture bubble that surrounded the demon-griffin broke with a loud pop. With Loincloth Man down, I could now focus on Polly-Wants-a-Cracker. I translocated past its still shivering form, but not before I made a vicious strike with my Bone Sword across the base of its elongated neck, decapitating the creature. This bone-headed move—the combination of translocating and swinging my sword for all that it was worth, despite Mr. Dexter's warning, at contact, dislocated my left shoulder.

Now well clear of the stricken griffin-demon, clouds of black ectoplasm poured out of its slack mouth and fountained from the base of its trunk. In fact, the entire demonic form broke down, sagged, and began to evaporate, creating a grayish-black fog.

Now for Loincloth Man. Well, he was unconscious, so I removed the leather pouch from around his neck and stomped down hard on his right hand, which made a sickening crunch. I didn't want him using it, if he should suddenly come to.

Meanwhile, only a black, and quickly dissipating diesel-like cloud remained of the fallen demon-griffin. Beneath where it had been was a pool of clear water and three broken throwing spears.

I quickly looked around, and remarkably, this entire mid-morning encounter had not been witnessed by a soul. Although I was willing to bet that President Silver Moon would want to know who did a job to her dorm parking lot.

I policed the area of the three broken spears, one vicious machete-like knife, a leather pouch, and the white ring fragments. These I pitched into the cab of my pickup truck, Old Faithful, which for some reason survived unscathed. Mr. Henry had been wrong. Then, I lowered my pickup's tailgate and muscled the still-limp Loincloth Man one handed. With my left shoulder screaming at me, I drove over to the campus clinic, parked in the Emergency Only lane with a lurch, levered myself out, and walked in requesting assistance for Loincloth Man.

My shoulder was now seriously doing a war dance. I pulled back my facemask and hood for some fresh air, which felt damn good, and flat passed out in the lobby of the Emergency intake. The combination of the shock of the injury and the adrenalin crash that *Monsieur* Dexter had warned me about, had firmly taken hold.

I quickly came to, only to discover that the friendly folks in the ER wanted to cut the UCS off my body instead of using its many zippers. It only took one look from me to shut down *that* asinine idea. Besides, whatever would they have cut the Kevlar suit with?

I looked the ER physician square in the eye and said, "Okay, doc. Here's how this is going down. It's the fourth quarter, we're behind, and I'm the star middle-linebacker. Now pop this sucker back in."

"No pain-killers?"

"Once you get it back in, doc, then we'll talk about those."

Well, I almost passed out twice before the doc finally got me put back together. I experienced what exquisite pain was—sharp, blinding, breathtaking, and sudden. But once my arm was back in where it belonged, the relief was tremendous. I thought I was floating.

I discharged myself from the ER against all objections. Now all dolled up in a beige sling with a heavy-duty prescription in hand, I walked back to my dorm room. Never before did just sitting down in my La-Z-Boy feel so good. While sleep was fast a-coming, I did manage to call Mr. Henry and Mel to tell them that I was okay and had survived the ordeal.

It was then I found out what that sneaky Alexandrian did to the demon-griffin. I wondered who had done that. She conjured that spell remotely, like all the way from Manhattan. Damn, I was grateful for her help, and mightily impressed as well. As I dozed off, I had to admit that Mel wasn't half bad after all. Not one bit. And no, I didn't tell either of them about my shoulder.

As for Loincloth Man, he was in a coma. No one had a clue as to who he was, so the ER intake designated him as a John Doe. While the majority of his injuries looked like he'd fallen off a motorcycle while riding without a helmet, that explanation quickly fell apart as it could not account for his bullet damaged left hand. But for now, he remained a mystery in the ICU. The next day I explained the entire situation.

*   *   *

"Mr. DeSalvo," Kiel said over the phone, "I have yet to hear from Mr. Gainsworthy and it has been a week, sir. What should I do?"

"Stop payment on his check. If he's still alive to claim it then we'll pay him with interest.

"On second thought, do we know where he was heading?"

"Western Pennsylvania, sir. The Old Oaks Academy, I'm afraid."

"*Dio mio*. Send a three-man team to scout out the nearby hospitals and clinics, and be sure that they check the local obits. In short, the usual for missing personnel."

"Yes, sir. But he's not of our Gathering."

"Yeah, I know. But he once was."

DeSalvo abruptly cutoff Kiel, and then asked himself: *What will it take to stop Stone?*

*   *   *

"Mr. Kiel," a breathless voice said on his smart phone, "we have found Gainsworthy."

"Where?"

"University of Pittsburg Medical Center, sir."

Western Pennsylvania. Why am I not surprised?

"Put Gainsworthy on the line."

"Can't do that, sir. He's in a coma."

"How bad?"

"He's not on life-support. The staff is optimistic that he'll come out of it when he's good and ready."

"Any other injuries?"

"Yeah, I was told that he was a real mess when they airlifted him in."

Airlifted?

"At first the ER staff thought that he was a motorcycle crash victim, because of Gainsworthy's extensive back lacerations and head trauma, but that diagnosis couldn't explain the man's left hand, which had been pretty much blown apart, probably by a gun or rifle."

Jesus Christ!

"Okay, you and your team stay put. Call me when Gainsworthy regains consciousness."

*   *   *

Two days later and after being comatose for almost two solid weeks, Gainsworthy's eyes finally fluttered open. Slowly he began to shift uncomfortably in his hospital bed. These movements kicked off an alarm at the nurse's central station, and in moments a white angel appeared.

"Where am I?" the man croaked out.

"You're in a hospital, sir. The University of Pittsburg Medical Center, in Pittsburg, Pennsylvania." She added unnecessarily. "Do you remember your name?"

Still blinking, the man tried to rub at his eyes but couldn't because his right hand was in a hard cast and his left was a round ball of bandage wrap. Seeing this, Gainsworthy said hoarsely, "Gainsworthy. Jeremy Gainsworthy. What the hell happened to my hands?"

Raising up the bed's mattress to thirty degrees, the critical care nurse fed her patient some ice water from a bendy straw. Gainsworthy drank deeply, let out cough, and then a sigh.

"Thank you, nurse. But what about my hands?" he asked again, this time with a frustrated tone, lifting them slightly.

"Well, Mr. Gainsworthy, your right hand was crushed and required surgery. It now has several screws and is on the mend. The left, however, was more badly damaged. I'm very sorry, sir, but you lost your thumb and forefinger. The surgeon, try as he might, couldn't save them."

A grunt was all that the patient could muster at that moment as the details of the fight with Stone, brief though it was, were all coming back to him in vivid detail, frame by frame.

The nurse continued. "Your back, sir, will have some scarring. You slid quite a ways on it. By the way, what did happen to you, sir?"

Looking down and seeing his heavily bandaged torso, he then registered the question, and lied, "Nurse, I really don't know."

* * *

A day later, Gainsworthy sat before DeSalvo in his Manhattan office. Bathed, shaved, and with an assistant to help him with all things that a set of hands should do, the assassin considered himself downright lucky. Never before had CMES leadership acted with such concern for a non-aligned asset. That meant, to Gainsworthy, that he had somehow remained valuable in some regard, and he suspected that he was about to find out why soon.

The assassin, dressed in a pair of loose-fitting blue jeans and a tight upscale collarless shirt that framed his taunt physique, sat leaning forward with his arms resting on his knees. His bandaged hands looked like boxing gloves.

"Mr. Gainsworthy, welcome back from the dead. I see that you have lived to fight another day."

"So it would seem, Mr. DeSalvo. However, precisely how I got to a hospital, is a question I cannot answer. Although, I have my suspicions."

"Stone?"

"Who else?"

"How long before the gloves come off?"

"I will be visiting with the doctor tomorrow. Both hands itch like hell, so that's good. As for their rehab, I haven't a clue as to how long that will take, much less what percentage of total facility can be regained."

The regional director sighed, "I totally understand. But can you tell me anything about what happened out there in Pennsylvania? To date, I have lost too many troops to this Stone."

A big sigh.

"Well, Mr. DeSalvo, first off, he's full of surprises. He wears some sort of adaptive camouflage for starters; that makes him very hard to spot. Next, he's extremely quick and fast. Quick in his reflexes; fast in sheer speed."

"Is there anything else that you care to share?"

"He shot the shit out of my left hand, so he carries a handgun of some sort. And he's accurate. He destroyed my handmade griffin ring with it."

"Which finger?"

"My thumb, sir. That's probably why I lost both my forefinger and thumb. He was out to destroy my griffin ring and they got in the way."

"Out of curiosity, how long did this encounter last, Mr. Gainsworthy?"

Silence, while the assassin considered the question.

"I would estimate under ten seconds, sir."

DeSalvo's eyebrows raised in surprise.

"Contrary to what most people think, such confrontations are extremely quick events. The reason for that is the enormous expenditure of energy that each of the combatants' use. But the point that I wish to emphasize, sir, is that Stone is extremely intelligent, well-equipped, and even better trained.

"Sir, I was caught unawares and put into a coma by a savage psychic casting that was delivered with a mere flick of the man's head. What that tells me is, that in addition to everything that I have already said, Stone is exceedingly conscious of his energy stockpile. For a big man, he moves effortlessly, with economy, and doesn't waste a single gesture. This alone is very telling of his training. Right now, he is damn near invincible."

Silence again. Then …

"And one other thing, Stone is beyond fast for a reason. I actually saw the man translocate several times."

"What?"

"Yes, sir. The man can translocate. I have never encountered a human who could do that before."

"When you're reasonably healthy, do you want another crack at him?"

"Absolutely, sir. A contract is a contract." The assassin said without hesitation.

"Good. In the meantime, our Gathering will take good care of you during your physical therapy. When all of this is over, then, perhaps, you might consider becoming a contributing member of my region. I am always looking for experience. And, I am willing to pay for it."

"Thank you, Mr. DeSalvo, for that offer, but I still have a contract to fulfill."

* * *

Mr. Henry and I hadn't gotten together for lunch for a good two weeks. Reason being, I had that little altercation and I was still rehabbing my left shoulder. So per our usual habit, we met at the Acorn at noon. The place, for some reason, was really hopping this time, so we couldn't sit at our usual table in the corner.

"Well, J.J., how did it go, this first encounter with a dark wizard?" My white-haired mentor in all things paranormal, asked over the rim of his beer.

"Mr. Henry, sir, I am not all that sure. I had considerable warning that something was up; both you and Mel warned with your concerns. I don't know how I would have fared without them. That fact alone sort of scares me."

A very pleased look formed on the old man's face.

"J.J., that's life. Premonitions happen for a reason. While I would never tell you to depend upon them, certainly wouldn't allow their help to detract from what you had to do, and when you had to do it.

"Now, who was it that dared to show up and take you on?"

Shaking my head, I admitted, "I don't know. Just some guy dressed in a furry loincloth or kilt with a tail. He carried three throwing spears and a big-ass knife over his back. But what was really interesting was his sidekick, a mythological animal, a griffin that he controlled with a white ring on his left thumb."

Holding up his hand for me to stop, Mr. Henry interrupted. "You mean to tell me that you took on a wizard *with* his griffin?"

"Yes, sir."

"J.J., there is only one adept that I know who fits that bill, a Brit named Jeremy Gainsworthy. His childhood was spent in Africa and later was trained by one of CMES' more blood-thirsty wizard-assassins, a man named Paine. No pun intended." He finished with more than a tinge of respect in his voice. "You were very fortunate, son. Now, tell me all about it, blow by blow, and in gruesome detail."

CHAPTER 21
The Tour

Mel struggled as she came to grips with her first official membership visit to the Gathering. Yes, outwardly, she told herself that it was just an exclusive spa, perhaps representing what life might have been like in a royal harem with attendants always within easy reach. Or, on the other hand, it represented Big Brother on steroids plucked right out of *1984*. Both were valid snippets and impressions, but overall there was an uncomfortable vibe to the place where everything and anything could be acquired, with a sense of "no limits."

Her orientation took place on the fourth floor, in an area marked Membership Services. There, in an exclusive, yet business-like setting, a stereo-optic picture was recorded, documents signed, and Mel was introduced to her personal valet and trainer, Arthur. At the end of the visit, the Alexandrian was formally presented with a black carbon-fiber and chipped ID card with her holographic image. The professor of Demotic and Coptic Literature was quite impressed. And yes, etched in low relief into the card's blank side was the omnipresent Celtic logo.

Arthur—or perhaps his original name might have been Arthuro—possessed a quietly dominant Latino personality, with curly black hair, a well-toned body, and impeccable grooming. Yet, Mel could tell that a black panther within yearned to be freed. A quick check of his aura and she judged him demon-free, but his hues lacked the usual luster of someone with his youthfulness and vigor. Clearly, he had made some choices that were not the best.

"Professor Makris, if you will follow me, then we can complete your installation."

"Installation?"

"Yes. That would include your assignment of a personal changing room. If after that you wish to set up a training regime, I can assist you with that as well."

After a brief journey on the elevator, Mel arrived at what looked like a hotel lobby with three receptionists behind another black granite desk decorated with five logos, which she judged as active.

"Professor Makris, kindly give your ID card to one of the receptionists so they can assign you your changing room."

The room assigned to her was number 6040. As for these receptionists, Makris judged them all to be fully human, while their dingy auras hinted at criminal backgrounds.

Anywhere else in Manhattan, Room 6040 would have been considered an outright suite, for it contained a bedroom, full bath, and a separate room with a small kitchen and office area. It was far nicer than Mel's flat on Third Avenue and had enough closet space to move in.

"Arthur?"

"Yes, Professor Makris."

"Is 6040 solely assigned to me?"

"Oh my, yes, Professor Makris. In fact, the Gathering encourages its membership to leave several changes of clothing and personal items behind for your convenience. Toting around bulky work out bags are not needed here. Additionally, several items have been provided for you if you wish to work out today, or go for a swim. You will find them hanging up in the bathroom closet area."

Curious, the Alexandrian went to look, and there hung a black, one-piece leotard and matching one-piece swimsuit, in exactly the right size.

"You certainly think of everything."

"We certainly try, Professor Makris. After their use, just put them in the hamper, and housekeeping will take care of them for you. Same goes for used towels and bedding. Even your personal clothing can be washed, dry-cleaned, and pressed if you wish.

"If you are ever hungry, please visit any one of our four award-winning restaurants on the twentieth through twenty-third floors. They are open twenty-four/seven and provide breathtaking views of the city."

"Arthur, during my orientation, I remember the mention of a lap pool. Where is that located?"

"Thirteenth floor, Professor Makris. If you wish to use those facilities, more traditional locker room arrangements are available there as well, as are several jetted hot tubs.

"Are the weight rooms also on the Thirteenth floor?"

"No, they are not. All of that section's physical fitness facilities can be found on the eleventh and twelfth floors. Additionally, our locker rooms on those floors have access to whirlpools—both hot and cold—a steam bath and sauna—including our massage and personal appearance facilities, such as hair styling, facials, manicures, and pedicures."

"Is it permitted to run the emergency fire stairwells, or, must I always use the elevators?"

That question actually caused the valet to frown

slightly.

"I am very sorry, Professor Makris, but typically we encourage our members to use the elevators. One moment and I will find out for you."

Out came his ubiquitous smart phone and after some furious texting, Arthur sent off his request.

"Do you wish to set up a fitness appraisal today?"

"No, Arthur, not today, but perhaps tomorrow. Do I need to set up an appointment to do so?"

"It would be preferred, but it isn't necessary. I am on staff daily from seven in the morning until five in the evening. Just ask for me at any reception desk and I will find you."

His smart phone rang. Reading its message, Arthur said, "Professor Makris, it is permitted to run the emergency fire stairwells. However, concern was expressed that if you slipped on a stair tread and injured yourself that emergency services might be delayed in getting to you."

"How would they find me?"

"Your ID card has a GPS chip."

"Oh, how comforting. "One last question before I leave for an appointment. I wish to enroll in some courses in self-development. How do I go about that?"

To this question, Arthur actually perked up. "That's easy, Professor Makris, return to the fourth floor, and they will be able to do so, and answer any other questions you might have."

"Thank you, Arthur. You have been most helpful. I'll see you tomorrow about that physical appraisal."

"I look forward to it, Professor Makris. Just be sure to hydrate sufficiently prior to it. It'll make things much easier."

*　　*　　*

Sweat dripped like a leaky faucet from the tip of Mel's nose. The deep burn in her thighs made her want to cry out for relief. Her numbed and slick hands on the stationary bike's handlebars threatened to lose their grip. Still, the Alexandrian wouldn't give up, wouldn't give that supercilious—no sadistic—grin on Arthur's face the satisfaction of breaking her. So, she endured an additional three minutes before punching the bike's cool down button.

Arthur's comment, "Not bad." Somehow Mel managed a quick and civil smile, while deep inside she wanted to tear out the twerp's heart.

Knees wobbly, the white witch made her way stiff-legged to the locker room for a hot shower and a massage. She figured she deserved it after that ride from hell.

Showered, deeply massaged, and, as a result, somewhat recovered, Mel exited the locker room facilities only to find Arthur waiting for her with a print out.

"Professor Makris. Congratulations. You attained the 94th percentile, which for your … *abilities* is quite remarkable." Clearly, the twerp almost slipped and said "age," but had caught himself.

"Why thank you, Arthur. What's your percentile?" Mel asked with a hard look.

No answer was forthcoming, just a smug smile.

"Be sure to hydrate, Professor Makris. It will help flush away all that lactic acid and speed your recovery," he helpfully added.

"Why, thank you, Arthur. What a wonderful

suggestion." Makris left that dangling phrase out there for him to chew on as either a straightforward compliment or a dismissive remark.

"Will I see you tomorrow, Professor Makris?"

"No, Arthur. I usually work out only every other day, and besides, tomorrow I have a personal development class. I will not be in need of your services."

*   *   *

The next day the introductory *Finding Your Center* personal development class was scheduled for eleven and met on the twenty-third floor. Upon exiting the elevator, Mel again noted the now all-too-familiar reception area layout and its three-man staff. Broad arched entrances to the right and left led to the restaurants that ringed the structure's perimeter. Just smelling those wonderfully wicked aromas threatened to put inches on Melaina's body. When the Alexandrian announced that she was there for a class, however, one of the guards guided her to a key-coded side door. He opened it and told her to proceed across a narrow fifty-foot hallway to the next door.

Once sealed within the cramped passage, Mel experienced, once again, the massive overpressure that was the building's magical defenses. But once through the doorway opposite, the pressure amped up to an almost intolerable level. Again confronted with a reception area and its staff, two of which were demon-possessed, the white witch was told by the human to enter the door marked "University," which Makris thought was a bit presumptuous. Once past its threshold, the near-blinding overpressure vanished.

On the other side, Mel walked up to a grandmotherly woman seated behind a heavily carved desk, which instinctively troubled her. Its design, shape, and vague aura looked more like something captured, rather than carved.

The woman, engrossed in her computer, now looked up to acknowledge her. With skin the color of ripe almonds and perfectly white teeth, she asked, "How might I help you, dear?"

This receptionist looked so much like Mel's mother that the Alexandrian struggled to keep her gaping mouth working.

"I am here for the introductory class on *Finding Your Center*. Where should I go?"

"Third door on the left, dear. Be sure to enjoy yourself." Then she returned to her work.

Half way down the hallway, Mel stopped, turned around, and saw that the elderly woman, now quite young, was observing her. Upon locking eyes, she smiled knowingly, and returned to her work. But then the Alexandrian noted her aura—a slimy black. At that, she immediately blocked her thoughts before allowing herself to think about what she had just seen.

Was that really a shape-shifting demon, or just a powerful telepath that was manipulating my thoughts?

Suddenly, as Mel now stood before the classroom's threshold, she came to the full realization of just how deep into enemy territory she really was.

*   *   *

There were only five people in Mel's class. They sat in moveable desks arranged in a circle. Front and center stood the severe instructor, Ms. Griffith—a nervous fidget, constantly on the move.

"Thank you for attending this introductory class in personal development," Griffith began with an odd accent that Mel could not place.

"This session will last forty minutes. Its purpose is to discover who is, and who isn't, prepared for the next class entitled *Paranormal Portals*. As a consequence, do not be surprised if you must repeat this introduction several times before you eventually make the grade."

Several in the class glanced about in surprise.

Griffith continued, "Magic is extremely serious business. Consequently, I will push you hard. Further, I believe the rod increases a student's attention."

So it began—a desperately savage probing of the id and ego, a contest of wills, along with some telepathic exercises involving playing cards. By its end, Mel thought she had developed a migraine as never before, since the Alexandrian witch had held her mental blocks up for such a long time.

Almost staggering out of the classroom, her mind still reeling, Ms. Griffith, unsmiling, stopped her and handed her a small linen envelope. Mel had been the only one to receive one.

Next stop was the twelfth floor as Makris sorely needed a massage to break her mental tension. As it turned out, it was a godsend, for in the locker room she finally read what the tiny envelope contained.

You have been invited to attend the next level in
your self-development process entitled:

Paranormal Portals

Be sure to present this invitation to your instructor
on your first day of class.—D.J. Griffith

*   *   *

Jenny Sauerbrünn carefully examined the four internal staff reports about a new member called Professor Melaina Makris. All of them noted her exceptional aura, mental acuity, and/or dogged stubbornness. That she could effectively block her thoughts—and for an extended period—was also critically appraised. To these, Sauerbrünn added her own privately held assessment; one admittedly tainted with pure and unadulterated lust. But in Sauerbrünn's mind, there remained one red flag that troubled her: Makris' early request to run the building's emergency fire stairs. That made her nervous, and made her wonder why.

CHAPTER 22
The Debrief

Two months into Professor Melaina Makris' orientation into the Gathering, she decided that it was time to report in. She made the call and took the train to Philadelphia the next day, a late Friday afternoon. Mr. Henry Johnson, her TIIIS contact, was assigned to debrief the Alexandrian white witch on her impressions. It was thought best that a Fourth-Class Adept do so for many reasons.

For Mel, the brief journey south she saw as a much-needed break from her research and the insane New York City tempo. She purposely left behind in her Manhattan flat, her ID card for the Gathering. As the train ride would take over an hour, Mel stopped by a bookstore, and on the recommendation of a good colleague at the MMA, bought *Sleeper Protocol* by Kevin Ikenberry. Not usually a reader of science fiction, Mel nonetheless was promised that the yarn was a real page-turner and potential tear-jerker. Sitting down in a window seat, the white witch curled up and began reading, even before the train even pulled out of Union Station.

Being a Friday, Mel's train pulled into Pennsylvania Station ten minutes late, but no matter, as Ikenberry's book about a soldier finding himself had completely captivated her. A quick cab ride later she checked into her hotel. Only then did she call Mr. Johnson, who was expecting it.

"Where are you staying, Professor Makris? Uh-huh. Give me twenty minutes, and I'll pick you up."

Standing at the curb of her hotel, Mel eagerly breathed in the evening air, with surprise that it didn't stink of the City. If anything, the air was clean and vaguely scented with salt water. She caught herself nearly hyperventilating in its richness, and something else, something primal, elemental, and welcoming.

Before she knew it, a bright red pickup truck with white Texas plates appeared under the hotel's veranda. The passenger, Mr. Henry Johnson, was easily identified by his white hair, big grin, and rippling blue aura. The driver was J.J. Stone. The Alexandrian witch's pulse raced, secretly overjoyed at seeing again the rangy, hunk of a Marine. Besides, Mel felt that the more people that she came in contact with within TIIIS the better. She was a big believer in getting to know people through their friends and colleagues.

This dynamic duo took her to a small Italian restaurant that was slotted into a narrow store front in a four-storey building of red brick. It was the kind of place with only six tables, where word-of-mouth and reservations were a must. Clean, neat, and care-worn, the smells that emanated from its kitchen were simply to die for.

Once there, Mel met another amazing person, President Betsy Silver Moon. A special treat.

The four were seated in an elegant converted pantry space in the back of the kitchen. It was cozy, quiet, and private, where they could talk, drink wine, and sample heaven only knows how many family specialties that came their way. Fresh-cooked, hyper-fresh ingredients, and all delicious, the variety reminded Mel of the Alexandrian marketplace. Yes, she felt homesick, but among these people, felt whole, somehow.

It was President Silver Moon who deftly shifted the conversation.

"Professor Makris, what brings you to the City of Brotherly Love? Surely, it can't be J.J.," she smirked. "I sense that there's something on your mind. Perhaps something that you wish to share?"

The debrief began. Sipping wine, nibbling on warm garlic bread, sampling some marvelous calamari, moving on to manageable portions of pasta, and finally, ending it all with an aromatic aperitif.

"Actually, Madam President, I have quite a bit to share. But first, I wish to thank all of you for putting together this lovely evening, and on such short notice. I haven't felt so unconditionally accepted since my mother's funeral."

Pause.

"Mr. Johnson, CMES' administrative core is to be found on the twentieth through twenty-third floors. I base this on the fact that the building's four restaurants surround this core and are arranged along the structure's perimeter windows. Additionally, when I went through the new membership process, all the interviews took place on these floors.

"In fact, the building itself is subdivided into three parts, each set apart with their own lap pool. Access to any of the building's floors is heavily defended in their elevator lobbies with magically empowered symbols; a complex Celtic knot that has embedded within it an inverted, five-pointed star."

At this last, President Silver Moon and the rest sat stone-faced.

"So," Mr. Johnson summarized, "you think the

building is a heavily buttressed, magical fortress compartmentalized into three sections. How did you arrive at that?"

"Actually, Mr. Johnson, I inferred it. When Director Sauerbrünn took me on the tour, one of the amenities was an eight-lane lap pool. She must have sensed that I was a swimmer and offhandedly mentioned that the building had three of them. When I expressed my surprise, she then added how green the building truly was, as each of the pools doubled as emergency fire reservoirs for the sprinkler system."

"Well, that sounds ingenious, and quite clever." Mr. Johnson said. "So, it is also your opinion that the administrative core you visited was literally buried in the center of the structure, without any obvious communication with the outside world, not even any windows."

"The security of the four administrative floors is absolutely oppressive. What I mean by that is that the paranormal overpressure of the defenses is staggering. I cannot imagine what would happen if their full force was unleashed."

Further silence.

"As for the personnel in that building, they all made me shiver. There is not a warm body in the entire facility. Even their Director of Membership, a cold and calculating Aryan blond, is some kind of sensory adept. Their security force is everywhere. Further, two-thirds of them possess the blackest of black auras. I have absolutely no idea what they are capable of."

"It was good that you came," President Silver Moon finally said. "Frankly, I was concerned about you visiting that facility, much less joining it." She paused, then asked with a penetrating look, "Have you noticed any subtle changes to your personality, research output, or outlook on life since you joined?"

"Absolutely, I am now getting into better physical shape. But with that, I have noticed that I have expectations, I am far more aggressive, assertive, and my patience has waned considerably. It's not that I snap at people. It's more like I'm constantly toe-tapping."

"Could it be, Mel," J.J. opined, "that you're just becoming a New Yorker?"

"I thought about that, J.J. But the Gathering exudes this extreme alpha-temperament, broadcasts it in open defiance of the religious edifices that surround it. In many ways, that structure is an evil dynamo that affects everyone inside it and near it."

More silence. Then Mr. Henry piped up. "Professor Makris, are you aware of ley lines?"

"I believe so. Alfred Watkins, in his book, *The Old Straight Track*, first coined the term. Why?"

"Are you aware that there are two kinds of ley lines?"

"No, I did not."

"Well, there are light and dark ley lines. Just as in the human body we have arteries and veins, so too does the earth have light and dark ley lines. Where a light one ends, a dark one begins. It is a sort of paranormal circulatory system that is extremely well-balanced."

Mr. Henry paused, and then continued.

"That said ley lines do select who or what they choose to link with. From all accounts, there is no rhyme or reason to this selection process—just that it is. Traditionally the most dangerous areas of the world are located near dark ley lines. For instance, New York,

Baghdad, Cairo, Barcelona, Hong Kong, Minsk, and Berlin are well-known hot spots powered by such dark ley lines.

"As a consequence, I suspect the overpressure, the psychic heaviness that you sensed at the Gathering building is the result of CMES' tap into a dark ley line. Out of curiosity—and I know that this was some time ago—what did you feel when you first set foot on New Mexican soil?"

Mel thought hard about that one, and then realized, "I was first impressed by the low humidity, clear air quality, and altitude. But I felt in the background something very primal, elemental, yet soothing and welcoming."

"See, there you go." President Silver Moon enthused. "That is because you were subconsciously tapping into the local ley line called the Silver Nile."

"Well, Professor Makris, that was some debrief," Mr. Henry Johnson said. "Without question, you are one brave woman. In many ways, your eyes on the ground have confirmed what we have learned through the building's architectural plans. In fact, your assessment dovetails perfectly with those plans, even to the division of the building into three subdivisions. It's almost like a vertical submarine with three bulkheads. All that we can say is, job well done."

At that, Mr. Johnson reached into his coat, removed an envelope, and placed it before the Alexandrian witch.

"Professor Makris. This envelope contains a rather sizable check made out to you. Might I suggest that you deposit it at your earliest convenience? It should amply cover your membership fees and, perhaps, some of your needs, while you are in Manhattan."

Reaching back into his coat, the man produced a card.

"Also, should a need arise, here is my contact information. Professor, consider me your banker, confidant, and ally."

*   *   *

Mel returned to Manhattan and over the next months allowed herself to fall into an easy groove of working out, immersing herself in research, and repeating what, by now, had become near ritual. She had specifically chosen, however, not to pursue the invitation to develop her paranormal skill set. Her reason, if asked, was that she couldn't devote sufficient time to the class, while in fact she was scared of what she might turn into.

Motivated by her pure hatred and wrath toward CMES and all that it stood for, by month three the effects of her early morning workouts had become apparent. Mel's leotard hung like an awning across a flat abdomen, her legs had become sculpted and defined, her endurance insane. Overall, she no longer wore clothing, it draped across her form. In parallel, her ongoing research into the Demotic and Coptic texts at the MMA progressed swimmingly, as her concentration and mental sharpness had reached a new plateau.

*   *   *

Sauerbrünn stared down at Professor Makris' latest fitness evaluation and her right eyebrow rose.

Arthur seems to think that you're ready for a New York marathon and after only twelve weeks of three-

days-a-week training sessions ... And I see that you have gracefully turned down, several times, our level two paranormal training ...

So what's up with you, professor?

*　　*　　*

"J.J., my boy, that Professor Makris is one formidable white witch," Mr. Henry began. "Never in my life have I ever met the like. Imagine—a white witch with such intelligence, fortitude, raw beauty, and sheer, unadulterated guts. She literally entered the lion's den and vowed to bring it down around her. The moxie of that gal positively gives me goose bumps!"

"So what are the chances that she can find us an angle to exploit?"

Shaking his head from side-to-side, I saw that Mr. Henry was *speechless*. Then, finally, "J.J., I don't know. CMES has built itself a magically secure blockhouse and then surrounded it with innocent human shields. But as they say, 'if there's a will, then there's a way.' If anyone can find a chink in CMES' armor, it's that witch."

*　　*　　*

That Saturday before Mel was due to return to Manhattan, Mr. Henry, President Silver Moon, and I met to discuss "how to do what" to the Gathering building. During a surprisingly frank conversation, our brain trust managed to conjure up a unique brand of mayhem.

"Given what we know about the structure and its many magical safeguards, we must assume a strategy that takes advantage of many different tactics," President Silver Moon said.

"In other words," I clarified, "you're advocating a multi-layered attack, fully expecting that one or more approaches will fail, while one or more approaches may succeed."

"Precisely," the president confirmed.

"So, gang, what do we have to work with?" Mr. Henry reasonably asked.

"I propose we plan the attack to happen in broad daylight, at high noon, and on a Wednesday."

"Why?" Mel replied with a cocked head. "What's the advantage? What's your thinking behind that time and day of the week."

"People will be thinking about lunch for one," I explained. "That means people will be the move, which causes traffic, potential confusion, and even panic."

"Okay. Let's consider that," President Silver Moon said.

"But, J.J., why a Wednesday?" Mel probed.

"Because it's Hump Day, the very middle of the week. People will begin thinking about their weekend plans. They'll be distracted."

"Interesting angle," the president said. "Now, people, what else?"

"We time an IT hack of their fire systems, building wide, which can occur to the second, potentially using any available operational remoras, I suppose." Mr. Henry offered.

"There's lots of 'what ifs' in that proposal, Horatio." President Silver Moon smiled. "But if IT and Security can swing it, we'll run with it. What else folks?"

"It seems to me," Mel offered, "that we first need to somehow debilitate their security and IT resources, so that they can't come to the rescue."

"And how could we pull that off within such a heavily defended environment?" The president said.

"Well," Mel continued, "I know how to send mail that is magically inert, undetectable, and untraceable by a spell whisperer."

"Holy shit!" blurted out Mr. Henry, who then immediately apologized for his indiscretion. "That's downright diabolical."

"That's awesome." I said. "But what kind of spell do you have in mind, Mel?"

"One that temporarily creates illness, fevers, and noisome boils."

"Damn. That sounds like a nerve gas attack!" I said, and Mr. Henry nodded in agreement. "It'll confuse the hell out of them."

"Another 'nice' thing about boils and illness is that I can specify a range of the effect. The usual measure is in terms of a Greek *plethron*, which is approximately one hundred feet. So, if I specify a cubic *plethron*, and send the same letter to say, five people on their security and IT floor, I could potentially blanket about three full floors of people."

Gawking silence.

"So, to again summarize," Silver Moon stated. "We want to hit them from multiple angles—broad daylight on a Wednesday for maximum impact; a well-timed high-tech hack; and stealth magic. This is a great start, but we need more, people. Think."

CHAPTER 23
A Virgin Oracle's Ire

A cloudless morning greeted the town's marketplace. Its square, filled with colorful stalls, gushed fresh bakery aromas, displayed still dewy vegetables, and many arrangements of fragrant cut flowers. Chuckling chatter between venders—mostly old friends with roots that went back before the construction of the cobblestoned street—filled the air. Gossip spread like wildfire between the stalls and with the many household shoppers. Some of them came early to select from the best of the best, while others took their leisure and strolled through, noting this and that. These patient ones drifted like vultures on the wing to make their purchases at the market's close, when the prices halved.

Valeria Costa counted herself among the former who demanded quality. Dressed in loose, comfortable jeans, sneakers, and a faded black AC/DC T-shirt, she wore her luxuriant hair down and took on the look of a mid-thirties rocker behind aviator sunglasses. More than one noted her sinuous progress with either outright lust or the sad regret of youthfulness lost. With a colorful wicker basket hanging from one arm, Valeria poked, sniffed, and squeezed her way through the many ripe and delicious items. Her basket began to fill.

In the Italian town of Tivoli, everyone knew everyone, what everyone did and where within the social strata someone fell. In Valeria's case, her always polite deference was noted with appreciation. Quick to wish someone well with a warm and genuine smile, the oracle felt safe within the confines of her town.

Valeria's quiet acts of charity were well-known, especially among the poor and sick, the *sfortunati,* "the unfortunate ones." In return, over the years she garnered a level of respect almost as great as that of the monsieur—but not quite.

Yes, it was whispered that Valeria was a powerful *strega*—a witch—but also on their lips appeared the qualifier *bianca*—white. Somehow, her family's restaurant and vineyard never suffered from this reputation within this staunchly Christian community, this Vatican summer retreat, but instead was only enhanced.

Valeria, with her basket now brimming, sauntered over to her favorite café bar, took a seat in the shade, and placed her sunglasses before her. Moments later, the waiter delivered her espresso with a small chilled bottle of sparkling water. For this prescient service, the young man received a radiant smile and a *"Grazie"* with a generous tip.

Valeria emptied the water bottle first and then stopped dead as she peered into her espresso cup. A swirling vortex had taken the place of the strong and dense brew.

A portent has arrived!

Uncharacteristically, Valeria left in a rush, leaving her espresso untouched and a bewildered waiter behind. During the ten-minute drive in her bright red Fiat 500, Valeria's mind ran through all the possibilities, but in the end gave up on speculating what the portent might be. Arriving at her home in a slide of tan dust, she dashed for the rough-hewn family grotto, leaving her spilled basket on the passenger seat. Gripping the sides of the silver basin, she entreated to its crystalline water:

I, Valeria, call upon Thou, oh ancient one.

I, Valeria, devoted high priestess of Vesta, seek a vision.

I, Valeria, spiritual daughter of Coelia Concordia, *Vergio Vestalis Maxima*, command you to do so.

I, Valeria, keeper of the most sacred flame of Rome, command you to do so *now*!

The waters stirred, became dark, and then lightened to reveal the back of a tall man and a slender woman in an intimate moment. He held her hand and placed within it a diamond ring. She, gasping in delight, put the ring on, and embraced him with tears in her eyes. The woman was stunning in an old-world sense, perhaps of Greek or Egyptian heritage. Her aura was a brilliant aquamarine that betrayed something else—she was a powerful witch. And the man … was … J.J. Stone.

The waters cleared and became still once again.

Head down and still holding the edge of the silver basin, but now in a death grip, Valeria did not know precisely what to make of her feelings. Her heart ached. Her head reeled. She felt isolated, alone. But above all, Valeria admitted to herself that she hated that witch who had the audacity to claim Stone for herself.

Cagna! (*Bitch!*)

Stone was to be my plaything.

And I was to deliver him to DeSalvo, once I had finished with him—had my way with him.

Valeria looked up from the waters with darkened eyes. Eyes filled with menace.

I must inform DeSalvo of this development. It is the least that I can do. Stone has a weakness that he can exploit.

CHAPTER 24
Interrupted Nuptials

DeSalvo just settled into his Manhattan office when his laptop pinged. The Italian e-mail address he recognized and so the Roman immediately opened it. On his first reading his eyes widened. On the second, he better understood what this opportunity represented and what he must do. He made a call. Moments later his phone rang.

"Mr. DeSalvo," Charlene said, "Ms. Sauerbrünn is on line one."

"Thank you." The regional director said as he put down his first coffee of the day.

"This is DeSalvo."

"Mr. DeSalvo," Jenny Sauerbrünn began, "I have an idea regarding Stone."

"Speak."

"Sir, I can secure for you an Icelandic Snow Banshee. Given what you have told me, would you wish to deploy it?"

"An Icelandic Snow Banshee …" DeSalvo whispered into the receiver.

"Yes, sir. It can be quite effective. And the best part is that it is a mortal construct, not of the Dark Realm. He'll never see it coming."

"Expensive?"

"Quite, sir. But I believe that you told me the chairman said to deal with Stone 'at any cost.'"

Pause.

Damn. She's right.

"Do it."

DeSalvo hung up the phone and smiled. One call to the right person produced results that no one else seemed to be capable of.

Jenny Sauerbrünn is formidable in ways that few understand. I'm glad that she's on my side.

As DeSalvo returned to savor his morning coffee he sighed with contentment.

And the ultimate indignity of having a snow banshee pissing over your remains. What a nice touch.

* * *

Two months later on a sundrenched Sunday morning, two earnest souls came forward to be joined as one. President Silver Moon remarked that it had been years since a nuptial ceremony had been held on the Old Oaks Academy's campus. As one, Melaina and Stone had chosen as their site of consecration the blackened remains of the old chapel. It seemed fitting, while the new edifice nearby had not yet reached completion. Besides, the blessing of such a union on the site consecrated it in a special way not easily duplicated. Someone had even thoughtfully arranged for fresh blooming flowers to be placed throughout the ruins, transforming it into a celebration of color and life.

The modest ceremony included only a handful of friends and colleagues. Mr. Henry agreed to be the best man, President Silver Moon as the maid of honor. Amazingly, both worried and fidgeted over the security of the wedding rings. Professor Peter Glass and his adoring wife Priscilla stood as witnesses, along with Regional Governor John Running Deer. An ebullient *Monsieur* Dexter manned the sound system, while Josh Remington and a select group of the IT and Security team surrounded the huddled group as if in an embrace.

Then, the first surprise appeared—A.R. and Constance Stone, J.J.'s sequestered parents, appeared at the last minute. The former Texas rancher, now rail thin, stood tall and proud, while his diminutive wife held his hand. J.J., at seeing his parents for the first time in a long time, broke down in greeting them and proudly introduced them to all present.

Two men of God presided, both members of TIIIS. One was a Coptic priest from Alexandria and a family friend of Melaina's, who had known her since childhood. He wore a simple white robe, and around his neck lay a resplendent and colorfully embroidered *epitrachelion* or stole. Layered atop that was a golden embroidered cape. A tall black miter covered his head. In his hands he carried a large, golden Hand Cross, and he wore a long gray beard, which caused Josh Remington to irreverently quip to one of his colleagues, "That dude should be with ZZ Top."

Standing next to the Coptic priest was a frail and white-haired Southern Baptist minister from Denton, Texas. Dressed in a severe black suit and white collar, he carried a thumb-worn Bible. He was the proud successor to the venerable Reverend Paul Roberts, the very man who defended the infant J.J. from a CMES assassin and had died in the process.

The bride, dressed in elegant, formal, white lace, was modestly covered to mid-neck. Her veil hid her face. White gloves completed her ensemble.

The groom stood rigidly at attention in formal black, his choice only because he had outgrown his dress Marine blues. He, too, wore white gloves.

As the pair slowly moved through an aisle of

flowers toward where the two men of God stood to receive them, *Monsieur* Dexter cued George Frederic Handel's *Water Music*. At the opening cords, the Frenchman seemed to grow even taller, stronger, and more imperial—if that were even possible.

Arriving before the men of God, the two turned to each other, bowed, and the Coptic priest began his blessing. It was an odd-sounding chant to western ears, filled with guttural stops and odd intonations, but to Melaina they brought tears to her eyes, which streamed freely down her cheeks.

Once finished, the Southern Baptist minister opened his Bible and read a passage from the Book of Genesis:

> So God created man in his own image, in the image of God he created him; male and female he created them. And God blessed them. And God said to them, "Be fruitful and multiply and fill the earth and subdue it and have dominion over the fish of the sea and over the birds of the heavens and over every living thing that moves on the earth."

Then the men of God strode forward and each took the hands of those to be wed, blessed them, and signaled for the rings.

Unknown to all, the surrounding oak trees were filled with the campus' diminutive guardians, the *Argenti*. They too were more than curious as to what the human kind were up to.

It was then that the second surprise showed up.

*   *   *

Three days later it would be reported in the media as a freak winter squall. Stone knew things like that just didn't happen in western Pennsylvania in mid-August, no matter what the weather experts said about El Niño winds.

Suddenly, gusting winds blew over all the carefully arranged flowers. Storm clouds appeared out of nowhere, as did the heavy dump of moisture-laden snow that fell in large, sticky flakes, best known as "cement."

It was then that the huddled wedding party first heard it, a blood-curdling scream coming out of the storm clouds that stopped hearts in mid-beat and reflexively caused all to shiver in sheer, primal fear.

Holy shit! What the hell was that? Stone thought.

For once, his cerebral occupant remained silent, and that fact alone worried him all the more.

Recognizing what that god-awful paean might represent, Stone screamed over the howling wind, "Mel, everybody, quick, get down in the crypt!" And the mad scramble was on.

Stone stood defiantly at the descending passage's entrance, guiding Mel and counting as the wedding party hurried for shelter.

Damn, I could use my UCS right now!

No, Soul Carrier, it is time that you used your other talents. Kick off your shoes and dig in your toes into the fertile earth beneath you.

So I did and immediately felt the surging power of the local ley line. My hair fluffed up with static electricity. In my mind, nothing would pass by me. The First Soul was right. I was far more than just the wearer of a high-tech battle uniform.

I stood next to the crypt's entrance in my black suit while snow accumulated on my head and shoulders. With my Mel and the rest of the wedding party now safely in the crypt, I jumped inside as well, and waited for what was about to arrive.

* * *

My brain, again, was psychically shaken by another one of those unearthly screams. This time, however, its ring was much, much closer, actually, right overhead, almost sonically pawing at the earth. As for the cry, it had taken on an altogether inhuman, and an emotionally ragged, quality that jarred nerves and defied description. What followed shortly thereafter were the sounds of crashing, thrashing, and the sound of heavy masonry thumping into the ground overhead. All of us in the crypt unconsciously ducked with each impact, expecting the native rock above to collapse, entombing us.

"Everyone," I commanded, "pair up and get into one of the nineteen burial trenches for added protection!" Seeing the hesitation is some, I emphasized, "Now!"

I helped my dad with mom into one of the three feet deep burial slots hoping that it wouldn't be permanent. Mel and I took the one nearest the entrance. The rest managed well enough.

But the ordeal was just beginning. Like frightened gophers, none of us dared to move out of sheer fear. I was covered with the slick rank sweat of pure terror. During my entire military career, I had never felt such pure and unadulterated fear. And then I asked myself, *Why was that?* Then and there I erected my mental blocks, finally realizing my incredible mistake. "Mel. Block your mind. It's listening for your fear."

Mel, wide-eyed, said, "You're probably right!"

"Everyone," I whispered to the rest of the wedding party, "listen to me very carefully. Block your mind if you can. If you can't, then pray, focus upon something peaceful, anything but your fear. Whatever's up there, it senses fear. It sniffs it out like a hound. Shut it down, now!"

And in direct response, again came that awful, terrible scream, but this time I could sense in it clear disappointment.

The above ground reaction to my order for mental focus was instantaneous. The ground shook, took a pounding, while thousands of discreet sounds filled the gale of that sunny day turned snowy night. Whatever was out there rummaged blindly around as it could no longer *hear* the fear of its prey. By my own watch, this frenzied thrashing continued on for almost an hour before, just as suddenly as it had appeared, it was gone.

All had gone silent. Only the steady dripping of water could be heard.

Perhaps out of prudent caution or extreme paranoia, I reminded everyone to remain mentally rigid in the crypt. "Seal your mind like a box turtle. Become a shadow without substance." Frankly, I suspected a return engagement.

But all remained silent.

After the passage of another hour, wet, mentally exhausted, and stiff-limbed, I emerged from the crypt feeling like the last man after the apocalypse. In a sense, I was, for, as a group, we had to dig past the heavy wet snow and rocky debris that clogged the crypt's entrance stairway. That chore alone took a good half hour of claustrophobic toil.

"Okay everybody, stay put until I give the word."

I emerged like a bear after its winter hibernation, blinking at the bright sunshine of a glorious Pennsylvania afternoon. Looking around, the old and new chapels had been leveled, as if stomped into the ground by the massive feet of a frustrated dinosaur. Nothing was intact, only a layer of snow. The devastation was so complete that I began playing "find anything that was intact." After several depressing minutes, I gave up.

Standing amid the chapel ruins with my hands on my hips, I tried to take it all in and utterly failed. The cleanup alone would take weeks. The only thing that seemed to have survived the destruction was the crypt dug out by the *Argenti*.

I asked myself, *Where were the Argenti during this attack? I thought the campus had a defensive pack with them.*

Then, on second thought, I pondered with concern. *Are the Argenti okay?*

Then, to my surprise, I heard a soft pop.

"Most Noble J.J.," the tiny creature said with dignity, "I am here."

Looking down, there at my feet stood the silver-streaked Rasha.

"Honorable Rasha!" I exclaimed, "Is your brood safe?"

"Very much so, Noble J.J., and I thank you for your concern. But it is you who has been injured. Your mating ceremony was interrupted and I and my brood could do absolutely nothing about it." She said as her head drooped. "We have failed you, Noble Lictor of Magic."

Sitting down heedlessly in the snow next to the plaintive brood mistress, I asked. "So, my good friend Rasha, what was it that prevented your brood from coming to our aid?"

"Most Noble J.J., our physiology is not suited to such a storm. We would have all frozen to death. By the way, have you noticed a rather particular smell?" She said with a twitching nose.

"Yeah, I do. A very heavy, almost musky scent. I first noticed it around the old chapel's foundations, or what's left of them. What is it?"

With her head held high the fastidious brood mistress of the *Argenti* stated with certainty and disdain, "It is a filthy practice. It is the urine of an Icelandic Snow Banshee. It marks as its own whatever it destroys."

* * *

Wet, muddy, shivering, and disheveled, we completed our vows after the attack without a hitch. *Monsieur* Dexter, now without his audio system to play, instead sang a beautiful hymn in praise of love and unity. President Silver Moon and Mr. Henry even managed to not lose our rings. Afterwards, after a celebratory wedding meal on campus, my parents were spirited away. It was a tearful parting. I didn't know if I would ever see them alive again. Dad sensed it, too.

"J.J. Son," the weathered old rancher said while gripped my shoulders with a strength that I didn't know he still possessed, "your mother and I are so very proud of you and what you have become."

His throat got all choked up. Tears began to stream down his craggy face. "Always remember that we love you fiercely. And as for Mel, well, she's just such a doll. Love and protect her, son."

Mother just hugged me with one of those hugs that said so much, with so much finality.

As they drove off in the heavily armored Suburban en route to God only knows where, Mel took my arm, rested her head against my shoulder, and murmured near my ear.

"They are such good people. I felt honored just to meet them, much less become their daughter-in-law. We are so blessed."

*　　*　　*

After mom and dad departed, we got down to business.

"Okay everybody, what the hell is an Icelandic Snow Banshee? Does anybody even know?" Stone queried the president, *Monsieur* Dexter, Mr. Henry, Peter Glass, and Mel.

"Where did you hear about that?" the white-haired Fourth-Class Adept countered in wide-eyed disbelief.

"From the Brood Mistress of the *Argenti* herself. Even I can smell the reek its piss all over the place!"

"Well now, J.J.," President Silver Moon observed, "let's review: First a highly unusual blizzard arrived; Then, according to the *Argenti*, a visit by an Icelandic Snow Banshee. By my count, that makes at least two conjurings—one by a weather witch, and another by a master conjurer. Plus the fact that someone knew they needed a particular type of weather that the *Argenti* couldn't handle. On top of that is the timing of the attack itself. So that makes, potentially, at least four culprits involved in this attack." She summarized.

"Fine, but what is this banshee thing?" I wanted to know.

"Now that is a good question," Peter said, "and it's one that cannot be precisely answered because few have even seen the creature, much less lived to tell the tale. All we positively know is from the forensics of its passing. It possesses extraordinary strength, is able to fly, and has claws or talons of some kind. You were the one who figured out that it can produce a psychic call that causes extreme fear and has the ability to sense that fear, which helps it to locate its prey."

"Well, Peter, it's got to be big, too, because it stomped the living crap out of these two chapels," I said while gesturing about the leveled landscape.

"Being underground seems to be a natural defense, and even though it can detect you, being underground frustrates it, which matches nicely with its serious attitude and temper. If it can't reach you, then it'll make a mess of everything that it can. Then for good measure, it will mark its territory in a pure fit of dominance. All in all, one nasty SOB."

Pause.

"What a time to go on a honeymoon," I said.

"And go you must," the president emphasized with a stern look. "Melaina, J.J., this is your time," she prodded. "Go. We will pick up the pieces."

*   *   *

Where do two telepathic sensitives go on their honeymoon? A cozy cabin in the Santa Fe National Forest, of course. High altitude, pine fresh air, beautiful vistas, better sunsets, and the proximity of the Silver

Nile ley line all combined to make our blissful moments even more so. Though we snuck into Santa Fe from time to time for some great meals. However, those trips were more grocery expeditions than anything else. But after a week, I had become antsy and itchy to get back to the Academy. Mel, for her part, felt much the same, as she wanted to establish her new routine at the Academy.

CHAPTER 25
Banshee Piss

A week later, Mel and I returned to the Academy, where the president had made arrangements for our new quarters within the visiting scholars' residence. Yeah, it was tiny, even cramped, but it was temporarily ours until we could find something better. Besides, the tight quarters gave us more opportunities to bump into each other.

While we were away, the Architecture Department had removed most of the wreckage from the chapels and had begun their restoration. President Silver Moon allowed no moss to grow under her feet.

At Mr. Henry's suggestion, I contacted one of TIIIS' recently vetted allies, a group called ACME, and asked their Help Line the following question: "Is it possible to track an Icelandic Snow Banshee by its urine?"

The answer I received after a lengthy pause did not sound encouraging.

"Potentially, yes, but as a demon's urine decomposes into ectoplasm very quickly, what's the point?" the ever-helpful Help Line representative asked.

I countered. "If the banshee urine decayed into ectoplasm, then why can I still smell it and see evidence of its stain after a full day?"

To this the Help Line didn't know, but in the spirit of scientific inquiry, ACME promised to send out a specialist to investigate.

The very next day I received word of her flight information, her expected arrival at the Latrobe Airport, and her name—Dr. Urdu Patel. At the appointed time, I stationed myself at the airport's baggage exit with a small sign that said "Patel Party."

The flight arrived on time. Urdu Patel turned out to be a tall Pakistani woman, dressed for success in a dark gray, pin-striped pant-suit, and short-heeled pumps. Since I met her in baggage, she assumed that I was her chauffer as I was dressed all in black. But before I could correct her, I was informed: "I have two checked bags. Please fetch them," she said as she proceeded to ignore me while examining the screen of her smart phone.

Interesting, I thought with hidden amusement. *Fine. Let's play this out and see where it goes.*

Her baggage turned out to be one luggage wheelie and an overloaded duffle bag that no thinking human being would voluntarily carry.

In the parking lot, I offered her the front passenger seat of my red Colorado, which she sneered at, and instead chose to sit in the cab.

Okay ...

So I innocently asked, "Would you like to first get changed and settled at the hotel, or go directly to the attack site?"

"The attack site. I have to be in LA this evening. I have a connection to make."

Right.

I drove in silence as Patel stared out the window with detached toleration. Sixty-seven minutes later we arrived at the Old Oaks Academy's campus. I parked my pickup in the dorm parking lot, got out, and opened her door. "Now we walk to the attack site."

With abhorrent shock on her face, she started.

"Why can't you drive me to the attack site?"

"Dr. Patel, the attack site is a muddy construction site. Do you have any hiking boots in that duffle bag of yours?"

"Yes."

"Good. Then I suggest you put them on."

After several minutes of obvious grousing and even some angry rocking of the truck, Patel emerged now fully booted up.

"Please follow me," I said with a welcoming gesture.

After slogging about one hundred steps, I know because I counted them, Patel finally exploded.

"Just what is the meaning of this! I demand to know what is going on here! I'm a respected ..."

I raised my hand palm facing toward her and softly said, "The attack site is just ahead, perhaps another one hundred feet. Kindly follow me." And I turned and began again, listening to her incomprehensible muttering.

Mere moments later.

"How much farther is it!" she demanded.

"Not far," I answered over my shoulder, while I continued on.

I must have been fifty feet from the old chapel's foundation when I began picking up the musty aroma of the banshee's urine, while Patel struggled through the sticky red clay mud, almost falling twice.

"Here we are," I announced. "This section was once the foundations of an old chapel. Over there, are the ruined remains of its replacement. Can you smell it, Dr. Patel?"

"Smell what?"

"A scent, vaguely musty, almost like mold."

"No, I cannot." She curtly said, "Besides, this is a damp construction site. It should be full of mold."

I rolled my eyes. "Then why are *you* here?" I reasonably asked, but now with my hands on my hips in mild frustration.

"I am here to investigate a purported attack by a mythological demon-creature called an Icelandic Snow Banshee. And from what I can see there is no evidence whatsoever of such an attack. Only those foundations that you are standing near."

I felt my temper building, but squelched it.

"All that I have seen is a total waste of my time and my organization's financial resources in making this emergency side trip. I haven't even been offered the opportunity to interrogate the individual in question."

"I see."

"Return me to the airport, forthwith."

"Who is it, Dr. Patel that you wished to 'interrogate'?"

"A certain Mr. Stone."

"Well, this is your lucky day, Dr. Patel. Ask away," I said with a strained smile.

Then and there the realization broke on her face. It was classic, her embarrassment complete and total in every way.

"Ah, ah, Mr. Stone, ah, I am so very sorry … I didn't realize."

I again raised my open palm in her direction.

"Dr. Patel. You're a scientist. Kindly step over here to this corner of the foundation. Do you see that large stain?"

"Why yes, I do."

"That large patch of discoloration was made by banshee urine. Now, doctor, why didn't that evaporate as ectoplasm usually does? Why didn't its noisome spoor dissipate? That's what I want to know, because that isn't what demon-produced material is supposed to do. It isn't supposed to persist in the mortal world, and I want to know why. Right now."

After some hand-holding, Dr. Patel finally got with the program, even though she was quite peeved that she had to return to the truck to retrieve her sampling equipment. And no, I did not assist her in any way. But if she had asked, I would have done so. As deeply embarrassed she was, Patel was just as stubborn.

To me the persistent banshee urine reek was more than troubling to my olfactory senses, it was downright disturbing, because it suggested that something was just not right between the various realms of the universe. As the Lictor of Magic, the investigation of such things was squarely in my wheel-house, so I had to find out what was what. Naturally, I contacted the only ones I knew who I could get the straight-skinny from.

Later that evening after I returned Dr. Patel to the airport took catch her ever important flight to LA, I sat in my dorm room thinking. I focused on a single mental message and before long I saw in my mind a familiar gray swirling column. I inwardly smiled and greeted this curious primordial being.

Hello to you, most Noble Lictor of Magic. It has been some time since we last communicated. How might I be of service?

"Venerable Ledger Keeper, I seek your wisdom. I suspect that there is yet again an imbalance between the mortal and dark realms. The vile urine of a demon-banshee has not dissipated into ectoplasm. Why is this so?"

Noble Lictor of Magic, it is not so much an imbalance between the realms, as a subtle shift in emphasis.

What an odd and puzzling answer. "I'm sorry, Venerable One, but I don't understand the meaning of your words."

Banshees, and in particular this Icelandic Snow Banshee, are not constructs that were created or reside in the dark demon-realm. They are instead manifestations of pure human madness, which can be directed to do the unspeakable. These are purely mortal constructs, hateful things of the mortal realm, Lictor of Magic. Find the one who directs it, and you can better address your concerns.

Ah-ha! So that's it!

However, Noble Lictor of Magic, the one who manifested this horrific creature resides no longer in mortal realm. I have recorded the passing of its tortured and deranged soul.

What?

Yes, Noble Lictor of Magic, the one who directed it last is the one responsible for the attack. Thereafter, it murdered she who manifested the banshee.

She?

Yes, a pitiful unfortunate, tremendously gifted, hopelessly misunderstood, and completely mad. Used as a tool, she has now been cruelly discarded.

Noble Lictor of Magic, be watchful with this mortal challenge. It will test your courage. Above all, it will test your humanity. Farewell, noble one.

*   *   *

Three days later, I received an e-mail from Dr. Patel. She had some news on the banshee pee.

Dear Mr. Stone:

The individual responsible for the generation of the Icelandic Snow Banshee is Ms. Jóhanna Jónsson, a gravely ill and aged psychiatric patient at the Kleppur Hospital in Reykjavík, Iceland.

This mental health hospital was founded in 1907, and Jóhanna, was its first patient at the age of eight years old.

She passed away two days ago.

Best regards,

Dr. Urdu Patel

I read and reread Dr. Patel's e-mail several times. While this poor Jóhanna had been identified as the source of the Icelandic Snow Banshee, I also knew that the harnessing and focusing of Jóhanna's highly charged imagery required someone else's manipulation. A poor analogy would be performing mechanical tasks with a car battery's energy through the mediation of a switch. The question was: Who was that switch? And by extension, is it possible that the postulated weather witch and this "switch" were one in the same? Somehow that made a whole lot of sense to me.

On an entirely different plane, a very humanistic one, I asked myself how anyone could take advantage of a crippled human's mind and weaponize it? That to me constituted outright slavery, not to mention a level of inhuman cruelty that I couldn't imagine, much less put a tag on. As a result, I vowed to find this fiend, this monster, whoever they were. This event had escalated way past a ruined wedding ceremony.

* * *

Right off I spoke to Mel, who was still busy wedging all of her things into our Academy accommodations in some imaginative of ways.

Much to the shock of her academic colleagues at Berkeley, Mel had accepted President Silver Moon's offer to teach in the fall and continue her research at the Academy. *Monsieur* Dexter's recommendation no doubt played a role in the president's decision. She was assigned a tiny office in Meyer's Hall, which she stuffed to the gills with bookcases.

It was Mr. Good's former office.

I needed to bounce my analysis off of Mel's cool, academic mind. It also gave me another opportunity to tell her how much I loved and appreciated her. By the way, loving sex between telepaths cannot be oversold.

"Hey there, professor, it's me. How are you doing?"

"Why J.J. What a surprise. Hand me that picture. What's up?"

"Got a moment?"

"Sure" Mel said with a wipe to her sweaty forehead.

"Well, I need your read on something that I stumbled across." And I laid it all out.

After some moments, I could hear her chewing on the situation. She finally said, "Well, J.J. That's quite a story. I know nothing of banshees. My culture doesn't have a tradition of them.

"To use in such a cold-blooded and premeditated fashion, another's mind for your own purposes. That takes horror to a completely new level.

"I agree. But is it possible for one individual to influence both the weather and manipulate a crippled intellect. The first thing that comes to mind was all the power that would be necessary to launch such a spell and then maintain it for several hours. I would suspect the use of a dark ley line to do that, and you should, too. Such power would be sufficient to amp up a mental delusion into a real, physical force, something truly difficult to contend with.

"What fascinates me the most about this banshee stuff is the way it psychically finds its prey. I'm convinced, J.J., that fear is the key to all of this."

"To summarize," I said, "a dark ley line for power and raw, primal fear used as a tool. Did I understand you correctly?"

"Quite well, actually. By the way, come here you hunk."

*   *   *

The next person I called up was Dr. Patel. I had a handful of questions and got lucky as she answered on the third ring.

"Good day, Dr. Patel. This is J.J. Stone. Do you have a few minutes?"

"Why, good day to you, too, Mr. Stone. What a pleasure. Certainly, I have some time. How may I be of service?"

"I just wish to clarify a few items from your e-mail.

The banshee urine was traced back solely to the mental patient in Iceland. Am I correct?"

"Yes."

"Good." I explained my theory about a single controlling conjurer, and then I asked, "Is it possible to detect who cast that spell? Both for the inclement weather and the banshee?"

"Mr. Stone, if one could cast both spells, that would take an enormous amount of energy, not to mention the ability to wield extraordinary control to independently manage such tasks. I do not think it's possible for one individual to do so."

"But it could be possible. Not impossible."

"Well, yes. Possible, but highly improbable."

"Will you at least try to trace the spells involved? Just in case the improbable turns out to be a reality?"

"Yes, Mr. Stone. I will try. Do you mind if I share this theory of yours with several of my colleagues at ACME?"

"Not at all, Dr. Patel. I'm just a guy looking for answers."

*　　*　　*

Stone was not finished. He had another idea. While Dr. Patel and ACME would no doubt do their best, he had this feeling that it wouldn't be enough. He needed another edge, avenue, what have you, and so he made another call, this time to his friend in TIIIS IT and Security, Josh Remington.

"May I speak to Mr. Remington, please?"

"One moment," the voice on the other end of the line said.

"This is Josh Remington."

"Josh, this is J.J. Stone. How are you today?"

"Just great, Mr. Stone. What can I do for you?"

"I need a search of the TIIIS and CMES human resources databases. I need the names of all the weather witches out there, pronto. Do you think that you can do that for me?"

"Not a problem. Do you want me to search the non-aligned universe as well?"

"Can you do that?"

"Yep. Sure can. When do you need this info?"

"Like yesterday."

"Well, sir, I'll do my best. Expect an e-mail soon."

"Thanks, Josh. I knew that I could depend on you."

"My pleasure, Mr. Stone."

*　　*　　*

Like most sensitives, Marjory Brown sought security within an ever more turbulent paranormal world. Part of her dilemma was that her real Danish name, Dagmar Overbye, she couldn't—wouldn't—use. It carried far too much baggage, and who needed that?

Still in her middle years, fit, and yet to have any gray hair, Marjory was proud of her appearance and more arcane abilities. She had to, because she was about to give herself up to someone whom Marjory considered the enemy. Bottom line: the woman was done running, hiding, and living a lie one step ahead of her pursuers.

Stepping off the long trans-Atlantic flight from Iceland, she endured the invasive passport control, snagged her single piece of luggage, passed under the "Welcome to Chicago" sign, and made for the cab stand outside O'Hare's International Terminal.

After TIIIS lost the Falls Church facility to a CMES goon raid, the operations, security, and IT resources for the U.S. Region ended up in Naperville, Illinois. Their new building was located within a high tech corridor that flanked Illinois Toll Road 88. Marjory handed the cabbie the address, sighed in resignation, and sat back in preparation for what she knew would be a long drive, in more ways than one.

The cab exited on Winfield Road, made a right turn, and wound its way to a complex of buildings that fronted on a pond and backed by the toll road. Cab paid and with her wheelie luggage in hand, Marjory straightened her shoulders and marched right up to the TIIIS U.S. Regional headquarters with purpose.

I'm running no more. But boy are they going to be surprised to see me.

* * *

Jóhanna had been a genuinely pretty child, outwardly perfect in every way, robust with a healthy pink complexion, rosebud lips, and hair like corn silk. Her disposition matched her looks. She greeted everyone with a bright smile, waving arms and kicking legs, excited gurgles, and dancing sky-blue eyes. The infant possessed such an innate personal magnetism that everyone felt compelled to fawn over her. Their lavish attentions had a profound effect, feeding the young one with boundless confidence.

Such characteristics might be considered a blessing, but to some, not so much in an imperfect world. At the time, many uncertainties loomed large, not to mention an impending world war.

The strangeness began innocently enough. The

family's home possessed air currents that slowly turned a colorful, multi-level, overhead mobile over her crib. Brightly painted animals of all descriptions hung to capture her attention and fuel her imagination. The pediatrician said that such things were good for developing eye muscles and focus in infants. As she tried to touch them, far beyond her reach, her parents saw that the mobile would tilt and sway under some unseen force. Quite literally their giggling daughter swatted the display this way and that ... somehow. One morning after several days of such abuse, she was discovered teething on the pink elephant, which had somehow found its way into her crib. As for the mobile overhead, something had contorted its wire framework.

Another instance involved Jóhanna's favorite toy ball, which had rolled just beyond the reach of her tiny, outstretched hand. Straining to grasp it, the colorful ball moved of its own accord until pudgy fingers took hold of it. Over time, this feat occurred numerous times and the child's parents didn't know what to make of it. She would clumsily throw the ball two-handed over her head and it would return of its own accord. They couldn't do this, so where did their little bundle of love learn such a feat? Surely, they couldn't have their little girl revealing this talent outside the family. After all, how would their rural church community react?

*   *   *

A lifetime later, Dagmar Overbye sat in a chair drained and exhausted. Her hands trembled uncontrollably. Eyes still closed, she took a deep cleansing breath to clear her mind of what she had just channeled. A shiver quaked throughout her body as that memory passed.

Opening her eyes, she glanced over to the now deeply sleeping figure. Impossibly old, but angelic-looking, her unwitting partner in this grand manifestation wore a smile. Her drawn and heavily wrinkled face was framed by a gossamer halo of stark white hair. The gentle rise and fall of the bed coverings hid the brutal-looking restraints that were deemed necessary with this one. She had worn them so long that a rough layer of callus had formed.

Jóhanna Jónsson was a remarkable paranormal with extraordinarily gifted abilities in astral projection, telekinesis, and corporeal imaging. Misdiagnosed early on, the young and sensitive Jóhanna became the victim of years of clinical ignorance and brutally antiquated mental health practices that included electroshock therapy, severe isolation, insulin-induced coma, and anti-psychotic drugs. That the patient survived was a miracle in itself, but as a consequence of her many treatments, she became stark, raving mad. Only one person seemed able to get through to her.

Dagmar rose from her chair, staggered a bit, and steadied herself. Her exhaustion, both physical and mental, was quite real, as this session in particular had lasted so long, nearly two hours of extreme focus, direction, and energy management. But the intermediary knew that her life would have been forfeit if she hadn't tapped into the ley line tributary that ran beneath this part of the clinic. That had helped greatly during the marathon session.

Finally, Dagmar smiled, her debt was now paid in full. She was free and no longer a bondage slave to CMES. Even better, she could walk away from that poor, tortured soul, Jóhanna, who, with only moments to go, should die a peaceful death enraptured in her wildest dreams. The morphine injection would see to that.

CHAPTER 26
Gearing Up

The sweeping multiple CMES attacks caused President Silver Moon to call an emergency meeting of all the governors and sub-governors of the U.S. Region to the Old Oaks Academy. She recognized that doing so potentially endangered the region with all of its leadership clustered in one place. She called it anyway.

Glancing around the conference table, the president saw concerned faces, which represented the governors of the Southwest, Northwest, Midwest, Southeast, Texas, and Great Lakes along with the sub-governors of Nevada and the Appalachians. They were all here. None had begged off. In all, counting her and Stone, there were eleven filled chairs around the large cherry wood conference table in the Vault, which included the Sub-governor of Central Canada, Sir James McElhinney, who insisted on attending. The presence of Central Canada only affirmed their resolve.

"Thank you all for responding on such short notice. Thank you, Sir James, for attending as well. While unorthodox, I have asked our Lictor of Magic, Mr. Stone here, to sit in on this meeting.

"Recent events have been extremely dark for our region. They came about by the most traditional of ways—treachery and betrayal. Today, I would like to discuss what we should do about it."

Silence fell across the table, while eyes were glancing about and throats suddenly turned dry.

"How can we truly hurt them?" asked the Governor of the Midwest, a woman of Polish descent by the name of Klara Kotula. "They just seem to bounce back whenever we ruin their Manhattan headquarters. What would it take to really cripple them?"

"Well," the president began, "we did take over two billion dollars in cash from them, ruined their international reputation, and purged their influence in Congress. I suppose that's a start. But I sense from your question, Klara, further doubt and frustration. That I cannot solve for you, only you can. The problem is that we do not have that ultimate target we can devastate in one blow. We can, however, continue to make CMES extremely uncomfortable in the U.S. Region, much like we have done in New Mexico and Pennsylvania."

"Okay, Betsy, I can support that, but what specifically do you have in mind?" Kotula followed up.

Perhaps unconsciously, President Silver Moon glanced over at Stone, who read the look as permission to speak.

"If I might, Madam President," Stone began, "as I see it, making CMES just uncomfortable is delaying the inevitable. Their seat of administration is in Manhattan. My suggestion would be to obliterate them, totally. Reduce their headquarters in such a way that it would have to be torn down. Up until now, we have been exceedingly careful about fatalities. I think that we should continue with that policy, but if you want to stop CMES, it has to be far more than a bloody nose."

"Mr. Stone," queried the Governor of the Great Lakes, Kevin Reiss, "you mentioned the obliteration of their building to the point that it is scrap. What did you have in mind?"

Thoughtful silence.

"Mr. Reiss, what I am suggesting is an aggressive,

outright, and blatant application of raw magic that consumes the Gathering building from within. In essence, transforming its exterior façade into a naked shell."

Stunned silence.

"Can that even be done?" an awed voice asked.

"Sadly, yes it can. Ask Sodom and Gomorrah. I have read a curse tablet that describes how it was accomplished. That spell even appeared in *The Book of Spells* that I took from the Dark One. Apparently, in antiquity, the spell was performed several times. Modern archaeology has only stumbled across one of these instances. What they found was quite extraordinary—a walled town gutted down to its oldest foundations. The interior surfaces of its fortifications transformed into a near glass-like material from the intense heat. The term used to describe this was vitrification. If one city was found so utterly destroyed, then I am quite sure there are more to be discovered." The sound of shifting bodies, a cough, and several clearings of throats broke up the silence. "The question, dear colleagues," Stone continued, "is just how bad do you want to rid yourselves of this moral cancer, this blight upon Manhattan, this affront to Western Civilization?"

To many, the imagery of cancer naturally brought on the subjects of chemo, pain, and lingering death. Stone had touched a nerve. The mention of blight pushed them farther. But the appeal to defend Western Civilization sealed the deal.

"This proposal of yours, Mr. Stone," stated the Governor of the Southeast, an imposing Afro-American Baptist minister with a well-deep voice to match, "just how contained can this immolation be? Manhattan is a cramped place with a population in the millions. If I understand you, you are describing the application of tremendous heat. Doesn't it have to go somewhere?" He concluded with his hands beckoning to the air above.

"Reverend Gregory, my proposal is just that. I can make no absolute guarantees, but rest assured there will be fallout from such a conflagration. It is up to everyone here present, to decide what we will ultimately do. I am, sir, just a tool."

Pause.

"Are there any other proposals that someone would like to make?" President Silver Moon inquired.

"What about the West Coast. What are we going to do about that rat's nest?" The Sub-governor of Nevada wanted to know.

"Mr. Ott," President Silver Moon said as she rummaged through some papers before her, "the membership statistics that we recovered from their human resources during our two raids on the Manhattan headquarters do not support your claim of a 'rat's nest.' One year ago the numbers were a little over three hundred in LA and something like forty-three in the Bay Area. While those are still substantial numbers, close to 350 in all, those are dwarfed by the CMES East Coast presence.

"Here are our current stats on the East Coast," the president continued, "again remembering that they are over a year old: Boston, four; Philly, eleven; Washington, DC, 156; the state of New York, 430; with Manhattan itself, 73. Now, given the grand opening of the Gathering, CMES membership has surged.

"So, Mr. Ott, while I understand your concern about the West Coast, can you give me a landmark target in that region that's better suited than the Gathering building? Because if you can, we'll target it."

To Ott's credit, he admitted, "I see your point, Madam President. This is more about making a firm statement than anything else."

"Are there any other ideas?" President Silver Moon doggedly pushed.

"I can now see that the Gathering is our primary target, but what can we do to suppress CMES subsequent to its destruction?" the Governor of the Northwest, Deirdre Meier, wanted to know.

"Believe it or not," Silver Moon sighed, "I have given that entire question considerable thought. Given how far apart our cultures are leaves little in the way of compromise. So where does that leave us? Public education as to what CMES is and what it represents? We have already done that. We really hurt them with our initial leaks of their confidential documents, so this effort will continue, relentlessly, until people realize that CMES is not all that attractive.

"Any other ideas?"

There were none.

*   *   *

For reasons of security, Stone's ops leadership also met in the Vault—Mel, Mr. Henry, and Peter Glass.

"Folks, thanks for coming." Stone stated simply. "Our president has tasked us to act against the CMES North American headquarters once again. We have her authorization to totally destroy the structure. That's quite a mandate, but it's doable.

"The plan that I have in mind, and which I wish to lay out before you, requires the specific talents each of you have. So here it is …"

*   *   *

On the way back to their apartment, Mel felt invigorated by what J.J. had outlined. His plan was sound, but was made more so by the fact that each team member had a critical piece to contribute. A total team effort was required.

Melaina, admit it, your husband is quite a find. He possesses an uncommon inner strength, give in to it. Yes, he can be a bit distant, but he's included you within his inner circle of friends—probably his only friends. So, Melaina, give into your feelings. Allow them to take you where they want to go. Don't suppress them like you usually do. He is, after all, the Carrier of the First Soul of Creation. He knows better than most what that means. Friends and loved ones are natural targets. So Melaina, can you handle being a target?

*   *   *

"Back in the saddle," is such a curious American expression, but today I understood it. Heaven knows how much I needed this workout. Arthur, for his part, really made me pay for the time taken off. What? Maybe two months.

As the Alexandrian wobble-legged her way to the elevator, Arthur surprised me. "What's up with you, Melaina? You've changed."

Blinking back at him, I thought. *Since when am I Melaina? Has my marriage to J.J. left some sort of obvious mark? Be strong, Melaina, and careful. He might be able to read minds.*

"Excuse me?" I snapped back. "Since when were we on a first name basis, Arthur?"

Well, it worked. Arthur blushed, stammered out some lame apology about having worked together for some time.

As I waited for my elevator to arrive, I noticed that the security staff—both possessed and not, were not the usual group of faces behind the reception counters.
Why so much change in only two months' time?

CHAPTER 27
A Devious Plan

Working in her Manhattan flat's kitchenette, Mel felt as if her mother was looking over her shoulder and guiding her fingers, just the way she had when the Alexandrian first learned how to knead bread. It was a warm feeling that made her happy and content.

Even better, Mel admitted she was embarking on something exciting and near and dear to her heart. She was a contributing member of a team, which for this traditional loner, was a new concept.

Per Stone's scheme for the ruination of the Gathering building, Mel was the first up to bat so her "stealth" magic could be in place to soften up the enemy's defenses. She had to think of it in those impersonal generalities because never before had the Alexandrian witch cast a spell of such global and indiscriminate effect.

The TIIIS IT and Security department gave Mel five names plundered from the raid on CMES' temporary headquarters. All the names provided were security and IT types. Their departments were the prime targets, along with their nearby colleagues—anyone who worked within one hundred feet of them. Truth be told, Mel added a sixth name to the mailing list, because, having developed a nasty impish streak, she couldn't resist.

Given the engrained proclivities of expert spell whisperers and extreme psychics, Mel fashioned her six mailings with the greatest of care. Her first concern was to make sure that not a trace of her DNA could be resurrected from them, so she went to a local hardware store and grocery to pick up her curious supplies. Supplies in hand, Mel transformed her Manhattan apartment into a witch's laboratory. After thoroughly vacuuming the tiny flat, she wiped down the kitchen area's surfaces with paper towels dripping with apple vinegar. Why apple vinegar? Because she liked the smell. All containers and mixing implements she put into the dish washer and sterilized. All her purchased ingredients Mel washed or sequestered in Ziploc bags until needed.

This entire process she performed while wearing a disposable HAZMAT suit, filter-paper mask, and latex gloves. Dripping wet from sweat within this near-surgical containment, Mel wondered what her neighbors might have thought if they chanced to see her—perhaps a marshmallow sprouting arms and legs. Once all was as it should be, Mel went to her bathroom, stripped, luxuriated in the shower, and got dressed in fresh protective gear.

The letters themselves she treated as if they were highly contagious, which in a way, they were. Mel even wore gloves when she printed the letters and address labels at the New York Public Library. She used their paper, at quite an outrageous cost per page, to remove herself as far as possible from detection, and to purposely introduce a red herring.

Next she added to the letters the variously layered spells and enchantments. To do so, Mel concocted a goodly amount of lemon ink, which while not totally invisible, is not readily perceivable either. This medium was unique in a very special way, for the Alexandrian affixed a spell to the liquid that hid her identity from even the very best of spell whisperers. Now she could write with total anonymity. Step one completed.

For step two, Mel wrote a spell, again using the lemon ink, written in ancient Egyptian Demotic, to the inside tear away flap of the six FedEx packets. This was tedious work that Mel performed with the sharpened end of a chopstick. With a care that she had learned at Oxford and perfected throughout her research career, Mel slowly wrote out the needful characters without one smear. She then placed the mail packets on the kitchen counter to dry.

The spell that Mel applied with such care remained inactive, dormant, and thus undetectable by any sensitive worth their salt. But the moment someone ripped open the mail packet, the spell's words would be rent, and the mechanical energy awakened the spell and made it effective. At this point, the crafted spell was capable of something, and that special something was simply to summon another spell. Step two completed.

Step three called for the precise application of the actual spell to be invoked. Here, Mel labored over each of the six letters and produced them all without blemish, all while within her confinement clothing.

The conjuring itself, also written in Demotic, Mel wrote on the backside of the printed pages along their four edges. This ensured that the magical words would come into direct contact with the letter's recipient, a critical detail for the spell's workings. Just as with the mail packet's spell, the letter's spell also remained in a dormant state until it was "called" and made effective by the triggering precursor spell on the envelope's flap.

Here is the content of the debilitating spell written on the backside of the computer generated letters:

Petbe, who is in the abyss,
I drag you up to ask you,
You whose front part looks like a lion,
Whose rear part looks like a hippopotamus,
Whose head is fixed in heaven,
Whose feet are fixed on earth,
The one with the head of bronze,
The one with the claws of iron.

I adjure you, Petbe, to cause illness, fevers, and
boils within the compass of this spell,
One plethron by one plethron by one plethron.

Petbe, allow the illness, fevers, and boils to cease
within two sunrises.

Petbe, who is in the abyss,
This, I ask of thee.

Before Mel could post her letters, someone
knocked on her door, which caused the Alexandrian to
jump. Peeking through the door's security lens she saw
J.J. eye's peeking in.

After entering, she closed the door, flung her arms
around Stone's neck, and admonished him for more
than several moments.

Finally coming up for air, Mel said, "You're late.
Let's get to work on Phase Two."

"Letters already done?"

"They're all ready to go."

"Excellent!"

*　　*　　*

Jamie Allison was always amazed at the delivery
consistency of their FedEx driver Juan. Rain or shine,

he showed up at the mail room between 10:08 to 10:15 in the morning. Perhaps it was magic.

How does he do it? Jamie thought while her rubber-tipped fingers quickly sorted through the heavier-than-usual Tuesday morning pile. With the mail cart's bins filled and sorted by floor and department, off she went on her rounds.

*   *   *

Susan Greer was frankly surprised that Jamie had stopped by her desk with a FedEx packet. Check that, Greer was more than a bit hesitant about the unexpected delivery. Turning the thin and stiff cardboard envelope in her hands, Greer speculated on its contents. Legal papers? An insurance notice? Maybe something even worse? She didn't have any idea and the longer Greer worried the envelope's corners, the greater that dread grew. Finally, biting her lower lip, Greer ripped open the packet, rummaged around, and finally found the single sheet of paper.

Damn, Susan! It's only a special vacation offer from your credit card company, which she immediately consigned, with relief, into the circular file.

That's a hell of an expensive way to advertise for Bahaman tourism!

By eleven that morning, Greer, and everyone around her cube were feeling ill. Then Greer lurched toward her trash can, made it just in the nick-of-time, and filled it with that morning's breakfast. In this universally recognized ritual, she found that she was not alone.

Nearing lunch time, the fevers began. And this wasn't only happening in Greer's department. She heard reports of the same thing breaking out throughout the administrative floors and three of the four perimeter restaurants.

Strangely none of the mixed security personnel, the in-house euphemism for "possessed," were so affected. Also not affected was William DeSalvo as he had been off site for an advertising brain-storming session. But when he was alerted by security as to what was happening, he wisely stayed away from the Gathering's building, and with good reason. The regional director didn't need to be psychic to recognize that his headquarters was once again under siege. But what was it this time? A chemical attack? Anthrax? Ricin? Bubonic plague? He didn't know, and not knowing drove the man to the edge, so DeSalvo did the right thing—he put all affected personnel on medical leave. Then he closed the facility to the public.

*   *   *

It didn't surprise the regional director that by the next day most of his administrative and IT staff were too sick to go to work. The building was populated with mixed security staff only. So before DeSalvo would allow any of his fully human staff or guests back into the building, the he had a sweep made by a private HAZMAT firm. To his great relief, after a thorough search of the premises, nothing was found or detected.

That same day, at 11:50 am, a crowd of over one hundred individuals, carrying signs that identified them as vocal Evangelical Christians, arrived at the main entrance of his the Gathering's building on Fifth Avenue. Chanting catchy slogans and waving their colorful placards with even more colorful barbs, each carried a white plastic grocery bag. While they circulated in an orderly fashion in front of the forty-one story building, they partially blocked pedestrian and vehicular traffic. DeSalvo ordered the lobby security to call the NYPD at the 17th Precinct Station.

At the strike of noon, the assembled crowd reached into their plastic bags and began hurling water balloons at the building and its entrance. By this time, several media sources had caught wind of the event and were recording the odd protest. In the process, and much to the surprise of the filming cameramen, they recorded energetic reactions whenever a water balloon stuck a Celtic knot logo above the main entrance or those affixed to the entrance doors. In every case, an explosion of steam would result. The crowd's discovery of this reaction caused them to focus upon these symbols of the Gathering more and more, to the point that a thick fog was quickly forming, obscuring the building's main entrance.

Meanwhile, William DeSalvo stood smoldering on the opposite side of Fifth Avenue. This sort of negative PR he didn't need. On top of that, he could only vaguely see his building's main entrance through all the fog. First the illnesses, now this collection of Bible-thumpers.

By 12:11, the NYPD finally appeared on the scene. They quickly dispersed the balloon-throwing pranksters, who by this time had run out of water balloons to throw.

At 12:15, DeSalvo's smart phone chimed with the announcement of a received e-mail. Unfortunately, he couldn't hear it over all the caterwauling demonstrators. But then his phone rang with an insistent tone. He dug the device out of his silk suit's coat pocket and on the third ring, answered it.

"DeSalvo."

"*Signore* DeSalvo! Your Gathering is in great danger!" the panic-stricken voice of Valeria Costa entreated.

"Is that you, *Signora* Costa? Please repeat what you said." DeSalvo said with one finger in his opposite ear.

"Your gathering is in grave danger!"

Turning to look up at the Gathering's building, DeSalvo saw nothing amiss, except for all the dissipating fog and pools of water. Yet, he had his oracle suffering from a panic attack.

What am I missing?

"*Signora* Costa, what should I be looking for?"

"Do not go to your office! Something terrible is about to happen! It must be bad, because something is preventing me from seeing clearly, *signore*!"

Unknown to either, Mel had almost completed her second circuit of the block, this time chanting a different spell with a devious purpose.

"Thank you, *signora*, for the warning, but I must go and see to the building." And with that, DeSalvo crossed the street, shouldered through the remaining demonstrators, and confronted he didn't know what.

His sudden and dark presence at the main reception desk snapped the security personnel to attend.

"I want a building security status report, right now!"

"What are we looking for?" One brave security staffer dared to ask.

"Damn it, man! Is anything attacking us?"

CHAPTER 28
Vitrification

In my utterly pristine Manhattan flat, we sat together hovering over my kitchen table like two mad scientists, me in my size small, he in a double-XL HAZMAT suit.

Preparing the six plague letters had been satisfying, but working with J.J. was the best. He shared the contents of this horrific spell that would gut the Gathering building and translated it, so I could better link it. That philological session was priceless. Here we were, two magicians, working side-by-side, employing two different languages, on a grand undertaking.

Per the instructions from an ancient tablet, J.J. said that he needed an incendiary metaphor of some kind, be it a pitch-covered torch or a brazier of red hot coals. Then, his eyes just lit up, full of mischievousness, because he just so happened to have in his old red truck a Roman candle from TNT Fireworks of Weatherford, Texas. Never mind why he carried such a thing about in a gasoline-powered vehicle.

We constructed the magical device around a six inch base of pure bees' wax that he got through a friend at the New York cathedral—the burned down end of a massive altar candle used for high masses. J.J. said the candle was consecrated, which held great importance for him. What that importance was totally escaped me.

On the bottom of this heavy wax base, J.J. attached a handwritten copy of the spell's text in Sumerian cuneiform. Around the four edges of this spell, I wrote, in my enchanted lemon ink, the Demotic "make effective" spell, which would set the Sumerian conjuring into motion. This, admittedly, was a special challenge as neither of us had never before built a magical device using two languages.

Next, J.J. mounted the Roman candle atop the wax so that it stood vertically. Far from finished, he then got down to the messy process of coating the Roman candle and its wax base in a heavy layer of pure honey. He used a sterilized table spoon to first heap on, and then smooth out, the sweet material.

Being curious, I asked about this bizarre detail, and in particular, why he chose this particular brand of honey.

"Mel, it's really quite simple. Both the consecrated nature of the wax base and the honey coating are insurance against anyone who is either a demon or demon-possessed. Such things are Kryptonite to them. As for the honey, it's the best and most dangerous for demons and their kind. It's produced by wild, Africanized bees. Now it's your turn to add to this surprise package."

That's when I attached to the Roman candle's wick, a long papyrus strip inscribed with a Demotic spell, again using my special, enchanted lemon ink. I carefully padded the papyrus down along the Roman candle's length.

Finally, Stone pressed into the honey encrusted wax base a disposable flip-phone. Between its clam shell lid and case, he inserted the end of my magical papyrus strip, and just for good measure, taped it closed.

Now completed, we sat back and critiqued our crude, but remotely triggered, magical incendiary device. In theory, when the phone vibrated, the energy would excite the triggering spell attached to the candle's wick, which, when ignited, would call the spell attached to the wax candle's base. A true Rube-Goldberg design to be sure, but one, if found, cannot be traced by a spell whisperer nor handled by a demon or demon-possessed individual.

"You know, Mel, such a cobbled together object, made up of such culturally different origins, may not work."

"You may be right," she said with a mischievous smile. "But even if it doesn't work, imagine their shock when they find it!"

* * *

Mr. Henry wanted dearly to play the role of the brown uniformed parcel delivery man, but I would have absolutely none of that. My Marine reasoning was flawless: if anything went wrong, and by definition it will, then I was the most survivable. That simple fact, when clearly enunciated to my proud and stubborn friend, finally won the day. Mr. Henry instead was relegated to being the getaway driver for Mel, Peter, and me.

"Bitch, bitch, bitch," was all I got in return from the man.

* * *

On the very day of the water balloon-throwing, Evangelical demonstration, just before noon, I arrived dressed as a UPS courier, with my UCS underneath, at the freight entrance of the Gathering building. I carried in my leather gloved hands an oddly shaped, tall parcel that was adorned with warning labels on all four sides, indicating vertical side up with large red arrows, along with several "FRAGILE" labels thrown in for good measure.

I fully expected that there would be a security guard at the freight entrance and wasn't disappointed. The fact that his aura was black didn't surprise me, either. The package's documentation on my clipboard indicated that its destination was the fourth floor, Membership Services, and that it required a signature. That meant I needed access to the premises.

The security guard first checked my ID badge, then the origin address of the parcel—Hallmark Birthday Surprises of Trenton, New Jersey. These seemed to satisfy the security guard, who then piped up.

"Where's the usual guy?"

"On vacation. I think he said the Bahamas," I invented.

"No shit. That lucky dog. I didn't know that you's guys made that much green."

I just shrugged my answer, activated the elevator's horizontal-split grating, got on, closed the grating behind me, and punched a button. What really bugged me, however, was that the security guard never once took his eyes off of me. As I disappeared from view I distinctly heard.

"Base. This is the West 53rd Street dock. We've got a live one on his way to the fourth floor. Watch for him."

I got off at the third floor. My suppressed 9mm was out behind my box. Fortunately, no one was there to greet me, but I knew that all hell was about to break loose, since I hadn't arrived at the fourth.

I stalled the elevator, stashed my precious surprise box behind the trash bin to the left of the elevator, got back in, and headed back down to the street level. As I descended I waited with my clipboard held before me and my 9mm behind it. Wearing a big smile as the elevator halted, its grating split across its middle, the security guard, now with a scowl, charged aggressively toward me. With the grating's gap only six inches wide I shot him right between the eyes. Mixed in with the flying gray matter was an all too distinct black cloud of ectoplasm that marked him as one of the damned.

Then, I triggered my throw-away flip-phone to a preprogrammed phone number, put it in the security guard's chest pocket, took off my hat, and stuffed it into a pocket. I heard the elevator engage behind me as I disappeared into the milling noontime crowd with my head on a swivel.

Now where is Mr. Henry's car?

Meanwhile, Peter Glass leaned against the stone façade of St. Thomas' Church, while sipping a soda. He was the one who had remotely pushed from across West 53rd, the elevator's fourth floor button with his astral finger. When he saw me exiting the freight dock, he sauntered off to find Mr. Henry's ride as well.

*   *   *

While my J.J. played daredevil, I walked the city block the building occupied, silently chanting a perimeter spell. Passersby thought I was a woman on her smart phone, since I wore some trendy orange ear buds. Nothing, however, could have been further from the truth, for my job was to keep the Hell's Own Fire strictly contained within that building.

*　　*　　*

It burned like a veritable Biblical pillar of fire, which, of course, it was. Unquenchable, unrelenting, it consuming all and everything within its carefully specified limits. Never once did the fires venture beyond the structure's outer walls. Never once did they extend below its first floor. Never once was the roof breached. Instead, that which burned within melted and settled like so much molten magma above the first floor, forming a vast pool that would take weeks, if not months, to cool. Throughout its progress, the conflagration spread slowly, steadily, and without pause, until those magically specified limits were reached. Then, and only then, did the flames turn inward to consume itself, utterly.

Such is the manageable nature of Hell's Own Fire, which provided the reason why the Fifth Avenue and 53rd Street Subway Station—which services the E and M lines beneath the Gathering building—remained intact and functional in every way.

CHAPTER 29
A Gutted Liability

Fifth Avenue Property Totaled By Fire

A fire consumed the renovated the Gathering building on Fifth Avenue. Fortunately, the fire's progress spread so slowly that there were no fatalities. The heat of the fire totally gutted the structure's interior leaving behind only what one expert called "a burned out shell."

An FDNY dispatcher admitted, "We only learned about the fire from 911 calls about smoke billowing from the building." Another mentioned that "it was a miracle that this didn't spread to the adjacent buildings." An FDNY forensics expert on the scene said, "I don't know how it's possible, but this fire bored right through the concrete and rebar of thirty-eight floors like a laser."

The recent history of this building is one of disaster. On July 17, 2009, its fire suppression system failed, flooding it out, and forcing its entire renovation, estimated in the hundreds of millions. Now, its fire system completely failed, resulting in a burned out shell. Cost? Priceless.

(*The New York News*, XXXIII 2011, Thursday, April 7, A1)

*   *   *

On that Thursday, William DeSalvo, Regional Director of CMES North America, was again an executive without an office. He smoldered over the fact that he had been played. He realized that the contamination, plague outbreak, whatever you want to call it, was a ruse to evacuate the facility. Worst of all, it was his own fault, for he had been duped into ordering it.

The emergency dockside warehouse that overlooked the Hudson, where he, his security, and entire administrative staff had evacuated to, would have to do for now. He was convinced that he would soon be out of a job as well. He didn't have to be psychic to sense the nearing shadow of a raven's beating wings. It just made good business sense. So he called his boss Feng Bai with the god-awful news.

"Good evening Mr. Chairman. This is William DeSalvo. I sincerely apologize for the lateness of this call."

"Mr. DeSalvo. I frankly didn't think I would ever hear from you again."

Silence. *What did that mean?*

"Mr. DeSalvo?" Feng Bai queried.

"Yes, sir. I am still here. What do you wish me to do?"

"Mr. DeSalvo, by calling me at this hour and asking me that question, you have temporarily redeemed yourself. Only a strong, responsible, and disciplined mind would have done so. Someone without those qualities would have run."

"Thank you, sir."

"Do not thank me quite yet, Mr. DeSalvo. I wish to sleep on your apology. Good evening."

* * *

"Mr. Kiel, how can we rid ourselves of Stone?" DeSalvo ranted.

"Sir, do you have any evidence that he did it?"

"Mr. Kiel, I don't need any evidence. The destruction of my headquarters is evidence enough!" DeSalvo emphasized this with his fist hammering the top of marred industrial gray, steel desk. The racket silenced the entire floor's activity as they stopped to listen in.

"Yes, sir," Kiel responded, perhaps too quickly.

"Do we know what happened to our headquarters?" DeSalvo wanted to know.

"No, sir. However, three spell whisperers are currently combing the structure's exterior. Their initial impressions are not good. They doubt anything can be gleaned from such horrifically vitrified material, so I contacted someone I know from Washington to look into the matter."

"Someone from Washington?"

"Yes, sir. He suggested that we get in contact with Professor Amelia Mazor. She is a Near Eastern archaeologist, a non-aligned paranormal, with a tight lip. She works at the Israeli Embassy here in Manhattan."

"An Israeli archaeologist?"

"Yes, sir. I'm going on a hunch. I just need her to confirm what I suspect."

*   *   *

"Mr. DeSalvo. The Chairman is on line one."

"Thank you, Charlene."

"DeSalvo, here."

"Mr. DeSalvo, are you making any progress in your investigations?"

"Yes, sir, I am, and it's intriguing."

"Mr. DeSalvo, your choice of vocabulary continues to amaze me. First, you apologize to me. Now, you find the destruction of your headquarters to be 'intriguing.' Mr. DeSalvo, what is it that you find so, intriguing?"

"The method used to destroy my headquarters, sir. An expert just provided me with evidence that something called Hell's Own Fire was employed here. The evidence, in her view, was unmistakable."

"I see. And who told you that, Mr. DeSalvo?" the chairman said with curiosity in his voice.

"A Near Eastern archaeologist, Mr. Chairman. One of her research specialties is searching for evidence of the use of Hell's Own Fire in the ancient world. She has confirmed five examples of its destructive power. And now, she has seen her sixth."

"Who could have done this, Mr. DeSalvo?"

"The archaeologist said that only one publication references such a spell that could create this kind of destructive fire. It was published last year. The book is called, *Curses and Demons: Dark Magic from Ancient Mesopotamia.* It was a *New York Times* best seller, and, its author was none other than Jonathan Joseph Stone."

"I know his book … I have read it. So what is your next move, Mr. DeSalvo?"

"Find Stone and kill him. Dead."

"Good luck, Mr. DeSalvo."

*   *   *

"Mr. Kiel, what happened when we last paid a visit to New Mexico?" DeSalvo queried.

"All of our troops were massacred."

"What happened when we sent mixed troops to Pennsylvania?"

"All the mixed troops were killed. Only one full human, Anderson, was returned."

"What happened when we raided TIIIS' Academy on Christmas Eve?"

"One of four helicopters returned with a partial load of troopers."

"What happened when we were suckered into that raid on a barbeque restaurant in Pennsylvania?"

"In that incident, only Randolph was lost. All the full humans were returned to us unharmed."

"Mr. Kiel, what did any of those returnees have to say about their engagements, about their opposition?"

"They raved on and on about Stone, how fast he moved, how hard it was to track him, much less see him. Then, there were reports about little, chipmunk-like creatures, which clawed and bit the mixed troops with great and telling effect."

"So what you're telling me is that all of our attacks have been conventional ones, with no magic involved."

"Yes, sir. No overt magic was used, other than the deployment of mixed security troops."

"Okay, Mr. Kiel. All of that changes as of right now. Am I understood?"

"Crystal, sir."

* * *

How the Mighty Have Fallen

Yesterday, the City of New York declared the ultra-glamorous the Gathering building, facing Fifth Avenue between 52nd and 53rd Streets, a hazardous liability. Its demolition will begin shortly.

Once considered an economic juggernaut, its carbon fiber membership card the ultimate symbol of societal prestige, and the hippest coven of all time, the Gathering building has been reduced to a molten, blackened, shell.

A flurry of lawsuits has been filed for denial of services. One lawyer quipped, "They'll have nothing to stand on. A fire is a fire—an Act of God." The owner of the property has not been available for comment.

(*The New York News*, XXXIV 2011)

So quietly ended Western Civilization's greatest moral threat.

*　　*　　*

Mr. Kiel was not all that sure just what CMES had in its arsenal, or for that matter, what advantages they might bring, so he contacted someone far wiser than he.

But before he did that, Kiel carefully reviewed all the post-op reports of the returnees. He was looking for some clue and found none. This train of thought was broken by the silent presence of a man.

"Yes?" he acknowledged.

The balding man with a peace wreath of grayish white hair stood at attention. Kiel's first impression of his erect posture and trim, well-tailored suit was that of an elite athlete now in his declining years. Why he thought that he could not say. It just fit.

"Sir, you called for the Armorer. I am he." Never before in Kiel's experience had such words been more formally presented. But when that utterance was coupled with the steady gaze of blue-white irises, Kiel knew for a fact that this man was somehow special.

"I see, Mister …?"

"Oliver Peabody, sir, at your service."

"Please take a box, Mr. Peabody. It's the best that I can offer you at the moment."

"Thank you, sir, but I prefer to stand. What is your desire?"

"Are you aware of the last operation to Pennsylvania and what happened to it?"

"Yes, sir. Our personnel were gassed, interrogated, and returned, while my predecessor was terminated," he said woodenly, with all the emotion of a sawhorse.

"Mr. DeSalvo wants Stone killed. Knowing what you know about our region's arsenal, what would you suggest?"

"Well, sir, we have several options. My first choice would be to send two of our Raven helicopter gunships loaded with Hellfire missiles and secondarily armed with GAU-2, 7.62 NATO mini-guns."

"How about something less extreme, Mr. Peabody, something with a distinctly magical bent."

This caused the man to blink, and when he did, the fingers of his right hand seemed to be manipulating something unseen in the air. Then, a right eyebrow arched.

"Mr. Kiel, several *things* come to mind."

The manner, in which Peabody said "things," caused the hair on the back of Kiel's neck to rise. The former government man then noted a subtle accent that troubled him to his core. While he couldn't place it, Peabody's voice now gave him the creeps.

"Such as?" Kiel bravely prodded.

"The first is an extremely corrosive gas-like being. It could easily kill Stone, but it is, unfortunately, quite uncontrollable in the open air. It is, however, excellent in all respects when utilized within the confines of a building.

"Another possibility to consider is a Sumatran Shadow Wing. It is swift, obedient, and above all, very deadly. It, however, cannot operate in broad daylight.

"What is a Sumatran Shadow Thing anyway?" Kiel asked.

"Sir, a Sumatran Shadow Wing is a nocturnal demon. Basically, it is a flying insect, part spider, part scorpion, the size of a medium-sized dog."

"Huh, a flying arachnid mix. How nice. What else can you recommend?"

"Perhaps the best choice, other than a human paranormal champion such as Jeremy Gainsworthy, would be to enlist the services of a dedicated human assassin. While I know that two such men have failed in the past to kill Stone as a youth, my analysis would suggest this time the selection of a woman, whose name is Nancy Forbes. Her professional nickname in the field is Sekhmet, after the ancient Egyptian lion goddess of destruction and chaos. She is very experienced, clever ..."

"Is she expensive?"

"Yes, sir. Forbes is a non-aligned mercenary, who prefers to live outside our Gathering." Pause. "Additionally, we have several conjurers within our Gathering who can bring forth demons of almost any stripe. Given the nature of the target, however, the adept or adepts deployed will have to be on site in order to manage their conjured entities.

"But, sir, if I may suggest, if it were *my* choice to make, I would select Forbes."

"Why specifically?"

"Forbes, sir, has a distinct advantage. She is utterly mad. Further, she seriously believes she is the embodiment of the goddess Sekhmet herself. Absolutely nothing fazes her."

"How quickly can we get Forbes under contract?"

"Unknown, Mr. Kiel," Peabody stated. "However, it is my responsibility to find out what her availability is."

"Let's go with your recommendation. And thank you, Mr. Peabody, you have been most helpful. And Mister Peabody, how long have you know of this Forbes woman?"

"Far too long for my liking, sir. I will be in touch."

*　　*　　*

DeSalvo bravely punched in the numbers. The call he dreaded to make, but make it he would.

"Mr. Chairman," DeSalvo began, "Good morning, sir. I am at a loss as to what to say. In three weeks begins the demolition of our headquarters property. That will be ably managed. I will need your guidance, sir, as to what to do with the property itself, once that process is complete.

"Currently, our regional staff is up and running in a satellite location on Manhattan's West Side. Our morale is building. We are no longer siloed into departments. Now we know each other's faces; hear each other's conversations. We are determined. We are an integrated team. Without question, we have been laid low, but we are holding up well."

"I see, Mr. DeSalvo," the chairman smoothly stated from his office just outside Rome. "I agree with you that we must decide on what to do with the Fifth Avenue property, and I can assure you that this very question has been handed off to a special committee formed two days ago."

At hearing this news, DeSalvo mentally exhaled with relief.

Finally, some external guidance.

"And I am pleased to hear about the morale of your staff, Mr. DeSalvo. That reflects positively on your management skills during this extraordinary turn of events."

"Thank you, Mr. Chairman. However, I have prepared a transition plan for my successor. All I need to know is to whom you wish me to send it."

Feng Bai, at hearing those words, was momentarily stunned, but quickly recovered. Never before in his experience had a Westerner offered himself up so professionally, so matter-of-factly. He made a decision.

"Mr. DeSalvo. You misunderstand the situation. I do not seek your replacement. At least, not yet. What your region is to do is find a solution for Stone. That task, Mr. DeSalvo, I wish you to solve."

And the chairman hung up.

DeSalvo sat in his used folding chair with dazed and glassy-eyes. Throughout the rest of the warehouse floor he could have easily heard a pin drop. His entire staff waited to hear what he had to say. Finding his voice, the Roman stood up and snarled with force, "We are going to kill that bastard Stone. Who's with me?"

The entire floor erupted.

*   *   *

The aftermath of the Gathering's fall made TIIIS giddy. For its besieged president, it was a much-needed win and reaffirmation of her external policy. As for the naysayers, they were conspicuously quiescent.

During Silver Moon's first encrypted video conference following the recent Manhattan event, she leveled a sobering warning.

"Dear colleagues. Let there be no mistake, the U.S. Region has been fortunate. The fatalities from the take down of the CMES North American headquarters were astonishingly low, if not nil. Our IT and Security Departments did very well.

"While at this moment we might be feeling our oats, get over it, quickly. Expect counter strikes. Our opponent is down, wounded, and still extremely dangerous.

"In short, remain vigilant." And with those words she abruptly ended the video conference, a new record in brevity.

CHAPTER 30
General Mobilization

War does not break out overnight. More often than not it is preceded by a long and protracted simmering period. Opponents posture, diplomatic messages are transmitted wherein veiled and not so veiled threats are exchanged, allies are found, and finally, the plowshares of peace are forged into the swords of war.

So it was with TIIIS and CMES, the philosophical opposites of the paranormal world. For the most part, CMES had ruled the roost for more than five thousand years, while TIIIS took its lumps and ducked its head—all to survive another day.

That all changed when I became TIIIS' Lictor of Magic. Perhaps for the first time since the good old days of Publius Cornelius Scipio Africanus, the first Lictor of Magic, did my society possess such a formidable package.

I'm not bragging when I say that. Don't believe me? Then consider this: I am a sum of many parts; the invincible First Soul of Creation that I carry guides this stubborn, gung-ho, U.S. Marine veteran; the Old Oaks Academy polished me; supercharged by the Silver Nile when I blundered into a tributary of that ley line; the *Argenti* taught me how to translocate; and finally, there is Mel. She represents my capstone.

*   *   *

Several weeks after the fall of the Gathering, seemingly right out of the blue, DeSalvo's presence was requested by Chairman Feng Bai. Not knowing what that meant, the regional director of CMES North America quickly put together a financial report, and, in a prescient moment, tucked into his baggage his current file on Stone—an accordion file that had taken on a pregnant appearance.

The weather in Rome, while dry and temperate, was debilitating due to the city's smog. After a half hour limo ride from the Leonardo da Vinci-Fiumicino Airport, DeSalvo was delivered to the CMES Rome Center campus. There, he was greeted, processed, and assigned quarters. An envelope was waiting for him at the main reception desk.

Dear Mr. DeSalvo:

You are invited for dinner

8 pm

Business casual

*   *   *

During a sumptuous multi-course meal, where each course offered its own wine pairing, DeSalvo chose not to drink. He needed his wits. When the dessert course was finished, Chairman Feng Bai stood, and addressed some fifty luminaries from the end of long banquet table.

"Ladies. Gentlemen. Thank you for responding to my invitation. I apologize for any inconvenience it may have caused you. What I wish to share with you will make my desires clear.

"As you all know, we, the *Consilium magorum et*

sagarum, have been under siege for the last two and a half years by a most unexpectedly capable opponent. Our cash treasury in North America was ransacked. Our financial and human resources data breached. Our good name smeared by the world media, which had previously swallowed whole the many lies fed to them."

The chairman paused to take sip of water.

"Today, at this very moment, we are in danger of losing our grip on the North American region."

This caused a clear ripple throughout the audience as everyone stole a glance in DeSalvo's direction, since he was its current regional director.

"How can I assess such a disastrous portent? First, our North American headquarters in Manhattan was rendered uninhabitable, its director hideously assassinated, and his *Book of Spells* stolen by this most capable opponent, who then shared it with the papists."

The magnitude of the situation was dawning on some of the less informed participants. This was not entirely about one region's bad luck, but rather about a paranormal power shift.

"Next, this same opponent massacred a North American security force of thirty-six in the mountains of the American West, near a place called Santa Fe, New Mexico. This emboldened opponent then raided the temporary North American headquarters, captured its freshly installed director, and then thoroughly squeezed him dry of information with drugs." The man invented. "Quite literally, they left the wretch babbling at the curbside like so much discarded trash."

All present knew about Mukhtar El-Najjar's fall from grace, but not the particulars, much less the context. As a result, a distinct growl of uneasiness was voiced. The chairman patiently waited until their emotion quelled to a simmer.

"Then there is the issue of my predecessor, Chairman Giovanni Presto, and his unexpected demise, a man cut down in the prime of life. Again, we highly suspect that it was this capable opponent."

A truly grim and determined look filled the faces of all those sitting before him.

"Recently, two other North American security forces were sent, this time to Pennsylvania. On one of those missions an extremely valuable asset was slaughtered, and the rest of the team gassed, captured, and *returned* to us unarmed and unharmed by this same capable opponent. The commander of this security detachment then delivered *us* a message from *them*. They *FORBADE* us, evermore, from setting foot in the U.S. states of New Mexico and Pennsylvania."

This last caused whistles and catcalls, some even irrationally called for the total destruction of every man, woman, and child in those states. The chairman raised his hands and signaled for quiet.

"Many of you are aware of the most recent attack on the New York headquarters. Our capable opponent burned it down from within with an all-consuming magical fire. The building cannot be saved. Once worth over two billion dollars, it is currently in the process of being demolished. Allow me to be clear. This could happen to any one of our Gatherings."

Reality had finally sunk in.

"Through a good part of this terrible history, one of our own continued to tirelessly fight back against this most capable opponent. And because of him, we now know, as a certainty, who our capable opponent is.

Again DeSalvo was glanced at, but the banquet room became as still as a church, waiting.

"Ladies. Gentlemen. Our capable opponent has a name, and it is called TIIIS."

The stunned audience took the news poorly and for good reason. TIIIS, for practically its entire history, had been considered a troublesome, but spineless entity, much like the village fool who was ready and willing to be kicked about.

"Mr. DeSalvo," the chairman continued, "I can see that your colleagues cannot believe their ears. Perhaps you could share with them your evidence.

DeSalvo stood up at his place, which was nearly opposite that of Feng Bai.

"Thank you, Mr. Chairman, for the opportunity to present my case.

"Ladies, Gentlemen, William Alexander is indeed very dead. He was assassinated by the current TIIIS Lictor of Magic along with two Vatican representatives of the Order of Saint Paul."

Silence.

"Make no mistake, the rumors of his survival were crafted TIIIS disinformation, as were the media leaks regarding our financial dealings with the U.S. Congress."

Again stunned silence.

"As some of you might remember, the former TIIIS Lictor of Magic was Peter Ignatius Edward Smithers, who served also as their president. He has been replaced by Jonathan Joseph Stone, a former U.S. Marine sergeant, a heavily-decorated, battle-hardened warrior. Stone is also a university scholar who graduated *cum laude*. Furthermore, this same man is a published expert in ancient Near Eastern demonology. As if those credentials are not enough, he currently carries the First Soul of Creation."

Gasps threatened to create a natural vacuum.

"Ladies. Gentlemen. In my opinion, Mr. Stone is the sole reason for why my region has fallen on such hard times. This individual, Stone, explains TIIIS' aggressive about face both for my region and *yours*."

Seeing several scoffing faces, DeSalvo doubled down.

"Don't believe me?" the Roman pointed at the three doubting Thomas'. Consider this: the remarkably orchestrated assaults on my headquarters, which have all the ear marks of a set-piece military operation—efficient, well-organized, and disciplined. Stone, with two Vatican minions, assassinated Regional Director Alexander. Stone plundered from Alexander his long-lived pride and joy, *The Book of Spells*. Stone single-handedly killed thirty-six mixed troops in New Mexico. Stone sprung a trap on twenty-one fully human troops, which he then so graciously returned to us. Also in that operation, he cut down Mitzi Randolph, *my* personal assistant and our region's armorer."

Many shook their heads upon hearing Randolph's name.

"Colleagues. Stone represents the head of the snake. I say cut it off. Cut it off and the snake dies," the Roman said while smashing his clenched fist into the table before him, upsetting wine glasses.

The place exploded with enthusiasm at DeSalvo's final words.

Feng Bai took note.

*   *   *

Half a world away, the Supreme Council of TIIIS met in the Vault, the subterranean, cave-like Colonial construction that made up a portion of Old Main's foundation on the Old Oak Academy campus. Thirty-three TIIIS representatives from around the world sat at the circular cherry wood conference table. Some were not happy about the requirement of their physical presence at the meeting, as they believed that a secure teleconference would have sufficed.

"Colleagues." President Silver Moon opened, "Thank you meeting today at Old Oaks Academy. I can assure you that what we will discuss today, I refuse to broadcast, no matter how encrypted or secure you think our video system is.

"Today I am placing the U.S. Region on a war footing against CMES."

President Silver Moon paused to let that statement sink in.

"Why? Because a former employee has defected and has informed CMES of our complicity in the events of the past two and a half years. Further, as I speak, there is a high-level CMES conference taking place in Rome where these facts will no doubt be shared.

"For the past two and a half years, like my predecessor, I, too, have consigned to the scrapheap our former external policy of passivity. In the past, this council was heavily divided about that proposed policy change. As a consequence, the U.S. Region went ahead and pursued that external policy of 'an eye for an eye' when dealing with CMES' acts of aggression. At that time, President Smithers also said that the U.S. Region will, and I quote, be 'an experimental case, while the remaining regions continue to follow the *status quo*.' That was then, and here is now.

"That said, the U.S. Region now wishes to know, who among you will stand beside us?"

The TIIIS Supreme Council, seldom a decisive, deliberative body, fell into a low murmur of turning heads. This, President Silver Moon knew, would be the case. It always was. After several moments of commiseration, Sub-governor Sir James McElhinney of Central Canada, asked and received permission to address the council.

"Colleagues," the sub-governor began, "while I readily admit the U.S. Region is probably daft in their proud pursuit of aggressive retribution for injuries incurred, I, in good conscience, cannot allow the U.S. Region to solely take on the brunt of this conflict. Consequently, Central Canada will stand behind the U.S. Region, Madam President."

Bless you, Sir James, President Silver Moon thought. *Now I wonder who else will throw their hat into the ring.*

Hasim Mohammed Nagi, the Governor of the Arab Republics, was the next who wished to speak.

"President Silver Moon. Do you expect this conflict with CMES to be purely regional in nature, or, one that will spread like a wild fire across a desiccated plain?"

President Silver Moon eyes squinted in thought as she formulated an answer.

"Mr. Nagi. Frankly, there is no telling what CMES' reaction will be. But I have a sense, especially given the character of their new CMES chairman, Feng Bai, that this conflict will remain regional. Our disinformation campaign has wounded CMES, causing them to back down and regroup in many industries and regions. Further, CMES has far more to lose in a wide-open conflict than us. Their exposure in the world economy is infinitely greater than ours."

This fact caused some uncomfortable shifting in seats.

"Further, my read on their Chairman, Feng Bai," President Silver Moon continued, "is that he is a patient man with his eye clearly on the future. As a consequence, he is the polar opposite of his predecessor, who shot first and asked questions later. On that basis, I believe hostilities will remain in North America. At least, that is my hope."

More intense murmuring and speculation.

Then Governor Kemal Kartal of Turkey spoke up.

"Madam President, my region will not participate in this policy of open hostilities and mad aggression," the Turk said as he pounded the conference table with his right fist for added emphasis.

"And as far as I am concerned," Kartel continued with passion, "President Smithers brought this on the U.S. Region, when he sanctioned the lawless use of our Lictor of Magic. He is the one who brought down the wrath of CMES upon the U.S. Region with his overwhelming pride of place. Be careful, Madam President, that you do not make the same jingoistic mistake. In fact, I openly challenge this entire change in external policy from our traditional and time-honored stance of live and let live."

At this, the now very ruddy-faced sub-governor of Central Canada blurted out.

"Now isn't that just wonderful, Governor Kartel," McElhinney said while slowly clapping his hands together in pure derision. "Go home, chappy, stick your head in the sand, and be sure to thoroughly grease your arse," the Canadian goaded while leaning forward with both of his hands on the conference table.

"Oh, and by the way, by not participating in this little North American dust up, you have aced yourself out of any of the spoils as well. Oops! I slipped. I forgot. You Turks historically never have had any interest in such things."

And so, on that hearty congenial note, the meeting ended after thirty minutes, instead of a productive day-long strategy session among peers.

*　　*　　*

Historians fiddle with facts while arguing their own cogent theories about whom or what ignited the conflict. Fine, let them postulate, formulate, and fulminate until they are blue in the face while seated in their padded leather chairs, set before roaring fires, safe and secure within their salons, far, far away from the frontlines.

But I was there. I was a participant in this hideous business. And I know for a fact what kicked off these hostilities. It all boiled down to one simple thing—the hubris of a flawed mindset, which believed that the *status quo* was immutable, and therefore eternal.

Like I said, I changed all of that, because I was the rogue variable, which the *status quo* could not account for.

In many ways, it was a blessing that the initial hostilities were largely contained within the North

American continent. The U.S. Region of TIIIS, as the proponent and initiator of this new TIIIS policy of "an eye for an eye," quickly found itself largely abandoned by the rest of the TIIIS international community. They, predictably, preferred to ignore everything, do nothing, and continue with the traditional box turtle defensive approach. This development was not unexpected.

As a consequence of this rapidly building storm, several non-aligned organizations, communities, societies, and communes chose to side with our cause. Sadly, many more fled to the other side. Throughout, extremely elevated, even furious, levels of diplomatic activity occurred between the principal antagonists. Here, the gruesome murders of well-known diplomats, fell squarely into context. In many ways, Paul's tragic death represented a bell-weather for that ever-building storm front.

Caught squarely in between, the non-aligned paranormals looked for that which was advantageous. Those with long standing ties sought out further concessions from their more powerful allies. But once the word got out of what TIIIS' did to the Gathering in Manhattan, defectors quietly trickled in. They offered their own special talents, acknowledged their global dissatisfaction with their former masters, and shared their insider knowledge of CMES' innermost workings.

Among those who came to the U.S. Region's aid included ACME, a star-studded collection of highly specialized paranormals—spell whisperers, dream and wind readers, ley line surveyors, and diviners of many stripes.

Next to step up was FIRST, a paramilitary mercenary organization best known for their ability to disappear and reappear. This remarkable talent was the result of a delightful mix of technology and telepathic skill. Their presence among our ranks was a true morale boost.

Less obvious, and therefore just as critical during a time of war, was our alliance with WHAMMO, a quirky tech organization that offered undetectable, unbreakable, and non-traditional communications and computing services among other dazzling, gee-whiz, techno-doohickeys.

RED STAR provided us with the ability to see in secret places. They were originally a Soviet paranormal group who specialized in remote viewing. Their core membership was made up of those who were originally the members of a discredited KGB experimental group.

With TIIIS' membership exceptionally strong in the American West and Southwest, THUNDERBIRD served as a clearing house for Native American shamans, witchdoctors, dream catchers, shape-shifters, and wind walkers. Not surprisingly, many members of TIIIS were already active within this UN-like organization, notably President Silver Moon and Governor John Running Deer of the Southwest.

Sometimes allies are more trouble than what they are worth. Such was the case with BAY CITY, an eclectic gathering of telepaths, telekinetic marvels, and outright head cases—just my opinion. Fortunately, the presence of the GREAT LAKES COMMUNE, a Midwestern, multi-state organization of well-grounded seers, psychics, and telepaths, provided a much-needed counterbalance to their West Coast colleagues.

These organizations were the U.S. Region's and Central Canada's allies. While few in number, they were mighty in capacity. Over the course of the war, others would flock to our banner, but these late comers would do so at great peril.

*   *   *

Following the banquet, Fang Bei signaled DeSalvo to follow him. Once in his private office, the Asian gestured for the Italian to sit.

"It is time, Mr. DeSalvo." Fang Bei quietly said to his regional director of New York. "You have done what you can to manage a horrendous series of events. I now want you to directly deal with the elusive Stone, and his troublesome organization.

"Be aware," he said with a raised finger for emphasis, "that I want this conflict to remain within the North American sphere. I wish to be clear, I do not want this war to bleed into the international arena. This is to be a North American phenomenon only."

"I understand, Mr. Chairman. Can I tap into any non-North American resources?"

"No, Mr. DeSalvo. Your region is on its own. Consequently, I would expect you to plan accordingly when dealing with your opposition."

CHAPTER 31
First Blood

During his flight back from Rome, DeSalvo reread Stone's ever thickening dossier one more time, but on this pass, he had his yellow legal pad at the ready. What the man looked for was Stone's associates, relatives, and friends—in short, anyone who had significant contact with him. He even threw in several others for hate's sake. By the time the aircraft touched down in Newark, his list was ready.

Once back at the West Side warehouse, he called Kiel over to his gray metal desk that served as his palatial office.

"Mr. Kiel, I'm putting you in charge of an assassination team. I want the targets handled in a professional and swift manner. I prefer a conventional approach that is not flashy. No magic, just results."

Tearing off a heavily marked up sheet of yellow legal paper from its pad, he handed it over to Kiel. "Here's my list. Eliminate them all, ASAP."

Kiel, who remained silent throughout, accepted the list with a nod. When he was finished reading and counting the twenty or so names, he grunted, nodded toward his boss, and got to work.

At his desk, the former government spook divided the names up geographically, and in so doing, realized that two were already dead—Mr. Theodore Good and Reverend Paul Roberts. These he crossed off.

In the end Kiel saw he needed potentially four wet professionals. His only uncertainty involved the location of Stone's parents, who had disappeared off the grid some time ago. That fact wouldn't stop him, however, from going forward with the rest. Their unknown status would just make them the last.

*   *   *

In a sea of college students during a period shift, one bobbing backpack looked pretty much like any other. Add a blond ponytail and a youthful face, the assassin blended in completely. With a PU campus map in hand, this job as contracted stipulated a quick and clean, in and out.

Connie Stark, age thirty-two, still had to endure the hassle of showing her ID at bars, but today it was distinctly her advantage. Dressed in jeans and a T-shirt, no one thought much about her within a campus of more than thirty thousand souls.

Finding the Ancient Near Eastern Languages and Cultures Department was a breeze. Bounding up the stairs to the third floor of Williams Hall, Stark wandered about the narrow corridors reading the names on office doors. One was open. It said, "P. Glass MA, PhD" in brass lettering edged in black. Peeking inside, she saw a tousled mop of curly salt and pepper hair studying something intently. She knocked on the door frame.

"Excuse me, but where can I get a department brochure? I'm thinking about taking a couple of classes."

Brightening at the request, the target stood up, smiled broadly, invited Stark in, and offered her a seat. She did, closed the office door, sat down, opened her backpack, and promptly shot the man dead with four sub-sonic and heavily suppressed rounds.

Quickly leaving the mess that she had made, Stark closed Glass' office door behind her and sauntered on down the hallway. Her next stop would be the Glass family residence, all because Peter Glass had been Stone's departmental chair and a member of TIIIS.

*   *   *

That same day in North Carolina a presentable young-looking man in a shirt, tie, and wearing a backpack entered a modern glass and aluminum corporate building. At the reception desk, he said, "Hello, I'm here to see a Mr. Sam Dempsey. Is he in?"

The protective receptionist reasonably asked, "Do you have an appointment?"

"No, I don't, but Sam told me to just drop by the next time I was in town. My name's Paul Crick."

"I see. One moment, please, Mr. Crick." The suspicious receptionist called Dempsey's office, explained the situation to his secretary and was surprised to hear that she should buzz the visitor in.

"Mr. Dempsey's office in on the second floor, Mr. Crick. Make a right when you get off the elevator."

"Thank you, ma'am." Crick smiled. He was in. Moments later, he was interrogated by Dempsey's private secretary about the reason for his visit.

"Ma'am, it's just this simple. I have a manuscript that's appropriate for your publishing house. Professor Peter Glass at the University of Pennsylvania suggested that I visit with you folks, and Mr. Dempsey in particular. That's my story."

After a brief conversation on the phone, moments later Dempsey's office door opened. "Please come in, Mr. Crick."

Dempsey, a balding, but very fit gentlemen with a firm handshake and a ready smile, offered Crick a chair. The two sat down. Crick removed his backpack.

"What can I do for you, Mr. Crick?"

"I have a manuscript for you, sir." And with that, Crick rummaged around in his pack, and killed Dempsey with several suppressed rounds. Just to make sure, the assassin waited two minutes for the body to bleed out. Satisfied, he left closing Dempsey's door behind him. He even thanked his secretary in passing and took the stairs. Walking confidently with his hands in his pockets and whistling lightly, he exited the building.

He, too, would finish off the Dempsey family, all because Dempsey's company had published Stone's book.

*   *   *

The third assassin ran into a hitch. Her target, Professor Melaina Makris, no longer taught at her institution. When she inquired where she might find Professor Makris, the officious secretary of the Ancient Near Eastern Languages Department told her to pound sand. Miffed, Clair Willis immediately contacted Kiel and told him precisely what she thought about his out-of-date intel.

*   *   *

The fourth assassin failed to get back with Kiel, as the Southwestern Regional Governor, John Running Deer, had personally taken care of her. This overt incident he swiftly shared with his good friend Betsy Silver Moon, who was already tallying up the names of the fallen. The common thread between them all was not hard to figure, so she put the Old Oaks Academy's staff and students on high alert. As far as Silver Moon was concerned, the war was now officially underway.

*   *   *

At this stage in the carnage, DeSalvo's directive had claimed only a portion of his list, mainly because they could be located. The regional director had emphasized swiftness. His subordinate had tried to deliver as best he could, on the basis of what their data said. Still and all, no one could have predicted that Professor Adam Gibson and his family would be out-of-the-country on an excavation somewhere in Turkey, and therefore, off limits. The locations of Mr. Henry Johnson and Professor Melaina Makris, while unknown to CMES, both resided now on the Old Oaks Academy campus. The location of Stone's parents, Andrew and Constance Stone, also were unknowns. As for President Betsy Silver Moon, one of DeSalvo's "for hate's sake" targets, Kiel concluded the woman must live perpetually on the move.

*   *   *

DeSalvo sat behind his gray metal desk on the West Side and coolly assessed his wins and losses. In all, he admitted to himself, he had gained practically nothing of value.

Okay. You win some, you lose some. But best of all, we drew first blood.

Then DeSalvo got an idea.

CHAPTER 32
The Challenge

DeSalvo told his assistant Kiel to canvas his region for paranormal combat champions and even those close to that potential. From the Roman's point of view, Gainsworthy's first encounter defeat by Stone was a function of his own overconfidence and dependence upon his Assyrian griffin. In essence, the man had to control the demon with one side of his brain, while the other was responsible for both protecting himself and attacking his prey. In short, Gainsworthy had overestimated his abilities to control his environment and completely underestimated Stone. After all, who could have known that the man could translocate?

Well, that was about to change as Stone was no longer an unknown commodity, for he had revealed quite a bit during that brief, though brutal, exchange with Gainsworthy. Stone had displayed once again his reluctance for killing full humans. For if he had, then these details would not have been revealed.

What DeSalvo wanted to create was a hit team of not one, but of several paranormal champions, who would finally put this Stone in the ground. The only question that remained in DeSalvo's mind was—could he find such individuals who were willing to act as a team, instead of lone wolves?

*   *   *

Such a spectacle had not occurred in centuries, at least not since the last standoff that had required it, which ultimately led to the Treaty of Tordesillas in 1494. The Challenge was designed from its inception as a peaceful method for avoiding all-out war between paranormal individuals and groups. The Challenge invocation triggered a time-honored process, which called for the establishment of a neutral tribunal to adjudicate the dispute. As CMES, the petitioner, had claimed first injury with the destruction of the Gathering building, they by right they chose the neutral tribunal's thirteen members, which in turn would decide how the claimed injury would be satisfied. Traditionally, such redress was reached through a calculation of *Wehrgeld*, "man-money." However, in this particular instance, the petitioner did not desire such payment, but rather pointedly requested champions from each side to meet in a dual to the death. Bowing to the injured party's wishes, the tribunal therefore selected a suitable site for the contest and drafted the Rules of Engagement.

After much deliberation, the tribunal uniquely found that four champions were to be arrayed—three against one. As one might imagine, many on the sidelines lived for the excitement of such a macabre drama. Only a chosen few would be allowed to witness the contest, but only at exorbitant cost. Certain favored gambling houses of Asia, Britain, and Monaco provided the rest their opportunity for thrills via a live video feed. On the week of the event, available hotel rooms at these locations were non-existent.

Those especially interested in the Challenge were a specialized group of paranormals known simply as *pugiles*, or "champions." Many hoped to be chosen to participate in this historic moment. Such rough and ready individuals typically stood apart, non-aligned, with any organization, society, or enclave, and for good reason. Their product was death. They were muscle for hire, trained specifically in the most deadly of martial arts, augmented with the most frightening of earthly and magical weaponry, all mated to a twisted sense of self and reality. Their day job was assassination for hire. Their handy and conveniently obtainable services prevented global war, internecine conflict, and dynastic disputes. For these practiced mercenaries of death, their reputation within the paranormal community was tantamount, as success was directly proportional to one's fee. A contest such as this represented target marketing on a global scale.

The hallowed process began with the Challenge Invocation, the formal serving of notice that a legal action had been recorded stipulating certain injuries. The delivery of said notice was via the arcane method of certified post. The Challenge Invocation also listed the composition of the thirteen tribunal members.

Truly, the calling for such a contest represented a surreal moment within the paranormal community. CMES, the tradition thug, had called foul upon its typically subservient counterpart, TIIIS, on account of its recent injuries, no matter the ultimate motivation for said misdeeds. To say there was a highly charged political component to the tribunal's proceedings would have been a waste of breath, since easily two thirds of that body, who examined the charges of *iniuriam*, or serious injury, was blood-bound by treaty to the plaintiff. So much for neutrality.

The tribunal met in late September and in Rome. Not surprisingly, it took only four days of deliberation to conclude that TIIIS was indeed guilty of six specific instances of *iniuriam*, while the antecedents presented by the defendant for justification were deemed spurious, fallacious, and *ad hominum*. Now at loggerheads as to what to assign as an appropriate punishment for this judgment, the tribunal received from the plaintiff, CMES, a simple request—that TIIIS sacrifice its greatest asset, its Lictor of Magic. Further, CMES stated that said sacrifice should be carried out by the injured, specifically, by three of its own champions. Only then, would satisfaction be reached.

After further deliberations, the tribunal assented to the plaintiff's motion, wishing to forestall any further injury within the paranormal community, and ordered, forthwith, the surrender of the sacrificial asset.

The TIIIS advocates present during the tribunal's deliberations were dumbfounded at the one-sidedness of the ruling. In a dramatic moment, the President of TIIIS, Betsy Silver Moon, who sat with the TIIIS contingent, placed her hand on the shoulder of their lead advocate, stood, and stated in ancient Greek— "Μολὼν λαβέ."

In essence, the TIIIS president said, "Come, take," as in, "I dare you," paraphrasing the famous words of King Leonidas to the Persian King's emissary, who sought the bloodless surrender of the Spartan King's sword at Thermopylae.

TIIIS' recalcitrant attitude vexed the tribunal, forcing their hand to find an appropriate, neutral location for the impending sacrifice. It meant that they had to organize and oversee the proceedings, establish rules, and not just blithely hand off a victim to an executioner. And along the way, several of their number began to sense a shift within the tribunal's resolve, for never before had this supposedly impartial judicial body been responsible for organizing such an event. Further, all sensed that there was far more afoot, and that the stakes had been raised considerably.

"If I understand the spirit behind the response from the defendant's contingent," the chair of the tribunal noted, indicating President Silver Moon, "then you have one week's time in which to prepare your sacrifice. One week from today he must appear at the very center of the Aralkum Desert, at sunrise, local time. Noncompliance with this direction is tantamount to an admission of guilt, which will be dealt with harshly and swiftly."

To this Draconian directive, President Silver Moon of TIIIS stood firm and addressed the tribune. "Bring it!"

Again, this extraordinarily confident demeanor on the part of TIIIS caused a stir within the paranormal community, causing some to ask. "What's suddenly gotten into TIIIS? Do they not know their place?" Meanwhile others took an entirely different view. "Such moxie. I have never seen their leadership so sure of themselves. What do they know that we don't?" Needless to say, the odds-makers at several gambling establishments did not know what to do either.

CHAPTER 33
Pre-Game Prep

At the Old Oaks Academy, I called a strategic and tactical powwow with *Monsieur* Dexter and Mr. Henry, because I wanted to pick their collective brains on a whole bunch of things. Both readily obliged. Our discussions went on for hours as scenarios, tactics, first moves, you name it, were hashed out. But one topic really got my attention.

"J.J.," Mr. Henry deadpanned, "what will you do, if one of your opponents is female?"

The question stopped me in my tracks. "A woman?"

"*Oui*, Sir Galahad, a beautiful woman," *Monsieur* Dexter pushed.

"Cut her down, I suppose."

At that lukewarm response *Monsieur* Dexter viciously back-handed me with a good bolt of energy across the face. My ears rung.

"*Non! Du tête de merde!*" he bellowed. "Have you completely forgotten your training? You destroy her like any demon-kind," the Frenchman spat. "She's not there to cuddle you with her tits, you baby-faced imbecile! She's there to tear out your guts, and then strangle you with them!

"*AM I CLEAR?*"

Monsieur Dexter has such an amazing way with words.

* * *

My training the next day, before I took the society's jet half way across the world, was devoted to stretching, personal maintenance, and physical and psychic drills that *Monsieur* Dexter and Mr. Henry personally designed for me. Our new armorer, a guy named Ian Crosby, rigged my UCS boots with spikes that provided better traction and contact with the earth. The Bone Sword I had cleaned and inspected. It cut like a laser. I added two new psychic defense moves. *Monsieur* Henry, ever one for authenticity, had me training with my dominant left hand bound, against three of TIIIS' best female security staff in the buff. Yeah, the man had gotten his point across, loud and clear.

*   *   *

Like many things about this arcane arrangement, I had disadvantages levied upon me left and right by the tribune and its rules. The desolate location of the Aralkum Desert represented just the opening salvo, with more sure to come.

I left four days early because the contest's site was so distant, not to mention that I'd be losing a day en route. TIIIS' flat black Gulfstream 528 took me, Ian Crowsby, and two of TIIIS' finest troopers on the journey, which went from Pittsburgh direct to the Ercan Airport at Nicosia, Cypress. There, we spent the night to stretch our legs after the nearly twelve-hour flight and refuel.

The next day, much refreshed, we took off again and finally landed at a small regional airport in Kazakhstan that serviced the village of Bozoy. With regards to its sketchy runway, I've seen better two-lane roads. While only a brief flight of some three and a half hours, it seemed as if we had landed on the dark side of moon. Nicosia, in contrast, was Las Vegas compared to this place. Nonetheless, we managed to get the plane refueled and ready to depart before our arranged-for ground transportation ferried us in a sketchy Land Rover Discovery the remaining one hundred and twenty-five miles.

All told, it took us almost four hours of overland trekking across a sandy terrain blown planar by the constant winds. Only birds seemed to populate this desolation of marginal grasslands.

The tribunal had thoughtfully provided me with a GPS location: Latitude 45° 07' 34.11" north by longitude 60° 38' 35.58" east. I now stood upon that spot, and since it was only five o'clock local in the afternoon, we set up camp.

Armed to the teeth, Ian, Joshua, and Paul acted as my companions/body guards, and if necessary, my pall bearers. Although, I sincerely hoped that would not be the case.

CHAPTER 34
Farce in the Desert

All games have rules, especially this one.

> **Rule Number One.** The sole defendant must occupy the tribunal's coordinates at dawn on the specified date. Otherwise, and regardless of any exigency, the defendant's legal position will be rendered null and void.

> **Rule Number Two**. The defendant must orient himself facing the rising sun. Once so oriented, the defendant cannot move until allowed to do so (See Rule Number Four).

> **Rule Number Three**. The plaintiff may, at their discretion, select as many as three champions to defend their claim against the defendant.

> **Rule Number Four**. The defendant cannot move to defend himself until a champion of the plaintiff moves first. Further, at least one of the plaintiff's champions must remain in plain sight of the defendant, even if that individual is not the first to move.

> **Rule Number Five**. Once any champion of the plaintiff moves, then the defendant may move in any manner of his choosing.

> **Rule Number Six**. All support personnel for the champions must be located one kilometer distant from the contest site, as measured from the central coordinates of the defendant, fifteen minutes prior to the contest's start.

*　　　*　　　*

After a fitful night/early morning, I probably got only about four hours of rest. Sunrise on the appointed day broke around 7:05 local, give or take. Two hours prior, we broke camp, loaded up the vehicle, and waited.

Per my usual pre-game ritual, I ate light and hydrated heavily. I was primed, ready, and just like my old high school football games of yore, I had my focus, my game face on. I was going to pancake them. They just didn't know it yet.

I was getting increasingly uncomfortable in my UCS as sand had somehow gotten into it. In fact, sand had managed to work its way into everything, even the packaged food. Go figure. It was Iraq all over again, which brought back some gruesome memories. Best thing about my condition, I knew how to live with it. I seriously doubted that my opponents could.

When the time came, my comrades, wishing me well, drove off to the distant ridgeline specified by the tribunal. Once there, they would provide whatever overwatch they could. We all knew that this entire scenario was bogus.

As I watched them drive off, I suddenly felt sad as I knew that I might not see them again—alive. I took my position per the coordinates, got into my stance, faced east, closed my eyes, and slipped into the zone. In spite of the UCS's marvelous ability to hide me, I knew that my form still threw a shadow, and at dawn's break I would stick out like a sore thumb for all to see, like the gnomon of a sundial. That was a serious disadvantage, not to mention the gloriously fair six rules that I enumerated above. Then a calming inner voice said.

"Steady, Soul Carrier.

"You are well prepared.

"Do not think.

"Act.

"Attack.

"Conquer."

After the First Soul's whisper of encouragement, I felt strangely reassured. It reminded me that I wasn't alone on that god-awful, wind-swept waste.

I allowed my focus to deepen to the point that time slowed. While the rising sun's glare gradually intensified and became a reddening sliver on the inside of my eyelids, I reached out to my immediate surroundings with all of my senses. Feeling emptiness, I extended that compass two-fold and clearly felt, much like the returning pulses on a radar set, the quiet approach of three individuals, each about one hundred yards away. Their formation was a classic equilateral triangle. I smiled and knew that once they stopped advancing, I would have to pay real close attention. Because once they moved again, it was game on.

*   *   *

DeSalvo and Kiel had put some serious thought into who would represent them as their champions. Gainsworthy, now well-mended, had prepared himself with a frightening will. Basically, for him this had become personal, for Stone had rendered him a man with only one hand, as his left, was essentially useless. Wearing his lion loincloth, the man held his three poison spears in his right hand and shouldered his machete's scabbard within easy reach. In situations such as this, the Brit knew for a fact that the London odds-makers did not favor him, even as he crept up on Stone's left rear quarter. Frankly, he didn't care. He was out for blood.

Jana Summers, also a non-aligned assassin, was best known for her marksmanship, knife throwing, hand-to-hand combat skills, and stunning beauty. She carried a three-barreled twelve gauge shot gun, two .45 automatics on her hips, and several throwing knives on her forearms. Tall, lanky, and extremely fluid in her movements, she faced Stone with a mind to transfix his concentration. The CMES team bet that the American's hormones would get him in trouble as Summers looked every bit the part of a blond Hollywood bombshell in her black, skin tight body suit that left nothing to the imagination. More predatory than a hungry lioness with several starving cubs, Summers was also unhinged. It was well known that she delighted in barbecuing and eating her victim's livers right before them.

Coming up on Stone's right rear padded the barefoot Oleg Gundersen. This massively muscled mountain of a Swede carried a double-bladed war axe in each hand. His bare upper body was covered with protective rune tattoos. A tight war knot bound his long grayish hair, pulled tightly back. Eminently practical, he was a man on a simple mission—to kill swiftly and collect his handsome fee even quicker.

Per their agreement, Summers, the distraction, would lay back for the *coup de grâce*. Gainsworthy, because of his prior injuries, was designated a first mover, while Gundersen would simultaneously fling his axes and bracket Stone. After all, the rules never mentioned that there couldn't be two, first movers.

This trio came to a halt thirty yards away from their prey, for Gainsworthy felt anything closer would be foolhardy. This displeased his two colleagues who preferred a swift and close-in encounter, but Gainsworthy's warnings had held the day as he was the only one who had any combat experience against this TIIIS Lictor of Magic.

Stone, with eyes closed and in deep focus, noted that one of his opponents had positioned themselves directly before him with the other two completing a perfect triangle covering his rear.

The local time was 7:04. Stone, still with eyes closed, stood relaxed, while he effortlessly listened in on their shielded minds. He sensed unbridled revenge, a perverse lust, and cool greed. But what he really waited for was the chemical snap neurons triggering their fast twitch muscles.

*   *   *

The TIIIS support team waited, too, leaning across the hood of their vehicle, each with binoculars glued to their eyes. They knew that once hostilities began, their optical equipment would be useless to follow the contest. Nonetheless, they had brought them.

"Damn, Ian, he looks so cool, calm, and collected out there. If that were me, I'd be shitting bricks." Joshua commented.

Crowsby, who after some time had taken a grudging shine to Stone, simply said, "And that, my boy, is why you're not the Lictor of Magic."

Then, Paul suddenly blurted out, "Holy shit! Did you see that!"

*   *   *

DeSalvo, unlike many within CMES, was not a betting man. While he had expected to spend a small fortune on his three champions, the Roman wanted to make sure that Stone would meet his end, come what may. To that end, and without his champions' knowledge, eight snipers in ghillie-suits had belly-crawled in during the early morning's darkness to the contest's one kilometer perimeter. Armed with suppressed, .50 caliber Barrett M82, semi-automatic rifles, each sniper had specific orders to open fire if Stone was the last man standing. And then there was that other contingency.

*   *   *

The throwing arm of Gainsworthy's jungle-trained, fast-twitch muscles began to move. Simultaneously, Gundersen's heavily muscled arms began their coil.

The neural explosions that these two warriors' muscles made sounded like firecrackers in Stone's head.

Patience ... patience ... now!

Their timing could not have been better. Gainsworthy launched three curare-tipped spears in a triangular formation that passed through the space once occupied by the extended shadow of a man, who had totally disappeared. Gundersen's two bracketing and rotating axes passed through the space as well, which actually struck two of the spear shafts, utterly shattering them.

This extraordinary display of weapons' craft caused Summers to gasp with dilated eyes of sheer pleasure. Temporarily mesmerized, that would be the last thought Summers would ever have.

At the precise moment when Stone knew that not one, but the two opponents behind him had moved, he had translocated fifty feet up, over, and behind the opponent before him. On his descent, he smoothly drew his Bone Sword and with one silent two-handed blow had spectacularly ended Summers day. Stone's brutal strength and the force of gravity combined into one felling, devastating blow that split Summers cleanly in two from head to crotch. The impact of the Bone Sword's passing created a sudden, balloon-like explosion of blood and gore as the two halves separated, fell to the earth, and grotesquely twitched.

Now grounded, Stone purposely dug in his modified boots into the dry sand, found what he was looking for, and head-flicked a vicious bolt of raw and unbridled energy into the chest of a charging, giant of a man. To Stone's surprise, the giant shrugged off the bolt like the splash of a bucket of water, though it did slow him some. So he translocated past the second, and struck him with a compact, scythe-like, two-handed blow squarely across his face, separating the cap of his head in a gushing fountain of blood. Now well past opponent number two, Stone turned to see the distinctive lion's tail kilt with its black tufted end.

Was that Gainsworthy? Again?

During that distracted moment of reflection, Gundersen blasted the former Marine near senseless with his own psychic bolt of directed energy. Just how Stone managed to remain alive was due to the fact that the full power of that bolt had missed him, gouging instead a twenty-foot furrow in the sand some four feet wide and behind him. What Stone had felt was only the roiling air of its passing. Gundersen had guessed where Stone would be, and missed.

Gundersen, now closing fast, reached out to what he thought was a stunned rag doll. But at the last moment, Stone translocated toward him, suddenly closing the gap, and plunging his silver-impregnated blade into the Swede's navel. With an upward grunt, Stone easily sliced through the man's sternum and, in the process, lifted the heavy-weight up on one foot. Stone then relaxed, and as the Swede's body slammed down, the American cruelly wrenched and twisted the blade across and through the man's upper rib cage severing his heart in two. There, the blade lodged itself firmly in a tangle of muscle, bone, and cartilage. The Swede, mouth coughing gouts of blood and with a totally wrecked torso, sagged to his knees. He grasped frantically at the sword's blade, trying furiously to dislodge it. He failed, but in the process, he did lose all of his fingers.

Total elapse time—mere moments.

The Bone Sword still wouldn't come free, so Stone had to leave it.

Why?

Danger! Soul Carrier!

Stone heard and sensed death was fast approaching. He translocated vertically again some fifty feet into the air. Nonetheless, one of the crisscrossing .50 caliber supersonic rounds clipped him in the right heel of his boot. While not damaging him in any way, the round's glancing impact rendered the foot numb and nearly useless. As for Gunderson, his body, caught in the crossfire, was further ruined as five rounds passed through his torso, exploding it.

* * *

"Sniper fire!" Crowsby barked at his men. "Mount up boys. Let's go get 'em."

"Weapons hot, full auto!" he unnecessarily added.

* * *

It's funny, but after dealing with those three, dealing with ordinary .50 cal. sniper fire seemed like child's play. Here I was, hop-skip-translocating toward where the sniper fire was coming from. Being that they had to be at least a kilometer out, I hoped my suit's camouflage would give them fits. I also knew that at least half of them might be able to spot me by my occasionally appearing, blurring shadow. Nonetheless, I charged forward, on the hunt for sharpshooters lying along the surrounding grassy ridge.

* * *

The first sniper Crowsby "accidentally" ran over. In his ghillie suit, he had been hard to spot. When he stopped the vehicle, Joshua dismounted and mercifully put a bullet in the unfortunate's head, took his weapon, and mounted up so his commander could continue looking for more.

* * *

After taking out my fifth sniper, I felt more than heard the rumbling sound of a C-130 Hercules transport plane laboring overhead. But what really got my attention was that its cargo ramp was down and that meant that someone or thing was in the process of being deployed. Then I saw it, the rolling cart, the coffin-sized object that separated from it, and the opening drag-chute.

My blood froze.

They've dropped a thermobaric fuel-air bomb ... My God ... They want to wipe the entire plain clean ... And they don't give a shit who they kill in the process.

Never before in my life did I translocate so fast away from that absolute horror of a weapon. The desert blurred around me. Miraculously, my numbed foot returned to service. Time slowed. My body ached from the strain. Maybe because I had reached Warp Nine. I didn't know. I just kept launching myself away from a blast zone that I knew for a fact would be a real bitch to survive. When it finally went off, I was in mid-transit and so I performed an artistic cart wheel in the air, only to pile in head over heels like a rag doll.

*   *   *

With Crowsby at the wheel, he saw the air drop first and reflexively jerked the vehicle away from it, causing Paul to rant.

"What the hell are you doing?"

Turning to his subordinate, he shouted in his face, "Shut the fuck up and pray we survive! They've dropped a daisy-cutter!"

Moments later the concussion moved their world sideways, shortly followed by the fuel-air fireball.

*   *   *

I survived, somehow.

While brushing off Lord knows how much sand and vegetation, I gazed back at the already breaking up, fireball's mushroom cloud in the distance. I thought about what I had just outrun—the most powerful device short of a tactical nuke. Hell, when I in the Marines, we trained with a version called the BLU-118/B, and they used it for clearing minefields a quarter mile at a time. Somebody clearly wanted to pulverize that desert plain real bad.

I took an inventory and found myself intact. Only then did I realize how far away I was, and immediately, frantically, thought about my mates.

I found their totaled and overturned vehicle several minutes later. All were more than just slightly crispy from the fireball. At the sight of them, I got angry. Then I gathered them together, hugged each, ignoring their wretched state, and whispered some words of a thankful farewell to friends forever lost.

Remarkably, one water bottle had not exploded in that concussive blast. I drained it in mere moments, sat down, and slouched against a displaced wheel waiting for the post-action adrenalin shock to hit me. Then I heard it, faintly, as my ears were still ringing. Ian's satellite radio was on and receiving something. Frantically I scrambled around on all fours trying to find it. I ended up prying it out of Ian's fingers.

"TIIIS team, come in. This is Stormbird. Over."

Stormbird was our Gulfstream 528's call-sign. I listened to its desperate call three times before I choked out.

"Stormbird. This is Stone. We have three KIAs and no land transport. Over."

"Stormbird acknowledges. Three KIAs and no land transport. Stay put at your location. Your GPS is wall-to-wall. Cavalry is on the way. Over."

*   *   *

There were forty paranormal witnesses at the contest—in addition to the tribune. They, as one, recorded the events of that day. From their vantage they saw it all, every detail, every treacherous act captured on video. They also saw the TIIIS Lictor of Magic escape and then return to his fallen retinue. They all sensed his freely gifted tears of anguish, his doting care over their remains. Meanwhile, no effort was made whatsoever by the plaintiff to do the same for their champions.

CHAPTER 35
An Unexpected Outcome

Much like the ripples formed when a pebble strikes a mirrored pond, so did the outcome in the Aralkum Desert reverberate and cascade throughout the paranormal communities of the world. Actions with this crowd count far more than the sycophantic judgments of a politically stacked tribunal. Additionally, the many explicit and implicit disadvantages placed against the defendant, and in particular, its champion, framed the contest more as an act of vendetta than true justice.

Those with any wits could not help but notice that CMES chose three champions to defend their injuries. Yet none came from within CMES' own ranks. All were non-aligned contractors.

"Why was that?" those with wits asked. Logic suggested that either CMES didn't possess anyone within their Gathering who could best the TIIIS Lictor of Magic, or, perhaps, their position as plaintiff in this legal action was contrived, baseless, and, hence, not worth potentially sacrificing one of their own. Either conclusion damned CMES' vaunted reputation, or perhaps better stated, what was left of it.

Another revelation from the contest in the desert regarded CMES' blood-lust and disregard for the tribunal's Rules of the Contest. With their three champions defeated, CMES' subsequent use of a sniper team, and, when that failed, a bomb drop, plunged the paranormal world, and most of CMES' own treaty-bound allies, into rebellion at the blatant treachery.

Rules of the Contest nit-pickers scoffed at CMES'

imaginative bending of those rules, when it came to their interpretation of what constituted the First Mover. Yes, they said, the tribunal had not specifically stated that there was to be only one, single, First Mover. But by the time these nit-pickers stood to declare their outrage, matters had already moved on to the far more serious charges of *crassus perfidiae*, "excessive treachery," and *summa iniquitatem*, "extreme lawlessness," which were being leveled squarely at CMES and its leadership.

The discussions did not stop there, however, for the entire composition of the tribunal had been brought into question. Again, those with wits quickly noted how many of the tribunal were in fact currently aligned members of CMES, instead of neutral parties. The putrid smell of cankerous cronyism and pestilential decay now wafted across the paranormal Internet. Rife snickering and even comparisons were made to the previous century's mayoral politics of Chicago.

As for the tribunal's selection of the Aralkum Desert, many openly challenged its purposely inconvenient location, not to mention, its rather checkered history as an ecological disaster and radioactive wasteland. But when events unfolded, even the totally witless breathlessly saw the blatant collusion between the tribunal and CMES' intent to rid itself of an irritant "at all costs."

All of these observations, however, coalesced into the global impression that the entire contest, and especially its tribunal, was nothing more than cheap, rigged theatre. A tawdry spectacle arranged specifically for the purpose of drawing out an allusive opponent, all to orchestrate his wonton destruction. What many found delicious was the fact that the sacrificial victim had not cooperated with this preordained fate. Among those, many quietly cheered for the underdog.

*   *   *

Naturally, President Silver Moon was livid with the entire course of events. Yet, across the entire planet, she could not ignore the tremendous outpouring of support and the tsunami-like shift of defecting members and non-aligned organizations. Many flocked to TIIIS' banner, applying for full membership, wishing for a full alliance, or at the very least, making generous offers of *bona fides*, "good will."

The "Farce in the Desert," as the contest came to be known, represented a public relations coup and membership blitz the likes of which TIIIS had never before experienced, and was ill-prepared to deal with. But as with any must-have commercial product, the consumers stood patiently in line, and endured TIIIS' careful selection process, all because they *believed* in its value.

*   *   *

The long flight back was not a satisfying one. I fought off dehydration, was speckled black and blue, and itchy from sand flea bites, but that was about all. Sadly, I lost my Bone Sword, but far worse, three comrades. Check that—three friends, now accompanied me home in body bags. I was not a happy camper.

My night arrival at the Arnold Palmer Regional Airport I will never forget. Stormbird was directed to a darkened hanger, and once inside, its vast bay doors quickly sealed. Then bright flood lights bathed the airframe.

As I started down the stairs, all was silent. Looking around, there were easily one hundred rigid, silent figures arrayed around the fuselage. Many of the faces, I recognized, many not. Some manned three carts to collect the fallen. Mr. Henry, of all people, met me at the base of the stairs with tears freely streaming down his craggy face. At his fatherly embrace my knees almost buckled, but like so many times, he caught me to free me from any embarrassment.

Next, came a firm-faced, but red-eyed President Silver Moon. Her embrace, her physical touch, transmitted a level of psychic contact that shook me to my very core.

"Welcome home, J.J.," she whispered in close.

That was the first time she had ever called me by my nick-name.

Thereafter, a long line of well-wishers continued— John Running Deer, *Monsieur* Dexter, Josh Remington, and on, and on.

And Mel. Frankly, I was more than glad to see her.

With me out of the way, ten kilted bagpipers, resplendent in a variety of tartans, fired up a soulful dirge. They filled the hanger with their soulful, heart-tugging paeans, creating a mournful symphony for welcoming home the dead. As I said before, I will never forget that arrival. There wasn't a dry eye in the house.

Afterwards, Mel stole me away for the journey back to the Academy. With the afterglow of the hanger ceremony behind us, I reached out, took her by the waist, squeezed her tight, and broke down. In response, she smoothed me with kisses, whispered words of everlasting endearment. She soothed me until my shakes went away.

"J.J.," the doe-eyed Alexandrian finally said, "You have become something of a sensation in the paranormal community. Did you know that?"

"What do you mean?"

"Since the contest, our society's diplomatic channels have been swamped with well-wishes directed at you, even marriage proposals; you name it.

"And, I might add, because of your heroic actions, many others wish to become part of the TIIIS family."

"You don't say," I said with a smile.

"And there's more. You now have fans."

"Does that make you one of my fans, too?"

"Indeed, mighty Lictor of Magic. I am yours to do with as you please," she said with eyes that could melt an iceberg.

I think I sat there open-mouthed for at least—well, I don't know how long. Meanwhile, Mel just sat next to me looking more and more beautiful by the second. Her smooth golden complexion, dark hair and eyes, and svelte bearing drove me crazy.

Then I said, "Do you have any idea how dangerous it is to be married to a Lictor of Magic? What sure peril you put yourself into?"

"Yes, J.J., I do. And I don't give a damn, because you're worth it."

CHAPTER 36
A Prize Find

As long as there has been human conflict, scavengers have benefited. Be it the biomass gleaned by the industry of crows, vultures, flies, and their offspring, or of humanity, which recycles whatever it deems valuable.

Today, the pinnacle of humanity's respectable scavengers is represented by the university-trained archaeologist. Proud, gritty, imaginative, and sometimes painfully aloof, these credentialed grave robbers examine the garbage of those who came before. Their published findings describe to the millimeter and pixel, and then dare in dense narrative an interpretation for the curious, extraordinary, or just plain pedestrian.

Professor Amelia Mazor, however, was a special sort of archaeologist. Being a shirt-tail paranormal member-in-good-standing with ACME, she was a living and breathing divining rod—a handy talent in her profession. As a member of the Israeli intelligence organization, Mossad, her talents made Mazor the go-to person on bomb detection, and a host of other things.

While Mazor the academic published widely on the lurid subjects of Sodom and Gomorrah, her archaeological research specifically delved into the destructive power of Hell's Own Fire, a phenomenon that she found evidence of in the near-vitrified ruins of several ancient Near Eastern tell sites. Because of this resume, the Israeli had been called in by CMES to inspect the ruins of the Gathering building in Manhattan. Based upon her assessment, Mazor positively reported that indeed Hell's Own Fire, an ancient Near Eastern magical weapon of frightening proportions, had caused the destruction. But that was before the Farce in the Aralkum Desert and her clan's decision to become a treaty-bound ally of TIIIS.

Now, here she was in the Aralkum Desert, on a personal contract executed by Oleg Gundersen's kin to find and retrieve his remains.

*   *   *

Travel to and within Kazakhstan was an absolute bitch. Now imagine the paperwork required for the retrieval of human remains.

Next, any tourist visit is limited to fifteen days, unless further paperwork is submitted. Given the country's paucity of transportation infrastructure, any travel across the country's broad expanses exceeded this time limit. Hence the need for a visa and several other miscellaneous slips of paper, required their important bureaucratic stamps.

Visas for someone like Mazor were nasty documents as they required a legal declaration that outlined the reason for the visit and one's occupation. Needless to say, the Kazakh authorities remained extremely leery of archaeologists, which for them was just a fancy term for a looter of their cultural heritage. This bureaucratic mindset in no way reflected upon what occurred while the country was a member of the Soviet Block.

Commercial flights in and out of the country were as scarce as hen's teeth and operated rarely, if ever, on schedule. When seats could be found, they were on airframes with dubious maintenance schedules. When planes fly, they must also land. Airports, as a consequence, were a direct reflection of the finely cared for and maintained aircraft that visited them.

Once in-country, the tourist is confronted with the crapshoot of securing in-country land transport. Vehicle reliability was never a question to ask about, much less amenities. If any vehicle can be rented, the transaction usually involved the exchange of several thick rolls of Kazakhstani Tenge, which did not include the driver's cut, the cost of fuel, nor of any repairs that are guaranteed to occur.

*   *   *

The cloudless Aralkum Desert in late October turned out to be not as brutal as Mazor anticipated, which widely ranged between 37 and 60 degrees Fahrenheit. What those figures did not take into account, however, was the ever-present wind and its bone chilling effects. But Mazor came prepared.

After calling in several favors owed and some serious bribery, the Israeli archaeologist finally got her hands on the coordinates that Stone had been instructed to occupy during the Farce. Now standing on them, she could sense the horror, tension, and anticipation of the moment. It was almost as if Stone had pissed himself, and now Mazor was picking up the latent scent of raw fear and adrenalin. Perhaps he had.

Spreading out her arms wide with fingers splayed, the slim archaeologist closed her brown eyes and felt for Gundersen's remains. In one of her pockets, a braid of the man's hair, aided her in her quest. It was a slow and patient process, one not to be rushed or hurried.

"Ah," Mazor whispered to the wind as a wisp of

her dark auburn hair tickled the tip of her nose, "there you are my friend," as the tingling in her fingertips registered a hit. Still with eyes closed, the archaeologist began shuffling slowly forward kicking up dust and sand. Slowly moving this way and that, she homed in. When the tingling became electric, the Israeli stopped, let her arms drop, and opened her eyes.

Looking down before her feet only smooth sand and dust could be seen.

"Time to dig, Amelia," she said as she fell to her knees, removing her backpack.

She removed her favorite folding military shovel and got down to work. It didn't take long before the archaeologist came upon the partially decayed and reeking remains of what once must have been a magnificent specimen. His spec sheet had said that he was six foot seven and from what she could see there was no reason to doubt it. Mazor reached into her pack and pulled out a pair of Latex gloves and a scented surgical mask.

Snapping them on, she began the grisly task of uncovering the decaying body. But before Amelia began the process of bagging the body for transport, Mazor came across an artifact that stopped her cold. Buried deeply in the corpse's upper left rib cage was a sword unlike anything she had ever seen before. Grabbing its handle with both hands, she could not dislodge it. So Mazor stood up, braced a foot against the remains, and wrenched it first this way and that. Finally, and after considerable grunting, the sword came free.

Standing with the sword, the archaeologist swung it several times to get a sense of its balance, which the qualitative side of her brain judged as superb. But what truly impressed Mazor was its perceived lightness, for it seemed to weigh but a feather, which, intellectually, she knew was pure hogwash. Now testing its edge with a low swing through a grassy tuft, the Israeli shook her head in admiration.

"This is damn sharp, dangerously so." As she carefully laid it aside beside her pack. Then she went back to the grisly task of bagging Gundersen's remains.

*   *   *

At the Kazakh custom's checkpoint, Mazor presented her papers, backpack, and the body bag for inspection. While the official made quite a scene of tearing apart the woman's backpack and displaying all of its contents on the stainless-steel table, he dared not touch the body bag both because of its latent stench and out of pure superstition, which the canny archaeologist had counted on.

*   *   *

Upon arriving in Stockholm's Arlanda Airport, Mazor was greeted by Gundersen's teary-eyed family—all near-giants themselves. The man's body bag, now sealed yet again, but this time within an airtight airline approved version, was directly transferred to the cart of an undertaker. The Israeli saw this, understood, but took the mortician aside.

"Within this burial bag you will find a very sharp and dangerous object. That object is mine. Do you understand?"

A thoughtful head nod, "*Ja.*"

Handing the man a business card, Mazor continued, "I want you to send this object to this address in New York, to the Israeli Embassy. I work there."

Then she handed the man a thick envelope. "In this envelope is ten thousand dollars, American. I believe that will cover the postage. Do you agree to this arrangement?"

"*Ja, gut*, I will do this thing."

One week later a long map tube about four inches in diameter arrived at the Israeli Embassy on Second Avenue in Manhattan. Mazor, twitching in anticipation and again with surgical gloves on, opened the seal at one end, experienced a gush of putrid air, gagged, and then pulled out a cylinder of bubble wrap. After removing about ten feet of the wrap, the gory sword lay before her.

"Time to clean you up big fella," The archaeologist said as she marched the sword over to a work bench in her laboratory. Placing it on a long pad for the purpose, Mazor attacked it with cotton balls soaked in rubbing alcohol and after a half hour's labor had the object clean and shiny. Best of all, it no longer stank.

But in the process of this careful cleaning, Amelia noted two odd things. Most glaring was that the blade was coated with a material the color of bone flecked with what appeared to be silver inclusions, instead of raw steel. The other strange characteristic was that the guard and grip changed color. At first she thought that she was just imagining it, but no, both perfectly mimicked their surroundings.

Is this sword enchanted? Mazor wondered.

So she stripped off her Latex gloves and slowly

passed her fingertips over the sword without actually touching it. Sensing absolutely nothing, she sat back.

Is this sword made with a new technology that I'm not aware of?

Impulsively, she reached out and picked up the sword by its grip and psychically received what amounted to a massive electrical shock. Reflexively, her hand spasmed open and she immediately dropped the sword back onto its padding.

Wowza! What was that!

Never ever have I heard of a weapon that was imprinted with its owner's personality. Enchanted weaponry, yes, there are plenty of those; even biometric fingerprint guns. But this was an individual's raw psychic energy, as if the sword was a storage battery. Just by holding it I got the shock of my life.

Now leaning against the work bench while gazing down at the subtle curve of its blade, Mazor reflected.

Without doubt this is Stone's weapon, which in the heat of battle or impending doom he discarded on the battlefield. My God, I can almost smell his adrenalin-rich sweat from that intense confrontation.

Mazor made a decision.

I've got to return this. It is totally useless to anyone else. Any attempt to sell it on the black market would be sheer idiocy. Besides, it would mean my banishment from my clan as we are now treaty-bound allies of TIIIS.

*　*　*

"Mr. Stone, this is Josh Remington of IT and Security."

"Josh! Great to hear from you. What's up in your neck-of-the-woods?"

"It seems that one of our new allies found something that you left behind in the Aralkum Desert. They want to return it to you."

Pause.

"You don't say."

"Yes, sir. They want to know if you can pick it up personally. They mentioned something about it being 'imprinted.'"

"Where are they located, Josh?"

"Where else? Manhattan. The Israeli Embassy."

"Josh, can you do me a favor."

"Shoot, Mr. Stone."

"I'll be there in two days' time. Tell them that I'll show up at eleven in the morning, and will take their representative out for lunch."

"Will do, Mr. Stone. I will relay the message."

"And Josh …"

"Yes, sir."

"Remember that lunch I took you to?"

"Yes, sir. I do. It was a blast."

"Okay, once again and repeat after me, my name is J.J."

"Yes, sir. Got it."

*　*　*

I drove from the Academy to Philadelphia, where I caught a train to Manhattan. Why? For one I needed the space for my body. For another, I've found train travel to be restful. Besides, Mel wanted me to read this book written by a guy named Ikenberry. So I did, to pass the time. On top of that, taking the train made for less hassle with my secured black leather sword case, which held only a scabbard and its shoulder webbing.

After arriving at Union Station, I grabbed a cab and gave the driver the address, 800 Second Avenue. He briefly paused, looked back at me in his rearview mirror, our eyes momentarily locked, and he said with a smile, "Welcome to New York."

The ride was quick. We rode in silence. Clearly, this guy knew how to get around. When it came time to pay up, the cabbie said, "Don't worry, Mr. Stone, this ride is on us."

Flabbergasted, I got out, and asked, "How did you know my name? And, who's 'us'?"

That earned me a big toothy grin from the swarthy young man. "Dude. You've got serious fans. Have a nice day." I stuffed ten bucks in his pocket anyhow and off he drove into the maelstrom that is Manhattan traffic.

To say that the Israelis take security to another level would be an understatement. Let's us just say both me and my leather sword case were carefully vetted, like at the molecular level. After that I was escorted high up into the building by two uniformed and armed security guards who, while polite, were not people to mess with. Arriving at the sixth floor, I was led by them past a security desk and down a hallway to a door that simply said LABORATORY. There, one of them knocked twice on its milky glass, and we waited until this little, itsy bit of a lady in a white lab coat opened the door, smiled, and said, "Thank you, gentlemen. I can take it from here."

As the security guards peeled off, she said while extending her hand, "Welcome, Mr. Stone. My name is Doctor Amelia Mazor. I have been looking forward to meeting you. Please come into my 'laboratory,'" she said with a flourishing gesture and a really good Boris Karlov accent.

Interesting ...

"Follow me," she said over her shoulder. I did and there she was, resting easy on a tufted pad, looking all shiny and new: my Bone Sword.

"How did you find it?" I asked with genuine curiosity.

"Mr. Stone, I'm an archaeologist. That's what we do," she said looking up at me with a broad grin. "But to be fair, I was on a contract to recover the remains of one of the other champions. I came across your sword by accident as it was firmly embedded in his rib cage." She stated with a cool clinical detachment.

Yeah, I remember that guy. He was a monster.

Dr. Mazor then continued. "That sword, Mr. Stone, is quite unique. Do you want to tell me about it?"

At that precise moment, my stomach growled quite loudly. I excused myself and said, "Well, how about this, Dr. Mazor: let's go to lunch and I'll tell you all about it."

Clearly pleased with my answer, she said, "Let me get my coat."

While she did that, my Bone Sword mated once again with its scabbard with a satisfying *snick*, and both were placed within my secured carrying case. Frankly, at holding it, it felt like an old lost friend who had been found.

Damn, girl. You are a beauty!

*   *   *

I hailed a cab and off we went to an address in Little Italy that was highly regarded by Mr. Henry and Mel.

In fact, when we entered the tiny place, both of them were already there. And from what I could see, they had enjoyed at least one glass of red wine each. How could I tell? The bottle was missing a third of its contents and Mr. Henry's cheeks were slightly flushed. Who knew that he liked that stuff?

Amelia Mazor, however, I could tell was taken aback as she started slightly and glanced up at me with a questioning look, when she saw that our lunch was not to be us alone.

After introductions were made, we sat down, Mel poured two more glasses of wine, and only then did Mr. Henry run with it.

"Doctor Mazor, my name is Henry Johnson and I wish to apologize on the behalf of our society for this surprise meeting. We just want to keep our conversation private and between allies. While we respect and wish only the very best relations with your nation's government and its security organization, some things, frankly, they should not be privy to."

"I think … I understand," a hesitant Mazor said.

"Wonderful!" Mr. Henry said effusively. "I do so hate misunderstandings. They lead to unnecessary bad blood."

"Sooo, Mr. Johnson, what indeed is the purpose of this lunch meeting?" Mazor probed.

"Several things, actually. First, to thank you and your nation for retrieving something quite valuable to our society. That, I believe, has been accomplished."

I nodded silently in confirmation.

"Second, we request that you do not reveal to your government anything about the object's unique qualities. Is that possible?"

"Mr. Johnson, sir, what you ask … it puts me in a very precarious position."

"Indeed, madam, it surely does, but the mere knowledge that paranormal technology exists is a far cry different from nuclear, or even biological, intelligence."

"Are you implying that my government would misuse such a technology?"

"Whether at a governmental or institutional level, most certainly. I can easily imagine any number of excuses that could be fabricated to justify the use of paranormal technology. And, I am equally sure that you can as well.

"So, Professor Mazor, can we count on your silence?"

In response, Mazor's shoulders dejectedly fell as she looked down, paused, and then reached into her purse. She held in her palm a tiny thumb drive.

"Here, Mr. Johnson, are my notes and images on that magnificent sword. That is my only copy and I recorded those on a device that I can readily destroy. Frankly, sir, I knew as soon as I found it, that it would come down to this … this difficult decision between our two worlds—the mortal and paranormal, and what was best for each."

Accepting the thumb drive, Mr. Johnson softly said. "Thank you, Professor Mazor. I agree, sometimes our most difficult decisions have nothing to do with national or institutional interests. I freely acknowledge that they have far-reaching consequences than most politicians are incapable of even understanding.

"That said, you need something from us to give back to your superiors; something to satisfy both your government *and* the fine security organization you quietly work for."

Mr. Johnson's slight emphasis on the connective caused Mazor's eyes to widen in surprise. Then I read her mind.

How can he know that?

"So please tell the appropriate individual or individuals that we, our society, owe them a big favor. And this is not me, speaking, I am directly paraphrasing our society's president, President Betsy Silver Moon's, own words.

"Kindly impress upon them that they now own a blue chip in the high-stakes game of life. That they can count on us. That they can trust us to come through for them whenever they choose to redeem that blue chip.

"Do you think that will do?"

"While I cannot speak for them, I believe your approach is sound."

"Now, can we order something, so J.J.'s stomach will stop complaining?" Mel said.

And at that very moment four calamari appetizers appeared as if by magic.

CHAPTER 37
Payback Is a Bitch

Pam Oliver, who hailed from the Hamptons, did not appreciate her sudden eviction from the Gathering. After all, she had blown a good portion of her inheritance to join because of its exclusivity, to find herself, and yes, to also spite her parents. Mid-twenties, a failed six-year project of a fancy New Hampshire college, and unashamed Goth, Pam didn't fit in with the family's country club set—hence the attraction of the Gathering. But what Pam's parents didn't know about their dear dimpled darling was that she possessed paranormal abilities—useful stuff like telepathy and understanding auras. Those talents revealed to Pam what people really thought about her, while their auras told more about their moral character than most were willing to admit. Frankly, what the woman saw on a daily basis scared the hell out of her. But at the Gathering, she fit in. There, Pam discovered that she wasn't a freak. As a result, she discovered that her Goth look wasn't working. Instead, it actually held her back from finding her true self—that of a witch.

With the fall of the Gathering and despondent about her prospects, Pam purposely wandered the streets of Manhattan, viewing auras and reading minds. Somehow, she had to pay the rent on her postage-stamp flat. She had angled, found a good job in tech, and got comfortably by. But it wasn't enough. On the side Pam became a watcher for CMES. Anything that she noted worthwhile, paid well.

One day Pam, with a to-go slice of pizza in hand,

was leaving Patsy's Pizzeria on Second Avenue, when she saw this giant of a man getting out of a yellow cab in front of the Israeli Embassy. Briefly, they locked eyes. What stopped Pam dead in her tracks was his bright electrum aura, a hue that she had never before seen. She admitted to herself that she trembled at seeing it, because it was so awesomely beautiful. Then a little voice said something in her head, it clicked, and she made a call.

*   *   *

Kiel rushed over to DeSalvo's gray metal desk.

"Mr. DeSalvo, Stone has been spotted in mid-town Manhattan," the former spook gasped out.

Putting down his pen and looking up, "When?"

"Three minutes ago. He entered the Israeli Embassy on Second Ave."

"Who spotted him?" DeSalvo asked with a rising voice.

"One of our street watchers named Pam Oliver."

The Roman now commanded, "Call her back. Tell her to stay on the scene. Meanwhile, put together a yellow cab with three of our people to meet her.

"This could be the chance of a lifetime, Kiel. Don't blow it."

*   *   *

The palms of Pete the driver were sweating as he worked his way through the pre-lunch hour traffic. Even so, and after who knows how many yellow stop lights, it took the three hit men twenty minutes to traverse from the West Side warehouse's parking lot to the Israeli Embassy over on Second Avenue.

Throughout, one of them was in constant contact with the watcher on the scene, who religiously checked in every thirty seconds with a status update. As they pulled up to the curb in front of the pizzeria, one of the men in the back seat spotted this reasonably attractive woman with a smart phone glued to her ear. He leaned out of the curbside window and asked, "Are you Oliver."

"Why yes, yes I am," said the excited voice. "Who are you?"

"I'm Roger, the guy on the phone."

"Oh, cool. He's still in the embassy, Roger," Pam said with genuine relief.

"Okay. Good job, Oliver. And thanks for looking out for us," the rugged looking man said, reaching out with a handshake. "In times like these, every little bit helps. We got this now. And thanks again."

With a satisfied smile and a wave goodbye Pam Oliver blithefully went on her way, knowing that she had done something important. She now felt a part of something greater—the direct telepathic bidding of the Devourer of Souls, who had so easily manipulated the woman's mind.

*   *   *

Their cab sat in front of a pizzeria idling, while they waited for their extremely high value target to appear from across the street.

"You guys know that you can't just spray him on the sidewalk of Second Avenue," Pete the driver said to his two companions in the back seat.

"Why not?" challenged Roger.

"Because idiot, that is the Israeli Embassy," Pete the driver lectured. "The area is loaded with cameras. And, if Stone walks out from their turf and is gunned down, we'll have Mossad all over us. No thanks. Besides, look at the traffic. It's almost noon. We'd be better off running to the subway, then trying to escape in this pig of a cab."

"Good point," the third man chimed in. His name was Karl.

"So what's the plan, Sam?" Roger wanted to know.

"We'll follow 'em. And when we find a good place, we'll finish our job," Peter the driver reasoned.

"Heads up, there he is. He's a big mother fucker. He's carrying something. Looks like a short gun case," Pete the driver said while craning his neck around looking for an opening in the traffic and seeing none.

"There are two of them," Karl said. "Fifty bucks says the woman is Mossad."

"How can you tell?" Roger asked.

"She just looks like trouble," Karl observed.

They watched while the couple hailed a yellow cab just like theirs.

"Roger, write down that cabbie's number, just in case," Pete the driver ordered, and as luck would have it, a rare break in the traffic allowed them to merge and pull a U-turn across the solid white line.

After a couple of minutes, Karl said, "Fifty bucks that they're going to Little Italy."

"Why there?" Roger wanted to know.

"Gut feeling."

Well, it really wasn't a "gut feeling" for Karl, for he was an extremely powerful telepath, which made him perfect for tailing people. After all, fifty bucks was fifty bucks and Karl saw no sense in advertising why his hunches were so good.

It took a good twenty minutes to get to Little Italy because the traffic was as thick as molasses on Second Avenue South and Houston.

"Back off, Pete," Karl said from the back seat. "That cab is trying to pull over. Yeah, that's what he's doing."

As the couple got out and paid their fare, the two in the back seat ducked down. Only Peter the driver actually saw them enter the restaurant.

"Okay. Now we have to wait this one out," Pete the driver said. "Roger, how about you get out and grab us something quick to eat?"

*　*　*

After a long wait and several "friendly" conversations with the same roving meter maid, not two, but four targets emerged from the restaurant.

"Who are all those guys?" Roger asked.

"Oh boy, guys, we've hit the jackpot," Karl said. "That old guy is Henry Johnson, a Fourth-Level Adept and a real, live mother-fucker. The brunette woman next to him is a white witch and Stone's wife. Her last name is something like Maki or Markus."

While Karl was telling his colleagues of their good fortune, Stone hailed a cab initially for Dr. Mazor. On a last-minute whim, Mel got in and joined her. In a flash, the cab took off, with the two women waving goodbye.

"So, which do we go for? The guys or the gals?" Roger asked.

"Stone and Johnson are our priorities." Pete the driver said.

"Okay, so how about right here?" Roger pressed.

"No," Pete the driver vetoed. "Let's get them in a confined space, like another cab. Then you guys can go to town."

"Makes sense," Karl agreed as he looked down and made sure the receiver on his suppressed .45 caliber ACP assault weapon had a round in it.

The twosome of Mr. Henry and Stone jumped into the back seat of the next yellow cab, with Stone entering last at curbside.

"This is perfect," Roger saw. "Now we've got them."

The first cab moved out, and a second, appearing disinterested, sauntered after it.

"Their heading for Union Station," Karl announced.

"Thanks" Pete the driver said.

As soon as the first cab made a right onto Centre Street heading north, the second did the same, accelerated, and pulled up along on its driver side.

*　　*　　*

Soul Carrier! Duck down! The First Soul screamed into Stone's inner ear. Reflexively, Stone did as he was ordered just as two suppressors from the neighboring cab hosed down with their ride with the coughing hail of sixty suppressed rounds.

Glass exploded.

Metal rent.

Blood spurted.

The cabbie and Mr. Henry, who didn't have a chance, were torn asunder in the opening salvo. The driver's body slumped against the steering wheel and the cab veered right, toward several parked cars and threatened an Asian restaurant.

Stone absorbed no less than fifteen rounds, which struck his left thigh, shoulder, and torso. Two rounds grazed the top of his head and right cheek, all which bled freely, transforming him into a bloody-looking zombie.

The cab itself, crashed to a halt against two parked cars on the right side of the street. The driver's foot still mashed the accelerator. The vehicle's right rear tire spun uncontrollably, enveloping the entire block with the acrid smoke of burnt rubber.

The second yellow cab drove on and disappeared into the northbound traffic.

CHAPTER 38
High Fives All Around

DeSalvo sat behind his gray steel desk in the West Side warehouse in quiet disbelief. Kiel had debriefed each of the three hit men immediately upon their return. He did so separately and in detail. Their stories jived even after Kiel rather painfully probed their minds. It was a skill he didn't often reveal, but in this case, he had to be sure. In all of their minds he saw a bullet riddled yellow cab, from three different perspectives.

"Are you absolutely sure?" the regional director asked the government man standing before him.

"As sure as three men can be," Kiel responded.

DeSalvo slumped in his office chair still unsure. "Do you have people watching the hospitals, the morgues?"

"Yes, sir. Even the neighborhood crisis clinics. If anyone survived that assault, and lived, we would know about it."

"Okay, then. Bonuses for our men. Tell your team 'well done.'"

"Yes, sir. Will do. Anything else?"

A shake of the head. Strangely, DeSalvo still felt the burden of Stone on his shoulders. He knew that he had tested out as a latent psychic, but he shrugged that off. Three men's testimony. Perhaps it was finally true.

"Mr. Kiel."

"Yes sir."

"Who alerted us about Stone being in Manhattan."

"One of our watchers, sir. A woman named Pam Oliver."

"Huh. Make sure that she gets a bonus check, as well. Hell, throw in a free membership for the next ten years. We need more reliable intel like that from the street."

"Will do, sir."

"And Mr. Kiel. Well done."

DeSalvo then dismissed Kiel and stood atop his desk so that all on the warehouse floor could see him.

"Members of our Gathering. I have good news— something rare these days. Stone has been killed!"

The entire floor of some seventy people went bananas at the news.

Returning to his chair, DeSalvo turned to his encrypted laptop. He crafted a brief e-mail, written in such a way that its content appeared innocuous. He told his boss, Chairman Feng Bai, that a platinum-colored Ferrari had been put out of commission. DeSalvo could not bring himself to use the term "dead," because he didn't have the man's body.

*   *   *

While the NYPD controlled the chaos and cordoned off the street, the FDNY used the Jaws of Life on the ruined doors and blood-splattered cab. None of the firemen believed that anyone within could still be alive, but while the sheet metal was being torn away in renting shrieks, one of the victims in the back seat stirred at the sound. Seeing that, the firemen redoubled their efforts and retrieved the lucky soul.

Once in the ambulance, the first responders got to work.

"I've a good pulse, Ricky, but his blood pressure is shocky as hell." Mike said.

"No surprise." Ricky replied, "Look what the dude's been through. I'm starting a saline drip."

Quickly swabbing their patient's blood-caked head, Mike observed. "His head and face wounds are superficial, but that left femur looks a wreck."

"Cut his pants away, Mike. Do a visual."

"Nice wool slacks, what a shame." Then, "Ricky, this dude has on some kind of strange, tightly fitting underwear on that I can't cut away, much less see to cut!"

"Whadda ya' mean? Is it Underarmor?"

"Nope, it sorta changes colors. Blends into the background. Ricky, I'm gonna bag the direct confirmation and just immobilized his left leg in an air splint. Let's leave the fancy undies to the hospital to deal with."

"Yo, Jerry! We have him stabilized. Let's roll!" Ricky shouted to the driver.

As soon as the wagon got rolling, dispatch contacted Jerry and redirected the ambulance to the Israeli Embassy on Second Avenue. Apparently, they had a helicopter and would transport the patient to the nearest hospital from there.

As the bright flashing lights and blaring staccato siren pulled up to the front of the embassy, a small army of heavily armed security and two white-coated doctors greeted them with a gurney.

"Okay guys, move the patient onto our gurney," ordered one of the doctors, a woman, to Ricky and Mike. "Careful with that IV drip!" she hectored, which had been inserted in the patient's neck.

Meanwhile, as the loaded gurney disappeared into the embassy, one of the security officers with short cropped gray-hair gathered the three first responders together.

"Okay guys, thanks for getting your patient here as quickly as you did. You did a fine job. Now, I need a big favor from you. This incident never happened. Got that? Never happened. Are we clear?"

"But what about the paperwork?" Jerry said. "Our time? Supplies?"

The security officer, now stone-faced, sighed heavily, and handed each of the trio a thick envelope. "Forget this mercy trip, gentlemen. That's all my country asks."

*   *   *

The Devourer of Souls faced its disappointment sourly. It had identified the opportunity. Yes, one had died, but his soul was so strong and filled with love that his ascent toward the light realm had already begun. The real prize, the First Soul's damned Soul Carrier, lived on.

"You vex me, foul soul! You caused your simpering carrier to hide behind his friend's shattered body. You coward! You are the one who fears a confrontation! I AM THE STORM! You are but garbage blown upon the wind before me!"

To this ranting, the First Soul responded. "There will be a time, you rotting piece of excrement, when I will walk upon your decayed dust."

*   *   *

Stabilized and heavily medicated because of my injuries, the Israeli's flew me directly to the Academy in less than two hours. All I can say is that must have been some corporate helicopter. I briefly became aware of my situation in mid-flight and hallucinated that I was back on an Apache in Somalia. The flight doctor, an intense woman with striking brown eyes, looked down at me and mouthed slowly.

"You have been injured.

"You're stable.

"We're en route to your Academy.

"Do you understand me?"

I nodded and grunted out, "What about the others?"

At that moment, her eyes softened. "I'm sorry. You were the only survivor."

At hearing that news, I closed my eyes which were awash with tears.

"Mr. Henry ..."

Mercifully, the doctor injected into the IV drip another bolus of sedative.

*　　*　　*

I woke up in a hospital bed, the left side of my body and top of my head heavily wrapped. It hurt to breathe. It hurt to move. It was a flashback to 2003 and my luxury stay on the *USNS Comfort* after that firefight at the cloverleaf in Nasiryiah.

I croaked out, "Where am I?"

The sound of my voice brought the face of a concerned nurse into my narrow field of vision.

"Blink if you can hear me."

So I blinked.

"Are you thirsty?"

Blink.

A bendy straw and a water bottle magically

appeared. I sucked hungrily at the cold liquid.

"Not so fast!" the nurse admonished.

Yeah. No shit. If I started coughing, damn that will hurt.

So I sipped, instead of chugged.

The nurse's face disappeared. I closed my eyes to sigh in relief. Just sucking on the water took the starch out of me. I concluded in my fuzzy head that I must have been really dehydrated.

You were most fortunate, Soul Carrier. You would have died if it weren't for your friend. He shielded you from the worst. The First Soul kindly informed me—the bastard. *What's with me and good friends anyways?*

I felt a soft breeze across my face that caused my eyes to open. There was a red-eyed President Silver Moon looking down on me. Frankly, she looked like shit. And there was Mel, too.

So what must I look like?

"Where am I?"

"At the Academy." Mel said.

"How did I get here?"

"Helicopter."

"Don't remember much about that."

"That's not surprising. You had us worried for quite some time, honey."

"It's bad, isn't it."

An affirmative shake of the head.

"Mr. Henry?"

Another grim shake of the head.

I sighed a very shaky, heaving sigh. And then the tears began to flow.

I choked out a whisper, "Why is it always me? Am I cursed?"

"No, you're not cursed." And then the president placed her two hands on either side of my head, just like she did that first time in Santa Fe. I felt my mind fog up, I relaxed, and fell into a deep sleep.

*   *   *

As this was my first ever serious injury, I found out what patience was. I had to relearn how to walk. I would learn to hate Pilates, but I didn't bitch once about all the plates and screws in my shattered thigh or the aches of my healing ribs and shoulder. I was alive, had a purpose, and was on the mend in a big way.

Two days into my hospitalization at the campus clinic, Mel and President Silver Moon stopped in.

"How are you feeling, honey?" Mel said taking my hand.

"Cruddy. It's just something that I have to fight through."

"Have you seen yourself in a mirror lately?" the president asked.

"Nope, but I probably look like a train wreck."

"Actually, more like a mummy, I have some bad news." Silver Moon said.

I remained silent. *What now?*

"Tomorrow a funeral will take place at the partially completed chapel. There will be two closed caskets— one for Mr. Henry Johnson, and one for yourself. Thereafter, your caskets will be placed in graves with granite markers next to the chapel. Obviously, you cannot attend."

I'm stone, cold, dead. My jaw sagged.

"Yes, J.J., as of tomorrow, you will be officially dead and off the grid. I even crafted your literary obituary that will appear in the *New York Times*. No one on campus, excepting of course your medical and security staff, will know of this most ancient of ruses. I suggest that you grow a beard and dye your blond hair."

"Hmm. I think that you would look quite dashing in a dark beard, my love."

"Wonderful."

"The doctors say," the president interjected, "that you'll need a good six months to recover and rehab. May I suggest that you do so, for I have plans for you, Lictor of Magic. Plans that will vex CMES to no end. All I ask is that you get well, listen to your doctors, and prepare, because when you are ready, I'm going to turn you lose upon the world.

"Deal?"

"You bet!"

The next day I watched my own funeral on the campus live feed. A tearful Mel was there dressed in black. Emotionally, I was a wreck. Heart-felt eulogies were delivered that stung my soul. The loss of Mr. Henry felt like ... I don't know. It just hurt real bad. God ... I just heaved and heaved, trapped in that hospital bed.

CHAPTER 39
Recuperation

After two weeks in a bed, just standing vertical caused the sweat to pop from my forehead, my arms vibrated like tuning forks while supporting my body weight. I felt light-headed. For a guy who had never been injured or sick before, these were new experiences—ones that made a humbling impression. In my current state, I was a sitting duck. President Silver Moon's scheme for me to play dead, now more than ever, made a whole lot of sense. Plus, it protected Mel.

Once the x-rays on my leg came in negative, off I went to the physical therapists, initially once-a-day, later twice, and the grueling process began. I won't comment on the perceived sadism that every patient believes their therapists possess. Instead, I just bit my lip, swore aplenty, and accepted their "attention" as an act of love—as they pushed and drove me back to near normal. But I didn't want to be "near normal." I wanted to be better than before. Besides, I admit I was burying my feelings. I was atoning for my survival. Fortunately, Mel visited me every day. That helped big-time with my isolation.

While I was getting intimately acquainted with a particularly hellish step machine during my first month, I rated my work out by the amount of sweat leaked upon it. It was a childish game, I know, creating those white blotches of salt that I would later mop up. But in my highly focused world, each droplet meant something quite dear.

Frankly, as isolated as I was, even with Mel's

visits, I got hungry to meet a new face. Then, out-of-the-blue, in walked this guy into the therapy room during my third workout of the day. A fit black man with streaks of gray at his temples—sorta like lightning bolts. His demeanor screamed that he was on a mission.

"You're looking well, Mr. Stone—for a dead man," the man said appraisingly. His accent was distinctly something, maybe Australian or New Zealander.

"And who are you?" Puff. "Got clearance to be here?" Puff.

"Indeed, I have. From the good president herself. I'm the new armorer, Mr. Stone. Name's Flynn, with a Y. I was Mr. Loomis' protégé."

"Right." Puff.

"I want to know about the injuries that you've sustained, Mr. Stone. I have half a mind to modify your UCS to prevent them in the future. Do you have a moment?"

I looked down at the step machine's dash and saw a minute, fifty-eight seconds left. "Almost finished"—puff—"Mr. Flynn." Puff. "Then we'll talk. Take a seat."

Finished, I plopped down in the chair opposite, the one usually occupied by one of my loving therapists, smiled in relief from beneath the towel over my head, and said, "Shoot," while I gathered myself.

"First off, that's a fine beard. It does indeed throw one off. As your armorer, sir, I am responsible for your welfare when it comes to the construction and fitting of your UCS. Clearly, the former suit saved you, but fell short in some ways. Tell me what you think it needs to be better."

"To be brutally honest, it's too flexible. While it provides me with a nearly impermeable second skin, it transmits shock instead of dampening it. Yeah, I know it's padded, but it isn't enough. My torso gets hammered, my shoulders, too."

While I spoke Flynn took notes, then he flipped over a sheet and began sketching a figure. Frankly, the man was an artist.

When he was finished, he said, "Mr. Stone, you're in luck. Technology relentlessly marches on. In your specific case, something called forged composite just might do the trick. Both Callaway Golf and Lamborghini pioneered the material and technique. Take a look at this."

I did, and what I saw looked like the body armor of an alligator. "How flexible would that configuration be?"

"Oh, quite. Such a design would provide you with far more resistance to internal injury. Imagine it this way—your old UCS with grafted on molded plates that interlock. Further, with these plates we can better protect your spine, back, thighs, forelegs, and arms."

"What about heavy rounds? How would those plates hold up? What would their impact feel like?"

"Currently, forged composite is being used for racing wheels and rims, so the material is extremely stout. The impact of heavy rounds will be spread over a greater area. Take a heavy .45 round, it will still hurt like the dickens, will still put you on the ground, but instead of a quarter-size impact, we now have a surface area eight to twelve inches across. We've effectively reduced the impact to light bruising instead of damaged cartilage and bone."

"I like that—a lot."

"Grand. I somehow thought you would. Do you have anything else for me before I rush off to the laboratory?"

"Yeah. I'm left-handed and like to draw my sword from across my back."

"Ah. Good point." Flynn began furiously erasing and sketching. "I can provide you a groove across your back for the scabbard. Any more Christmas wishes?" the man said expectantly.

"No, just that I have the usual provisions for my knife, 9mm, mags, etc."

"Done. Very good, then. I will stop by again in a few weeks' time … and Mr. Stone, I wish you to know that I understand what you are going through. I lost two good friends during the Christmas Eve Raid. Your heroic actions in our defense, sir, will never be forgotten. Ever."

* * *

Later that evening I finally snuck out of the clinic and like a wraith in the night visited, for the first time, the grave of Mr. Henry. I fell to my knees when I confronted the reality of touching his grave marker, and traced its inscription with my fingertips. That emotional act, its finality, delivered quite an emotional message.

I realized that I had nothing to give or leave behind. I came empty handed. Instead, I left my tears.

* * *

With my body well on the mend, I felt the need for a full-on refresher of my other skills. I chose to begin with *Monsieur* Dexter, my magical mentor in offensive and defensive magic. Because of my rather unique status as a dead man, the good Frenchman agreed to meet me at my new quarters within the campus clinic.

"Good morning, *Monsieur* Stone. I am so happy to learn that you are among the living," the man clapped, "and what a magnificent beard, *monsieur*! Your darkened hair color completely transforms you. No longer are you that golden angel, but now a dark and brooding philosopher. I like the new look."

To this assessment, I scowled.

"*Monsieur* Stone," the man chided, "sometimes subterfuge is a requirement, if not an advantageous ploy. Besides, *mon ami*, your appearance is quite emblematic of your darkened aura. It's still quite magnificent, but now it possesses darkened tones that add relief."

After a brief pause, he continued, "And please accept my sincerest condolences regarding *Monsieur* Henry Johnson. I know that you were close. His loss, I can assure you, is felt by all."

"So, why am I here?" the man asked.

"I need a refresher, *Monsieur* Dexter."

"Eh? I see. Then *monsieur*, *en garde!*"

Precisely one hour later, I was a sweat-soaked mess with more new bruises than I am willing to admit. *Monsieur* Dexter, for his part, more than held his own, although I did surprise him several times.

"*Monsieur* Stone," *Monsieur* Dexter said while wiping his brow with a gym towel, "that was a most energetic session."

*   *   *

Next on my list, I pinged Mr. Flynn, our new armorer, who agreed to meet me at the campus clinic.

"Mr. Stone. You are looking well. What can I do for you?"

"Mr. Flynn. I would like a refresher in swordsmanship."

"May I ask why?"

"Your predecessor began my training. I'm not blind to the fact every armorer has their own style, preferences, and skills. I suspect that you have plenty to share."

"When will you be … available?"

"The docs say in two weeks."

"All right, then. So, when are you officially 'coming out' as a member of the living?" Flynn reasonably asked.

"I'm not."

"I see. I'll have to secure a secluded place where we can train. Thank you for the two-weeks heads up. I'll get back to you on that."

The armorer's eyes then appraised me.

"Your body's profile has changed, Mr. Stone. You're leaner. I'll need some measurements for your new UCS. Have a moment?"

"I'm all yours."

Two weeks later, Flynn told me to report early to a glen within the surrounding oak forest. Flynn's e-mail provided the GPS coordinates of the glen, which I could follow on my throw-away smart phone. He also mentioned that I should leave my Bone Sword behind and show up in sweats.

The walk to the appointed location turned out to be a joy. Granted, part of it was because I was loose from the confines of the clinic. I took the same narrow tarmac road that passed the entrance tree to the Pressure Cooker, but this time I continued past and rounded the bend.

The dense oak woods twittered with a variety of bird calls and smelled of decaying leaves, wild flowers, and rich heavy loam. Mother Nature was on full display. My silent approach even spooked several white-tailed deer—a doe with two downy fawns. In many ways the walk reminded me of my rich childhood memories on the ranch.

I followed a freshly-cut path that led off the black topped lane through a dense copse of trees. And there was the glen, a perfect stadium formed by the forest. A heavily padded figure stood waiting in its center. Next to him, I saw a pile of similar gear.

"Good morning, Mr. Flynn," I cheerfully greeted.

"What do you know about *kendo*—'the way of the sword,' Mr. Stone?"

"Zero, zip, nada."

"I thought so. First, let's get you into this padded equipment. Then, I'll begin your education."

It started out so innocently—stance, block, thrust, and block again with a practice sword called a *shinai*—a thin bundle of bamboo with a long, generous, double-griped pommel at one end. After a fashion, Flynn thought nothing of whacking me at every opportunity. Even through the padded equipment, the blows really stung. Now with my attention fully focused, I probed his mind, trying to anticipate his next attack.

"Not so fast Lictor of Magic. That Jedi trick won't work on me!" the man taunted as he attacked again.

I focused now on his aura, which told me

something that I didn't expect—he was grounded, linked to a ley line through his thinly soled leather shoes.

This time I refocused, thinking about the push and pull of combat, the ebb and flow, and allowed the man to come to me, instead of me attempting to bash him. That seemed to work, as now I was blocking everything he did. I waited for an opening, translocated just a few feet to his left, and delivered a good whack across his back.

This infuriated the man, and in his zeal, left himself open twice more.

Then, he signaled for a stoppage. Breathing heavily he said, "Break for water."

I must have guzzled a gallon on my own. While wet with sweat, my stamina I rated okay.

"How do you feel, Mr. Stone?"

"Well exercised, but I'll need a whirlpool for some of your strikes."

"For a man who knows nothing of *kendo*, you're a quite a gamer. How about we meet again in two days, same time, same place. Is that agreeable?"

And for the next two weeks, we learned much about each other, neither giving the other any quarter. On the last day, after an exceptionally vigorous and long session, I realized something. I had forgotten about my left leg, ribs, and shoulder. I was engaging at full force, without pause, and for an extended period of time. Best of all, my reflexes had returned.

"Mr. Flynn, you are ever the devious one."

"Meaning?"

"You successfully challenged me to work past my injuries, and for that I'm most grateful."

"Mr. Stone, that's my job. Now, let's properly fit you up for your new armored UCS."

*   *   *

During my dueling with Mr. Flynn, I finally made a nighttime visit to Mel at our campus apartment. It was the first time since the hit in Manhattan. I was immediately greeted by her explosive, smothering energy. It felt great, normal, and better than any second honeymoon could ever be.

Only later, in a moment of near exhaustion, did I see on the bed stand her family's book of spells, seemingly waiting for me. For some reason I rolled over and picked up the ancient family treasure. With care I opened it, and paged through its many leaves written in Egyptian Demotic, each penned by different hands, finally reaching the end where I found what looked like a long list of names. Even though I cannot read Demotic, I still could make out Mel's name as the last insertion. I reverently ran my fingertips over it.

Then and there I knew that I had to learn to read Demotic.

*   *   *

Contrary to everything that my physician's said, I was raring to go in a little over four months. Physically, I felt at my peak as a leaner version of my former self. The two weeks of *kendo*, in addition to all of my therapy sessions, had worked wonders. And so had Mel's support.

The next day I had just finished a grueling therapy session and was still moist from my shower, when I heard a knock at my door. It was President Silver Moon.

I offered her my only chair and the president opened with, "As I understand from Mr. Flynn, you have become quite the swordsman."

"Madam President, the man beat the devil out of me."

"So he says. It is quite apparent that you've slimmed down some. How does the UCS fit?"

"Beautifully—the armor does not hinder any movement or bind whatsoever. In all respects, Flynn is a genius."

"And *Monsieur* Dexter, who incidentally is unabashedly a big fan of yours, reports much the same. So, J.J., how do you feel?"

"Ready."

"Good, because I have quite an agenda for you to fulfill. And if you're even half successful, you will put the fear of God into CMES."

"What do you have in mind, Madam President?"

CHAPTER 40
West Side Renovation

Following the tragic death of my good friend Mr. Henry, I became Death. Bearded and with long, flowing dark hair, I was no longer the brooding philosopher of *Monsieur* Dexter's imagination. Rather, I became a man with a tight and narrow focus, much like a race car driver entering a high-speed turn, floating in the tight seat's harness under heavy deceleration, all the while manipulating three pedals, a stick, and a wheel.

Strangely, my spiritual tenant, the First Soul, was good with the situation. In fact, if he had had hands, he would have rubbed them together in anticipation, or simply applauded. For many dark souls had crossed over into the mortal realm, who had absolutely no business being there. They, in point of fact, were cosmic interlopers who had taken advantage of the rift between the dark and mortal realms before I closed it. Now trapped in the mortal realm, their culling was needed. Balance had to be restored.

My society granted me the means and support to wreak havoc upon CMES and its darkest minions. All I had to do was execute. What CMES was about to experience hadn't occurred since the sack of their beloved Mother Ur so very long ago. It was time for a reprise, and I was fine to be the instrument.

In anticipation of any knee-jerk reactions by CMES on account of my predations, President Silver Moon evacuated all non-essential personnel from the Old Oaks Academy's campus. She sent them all west, sprinkling them throughout the Midwest, TIIIS' Illinois facility, and sent some as far as Santa Fe. That's where Mel ended up. A mass purchase of used cars now filled the campus parking lots in an attempt at subterfuge. Meanwhile, TIIIS' IT and Security hunkered down on full alert awaiting any mischief.

*　　*　　*

"Where do you think CMES has slunk off to?" I asked President Silver Moon as we sat in a busy Times Square Starbuck's drinking coffee. Between my trimmed beard, my dark hair down over my ears and collar, and my Ray-ban aviator sunglasses, I had rendered myself invisible. No facial recognition software could have identified me. If anything, I looked like some Madison Avenue poster boy.

"Most likely somewhere within the Tri-state area." she suggested.

"That's a pretty big footprint," I glumly allowed.

"Okay then, J.J., how do we narrow it down?" she encouraged. "Is there some way to track them? I see so many sketchy auras."

"Nearly six months after we turned their house into a burned-out cinder? Not likely. They've had plenty of time to settle into their new nest," I countered. "If anything, they're holed up in what amounts to a safe house. It'll be well-stocked, something low profile, ordinary, and in a place no one would expect."

"Well, that really narrows it down." Silver Moon sarcastically quipped.

"Facts are facts. We evicted them. Now what did you expect them to do? Run away whimpering on the next flight to Rome lock, stock, and barrel?" I retorted. "If anything, while they're tearing down their former headquarters, they're probably wondering how to evade the wrath of Rome far more than worrying about us. The time is perfect."

"You're right, J.J., our timing couldn't be more perfect," a thoughtful president said. "And J.J., just to be clear, what would you do if we knew their location?"

"I'm not sure," I admitted. "Too many variables."

"Indeed," the president concluded. "And just for the record, that was the precisely right answer. Which takes me back to the question, 'how do we track them'?"

Then, I saw it—a woman with a dark aura, who had just purchased a coffee to go. As she exited the coffee shop, I had this odd feeling, her face was familiar. I got up and said, "Excuse me, Madam President, but Providence just provided us with a possible lead."

*   *   *

Pam Oliver bubbled with delight. Morning coffee in hand, she was off to the subway, and her new full-time tech-gig with the Gathering. Ever since their surprise generosity and membership for her tip on the man with the strangely beautiful aura, Pam had become one of them. Best of all, because of her technical skills, the head of HR hired her on the spot and then helped her with her self-image and clothing choices. In retrospect, Pam now understood the Gothic look had been a defense mechanism; it wasn't her. Now, she felt pretty. The tall dark-haired man who discretely followed her from a distance, Pam never saw because her nose was buried in her device.

*   *   *

It took me several minutes to piece together where I had seen this woman before with her dingy signature aura. And then I had it, it was on Second Avenue, in front of the Israeli Embassy as I got out of the cab, just before I retrieved my Bone Sword from Dr. Mazor, just before that lunch in Little Italy, just before …

But now she wasn't dressed all in black with heavy eye makeup. Someone must have gotten to her, because her appearance had lightened up considerably. Or, J.J., was that Goth-look just her other side? An alter-ego, maybe a cover?

We took the Black Line west toward the Hudson, got off at Eighth Avenue, transferred to the Blue Line south, and finally got off at the 23rd Street/Eighth Avenue station. We emerged on the West Side in a seedy neighborhood. *Perfect.* It was Hell's Kitchen. *Even better.*

Now things got a bit tricky. Stalking in a jungle or forest is relatively easy, move quietly and use cover. But within an urban environment, an entirely different set of rules applied. Stuff like walking on the opposite side of the street, walking with purpose, no eye-contact, and absolutely no Hollywood moves with newspapers-up, or ditching into store fronts or gangways.

She walked west to Eleventh Avenue and then turned north. At this point I had no cover, so I continued on to Tenth Avenue and paralleled her, watching her progress from each corner. At the fifth corner, she disappeared, which meant to me an address on Eleventh Avenue between 27th and 28th Streets. That's all I needed.

* * *

When I called President Silver Moon with what I found, she said that she'd look into it. True to her word, two hours later I got a call.

"J.J., you really shouldn't be traipsing around a neighborhood like that, even in broad daylight. That neighborhood is not the best.

"That said, our recon team found out that a warehouse that takes up the entire block. It's camouflaged as a Con Edison facility. The uniformed security guard at its entrance has the black aura of a demon-possessed. That makes him CMES security and not an electric company employee, all jokes aside. The two-storey building itself is L-shaped with a flat roof. Its parking lot takes up the rest of the block with cyclone fencing screened with canvas and topped with loops of razor wire.

"The team also noted rippling vortices of defensive magic along the edge of the roofline. I would not recommend an assault from above."

"Finally, of interest are several taller buildings that overlook this address, from directly across the street and to the south of it. Both front Eleventh Avenue. These might be worthwhile looking into as observation posts.

"Want me to set up some observation posts, J.J.?"

"You bet."

* * *

The next day three TIIIS observation posts were up and running. After a week of visual and infrared video, we knew that about eighty-three employees regularly worked in the building from nine to five—typical banker's hours. The U.S. mail carrier made his delivery just after ten. Thereafter, only a skeleton crew of fifteen to seventeen watched over the building and its parking lot. We assumed that these were security types, maybe even mixed personnel.

These numbers we compared against the HR data that we took during our previous raids on their headquarters. And Shazam, the current numbers reflected a shortfall of some forty-odd people. Nonetheless, we now had a long list of names and e-mail addresses.

*   *   *

Dear [NAME]:

Hello.

I am contacting you today as a courtesy. Your current place of employment is in serious jeopardy. Don't believe me? Look east at your once grand headquarters building that is under demolition.

What to do? Be wise and take all your hoarded vacation time before you lose it. While relaxing at that special someplace, ask yourself, "Why do I work for CMES North America?"

The above missive we posted at Manhattan's General Post Office two days prior to its identical transmission via e-mail. When the snail mail arrived at the warehouse's address that Wednesday morning, we allowed one hour for its distribution before we transmitted the e-mail storm.

To our endless surprise, the building's personnel

decided to take an early lunch that began at eleven. Cars left the parking lot a full hour ahead of the usual noon-hour lunch break. By high noon, the infrared body count was down to twenty-two—nearly that of the overnight skeleton crew. Apparently, most of CMES' staff took our suggestion seriously.

*   *   *

Jenny Sauerbrünn, now the Director of Membership and Human Resources, was fit to be tied. Even that CFO squirrel of a man, Vince Spence, had fled the premises. Only a handful of human personnel remained at their desks in IT and Security, while the remainder comprised those damned abominations.

With the regional director again in Rome, Sauerbrünn acknowledged the loneliness of leadership in a time of crisis. She quickly forwarded DeSalvo the manifesto. She didn't know that he had already received his own copy.

She reached down into her waste basket and retrieved the balled-up envelope and letter. Smoothing out its crinkles, she read the letter again and mouthed its words. At first, she could feel nothing from the computer-generated missive. But this time, Sauerbrünn stopped, focused, and gently reran her hyper-sensitive fingertips across it. A thrill ran through her. She could tangibly feel the power of its creator, his strength, his sense of righteous purpose.

Oh, how I want you dead! But you already are! She thought in complete confusion.

*   *   *

Valeria Costa had finished her dinner—a garden salad, bowl of buttered linguini, mushrooms, and garlic, and a delicious glass of red wine from her family's stock. Through her kitchen window, Valeria gazed out across the terrazzo patio toward the setting sun. She smiled in total contentment. Sighing with her chin in her palm, she goaded herself to get up and do the dishes. The warm soapy water quickly cut through the butter and olive oil residues of her repast.

Then her hands shook uncontrollably. In the process, the treaty-bound oracle of William DeSalvo dropped the dish she had been drying. When it crashed onto her kitchen's stone flooring, its fragments crudely formed the word *pietra*—stone ...

Stone?

What does that mean, Valeria?

Stone is dead.

At her denial, her hands shook even harder, as if to emphasize what her eyes refused to acknowledge.

Stone is alive?

With that thought her hands settled, yet Valeria's pulse raced. She knew what do and reached for her phone.

*   *   *

Noon came and went. The parking lot was practically empty, the TIIIS observers reported the remaining twenty-two infrared signatures were no longer stragglers, but stubborn defenders. To this information, I grunted and accepted the number as reasonable.

"Mr. Donaldson." I said from my observation post high up the building opposite that overlooked the entire scene. "Let 'er roll."

"Acknowledged," the new head of TIIIS IT and Security said in his heavy Irish tongue as he turned to face the waiting soldiers, giving them a twirling finger in the air.

Parked on Twelfth Street and almost taking up the entire city block, sat a massive flatbed semi. Its spot had been reserved by a long string of orange, NYPD traffic cones, courtesy of a helpful police sergeant that Meneer/Grimes knew at the 17th Precinct Station. In all, some twenty of New York's finest were on the scene to redirect traffic away from the future demolition site. Sprinkled liberally among them were TIIIS Security personnel who were there to "assist" as necessary.

While the flatbed was ordinary, what it carried was anything but—a desert camouflaged M1A Abrams tank. This particular vehicle, a tried and true veteran of the Gulf Wars, was on loan from Fort Dix. Eight uniformed soldiers, who had accompanied their vehicle, rapidly rolled up the tarp that shrouded the nearly seventy-ton beast, loosed its securing chains, and lowered the flatbed's ramps. When the Honeywell turbine fired up, the shriek of its jet turbine's fifteen hundred horsepower echoed off the neighborhood's buildings.

Even with its rubber treads, the unloaded metal monster creaked and rumbled its way south on Twelfth Avenue past its flatbed carrier en route to West 28th Street. The street's pavement freely buckled under its weight, leaving behind two clear ruts in the tarmac.

Just short of the corner of Eleventh and West 28th, the tank stopped, its turret and main gun faced rearward. Then it pivoted smartly to the left, mounted the curbing, and plowed right through the cyclone fencing of the CMES property, flattening it. The metal beast relentlessly accelerated through the mostly empty parking lot, sending two columns of roaring superheated turbine exhaust straight into the air. The two parked vehicles in its path were pancaked. Still accelerating, the tank struck the western end of the CMES warehouse at nearly forty miles an hour. With its treads churning up the parking lot's asphalt like so much mud, it disappeared beneath the structure's roofline.

Overhead, the tank's wake became obvious as the building's roofing failed. The behemoth continued right on through its mostly hollow interior until it breached on Eleventh Avenue like a surfacing whale. Covered in a layer of ruined plaster board, the vehicle looked like a dusty ghost. Halting at the curb briefly, it then turned and proceeded north on Eleventh, and then up West 29th to reload onto its flatbed, its victory lap done.

Ten minutes later, the flatbed loaded, secured, and tarp shrouded, the big rig rolled south on Twelfth Avenue heading for the Lincoln Tunnel, New Jersey, and the long drive south back to Fort Dix.

Witnessing all of this excitement from Eleventh Avenue, one cop said to a TIIIS security guard, "Ya know dat Streets and Sanitation will not like this one bit."

This brought a big grin on the TIIIS guard's face, "Not a problem officer. We'll be happy to pay for the repaving," Josh Remington gloated from behind the Lexan shield of his riot helmet.

*   *   *

At the initial starting of the M1A, many within the CMES warehouse looked up when they heard its deafening roar, but only one human of the security team recognized that distinctive turbine whine.

"What the fuck! That just can't be."

Moments later, their world came crashing down. Staffers scattered before the tank's onrush, but twelve mixed security dumbly stood their ground and unleashed a fusillade of handgun and automatic rifle fire at the armored battering ram to no effect. As it turned out, those were the only casualties as the full humans had the common sense to get out of the way.

In all, TIIIS medics transported fourteen dazed CMES survivors to a local emergency clinic. As for Sauerbrünn, she was in total shock. Her hyper-sensitivity, ratcheted up to overload at the sight of the tank bearing down on her, had turned her into a babbling automaton. When the survivors began stumbling out of the stricken building, all looked like ghosts, covered as they were, head to toe, in building dust.

*　　*　　*

Being summoned to Rome was not exactly DeSalvo's cup of tea. Then again, the Italian reasoned, at least he was still upright to defend himself. At the same time, he couldn't be in two places at once. While his region was monitoring the demolition of the Gathering property, the financial department oversaw the refund of unfulfilled spa memberships. As for the disposition of the property itself and its future, that remained a very sensitive hot potato—hence the real reason behind his Rome visit.

While en route to CMES' Roman campus, his cell unexpectedly rang. Displayed on its screen was an all too familiar exchange. DeSalvo, pulled over to the side of the road and with dread answered, *"Ciao?"*

"*Signore* DeSalvo, Stone is not dead! He's very much alive!" Valeria Costa gushed without preamble.

Pause.

"And he's up to something. I can feel it."

"Are you absolutely sure?" the blind-sided regional director asked, who now held his head in one hand.

"Sí."

"*Grazie*, Valeria. You probably just saved my life."

With his oracle's warning still tumbling around in his head, DeSalvo somehow remerged into traffic. While he fully expected not to use his return ticket, the Roman was not prepared for Feng Bai's furor.

"Thank you for coming, Mr. DeSalvo." The chairman cooed from behind his new piece of furniture—an ornately carved and gilded dragon desk. DeSalvo had heard about it, but the descriptions didn't do its artistry justice. The piece appeared to be that of a slumbering reptile, complete with a massive tail that was wrapped, protectively, around its feet. DeSalvo also observed the chairman did not shake his hand.

Yes, I have become officially toxic. The Roman concluded while he offered a generous bow from the waist to his superior.

"Mr. DeSalvo, either you are the most unlucky man that I have ever met, or, the most incompetent. This, I have yet to decide. At least, to your credit, you have solved the Stone issue.

Or have I?

"However, the diplomatic blow-back from the

contest in the Aralkum Desert cannot be brushed aside. The fallout is most disquieting for our society. You have caused us to lose face, Mr. DeSalvo.

"The disgrace of the North American Region reflects poorly upon us all. Traditional treaty-bound allies and individuals are fleeing in droves. Worse, CMES appears weak, and incompetent. Confidence in us, our very philosophy, has been questioned. Our long-held suzerainty, some have intimated, has come to an end.

"THIS I WILL NOT TOLERATE ..." the chairman stated with such steel in his voice that DeSalvo felt a preternatural heat in the air. The man glowed. " ... even from you, Mr. DeSalvo.

"Further, I have just learned that you now have two properties under demolition in Manhattan."

"What?"

"Yes, Mr. DeSalvo, moments ago someone demolished your temporary headquarters in Hell's Kitchen."

Valeria was right, yet again!

"By the way, what a memorable name.

"It seems that someone has a sense of humor. They drove a military tank right through the building, rendering the structure useless. Those who stood their ground were either run over or taken away. As for the rest of your staff, they scattered to the four winds, frightened away by a posted letter and e-mail suggesting that they flee."

At this bone-crushing news, DeSalvo's checked his e-mail and there it was—the warning. His entire posture took on the wilted pose of a defeated man.

Seeing this, Feng Bai remarked. "Mr. DeSalvo, you

have a choice to make. You no longer have a headquarters to return to. So, what will you do?"

Contemplative silence.

"Mr. Chairman," DeSalvo said, "I would prefer the opportunity to stay in Italy and live out my days in quiet obscurity."

Nodding, Feng Bai said, "This you may do, Mr. DeSalvo, but your future will be anything but obscure, because I am ordering you to perform one, and only one thing—find out who did this. Once that is complete, then, and only then, can you enjoy your much-desired obscurity."

In truth, DeSalvo had forgotten what it was like to be on the outside, on his own, without the incessant pressure of operational responsibilities, without a staff. What made his present situation scary was his boss' mandate to identify an unknown. Even more unnerving was the distinct possibility that the unknown might be someone who, for all practical purposes, seemed invincible.

If Stone indeed was alive, as Valeria reported, this menace had destroyed his career within CMES with his repeated attacks and destruction of everything that DeSalvo had built, and re-built. Railing on and on about this ghost of a man and his odious accomplishments, provided nothing productive. Instead, the Italian reread again his dossier, which no longer was a thin manila folder, but rather had swelled to a voluminous accordion ledger.

Weaknesses? Yes, we killed his friends and colleagues. The man's parents survived, but had been relocated twice, but to where? The crafty Roman noodled briefly on this factoid and decided to let it go.

He made that decision because down deep he didn't have the will to harm the aged and defenseless. On the other hand, Stone senior proved himself to be hardly helpless, DeSalvo reminded himself. *Maybe there's something special in that family's gene pool*?

As for his wife and her location, he possessed only pure speculation.

What else William? What else am I missing?

CHAPTER 41
Irony

In perhaps the greatest irony of New York City lore, an international consortium bought the ruined Gathering property. Word on the street said they paid too much. Most of its partners were not known, the list made up of alphabet soup corporations that included an odd paranormal research society. One partner, however, stuck out from the rest, the consortium's principal investor—the Roman Catholic Diocese of New York. Hence, the irony.

*   *   *

One month after the finalization of the Fifth Avenue property's sale, I and my president were invited to the rectory of St. Patrick's Cathedral. Cardinal Dominic Ricco, recently appointed by His Holiness, requested the visit.

The meeting itself turned out to be a low-key affair. The cardinal selected several vintage reds for the event, along with various cheeses, fruits, and breads that he favored, and hoped, that we might as well.

Cardinal Ricco was young for such an important post within the Vatican network. In his forties, lean, and of medium build, he bore the dark complexion so typical of southern Italy. With a narrow face and prominent nose that emphasized his large brown eyes and lashes, I had the feeling that the man could actually see into my soul, and as it turned out, I wasn't all that wrong. For when we were first introduced, the cardinal greeted us with a small bow, and in turn, took both of our hands in his.

"Madam President, I am most pleased that you could come. And, I must say, that your aura is as breath-taking as the energy that vibrates throughout your being."

When the cardinal came to me, he smiled and shook his head. "You, sir, can only be *the* Jonathan Joseph Stone that Father Flanagan told me so much about. I am honored to meet you, and for all the things that you did for my good friend, Antonio Garibaldi." Then he surprised me as he partially turned me to the right, while he peeked behind me. "I see that you hide your dark wings well, oh mighty Lictor of Magic," he added with a chuckle.

With his arms now out from his sides, Cardinal Ricco announced, "Please, sit, and be at ease."

After some small talk, Father Flanagan appeared and did the honors with pouring the wine. While we poked at the cheeses, Cardinal Ricco got down to brass tacks.

"Madam President, His Holiness wishes to thank you and your organization for all the things that you have done on behalf of this diocese over the years, and especially during the past three years. Additionally, and admittedly because of your generous gift of a certain document, he is in the process of generating a formal, but secret document wherein your organization will be diplomatically recognized by the Holy See. The Holy Father sees this as the cornerstone for establishing a new relationship between Holy Mother Church and TIIIS. Naturally, your organization may wish to not accept this overture. But I sincerely hope that you will."

The shock on President Silver Moon's face was classic. "Cardinal Ricco, I can assure you that my society will seriously consider your offer. Do you know if this is a precursor step to an alliance of some sort, or, would that be something later to be discussed?"

"Madam President, I can assure you that this is a most serious offer from the Holy See. With it comes, how do you say, many benefits up front. As with everything, the Holy See and its many roots and branches reach nearly everywhere. The term 'alliance' is a very strong and legalistic term, which invokes terms, agreements, and limits. Sometimes a declaration of friendship is far stronger, flexible, and more meaningful."

While the Cardinal paused to sip at his wine, my mouth babbled out.

"Cardinal Ricco, you said earlier that Cardinal Garibaldi and you were friends. What did you mean by that?"

"Mr. Stone, Antonio and I were both brothers of the Society of Saint Paul. That makes us both psychic sensitives and trained exorcists. And from what Father Flanagan tells me, both you and Antonio worked together quite well as a team. I would hope that we might continue that tradition."

"I would be honored, Cardinal Ricco," I forthrightly stated as I straightened in my chair.

"Wonderful."

Then shifting gears, the cardinal continued.

"Madam President, His Holiness also wishes to express his … surprise at TIIIS' participation in the recent purchase of a piece of Fifth Avenue property. He asks, why?"

"That is easy to answer, Cardinal Ricco. It is in TIIIS' best interest to see CMES' North American Region in full retreat and disarray. While our financial position in this purchase was considerable, we prefer to have that property in the hands of the Roman Church, someone whom we know, someone with whom we have a working relationship. The decision to do so was based purely on those pragmatic considerations."

"I see," the cardinal said. "I will relay this to His Holiness. And thank you for your candor. It is most refreshing."

"So, Cardinal Ricco," I said, "since the Roman Catholic Diocese of New York is the principal entity listed in this purchase, what are your plans for it?"

Raising his wine glass in my direction the cardinal answered. "The frank answer is, right now, right this moment, we're not sure. But whatever we come up with, the final decision will be one arrived at with *all* of the consortium members' input. As for myself, I favor a non-denominational humanitarian complex, where food, medical services, and the like, are freely available to those in need, all packaged in way that does not disrupt the Fifth Avenue vibe. Mr. Stone, I do believe that the homeless can co-exist with Prada."

CHAPTER 42
European Rampage

Following the recent Hell's Kitchen op, President Silver Moon met with me for lunch at a raucous brew pub called Empire Burgers & Brew in downtown Naperville, Illinois. The trendy and airy place screamed atmosphere with its overlook of the Du Page River. Best of all, it held the promise of good food and beer. While such establishments were not exactly on the president's A-list, she knew that Mr. Henry and I had made a practice of frequenting quite a few. Besides, I insisted on the place.

"Nice place," the president said with her head on a spin as we sat down at an ultra-modern bar enclosed from the elements by walls and a roof made of glass. A typical Midwestern thunderhead had just passed through, which marred those transparent surfaces with pebbled rain drops.

"All this glass makes me feel exposed," she said, "especially for what we'll be discussing."

"Do you want to leave?" I asked.

"No. But let's remain discrete."

At that moment, the bartender appeared with an expectant smile. "Menus?"

"Yes, please." I said.

"Perhaps something to wet your whistle?" the bartender named Craig reasonably asked.

"How about a sampler of your six best, and we'll go from there." I countered.

"Coming right up!"

"Thank you, J.J. for handling that," she said while

scanning the menu. "Some of these names are simply outlandish," the president observed.

"Welcome to the world of craft brewing, Madam President—the Wild West of branding."

When the sampler appeared, we ordered our food, and then got down to business.

"J.J.," my boss began, "I want you to review the files on this thumb drive. It contains the profiles of several European leaders and the antics of one enclave in particular."

I slipped the drive into the hip pocket of my jeans. "Okay, what do you have in mind?"

"That, Lictor of Magic, I will leave for you to decide."

"That bad?" I said with clear surprise on my face.

"Oh my, yes."

When we returned to the nearby TIIIS facility off of Highway 88, I got down to exploring what was on that drive. After a good two and a half hours of gruesome reading, I thoroughly understood.

And just to close the loop, the president really liked the Solemn Oath Snaggletooth IPA. She has promise.

*   *   *

As I flew east-bound in our society's private jet, my intended itinerary started in Budapest. Thereafter, I would work my way west through Berlin, Paris, and Barcelona, where I had a hard date with its enclave. That was the plan when I took off from Latrobe. Mel, bless her heart, saw me off.

In all, it took a brutal thirteen hours of flight time to reach Budapest after a refueling and change of crew in Zurich. I tried to sleep, but ended up rereading all the dossiers that President Silver Moon had shared. Their content removed any remaining possibility of slumber.

Budapest is a beautiful, architectural jewel divided by the majestic Danube River. Frankly, I had expected a dark and desolate post-Soviet city. I couldn't have been more wrong. Its people share a ready smile to foreigners. I had to pinch myself that a monster lived among them.

Her name—Éva Szilagyi. Her file stated she ruled her Hungarian enclave with an iron fist caked with blood. It pointed out that Szilagyi's formidable powers of telepathy and telekinesis probably benefited from the use of a dark ley line. It was unknown if she was demon-possessed, but gifted eye-witnesses reported Szilagyi's aura as the blackest of the black.

As to why President Silver Moon had pulled her jacket, Szilagyi's list of atrocious atrocities dove-tailed with her clear Neo-Nazi political ideology. Reportedly, she delighted at lowering the city's minority populations in the most diabolical of ways—the details of which formed the fodder of a purely insane nightmare.

I had to find and kill this monster without her keen awareness detecting me. Fortunately, the local TIIIS community readily provided me with the former and a recent image. Apparently, Szilagyi's dark preference was to stroll with her entourage through the city's Great Market Hall, a grand structure of decorative brick and stone that takes up a complete city block. Within its crowded and cavernous interior of countless aisles filled with shops, Szilagyi would make her random selection based on ethnicity or religion.

I visited this market, trying to focus on the job at

hand instead of its delicious aromas. The cramped environment nixed the use of my Bone Sword, however, my heavily suppressed 9mm would be perfect for a quick and dirty pass-by encounter.

I waited two days before the monster appeared. With mind-blocking TIIIS spotters sprinkled around the market's exterior, I learned where they entered, and merged that with a plan of the first floor. Immediately, I saw several ambush points.

Since the weather was coolish, I wore my hoodless UCS under loose clothing and a long trench coat. My neatly trimmed beard and hair style fit in seamlessly among the throng of shoppers. I stood against a massive brick pillar along an aisle with my mental blocks on max. I became the brick and waited to catch sight of my prey.

In all, there were five of them—a square formation of four human goons with the monster in between. Szilagyi, dressed in a pricy dark coat and skirt combo looked every bit the executive, crisply put together and elegantly turned out. With her head on a swivel, she scanned the crowds with the cold look of a hungry butcher. She owned the place. This was her turf. Szilagyi was way too over confident.

I didn't move a muscle. At the periphery of my mind, I sensed her blatant telepathic probing. As they passed by my pillar, onlookers turned, moved away, or stared back at the intrusive procession, not knowing why. The entourage continued to casually move on, relentlessly, like a great white shark swimming in a school of spawning mackerel.

At a small gap in the crowd, I slid in behind and between two of the goons using several innocents for visual cover. Two sub-sonic rounds coughed into the back of the monster's head, destroying it utterly. Her bodyguards turned to react, but no one was there, only wisps of gun smoke that hung in the air. In a series of quick translocations, I had already left the market.

One down.

*   *   *

My next two appointments took place in quick succession on the following days in Berlin and Paris. They were pretty much carbon-copies of the Budapest hit. I simply got up close, used my suppressed 9mm, and translocated away. It was almost too easy.

Berlin's monster was a cruel and thuggish buffoon named Hans Gross, who delighted in indiscriminately frying people on the open street. A really big guy, tall and broad at the shoulders, Gross fancied himself a serious warlock and looked the part in his tight leathers, shaved head with a tall mohawk, and tattooed runes across half his face. Frankly, I was good with the look, but didn't understand the black eye shadow.

This dude was always linked to his dark ley line. Even when it snowed, the man reportedly traipsed around barefoot. Continuous ley line hook-ups like that do strange things to you. All that power can fry your nervous system, causing a host of neurological issues.

As proof of such damage, the passage of his castings roiled the atmosphere with superheated air. Bystanders beware, of which there were many. With this guy, Gross always used a sledgehammer to crush a bug, when a far lighter touch would have been fine. Everything had to be done in excess. The word finesse didn't appear anywhere in his vocabulary. Maybe he just couldn't control himself. Again, those neurological issues.

Regardless of his heavy-handedness, Gross had two sure weaknesses—late night partying and his smart phone's camera. Gross loved to photograph his victims. To memorialize his well-known traits, while his attention was thoroughly distracted, I drilled him at point-blank range right through his mobile device in front of the *Tresor* nightclub on Köpenicker Strasse. Picture that!

Two down.

One of Gross' angry followers with spiked purple hair, however, nicked my UCS' armor with several carelessly scattered rounds from his machine pistol, which went on to hit several innocents. I grabbed his leather-wrapped wrist, viciously twisted it, stabbed my still hot suppressor into his left armpit, and fired twice under his body armor, ruining his heart and lungs.

*   *   *

Paris' monster was this freak who thought she was a vampire. Plainly a nut-case, Francine Blauh, aka Madam Scarlet Moulin, worshipped, and acted out, Anne Rice's vampire series. Her "lover" reportedly was even named Lestat de Lioncourt. Who knew how many died to fulfill this one's fantasy of eternal life fueled by human blood. But she had to go, so I obliged Madam Scarlet. As she floated about looking for victims on the streets of the Left Bank, she encountered Death itself. In front of a small shop called Coisas de Brazil, two of my suppressed rounds found her left temple.

Three down.

*　*　*

Then there was the CMES enclave in Barcelona.

On a glorious fall evening near ten o'clock, the entire Barcelona enclave met on the sidewalk outside a neighborhood restaurant called Racó de la Vila on the Carrer de la Ciutat de Granada 33, a brief walk away from the Llacuna Metro stop. Numbering about sixty and all dressed in black for the occasion—the election of their new Tribune—a grand feast had been arranged to celebrate her formal installation.

As I scanned the crowd from the shadow of a storefront, not one possessed a clear aura. Instead, all had muddied, dark colors, indicative of extreme criminality at best. In fact, over half were so black I wondered how they managed it. Then I recalled their file, *With this group, they had all gleefully earned that darkness.*

The Barcelona Gathering held a pride of place among CMES for their extreme depravity, earning a notorious reputation for their inhuman treatment of anyone they considered their paranormal lesser. No one would engage in treaty talks with this bunch. Having read about their many predations, all deserved a harsh judgment—something more in keeping with their lingering, inflicted atrocities, but that was not my style.

This moonless night I emerged from the shadowed storefront onto the poorly lit, tree lined street, and struck. The reactive camouflage of my armored UCS hid me, while I reached out with my hideously sharp Bone Sword. I moved in a counter-clockwise direction, encircling the crowd, herding them, as a barely seen blur. I translocated often, in brief jumps, sundering them. My sword became a scythe that laid low the tightly packed crowd, mowing them down like ripe wheat. I swirled around their perimeter, easily catching stragglers, felling them. My frenetic attack felt like a *kendo* exercise, only far more savage.

They fought back as only they knew how. The remnant, stood back to back, casting blindly their deadly magic. Rippling bolts of energy reached out and noisily gouged the concrete sidewalk and macadam pavement. A parked car, caught in their barrage, was crushed in like an aluminum can, fountained out its shattered glass. A section of a nearby tree trunk, precariously shredded, began its slow, sagging topple. None of these blind and desperate attempts found me, while they continued to succumb to the Bone Sword.

It didn't take long before all lay dead or nearly so. I scanned their auras looking for survivors. Finding two, I finished them.

It has been a good harvest, the First Soul drily commented.

I couldn't disagree, as I had encountered two demon-kind among them. When struck, they had exploded spectacularly into black ectoplasmic clouds that rapidly evaporated away. Otherwise, blood and gore slicked the sidewalk and streamed into the curbing's gutter, causing a sudden flood that washed away the dried tree leaves into the sewer.

Without question, CMES suffered another loss to their membership, but upon investigation they would find no magic involved, and therefore, precious little to trace. This dark enclave I eradicated from this fair city. CMES might recolonize it, but given this night's carnage, that job would be a hard one to do.

After several translocations, I made my escape to an awaiting bread van two blocks away, driven by two local TIIIS members. While they drove me to the airport and our society's private jet, unlike with the other three, this time I broke down into a shaking post-op mess, while I relived each and every strike, each execution. A part of me said they deserved it, but the other was aghast at my wonton savagery. So I did the sensible thing and filled two airsick bags, which had been thoughtfully provided.

Barcelona was my fourth stop on my whirlwind tour of the Continent. The first I performed in broad daylight, the rest took place in the inky dark where my UCS concealed me from their eyes. After all, who had the wits to look for my shadow cast in the night?

After this one week's labor, TIIIS' IT and Security informed me that all public appearances of the Gathering's leadership had been globally canceled. CMES raised their institutional security to an all-time high. For once in their existence, the Gathering was looking over its shoulder. Someone was actually hunting them down, and they didn't like it.

*   *   *

Deep within the endless abyss that is the Dark Realm, The Devourer of Souls became inundated with the shattered remains of two demons and over fifty dark-stained souls. All shared one characteristic—the mark of the First Soul and a rash of silver poisoning.

"You tax me, First Soul. Do not revel overly in this carnage, for you will be next!"

"Carnage?" the First Soul retorted. "You do not know what carnage is, for I AM THE STORM!"

CHAPTER 43
Surprise Visit

While sitting on the tarmac of the Barcelona-El Prat Airport, I got a crazy-insane idea, while I fingered the worn edge of Valeria Costa's business card that said, "Personal Advisor." This once blood-bound oracle of Vesta served a former CMES chairman that I assassinated with her help. With her kind of black widow reputation, what could possibly go wrong? So I sent her a text and postponed my return home with a short side trip to Rome. All it said was "Lunch?"

Sig.ra V. Costa
Tivoli, ITALIA
+39 774 335281
sigravcosta@fastweb.it

*　　*　　*

A day later, I again strolled the cobblestone streets of ancient Tivoli, a wonderful town so in touch with its Roman roots, and yet so alive. As I made my way to a certain side street restaurant, memories flooded my mind of a dark night and the high-tech murder in a villa that overlooked the town.

Then, suddenly, I found myself standing before a quaint restaurant. How I got there, I cannot say, but I've been there before and my stomach probably told my feet. Instinctively, I put my mental blocks on full.

Valeria's brother's restaurant breathed out the luscious smells of freshly baked bread, grilled onions and garlic, fish, and Lord only knows what else. Then it hit me—under no circumstances could a demon or demon-possessed person approach this place. How clever. At that inside baseball revelation, I shook my head in appreciation and entered.

Ducking under the wooden lintel, I transitioned from the bright sunshine to a pleasantly dim atmosphere of linen tables, precisely laid out silverware and napkins, and sparkling wine glasses. The place was nearly vacant given the early hour, excepting the one table in the corner occupied by Valeria Costa, who sipped a glass of red wine.

Valeria genuinely smiled up at me, gestured with her glass to join her, and so I did.

"J.J., your new look nearly stopped my heart. You're suddenly so 'Italian' ... and not to mention, so alive."

That last comment told me a lot, and probably more than she intended. *Was she somehow involved with the hit on Mr. Henry and me? Or even the attack on my wedding day? Upon considering that possibility, a distinct coolness ran through my heart.*

"Wine?" she followed up with a raise of her near-empty glass.

"Only if it comes from your family's vineyard."

She poured. "How kind of you to remember."

Then the powerful oracle's eyes hardened to all business, "Why did you wish to see me?"

Instead of immediately answering, I swirled the red, breathed in its bouquet, took a sip, and once again this beer guy was overcome by its smooth finish. I shook my head in frank appreciation.

"Valeria, has your family been in any way impacted by the passing of the former chairman?"

Valeria sat back and crossed her arms with her glass of wine. "No," she guardedly said.

"Good. I was concerned." Especially since she had warned me about the three demon-dogs posted outside of the chairman's villa. "And thank you again for that tip about his *dogs*."

She waved her hand in dismissal as if her warning had been but a trifle. Then, with penetrating eyes, she asked, "Have you heard anything about the murders in Berlin, Budapest, Paris, or Barcelona last week?"

"Nope," I deadpanned with my very best poker face. "Which murders? Who?"

Now looking at me sideways, "The near surgical murders of high-ranking officials of the Gathering."

"Did those animals deserve it?" I thoughtfully asked.

"'Animals,' an interesting choice of words, Lictor of Magic. Did you claim them?" Her words were like ice picks as my mental blocking blunted her thoughts.

I countered, "Is your Gathering better today because of their passing? Were they, perhaps, an excessive embarrassment?"

"Perhaps."

I raised my glass, "Then let's toast to their unexpected passing."

I drank deeply.

She didn't.

"You murdered them all." A flatly stated accusation if there ever was one.

"I murder no one."

Again, with that sideways look and crossed arms. Her heavily shielded thoughts said, *Is he telling me the truth?*

"By the way, speaking of murders, have you heard about the TIIIS adept recently killed in Manhattan?"

The question caused the oracle to stumble out, *"Sí."*

Then I heard in her mind, *You should know. You were supposedly there.*

"Indeed, Valeria. I was indeed there."

With wide eyes she said, "How, how can you ..."

"I've evolved, Valeria, remember? You already know that I am joined to the ley line system. Of that I'm sure. But to return to the Manhattan hit, the man in that yellow cab was a very dear friend," I said with a whisper.

Valeria covered her mouth with her hands, her mind an explosion of emotions difficult to untangle, so I didn't bother. I suspected that she was purposely doing so, in an attempt to hide something.

So I changed the topic. It seemed appropriate.

"Valeria, have you ever heard of anyone being able to cast a spell remotely?"

At the question, she blinked.

"What do you mean, J.J?"

"A spell cast without the practitioner present."

She put down her glass, squinted at the ceiling, and again crossed her arms, this time in thought.

After the passage of several moments, she looked at me and said, "Only once in my lifetime."

"Care to tell me about it?" I fished.

With her elbows on the linen she said, "It was in the early 90's, in Alexandria, Egypt, as I recall. Someone murdered one of our Gathering, a physician, a gynecologist, most horribly. It was the subject of much discussion and concern."

"How was the casting done without the practitioner being present? Where did the energy for the casting come from?" I reasonably asked.

"I remember now more clearly. The casting was accomplished using an Egyptian figurine as an intermediary. It was discovered that the artifact was empowered by a second triggering spell. The energy came from the opening of the figurine's parcel."

I held my head in my hands in astonishment.

"What about consulting a spell whisperer?" I prodded hopefully.

"There was nothing to detect, as the figurine and spells had been guarded with an entirely unknown enchantment.

"Damn." *Way to go Mel!*

"Indeed, J.J. Fortunately, that event has not been repeated. Now, J.J., why all these questions?"

"Because what I need to know, Valeria, is whether the death wish spell—the one that your religious order and my society cooked up way back when, can be remotely invoked."

At that question, her eyes widened.

"*Signore* Stone," she uncharacteristically said, signaling her concern, displeasure, whatever, "that spell is a very sensitive subject between my order and yours, and one that is not widely known. What do you have in mind?"

Now I leaned forward on the starched white linen. "*Signora* Costa, everybody knows that a spell's casting is only as powerful as the practitioner who casts it. We are talking about the simple transfer of energy. I'm wondering whether it would be possible to digitally send a voice recording of the spell's casting, thereby saving the practitioner from becoming a victim of the spell itself."

A long, manicured fingernail now tapped her front teeth in thought. "Interesting, but the spell would not work, because the fundamental *quid pro quo* of the spell would not be satisfied. A sacrifice must be present. So, no, I don't think so. This is something that would require experimentation, surely *not* something for the table of a restaurant."

"I see." I took another sip of that red ambrosia.

"J.J., I am sorry for your loss."

"I am, too."

Another sip.

"Did you watch the Olympics, Valeria?"

"*Sí.* Who didn't?"

"Then consider this. At rest a human puts out about eighty watts of energy. An Olympian, like Usain Bolt, perhaps two thousand during a one-hundred-meter sprint. In your experience, how much effort do you expend in your highly specialized work?"

Valeria smiled wistfully, "J.J., what you ask needs a laboratory to make measurements. But just for the sake of argument, some 'highly specialized work' requires more energy, some less. But if *Signore* Bolt exerts himself for nine seconds and uses *duemila* watts, that should be the upper limit, I would suppose."

"Yes, I totally agree, but are there adepts who could exceed such a biological limit through other means, such as meditation or trance?"

Again, with that tapping fingernail. Then, finally, she said, "Perhaps. In my experience, one's training in 'highly specialized work' always emphasizes the need for restraint and managing one's actions, in order to better recover from the physical strain. Otherwise, you could endanger, or even permanently harm, yourself." Then her eyebrows rose. "But, J.J., what if one is connected to a ley line, eh?"

"Good point."

"But again, why, J.J., are you asking about these things?"

"Because you are an experienced practitioner, Valeria. You have done these highly specialized things all your life. You know what your body goes through when performing them."

"Yes. That is indeed so," Valeria murmured more to herself as she looked down at her hands. "In the end, J.J., it would depend on how powerful you wish to make the spell. The one that you mentioned before actually allows the practitioner to set limits on its effect. The broader the limits, the more power needed."

I pinched my lower lip and said, "I see. I have one more question for you. Do you listen to music, Valeria?"

"Why, yes, I do."

"What is the medium that you use—digital or vinyl?"

"*Sí*. I play records."

"What kinds of music do you listen to?"

"Many, but mostly jazz and classical."

"When you play your records, Valeria, in a purely magical sense, do you invoke the sound by playing the record or does the record invoke the sound on its own?"

"Why, J.J., what a silly question. I invoke the music by playing the record."

"So where is the *quid pro quo*? With you or the record?"

The oracle sat opposite me with ever-widening eyes. "So you were the one who cast those remote spells," she whispered.

"No, Valeria." I said shaking my head. "That wasn't me."

I pressed, "By the way, since we're catching up on current events, have you found a new sponsor, now that the old one has passed?"

That question again triggered the crossed arms. "If you're so curious, J.J., why don't you just read my mind?" the oracle said.

I already had: *William DeSalvo, the former regional director of Manhattan.*

"Because that would be impolite, Valeria. There, I said it. I apologize for intruding on your thoughts."

"You have changed, J.J." She said while hard eyes tried to drill holes through my mental shield.

"The death of those close to you, Valeria, does that to you."

After a few moments she shifted subjects. "Yes, J.J., I have found a new sponsor. He holds great promise."

"Is he a member of the Gathering?"

"Yes, but is no longer of any importance."

"If that is the case, Valeria, protect him, for his fortunes may change. Tell him to stay clear of the Rome campus."

At this point, Valeria's brother Richardo appeared with a covered basket of fresh, hot bread, and a bottle of olive oil.

Valeria swallowed hard at that nugget and said, "I will order for you, J.J. You have been thinking too hard. I just heard your stomach growl."

*   *   *

Back at Ciampino Airport, southeast of Rome proper, I made an encrypted call from the TIIIS plane. I was trying to reach my old buddy Josh Remington in the IT and Security Department and got lucky.

"Mr. Stone! What a surprise! What can I do for you? Where are you, anyway?" the excited professional said.

"For starters, Rome. Now, Josh, how much energy does a typical laptop or standalone computer use?"

"Like anything, that depends, but most laptops are built to run efficiently on a battery and so use anywhere between twenty and one hundred watts, while a standalone, heck, can pull twelve thousand-plus watts right out of a wall socket all day."

"Does your security department depend on laptops or standalones?"

"We're mostly standalones with multiple screens, but in the field, we shift to laptops and smart phones."

"You don't say. Next question, Josh—can you add something to an e-mail that the recipient couldn't see?"

"Sure, that happens all the time. They're called attachments. One click of the mouse opens them up. They're usually images, spreadsheets, and the like."

"No, Josh, what I'm envisioning is an e-mail that has several hidden commands, which once opened, are automatically triggered into action."

Josh's voice suddenly got small on me, almost a whisper.

"Ah, Mr. Stone, what you're describing is some pretty sophisticated coding. What sort of commands would you want embedded in this e-mail of yours?"

I rubbed my chin in thought. "Well, after about two minutes I want the e-mail to erase itself and any trail of its existence within the CMES system. But before that happens, I'd want to play a recorded message, at the end of which a specific amount of electrical power would drain from the computer's power source."

While I described my idea, Josh took notes; I had to repeat several of them in detail.

"Well, Mr. Stone, what you have just described is called a worm, which can be coded and kicked off to erase an e-mail after a specified period. Another worm can do the same to delete an e-mail within CMES' e-mail server. But to automatically play an audio message in the background, that I have never heard of. Usually, when people want to hear audio they click on an executable button that says PLAY. My first thought about the audio file is that it will get flagged. Such self-executable files in e-mails are caught by most spam filters, which will detect the embedded file as a potential virus or malware. Mr. Stone, my suggestion would be to create an innocent attachment that looks legit so an operator executes it. Then to make sure that it does, I'd send it to multiple users."

"Now Josh, who should I talk to about making this coding happen?"

"That would be me, sir."

"Excellent."

CHAPTER 44
The Trojan Horse

DeSalvo's villa, located in the tiny mountain village of Orvieto north of Rome, sat atop an outcrop of uplifted stone. Its leaded-in windows faced a magnificent view of the western Sabine foothills. This morning he sat on his shaded patio and was taking in this glorious panorama, when his phone rang. Putting down his breakfast coffee, he answered.

"Ciao?"

"Signore DeSalvo?"

"Sí."

"I have received an urgent portent!" Valeria Costa breathlessly gasped.

"And?"

"Under no circumstances visit the Rome Center anytime soon!"

"That's an odd message, *Signora* Costa, but I will honor it nonetheless. *Grazie.*"

Moments later, his phone chimed, but this time with an encrypted e-mail. It read,

Critical Meeting. Tomorrow. 9 am.

Since DeSalvo received this missive, he logically assumed that he was invited. However, given what had recently transpired with his chairman, DeSalvo paused, unsure. To casually disregard such a "critical meeting" was difficult for the Roman, made more so given his oracle's recent warning.

What to do?

*　　*　　*

While I flew back, Josh wasted no time and ginned up the two worms and an attractive attachment. We figured if the sender was Feng Bai, the odds would be good that the addressees would open it. Now back at the Academy, a virtual ghost town with its non-essential staff and students relocated hither and yon, Josh Remington and I went over some last-minute details prior to its launch.

As for the attachment, Josh outdid himself. Its content was the Latin text that typically appears in website design as content placeholders. To wit: *Lorem ipsum dolor sit amet, ex labores admodum epicurei vis* ... Which is nothing more than a dreadful mash-up of Ciceronian Latin taken from his work, *De Finibus Bonorum et Malorum*, "On the Extremes of Good and Evil." The reason Josh used this particularly well-known text was to befuddle the reader for a sufficient amount of time, while the Latin death wish played in the background. Josh, bless his soul, thought his prank appropriate. When I saw it, I screamed with laughter. Our president thought we had both gone insane.

At five that next morning, President Silver Moon authorized the attack when she pressed the ENTER key, sending off our Trojan horse. We three watched in anticipation from Josh's security station. In the blink of an eye, the status of the e-mail changed from SENT to RECEIVED by the CMES Rome e-mail server. Its time stamp read eleven in the morning Rome time. From the HR data plundered from the North American headquarters, we selected twelve e-mail addresses hoping one would open it.

*   *   *

Gina Ferrache looked forward to her lunch break and daily hike around the campus. Even though today's weather forecast was for sunshine and heat, she relished any opportunity to get out of her cramped cubical in the Communications and Security Department. Then her computer station chimed for perhaps the billionth time that day.

Another damn virus e-mail.

Dragging her cursor over from her coding project on one screen to the other with the e-mail server's in-tray, she saw that the e-mail vetted by the fire wall for her attention. It carried a large attachment with a .wav-file.

A .wav-file?

Gina saw it was addressed to twelve individuals who she knew, and stopped right there.

Is this spam? The e-mail and its attachment made it through the normal filters, but the virus detection still flagged it.

Then she noted *Signore* Feng Bai's name as the e-mail's point-of-origin.

Gina thought again for about five seconds, made her decision, and dragged the e-mail and its attachment into the secure environment for delivery.

Six minutes later, Gina felt an oppressive pressure in her head, blood dripped out of her ears, nose, and eyes. Her breathing became labored. She gripped her desk for support, while her last thoughts centered on the framed picture of her husband Gino, and one-year-old baby boy, Paulo.

*   *   *

Four addressees were curious enough to open the e-mail's attachment. All four did so from computer stations powered by 240-volt electrical outlets—the European standard. While the attachment's oddly familiar content presented itself with a computer-generated audio accompaniment, the death wish succeeded in replicating itself four times, because the addressees who had chosen to open the attachment had become the *quid pro quo* sacrifices.

Given the spell's stipulated range of two *stadia*, a sphere some 1030-feet in diameter, the spell sterilized the CMES Rome campus, its villa, and extensive catacombs four times of all life. Insects ceased to move. Reptiles and vermin exploded. Birds fell from the sky.

Over two hundred souls died, including forty-seven possessed, who were mostly security. The CMES chairman and twenty-one high level CMES officials, members, and staff perished.

Then the e-mail's worms took over, erasing all evidence of its presence throughout the CMES computer system.

Now devoid of all life, even bacteria, the CMES Rome campus became a quiet tomb with only chiming computers and the ringing of unanswered telephones.

*   *   *

The Devourer of Souls received in silent rage an inundation of dark souls and the tattered remains of many old demons. This time it did not cry out, for the mark of the First Soul was not on any of them. But the arch-demon of the Dark Realm knew better. His kin had been tricked. Something most foul had been perpetrated upon them.

The First Soul, however, reminded this dark denizen with a wag of its finger, "This is carnage! Most foul one! Never forget, I AM THE STORM!"

*　*　*

The Ledger Keeper, that eternal entity which monitored the comings and goings of souls between the Light, Dark, and Mortal Realms, was supremely satisfied. The First Soul brought into balance the number of souls, each to their realm, as it was prior to the discovery of the Great Rent in AD 1431—that unfortunate time when the Mortal Realm suffered the unchecked invasion of dark souls. Now, with its ledgers again in equilibrium, it sighed with immense satisfaction.

*　*　*

In the aftermath of "The Fall," as the event later became known, CMES was staggered. In this vacuum, William DeSalvo offered himself as a candidate for the chairmanship at his oracle's suggestion. The selection committee, cobbled together from the three surviving regional directors, agreed that DeSalvo offered the most experience. While his reputation was sullied by his brief stint as the North American regional director, the man had his successes, was considered level-headed, with a creative management style. In the final analysis, truly none of the surviving regional directors wanted any part of the chairmanship.

*　　*　　*

After the long removal of remains and the cleanup of the Rome campus, which took over a month, DeSalvo staffed the facility with CMES members predominately from Europe and Asia. With the campus once again up and running, only then did he commission a team of non-aligned spell whispers to assess what had happened.

Four days into their investigation the spell whispers stopped, for they could not find one shred of culprit magic—much less identify who had cast the supposed spell. While they all agreed that "The Fall" probably was attributable to some sort of global death spell, they could in no way prove it.

In one of his first directives, Chairman DeSalvo removed all trace of his predecessor's mark and replaced it with monk-like austerity. The former chairman's office became an open reception area filled with plush furniture and seating, while his own office became a cubical located deep within the catacombs.

CHAPTER 45
Peace

President Silver Moon sat at the conference table within the Academy's Vault. She was pleased to note that all thirty-three TIIIS representatives were present in hushed anticipation. Apparently, she thought, they all had put two and two together after the rumored rumblings of "The Fall."

"Dear colleagues," she began, "thank you for attending at such a short notice. I can assure you that it was quite unavoidable.

"Today is a momentous one. I am pleased to report that CMES has quietly approached us requesting the establishment of diplomatic relations."

The bugged-out eyes and intake of breath at this extraordinary announcement threatened to create a vacuum in the vast underground chamber.

"Apparently, their new chairman, William DeSalvo, is genuinely concerned that we keep our Lictor of Magic 'on a tight leash'—his words.

"So, dear colleagues, it appears that the US Region's external policy of 'an eye for an eye' is quite effective. Our membership rolls have swelled. New alliances are crafted daily with the non-aligned. While I do not wish to be too sanguine about these developments, I cannot help but be pleased. No doubt, our future talks with CMES will be very interesting.

"May I now suggest that we begin preparations for those upcoming talks? To begin—do we appoint a committee to deal with CMES face-to-face, or, do you wish to authorize me to personally broker the deal?"

*   *   *

Peace.

"Mr. Henry, it's no secret. It's every soldier's dream to return to the ranch, farm, or city, and pretend everything's back to normal—the way things were. But I can't drink that Kool Aid. Nothing ever gets back to normal, whatever normal is. CMES, sure, is at the moment down for the count, but that will change. In time they'll return to their old ways as sure as the sun rises in the east. Meanwhile, the world remains a dangerous place that needs an enforcer to deal with the inevitable crazies out there. The three realms need me to maintain their balance. Someone has to provide that. That's what I do. It's my job."

You have done well, Soul Carrier, the First Soul chimed in. *But you are correct, balance is all and you will be busy. It is the natural way of things.*

This private conversation took place while I stood at Mr. Henry's graveside with my beloved Mel. I chugged my beer and placed it next to his gravestone. I did this often, like every Wednesday at noon. He was such a good listener and advisor. He understood. Then my thoughts were broken by a familiar voice.

"J.J., I hope that I'm not interrupting something."

"No, Madam President. You aren't."

The presence of the empty beer bottle next to the gravestone suggested quite the opposite.

"Do you come here often?"

"Every Wednesday at noon, ma'am."

"I see. Well given the current hiatus of hostilities, have you ever considered taking on another challenge beyond that of the Lictor of Magic? Perhaps becoming an instructor at the Academy?"

The suggestion surprised me and the president plainly saw it on my face.

"What a marvelous idea," piped Mel. "You'd make a wonderful instructor."

"What specifically do you have in mind, Madam President?" I countered.

"Oh, I suspect the possibilities are endless. You're a fine writer. You make the ancient world of magic sing to the everyday reader. I know that you enjoy research. I have even heard that you're taking up a new ancient language. But I think that you would be a wonderful fit for *Intro to Demonology*. What do you think?"

"You mean Mr. Good's old class?"

"Yes. I have this sense that you could liven up the material."

After a moment of consideration, I glanced at a beaming Mel. Then I said in deference to my spiritual companion, "My duties to the three realms come first, ma'am."

"Of course, they do."

"In that case, you're on!"

ABOUT THE AUTHOR

For W.J. Cherf, this is his third journey into the realm of paranormal, action-adventure literature. *The First Soul* is the first book in the series entitled, The Adventures of J. J. Stone, and *The Lictor of Magic* is the second installment. This book completes the trilogy.

Cherf is also known for his works in "historical science fiction," specifically his award-winning five-volume time traveling series, The Manuscripts of the Richards' Trust, which take place in Ancient Egypt and early Medieval France. They are full of adventure, intrigue, wonder, and vivid description.

As to why Cherf writes in his retirement years, he says, "I always wanted to write a book without footnotes." This is an oblique reference to his treadmill "publish or perish" days as a professor of ancient history and archaeology.

To find reviews and free chapters to all of his works, not to mention a handy source for the latest news in Egyptology, go to www.wjcherf.com.